The *New York Times* bestselling
anthology series . . .

Once Upon a Kiss
Once Upon a Rose
Once Upon a Dream
Once Upon a Star
Once Upon a Castle

"Excellent stories."
—*Rendezvous*

"Four of America's most beloved
romance authors."
—*Publishers Weekly*

Once Upon a Midnight

NORA ROBERTS
JILL GREGORY
RUTH RYAN LANGAN
MARIANNE WILLMAN

JOVE BOOKS, NEW YORK

These are works of fiction. Names, characters, places, and incidents either are the product of the authors' imaginations or are used fictitiously, and any resemblance to actual persons, living or dead, business establishments, events, or locales is entirely coincidental.

ONCE UPON A MIDNIGHT

A Jove Book / published by arrangement with the authors

PRINTING HISTORY
Jove edition / October 2003

ISBN: 0-515-13619-0

A JOVE BOOK®
Jove Books are published by The Berkley Publishing Group, a division of Penguin Group (USA) Inc., 375 Hudson Street, New York, New York 10014. JOVE and the "J" design are trademarks belonging to Penguin Group (USA) Inc.

PRINTED IN THE UNITED STATES OF AMERICA

10 9 8 7 6 5 4 3 2 1

CONTENTS

THE WITCHING HOUR

Nora Roberts

Prologue

In a distant time, in a distant place, the great island of Twylia swam in the vast blue Sea of Wonders. It was a land of mountains and valleys, of green forests and silver rivers, of wide fertile fields and quiet lakes. To those who lived there, it was the whole of the world.

Some said that once, in the dawn of beginnings, there was a bridge of land that led to other worlds, and back again to Twylia. A bridge of rock and earth conjured by the great wizard-god Draco, and so destroyed by him when the world beyond became a battlefield of greed and sorrow.

For on Twylia peace and prosperity prevailed for a thousand seasons.

But a time came when men—some men—sought more. When the more they sought was riches not earned, women not wooed, land not honored. And power, most of all—power not respected.

3

With this avarice, war and death, treachery and fear infected Twylia so that Draco, and those who came from him, wept to see the green fields stained with blood and the valleys echoing with the cries of starving children. He vowed, as he stood on the peak of Sorcerer's Mountain, in the light of the moon, on the night of the solstice, that peace would return to the world.

It would come through blood, and courage, through pure love and willing sacrifice. After dark days, the light would shine again. And so he cast his spell.

There will be one born in the darkest hour of the darkest night who will wield the power and bring the light. The Crown of Stars only one will wear to prove this be my one true heir. Through blood and valor, through grief and joy, the True One shields what greed would destroy. But one seeks another, woman to man, heart to heart, and hand to hand. So warrior, witch, daughter, and son, will complete what has begun. If there is strength and hearts are pure, this land of Twylia will endure.

The midnight hour will forge their power to free this world of tyranny. As I will, so mote it be.

From the peak of Sorcerer's Mountain, to the Valley of Faeries far below, across the fields and lakes and forests, the length and breadth of the island trembled from the might of the spell. Wind swirled and lightning spat.

So Draco sat atop his mountain and watched in glass and fire, in star and water as years passed.

As Draco bided, the world struggled. Good against evil, hope against despair. Magic dimmed in all but the secret places, and some grew to fear as much as covet it.

For a time, a short time, light bloomed again when good Queen Gwynn took the throne. The blood of the sorcerer ran in her veins, as did his love for the world. She was fair of face and of heart and ruled with a firm and loving hand beside her husband, the warrior-king Rhys. Together, they worked to heal the world, to rebuild the once grand City of Stars, to make the forests and fertile valleys safe again for the people of the world.

Hope shimmered into light, but its opposite lurked, and plotted. The shadows of envy and greed slithered in the corners and the caves of Twylia. And those shadows, under the guise of peace and reconciliation, armed for war and treachery. They marched into the City of Stars on a cold December morning, led by Lorcan, whose mark was the snake. And he would be king at any cost.

Blood and smoke and death followed. Come the dawn, the valiant Rhys lay dead and many who had fought with him slaughtered. Of the queen there was no sign.

On the eve of the solstice, Lorcan proclaimed himself king of Twylia and celebrated in the great hall of the castle, where royal blood stained the stones.

1

Snow fell in streams of icy white. It chilled to the bone, but she didn't curse it. It would blind any who pursued, and cover the trail. The bitter white cold was a blessing.

Her heart was broken, and her body nearly done. But she could not, would not yield. Rhys spoke to her, a spirit whisper in her mind that urged her to be strong.

She did not weep for his death. The tears, a woman's tears for the man she loved, were frozen inside her. She did not cry out against the pain, though the pain was great. She was more than a woman. More even than a witch.

She was a queen.

Her mount plowed through the snow, surefooted and loyal. As loyal, she knew, as the man who rode in silence beside her. She would need the loyalty of the faithful Gwayne, for she knew what was coming, what she could not stop. Though she hadn't seen her beloved Rhys's death, she knew the instant the usurper's sword had struck him down. So inside her cold and shattered heart she was prepared for what was to come.

She bit back a moan as the pain tore through her, breathed fast through her teeth until it eased again and she could say what needed to be said to Gwayne's silence.

"You could not have saved him. Nor could I." Tears stung her eyes and were viciously willed away. "Nor could I," she said again. "You served him, and me, by obeying his last order to you. I regret . . . I'm sorry that I made it difficult for you to do so."

"I am the queen's man, my lady."

She smiled a little. "And so you will continue to be. Your king thought of me. Even in the heat of battle, he thought of me, and our world. And our child." She pressed a hand to her heavy belly, to the life that beat there. "They will sing songs of him long after . . ." The pain ripped a gasp from her, had her fumbling the reins.

"My lady!" Gwayne grabbed her reins to steady her mount. "You cannot ride."

"I can. I will." She turned her head, and her eyes were a fierce and angry green in a face as pale as the snow. "Lorcan will not find my child. It's not time. It's not yet time. There will be a light." Exhausted, she slumped over the neck of her horse. "You must watch for the light, and guide us to it."

A light, Gwayne thought, as they trudged through the forest. Night was falling, and they were miles from the City of Stars, miles from any village or settlement he knew. Nothing lived in these woods but faeries and elves, and what good were they to a soldier and a woman—queen or no—who was great with child?

But here, into the Lost Forest, was where she'd ordered him to take her. She'd fought him, that was true enough, when he bowed to the king's command and dragged her from the castle. He had no choice but to lift her bodily onto the horse and whip her mount into a run.

They fled from the battle, from the stench of smoke and blood, from the screams of the dying. And royal command or not, he felt a coward for being alive while his king, his people, his friends were dead.

Still, he would guard the queen with his sword, with his shield, with his life. When she was safe, he would go back. He would slay the murderous Lorcan, or die trying.

There was murmuring under the wind, but it was nothing human, so didn't concern him. Magic didn't worry him. Men did. There may have been sorcery in Lorcan's ambush, but it was men who had carried it out. It had been lies as much as spells that had opened the doors for him, allowed him to walk into the castle under the flag of diplomacy.

And all the while his men—those as vicious as he, and others he'd gathered from the far edges of the world and paid to fight in his name,—had prepared for the slaughter.

Not war, Gwayne thought grimly. It wasn't war when men slit the throats of women, stabbed unarmed men in the back, killed and burned for the joy of it.

He glanced toward the queen. Her eyes stared straight ahead, but seemed blind to him. As if, he thought, she was in some sort of trance. He wondered why she hadn't seen the deception, the bloodbath to come. Though he was a queen's man in spite of her reputed powers rather than because of them, he figured sorcerer's blood should have some vision.

Maybe it had something to do with her condition. He didn't know anything about increasing women, either. He hadn't wed, and didn't intend to. He was a soldier, and in his mind a soldier had no need of wiving.

And what would he do when the time came for the babe? He prayed to every god who walked or flew that the queen would know what to do—in the way he assumed a woman knew of such matters.

The heir to Twylia born in a snowbank in the Lost Forest during a winter storm. It wasn't right. It wasn't seemly.

And it terrified him more than any enemy's sword.

They must stop soon, for their mounts were near exhaustion. He would do what he could to make a shelter for her. Build a fire. Then, gods willing, things would . . . progress as nature demanded they progress.

When it was done, and they'd rested, he would get them—somehow—to the Valley of Secrets, and the settlement of women—some said enchantresses—who lived there.

The queen and the child would be safe, and he would go back—go back and drive his sword through Lorcan's throat.

He heard a sound—it was like music through the soughing wind. And looking to the west, he saw a glimmer of light through the stormy dark.

"My lady! A light."

"Yes. Yes. Hurry. There isn't much time."

He pushed the mounts off the path, so they were forced to wade through the sea of snow, to wind around ice-sheathed trees toward that small flicker of light. The wind brought the smell of smoke to him, and his fingers gripped the hilt of his sword.

Ghosts slipped out of the dark, with arrows notched.

He counted six, and his soldier's sense warned him there were more. "We have no gold," he shouted. "We have nothing to steal."

"That's your misfortune." One of the ghosts stepped forward, and he saw it a was a man. Only a man, and a Traveler at that. "Why do you journey here, and on such a night?"

Travelers might steal, Gwayne knew, for the sport of it. But they wouldn't attack unprovoked, and their reputation for hospitality was as renowned as their love of the road.

"Our business is our own, and we want no trouble from you, but only some of the warmth of your fire. I have a lady with me. She is near her time. She needs women to help her with the birthing."

"Throw down your sword."

"I will not. Nor will I raise it against you unless you seek to harm my lady. Even a Traveler should honor and respect a woman about to give birth."

The man grinned, and under his hood his face was brown as a nut and just as hard. "Even a soldier should honor and respect men with arrows pointed at his heart."

"Enough." Gwynn threw her hood back, gathered her strength to raise her voice. "I am Gwynn, Queen of Twylia. Have you not seen the portents even through the storm of snow? Have you not seen the black snake slither over the sky this night to snuff out the stars?"

"We have seen, Majesty." The man and those with him lowered to one knee in the snow. "My wife, our wisewoman, told us to wait, to watch for you. What has happened?"

"Lorcan has overthrown the City of Stars. He has murdered your king."

The man rose, laid a fist on his heart. "We are not warriors, my lady queen, but if you bid it, we will arm and band and march against the snake in your name."

"So you will, but not tonight, and not in my name but in the name of one yet to come. Your name, sir?"

"I am Rohan, my lady."

"Rohan of the Travelers, I have sought you for a great task, and now I ask your help, for without it, all is lost. This child seeks to be born. Draco's blood runs through me, and through this baby. You share this blood. Will you help me?"

"My lady, I and all I have are yours to command." He took her horse's halter. "Go back," he shouted to one of his men. "Tell Nara and the women to prepare for a birth. A royal birth," he added, his teeth flashing in a smile. "We welcome a cousin." He pulled the horse toward the camp. "And enjoy a fight. Though Travelers pay little mind to the changing wind of politics, you will find none among us who has love for Lorcan."

"Politics play no part in murder done under a flag of truce. And your fate is tied to what happens this night."

He looked back at her and fought off a shudder. It seemed her eyes burned through the dark and into him. "I give you my sympathies for the loss of your husband."

"It is more than that." She reached down, gripped his hand with an urgency that ground bone to bone. "You know the Last Spell of Draco?"

"Everyone knows it, my lady. The song of it is passed generation to generation." And he, a man who feared little, felt his hand tremble in hers. "This child?"

"This child. This night. It is destiny, and we must not fail to meet it."

The pain seized her, and she swooned. She heard voices, dim and distant. A hundred voices, it seemed, rising up in a flood. Hands reached for her, lifted her down from her mount as the birth pangs ripped a cry from her throat.

She smelled pine, and snow and smoke, felt something cool pressed to her brow. When she came back to herself, she saw a young woman with bright red hair that gleamed in the firelight. "I am Rhiann, sister of Rohan. Drink a little, my lady. It will ease you."

She sipped from the cup held to her lips and saw she was in a rough shelter of branches. A fire burned nearby. "Gwayne?"

"Your man is just outside, my lady."

"This is women's work, and men are useless here, be they warrior or scholar."

"My mother," Rhiann said. "Nara."

Gwynn looked at the woman busily tearing cloth. "I'm grateful to you."

"Let's get this baby into the world, such as it is, then you can be grateful. Get that water on the fire. Fetch my herbs." The orders were snapped out as Gwynn felt the grip of the next pang.

Through the blurring of her vision she saw movement, heard chatter. More women. Women's work. Birth was the work of women, and death, it seemed, the work of men. Tears she'd conquered earlier now began to spill.

More voices spoke to her, inside her head, and told her what she already knew. But they were small comfort as she fought to give her child life.

"Midnight approaches." She turned her head against Rhiann's bracing shoulder. "The solstice. The darkest hour of the darkest day."

"Push," Nara ordered. "Push!"

"The bells, the bells strike the hour."

"There are no bells here, my lady." Rhiann watched the cloths go red with blood. Too much blood.

"In the City of Stars, Lorcan has the bells rung. For his celebration, he thinks. But they ring out for the child, for the beginning. Oh! Now!"

Rearing back, she pushed the child into life. She heard the cries and laughed through her own weeping.

"This is her hour, this is her time. The witching hour between night and day. I must hold her."

"You're weak, my lady." Nara passed the squalling baby to Rhiann.

"You know as well as I, I'm dying. Your skill, Nara, your herbs, even your magic can't stop my fate. Give me my child."

She held out her arms, and smiled at Rhiann. "You have a kind heart to weep for me."

"My lady."

"I must speak to Gwayne. Quickly," she said as Rhiann put the baby in her arms. "There's little time. Ah, there you are. There you are, my sweet girl." She pressed a kiss on the baby's head. "You've healed my heart, and now it tears in two again. Part to stay here with you, part to go to your father. How I grieve to leave you, my own. You will have his eyes, and his courage. My mouth, I think," she murmured and kissed it, "and what runs in my blood. So much depends on you. Such a small hand to hold the world."

She smiled over the baby's head. "She will need you," she said to Nara. "You will teach her what women need to know."

"You would put your child into the hands of a woman you don't know?"

"You heard the bells."

Nara opened her mouth, then sighed. "Yes, I heard them." And she had seen, with a woman's heavy heart, what would pass this night.

Gwayne came into the shelter, fell to his knees beside her. "My lady."

"She is Aurora. She is your light, your queen, your charge. Will you swear your fealty to her?"

"I will. I do."

"You cannot leave her."

"My lady, I must—"

"You cannot go back. You must swear to me to stay beside her. Keep her safe. You must swear on my blood that you will protect her as you have protected me." She took his hand, laid it on the child. "Gwayne, my white hawk. You are hers now. Swear it."

"I swear it."

"You will teach her what a warrior needs to know. She will stay with the Travelers. Hidden in the hills, and in the shadows of the forest. When it is time . . . you will know, you will tell her what she is." She turned the child so he could see the birthmark, a pale star, on the baby's right thigh. "All she is. Until then, Lorcan must not know of her. He will want her death above all things."

"I will guard her, on my life."

"She has her hawk, and her dragon watches from the highest point of the world," she murmured. "Her wolf will come when he's needed. Oh, my heart, my own." She pressed her lips to the child's cheeks. "This is why I was born, why I loved, why I died. And still, I grieve to leave you." She drew a trembling breath. "I give her into your hands." She held the baby out to Gwayne.

Then she held out her own, palms up. "I still have something left in me. She will have it." Light spun over her hands, whirled and caught the red, the gold from the fire. Then with a flash, what lay in Gwynn's hands became a star and a moon, both clear as ice.

"Keep them for her," she said to Nara.

The good queen closed her eyes and slipped away. The young queen wailed in the arms of a grieving soldier.

2

SEASONS PASSED, AND the world suffered under the harsh reign of King Lorcan. Small rebellions were crushed with a brutality that washed the land with blood and sent even the valiant into hiding. Faeries, witches, seers, and all who dwelt within the Realm of Magicks were outlawed and hunted like wild beasts by the mercenaries who came to be known as Lorcan's dogs.

Those who rose up against the usurper—and many who didn't—were executed. The dungeon in the castle filled with the tortured and forgotten, the innocent and the damned.

Lorcan grew rich, lining his coffers with taxes, increasing his holdings with land taken by force from those who had held it, worked it, honored it for generations. He dined off plates of gold and drank his wine from goblets of crystal while the people starved.

Those who spoke against him during the dark times spoke in whispers, and in secret.

Many of the displaced took to the high hills or the Lost Forest. There magic was practiced still, and the faithful searched the sky for portents of the True One who would vanquish the snake and bring light back to the world.

There, among the farmers and merchants, the millers and artists who had become outlaws, among the faeries and elves and witches with bounties on their heads, the Travelers roamed.

"Again!" Aurora thrust with the sword and thrilled to the ring of steel against steel. She drove her opponent back, parried, pivoted.

"Balance," Gwayne warned.

"I have my balance." To prove it, she leapt nimbly over the sword swept at her feet, landed lightly.

Swords crossed, slid hilt to hilt. And she came up with a dagger, pressing the point to his throat. "And the kill," she added. "I like to win."

Gwayne gave her a little poke with the dagger he held to her belly. "So do I."

She laughed, stepped back, then gave him a courtly bow. "We both died well. Sit. You're winded."

"I am not." But he was, and he rested on a stump while she fetched a skin of water.

She has her father's eyes, he thought. Gray as woodsmoke. And her mother's soft and generous mouth. Gwynn had been right—about so many things.

The child had grown into a lithe and lovely young woman, with skin the color of pale, pure honey, hair black as midnight. A strong chin, he judged, murmuring a thanks when she offered the water. Stubborn. He hadn't known a girl-child could *be* so stubborn.

There was a light in her, so bright he wondered that those who looked on her didn't fall to their knees. She was, though garbed in hunting green and worn boots, every inch a queen.

He had done what he had been asked. She was trained in the ways of a warrior. In sword and arrow and pike, in hand against hand. She could hunt and fight and ride as well as any man he'd trained. And she could think. That was his pride in her.

Nara and Rhiann had schooled her in women's work, and in magicks. Rohan had tutored her in scholarly matters, and her mind, her thirsty mind, soaked up the songs, the stories of their people.

She could read and write, she could cipher and chart. She could make the cold fire with a thought, stitch a wound, and—these days—take him in a sword fight.

And still, how could a girl of barely twenty seasons lead her people into battle and save the world?

It haunted him at night when he lay beside Rhiann, who had become his wife. How could he honor his vow to keep her safe and honor his vow to tell her of her birthright?

"I heard the dragon in the night."

His fingers squeezed the skin. "What?"

"I heard it roar, in my dreams that were not dreams. The red dragon who flies in the night sky. And in his claws was a crown of stars. My wolf was with me." She turned her head, smiled at Gwayne. "He is always with me, it seems. So handsome and strong, with his sad eyes green as the grass on the Hills of Never."

Even speaking of the man she thought of as her wolf had her blood warming. "We lay on the floor of the forest and watched the sky, and when the dragon came with his crown, I felt such a thrill. Fear and wonder and joy. As I reached up, through a great wind that blew, the sky grew brighter than day, stronger than the faerie fire. And I stood beside my wolf in the blinding brightness, with blood at my feet."

She sat on the ground, resting her back against the stump. With a careless gesture, she flipped the long, fat braid she wore behind her shoulder. "I don't know what it means, but I wonder if I will fight for the True One. If his time draws near. I wonder if I will, at last, find the warrior who is my wolf and stand with him to lift my sword for the true king."

She had spoken of the wolf since she could form words—the boy, and now the man, she loved. But never before had she spoken of seeing the dragon. "Is that all the dream?"

"No." Comfortably, she rested her head against his knee. "In the dream that was not a dream, I saw a lady. A beautiful lady with green eyes and dark hair, and she wore the robes of royalty. She was weeping, so I said, My lady, why do you weep? She answered, I weep for the world while the world waits. It waits for the True One, I said to her, and asked, Why doesn't he come? When will he strike at Lorcan and bring peace to Twylia?"

Gwayne looked into the forest, gently stroking her hair. "What did she say to you?"

"She said the True One's hour is midnight, in birth, in death. Then she held out her hands, and in them were a globe, bright as the moon, and a star, clear as water. Take them, she told me. You will need them. Then she was gone."

She rubbed her cheek against his knee as the sadness she'd felt came back on her. "She was gone, Gwayne, and I ached in my heart. Beside me stood my wolf with his green eyes and dark hair. I think he was the True One, and that I'll fight for him. I think this dream was a portent, for when I woke, there was blood on the moon. A battle is coming."

Gwynn had said he would know when it was time. He knew, sitting in the quiet forest with spring freshening the air. He knew, and it grieved him.

"Not all battles are fought and won with the sword."

"I know. Mind and heart, vision and magic. Strategy and treachery. I feel . . ." She rose, wandered away to pluck up a stone and cast it into the silver water of the river.

"Tell me what you feel."

She looked back. There was silver, bright as the river water, mixed with the gold of his hair, and in his beard. His eyes were a pale blue, and it seemed to her there was a shadow in them now. He was not her father. She knew her sire had fought and died in the Battle of the Stars, but Gwayne had been her father in all but blood all of her life.

There was nothing she couldn't tell him.

"I feel . . . as if something inside me is waiting, as the world is waiting. I feel there is something I must do, must be beyond what I am, what I do know." She hurried back to him, knelt at his feet. "I feel I must find my wolf. My love for him is so great, I will never know another. If he's the one of prophecy, I want to serve him. I honor what you've given me, Gwayne. You and Rhiann, Nara and Rohan and all my family. But there's something inside me, stretching, growing restless, because it *knows*. It knows, but I can't see it."

She rapped a fist against his leg in frustration. "I can't see. Not yet. Not in my dreams or in the fire or the glass. When I seek, it's as if a film covers my vision and there are only shadows behind it. In the shadows I see the snake, and in the shadows my wolf is chained and bleeding."

She rose again, impatient with herself. "A man who might be king, a woman who was a queen. I know she was a queen, and she offered me the moon and a star. And while I wanted them with a kind of burning hunger, I feared them. Somehow, I know if I took them, everything would change."

"I have no magic. I'm only a soldier, and it's been too long since my courage was tested. Now I taste fear, and it makes me an old man."

"You're not old, and you're never afraid."

"I thought there would be more time." He got to his feet, just looked at her. "You're so young."

"Older than your Cyra, and she marries at the next equinox."

"The first year of your life I thought the days would never end, and time would never pass."

She laughed. "Was I so troublesome an infant?"

"Restless and willful." He reached out to touch her cheek. "Then time flew. And here we are. Come, sit with me on the riverbank. I have many things to tell you."

She sat with him, and watched a hawk circle in the sky. "There is your talisman. The hawk."

"Once, long ago, and most often behind my back, I was called the queen's hawk."

"The queen?" Aurora looked back sharply. "You were the queen's man? You never told me. You said you fought with my father in the great battle, but not that you were the queen's man."

"I told you that I brought your mother out of the city, into the Lost Forest. That Rohan and the Travelers took us in, and you were born that night in the snow."

"And she died giving me life."

"I didn't tell you that it was she who led me, and that I left the battle with her on orders from the king. She did not want to leave him." Though his words were spoken softly, his gaze was keen on her face. "She fought me. She was heavy with you, but still she fought like a warrior to stay with her king. With her husband."

"My mother." The breath caught in her throat. "In my dream. It was my mother."

"It was cold, and bitter, and she was in great pain. Body and heart. But she would not stop and rest. She guided me, and we came to the camp, to the place of your birth. She wept to leave you, and held you to her breast. She charged me to keep you safe, to train you, as she charged Nara to train you. To keep the truth of your birth from you until the time had come. Then she gave you to my hands, she put you in my hands."

He looked down at them now. "You were born at midnight. She heard the bells, miles away in the city. Your hour is midnight. You are the True One, Aurora, and as I love you, I wish it were another."

"How can this be?" Her heart trembled as she got to her feet, and she knew fear, the first true fear of her life. "How can I be the one? I'm no queen, Gwayne, no ruler."

"You are. It is your blood. From the first moment I held you in my hands, I knew this day would come. But beyond this I can see nothing." He rose, only to kneel before her. "I am the queen's man, and serve at your hand."

"Don't." Panicked, she dropped to her knees as well, gripped his shoulders. "By Draco and all the gods, what will I do? How could I have lived all my life in comfort, never knowing true hunger or hurts while the people of the world waited? How can I stand for them, free them, when I've hidden away like a coward while Lorcan rules?"

"You were kept in safety, your mother's dying wish." He stood, taking her arm to pull her up with him. "You have not been a coward. Nor will you shame the memory of your mother, your father, and play the coward now. This is your fate. I have trained you as a warrior. Be a warrior."

"I would fight." She slapped a hand to her sword as if to prove it. "I would pledge sword and magic, my *life*, without reserve. But to lead?" She drew a shaky breath and stared out over the river. "Nothing is as it was only a moment ago. I need time to think." She shut her eyes tightly. "To breathe. I need to be alone. Give me *time*, Gwayne," she said before he could argue. "If you must break camp and move on, I'll find you. I need to find my way. Leave me." She stepped aside as he reached out to touch her. "Go."

When she knew she was alone, she stood by the banks of the silver river and grieved for her parents, her people, and herself.

And longed for the comfort of the lover she called her wolf.

She walked deep into the forest, beyond the known and into the realm of faeries. There she cast the circle, made the fire, and sang the song for vision. She would see what had been—and what would be.

In the flames, while the moon rose and the single star that dogged it blinked to life, she saw the Battle of the Stars. She saw the bodies of servants, of children as well as soldiers. She saw the king—her father—fight like a demon, driving back the greater forces. She heard the screams, and smelled the blood.

Her father's voice came to her ears, a shouted order to Gwayne, who fought beside him, to get the queen, and the child she carried, to safety. To do this thing, as a soldier, even against the queen's orders, for the world. For the True One.

She saw her father's death, and her own birth. She tasted her mother's tears, and felt the force of love beam through the magic.

And with it, the force of duty.

"You will not shirk it."

"Am I enough?" Aurora asked the image of her mother.

"You are the True One. There is no other. You are hope, Aurora. And you are pride. And you are duty. You cannot turn from this."

Aurora watched the battle, and knew it was what would come, not what had. This blood, this death, would be by her own hands. On her own hands. Even if it meant her end, she must begin. "I have power, Mother, but it is a woman's power. Small magic. I'm strong, but I'm not seasoned. How can I lead, and rule, with so little to offer?"

"You will be more. Sleep now. Dream now."

So she dreamed again of her wolf, her warrior with eyes as green as the hills. He was tall, and broad of shoulder. His hair, dark as her own, swept back from a face of sharp planes and angles, and a white scar slashed through his left brow like a bolt of lightning. She felt a curling in her belly that she knew for desire, one she had felt for no one but him.

"What will you be to me?" she asked him. "What will I be to you?"

"I know only that you're my beloved. You and you alone. I've dreamed of you through my life, waking and sleeping, only of you." He reached out, and she felt the brush of his fingers over her cheek. "Where are you?"

"Close, I think. Close. Are you a soldier?"

He looked down at the sword in his hand, and as disgust rippled over his face he shoved its point into the ground. "I am nothing."

"I think you are many things, and one of those is mine." Giving in to curiosity, following her own will, she pulled him to her and pressed her lips to his.

The wind swirled around them, a warm wind stirred by the great beating of faerie wings. The song rose up inside her, and beat in her blood.

She would have love, she thought, even if death followed.

"I must be a woman to become what I am to become." She stepped back, drew off her hunting tunic. "Teach me what a woman knows. Love me in visions."

His gaze swept down her as she stood before him, dressed only in moonbeams within the shimmering circle of magic. "I've loved you all my life," he said. "And feared you."

"I've looked for you all of mine, and come to you here, fearing everything. Will you turn from me? Will I be alone?"

"I'll never turn from you." He drew her to him. "I'll never leave you."

With his lips on hers, he lowered her to the soft floor of the forest. She knew the thrill of his hands, the taste of his skin, and a pleasure, a deep and drugging pleasure that caused her body to quake. Flames leapt beside them, and inside her.

"I love you." She murmured it as she raced her lips over his face. "I'm not afraid."

She rose to him, opened to him, entreated. When he joined with her, she knew the power of being a woman, and the delights.

When she woke at dawn, alone, with the fire gone to ash, she knew the cold kiss of duty.

•　•　•

"You should not have let her go alone."

Gwayne sat honing his sword while Rhiann scolded and made oatcakes. The morning sounds of the camp stirred around them. Horses, dogs, women cooking at pots, children chattering, and men readying to hunt.

"It was her wish." He spoke more sharply than he intended. "Her command. You fret over her like a mother."

"And what am I to her if not a mother? Two days, Gwayne, two nights."

"If she can't stay two nights alone in the forest, she can hardly rule Twylia."

"She's just a girl!" Rhiann slammed down her spoon. "It was too soon to tell her of this."

"It was time. I gave my oath on it, and it was time! Do you think I have no worries? Is there anything I would not do to keep her from harm, even to giving my life?"

She blinked back hot tears and took his hand. "No. No. But she is like our own, as much as Cyra and young Rhys are. I want her here, sitting by the fire, putting too much honey on her oatcake, laughing. It will never be like that again."

He set aside his sword to rise and take his wife in his arms. "She is not ours to keep."

Over Rhiann's head, he saw her come out of the forest, through the mists of the morning. She was tall—tall for a girl, he thought now. Straight as a soldier. She looked pale, but her eyes were clear. They met his, held.

"She is come," Gwayne said.

Aurora heard the murmurs as she walked through camp. They had been told, she thought, and now they waited. Her family, her friends, stood beside their colorful wagons, or stepped out of them to watch her.

She stopped, waited until all was quiet. "There is much to be done." She lifted her voice so that it echoed through camp, and beyond. "Eat, then come to me. I'll tell you how we will defeat Lorcan and take back our world."

Someone cheered. She saw it was young Rhys, barely twelve, and smiled back at him. Others took up the shouts, so that she walked through the celebration of them on her way to Gwayne.

Rhys dashed to her. "I'm not going to have to bow, am I?"

"You might, but not just now." She ruffled his mop of golden hair.

"Good. When do we fight?"

Her stomach clutched. He was a boy, only a boy. How many boys would she send into battle? And into death? "Soon enough."

She stepped to Gwayne, touched Rhiann's arm to comfort her. "I've seen the way," she said. "The way to begin. I'll need my hawk."

"I'm yours." He bowed, deep. "Majesty."

"Don't give me the title until I've earned it." She sat, took an oatcake, and drenched it with honey. Beside her, Rhiann buried her face in her apron and sobbed.

"Don't weep." Aurora rose again to gather Rhiann close. "This is a good day." She looked at Gwayne. "A new day. It's not only because of what's in my blood that I can do this, but because of what you've taught me. Both of you. All of you. You've given me everything I need to meet my destiny. Rhys, will you ask Nara and Rohan to join us and break fast?"

She pressed a kiss to Rhiann's cheek as Rhys ran off. "I've fasted for two days. I'm hungry," she said, and with a wide grin she sat to devour her oatcakes.

3

He had known her all his life, in his mind, in his heart. She came to him first as a child, laughing as she splashed in the silver river of a deep forest.

In those days they played together, as children do. And when he knew hunger and hurt, cold and a loneliness sharper than a blade, she would comfort him.

She called him her wolf. To him she was the light.

When they were no longer children, they walked together. He knew the sound of her voice, the scent of her hair, the taste of her lips.

She was his beloved, and though he thought her only a fantasy, he clung to her for his sanity. She was the single light in a world of darkness, the only joy in a world of despair.

With her he watched the dragon roar across the sky with the crown of prophecy in its claws. Through the magic light that followed, he saw the blood stain the ground at her feet, and he felt the smooth hilt of a sword in his hand.

But he dared not hope that he would be free, at long last, to lift that sword and serve her.

He dared not hope that she was real, and that someday she would belong to him.

"Will you give me the gifts from my mother?" Aurora asked Nara.

"I've kept them for you. Rohan made this box, to keep them." An old woman with a face scored by many seasons, Nara held out a box of polished applewood, scribed with the symbol of star and moon. It had been the royal seal of Twylia before Lorcan had ordered all such symbols outlawed.

"It's beautiful. You honor my mother, Rohan."

"She was a great lady."

She opened the box and saw the clear globe, the clear star lying on dark velvet. Like the moon and star she'd seen in the night sky. "Conjured from love and grief, from joy and tears. Can there be stronger magic?"

When she lifted the globe, the light exploded in her hand. She saw through it, into the glass, into the world. Green fields sparkling in summer sunlight, wide rivers teeming with fish, thick forests where game grew fat. Cities with silver towers.

Men worked the fields, hunted the forests, fished the rivers, brought their wares to the city.

The mountains speared up, white at the peaks where the snow never melted. Beyond them, the Sea of Wonders fanned out. Other lands rose and spread. Other fields, other cities.

So they were not the world, she thought. But this was hers, to guard, to rule.

She took the star in her other hand and felt its heat, the flame of its power, fly into her.

"And the star shall burn with the blood of the dragon. Come as a lamb, mate with the wolf. Under truth is lies, under lies, truth. And valor holds its light under the coward's guise. When the witching hour comes, when the blood of the true one spills on the moon, the snake shall be vanquished, torn by the fangs of the wolf."

She swayed, lowered the crystals in her hands. "Who spoke?"

"You." Gwayne's voice was thin as he stared at her. Her hair had flown out as if on a wind, and her face had been full of light, her eyes full of power. Power that struck even a warrior with edges of fear and superstition.

"I am who I was. And more. It's time to begin. To tell you, tell everyone."

"I had visions," Aurora said when everyone gathered around. "Waking and dreaming. Some were shown and some were told to me, and some I know because it is my blood. I must go to the City of Stars and take my place on the throne."

"When do we march?" Rhys shouted, and was lightly cuffed by his father.

"We will march, and we'll fight, and some of us will fall. But the world will not be freed by only the slice of a sword. It is not only might that will win what was taken from us."

"Magic." Rohan nodded. "And logic."

"Magic, logic," Aurora agreed. "Strategy and steel. And wiles," she added with a sly smile. "A woman's wiles. Cyra, what was most talked of in the village where we last stopped for supplies?"

Cyra, a blooming sixteen, still struggled not to stare at Aurora with awe. "Prince Owen, son of Lorcan. He seeks a bride among the ranking ladies across Twylia. Orders have gone out for any knights or lords still with holdings to send their eligible daughters to the city."

"So Owen can pick and pluck," Aurora said with disgust. "There will be feasting, and a grand ball, will there not, while ladies are paraded before the son of the snake like mares at auction?"

"So it's said, my . . . my lady."

"My sister," Aurora corrected, and made Cyra smile. "I will go as the lamb. Can you make me look the lady, Rhiann?"

"To ride into the city unarmed—"

"I won't be unarmed." Aurora looked at the crystals, and the sword she'd laid beside them. "Or alone. I'll have an escort, as befits a lady of quality, and servants." She tugged the hem of her hunting tunic. "And a wardrobe. And so . . . garbed, I will gain access to the castle. I need men."

Excitement rose in her. What had been stretching inside her had found its shape. She bounded onto the table, lifted her voice. "I need men to ride out, to find the pockets of rebels, of soldiers whose swords grow dull and rusted, of their sons and daughters who would follow the True One. Find farmers willing to set aside their plows, and craftsmen willing to forge weapons for them. They must be trained, they must be forged, even as the weapons are forged, into an army. In secret, in haste."

She looked into the forest, into the deep green of summer. "I swear to you, before the first frost bites the air we will take the city, we will take the world, and I will have the head of the snake in my hand."

She looked down at Gwayne. "Will you raise my army?"

His soldier's heart thrilled. "I will, my lady."

"When it's time to strike, I'll send you a sign. You'll know it. Rohan, I need your maps, and your logic."

"You'll have them."

"Rhiann." Aurora spread her arms. "I need a gown."

She was groomed and tutored, gowned and schooled. Even as Rhiann and those she deemed could run a passable seam worked on silks and velvets, Aurora practiced with sword and arrow.

She gritted her teeth as lotions were rubbed into her skin, as Cyra practiced dressing her hair. And she planned her strategy over bowls of mead, read dispatches from Gwayne, and sent them.

It was the far edge of summer when she set out, garbed in a traveling cloak of dark blue, with Cyra and Rhiann as her handmaidens and Rohan, young Rhys, and three other men as her escorts.

She would play her part, Aurora promised herself. The gods knew she looked the pampered lady. She would charm and beguile, seduce if need be. And she would take the castle from the inside, while the army Gwayne was training came over the city walls.

It was a long journey, but she was grateful for the time. She used it to hone her vision, gather her courage, strengthen her purpose.

The fields were still green, she noted, whoever ruled. But she'd seen the fear, the distrust, and the anger in the eyes of men they passed on the road. She'd seen the crows picking at the bones of those who had been unlucky enough to be set upon by thieves, or Lorcan's dogs.

Children, their faces pinched with hunger, begged for food or coin. She saw what was left of homes that had been burned to the ground, and the desperate eyes of women with no man left to protect them.

Had she not looked so closely before? Aurora wondered. Had she been so content to run through the forest, to sing in the hills, that she hadn't seen the utter despair of her people, the waste of her land?

She would give her life to put it right again.

"It seems so strange to see Grandfather garbed so richly," Cyra said.

"You must not call him Grandfather."

"No, I'll remember. Are you afraid, Aurora?"

"I am. But it's a good fear. The kind that tells me something will happen."

"You look beautiful."

Aurora smiled, and struggled not to tug at the confining gown. "It's only another weapon, and one I find I don't mind wielding. A sprinkle of witchcraft and . . . he'll look on me, won't he, this son of a demon? He'll look on me and want?"

"Any man would."

Satisfied, Aurora nodded. While he looked, and wanted, she would seek another. She would seek her wolf.

He was there. Waiting. She felt him in her blood, and with every league they traveled, that blood warmed.

She would find her love, at last, in the City of Stars.

And her destiny.

"Oh, look!" Cyra bounced in her seat. "The city. See how the towers shine."

Aurora saw it, in the distance, the silver and gilt that spread up into the sky. The grand towers of the castle gleamed, and on the topmost, the black flag with its coiled red snake flew.

She would burn it, she vowed. Burn it to ash and hoist her family crest in its place. The gold dragon on its white field would fly again.

"Twenty men on the castle walls," Rohan said quietly as he rode his mount sedately toward her.

"Yes, I see them. And more at the city gates. He will have a personal guard as well, others at the castle gates. Some will slip away once Lorcan is dead, some will certainly join our cause. But others will fight. We'll need to know the castle, every foot of it. Gwayne's drawings are a start, but it's likely Lorcan has changed some of it over the years."

"On the sweat and blood of the people," Rohan agreed. "Building fine rooms and thicker walls." He had to remind himself not to spit. "However fine the gilt, he's turned the City of Stars into the pit of a snake."

"And I will bury him in it."

She fixed a bored expression on her face, and watched everything, as they rode through the gates of the city.

In the stables, Thane groomed the roan mare. He worked alone, and the work was endless. But he was used to that, to the aching muscles, the weary bones at the end of the day.

And he had come to prize his solitude.

He loved the horses. That was his secret. If Owen and Lorcan knew he enjoyed them, they would cast him out of the stables and the dim quiet that brought him some measure, at least, of peace. They would find him other drudgery, he thought. It pleased them to do so. He was used to that as well.

He'd learned as a very young boy to keep his words and his opinions to himself, to do his work, expect nothing—unless it was the heel of a boot in the ass. As long as he controlled his temper, his fury, his hatred, he had the gift of alone.

And those he loved were safe.

The mare blew softly as he ran a hand over her silky neck. For a moment, Thane laid his cheek to hers, shut his eyes. He was exhausted. Dreams plagued him, night after night, so that he woke hot and hard and needy. Voices and visions ran through his head and gave him no answers, and no relief.

Even his light, his love, brought a strange restlessness to him.

He could not war, could not find peace, so there seemed nothing for him but hours of work.

He stepped away from the mare, ran a hand through his unruly black hair. He would have gone to the next mount, but something stirred in his belly, a kind of hunger that had nothing to do with desire for food.

He felt his heart thudding in his chest as he walked past the stalls, toward the stable entrance, where the light fell like a curtain of gold.

He lifted his hand to shield his eyes from the glare and saw her, his vision, mounted on a white stallion. Blood roared into his head, made him giddy as he stared.

She was smiling, her lashes downcast. And he knew—he *knew* the eyes they hid were gray as smoke. Dimly, he heard her voice, heard her laugh—how well he knew that voice, that laugh—as she offered Owen her hand.

"Servants will see to your horses, my lady . . ."

"I am Aurora, daughter of Ute of the westland. My father sends his regrets for not accompanying me to honor you, Prince Owen. He is unwell."

"He is forgiven for sending such a jewel."

She did her best to work up a flush, and fluttered her lashes. He was handsome, with the look of a young, golden god. Unless you looked in his eyes, as she did. There was the snake. He was his father's son.

"You flatter me, sir, and I thank you. I must beg your indulgence. My horses are precious to me, I fear I fret over them like a hen over chicks. I'd like to see the stables, if you please, and speak with the grooms about their care."

"Of course." He put his hands around her waist. She didn't stiffen as she wished to, but smiled prettily as he lifted her down.

"The city is magnificent." She brushed a hand over her headdress as if to fuss it into place. "A country lass like myself is awed by so much"—she looked back at him now deliberately provocative—"glamour."

"It dulls before you, Lady Aurora." Then he turned, and she saw his handsome face go hard with temper and those dark eyes gleam with hate.

She followed his glance and felt her world tilt.

She had found her wolf. He was dressed in rags, with the sweat of labor staining them. His dark hair curled madly around a face smudged with stable dirt. And in his hand he carried not a sword but a currycomb.

Their eyes met, and in that single instant she felt the shock of knowledge, and of disbelief.

He took one step toward her, like a man in a trance.

In three strides, Owen stormed to Thane and used the back of his hand to deliver a vicious blow that drew blood. For an instant, only an instant, rage flamed in Thane's eyes. Then he lowered them, as Owen struck again.

"On your knees, worthless cur. You dare cast your eyes on a lady. You'll be whipped for this insult."

Head down, Thane lowered to his knees. "Your pardon, my lord prince."

"If you have time to stand and stare at your betters, you must not have enough to do." Owen pulled out his riding crop, raised it.

To Aurora's disappointment, the wolf of her visions stayed down like a cowed dog.

"Prince Owen." Her knees shook, and her heart thundered. Every instinct had to be denied. She couldn't go to him, speak to him. She must instead play the pampered lady. However it scored her pride, Aurora laid the back of her hand on her brow and pretended to swoon. "I can't bear violence," she said weakly when he rushed back to catch her. "I feel . . . unwell."

"Lady, I'm sorry you had to witness such a . . . display." He looked down on Thane with derision. "This stableboy has some skill with horses, but too often forgets his place."

"Please, don't punish him on my account. I couldn't bear the thought of it." She waved a hand, and after a moment's confusion, Cyra rushed forward with a bottle of salts to hold under Aurora's nose.

"Enough, enough." Aurora nudged her away as the salts made her eyes water. "If you could assist me, my lord, out of the sun?"

"Forgive me, Lady Aurora. Let me take you inside, offer you some refreshment."

"Oh, yes." She leaned against him. "Traveling is so wearing, isn't it?"

She let him lead her away from the stables. Her heart was heavy to find her wolf, at last, and learn he had neither fang nor claw.

Feigning light-headedness, she let herself be led across a courtyard and into the keep. And she noted every detail. The number of guards and their weapons, the richness of the tapestries and tiles, the placement of windows and doors and stairs.

She noted the stone faces and downcast eyes of servants, and the demeanor of the other women, other ladies brought in like broodmares for display.

Some, it seemed to her, were pleased to be considered worthy of Prince Owen's regard. In others, she saw fear lurking in the eyes.

Women were chattel under Lorcan's reign. Property to be owned by father, husband, brother, or any man with the price. Any suspected of witchcraft were burned.

Women were lesser creatures, Rohan had told her, in Lorcan's world. All the better, she thought. He would hardly suspect that the True One was a woman, and that she bided under his roof until she could slit his throat.

She fluttered and flushed and begged Owen that she be taken to her chambers to rest away the fatigue of the journey.

When she had safely arrived there, she balled her hands into fists. "Simpleton. Bully. Bastard." She took a deep breath and fought for control. "Calling him prince makes my tongue ache."

"He was cruel to that boy," Rhiann murmured.

"It wasn't a boy, but a man. A man without a backbone." With a hiss of rage, she dropped into a chair. The man of her dreams would not grovel in the dirt. She would *not* love a man who would beg pardon of an ass.

So she would forget him. She had to forget him and her woman's heart, and do what came next.

"We're inside," she said to Rhiann. "I'll write a dispatch to Gwayne. See that it's sent today."

4

Aurora dressed with great care in a gown of blue velvet piped with gold. With Cyra's help her heavy hair was tamed into a gold snood. She wore small blue stones at her ears, a delicate pearl cross at her throat. And a dagger strapped to her thigh.

After practicing her smiles and simpers in the glass, she deemed herself ready. She wandered the gallery, knowing that the art and furnishings there had been stolen from her parents or looted from other provinces. She gazed out the windows at the gardens and mazes and lands that had been tended by her forebears, then taken by force for another's pride and greed.

And she noted the numbers and locations of guards at every post. She swept down the stairs, meandered into rooms, watched the servants and guests and courtiers.

It pleased her to be able to move freely through the castle, around the gardens. What threat was a woman after all, she thought as she stopped to smell the golden roses and study the rank of guards along the seawall. She was simply a candidate for Owen's hand, sent to offer herself like a ripe fruit for the plucking.

"Where is the music?" she asked Cyra. "Where is the laughter? There are no songs in Lorcan's kingdom, no joy. He rules shadows."

"You will bring back the light."

"I swear that I will." Or die in the attempt, she vowed silently. "There's such beauty here, but it's like beauty trapped behind a locked glass. Imprisoned, waiting. We must shatter the glass."

She rounded a bend in the path and saw a woman seated on a bench with a young girl kneeling at her feet, weeping. The woman wore a small crown atop her golden hair. She looked brittle and thin in her rich robes, and though her face held beauty, it was pale and tired.

"She who calls herself queen." Aurora spoke softly and fought to keep the fury out of her eyes. "Lorcan's wife, who was my mother's woman. There's time before the banquet. We'll see if she can be of use."

Folding her hands at her waist, Aurora stepped forward. She saw the queen start, saw her hand close tight over the girl's shoulder. "Majesty." Aurora dropped into a deep curtsy. "I am Lady Aurora, and beg pardon for disturbing you. May I help?"

The girl had shut off her tears, and though her pretty face was ravaged by them, she got to her feet, bowed. "You are welcome, lady. You will excuse my behavior. It was only a childish trifle that had me seeking my mother's knee. I am Dira, and I welcome you to the City of Stars and our home."

"Highness." Aurora curtsied, then took the hand the queen offered.

"I am Brynn. I hope you have all that you require here."

"Yes, my lady. I thought to walk the gardens before the sun set. They are so lovely, and with summer nearly done, transient."

"It grows cold at twilight." Brynn gathered her cloak at her throat as if she could already feel the oncoming winter. When Brynn rose, Aurora noted that her eyes were strongly blue, and unbearably sad. "Will you accompany us inside? It's nearly time for feasting."

"With pleasure, my lady. We live quiet in the west," she continued. "I look forward to the dancing and feasting, and the time with other women."

"Partridges and peahens," Dira whispered.

"Dira!"

But Aurora laughed over the queen's sharp rebuke, and glanced at the girl with more interest. "So we must seem to you, Highness. Country girls parading in their finery with hopes that Prince Owen will show favor."

"I meant no offense."

"And none was given. It must be wearying to have so much female chattering about day and night. You'll be happy, I'm sure, when the prince has chosen his bride. Then you will have a sister, will you not?"

Dira looked away, toward the seawall. "So it would seem."

A shadow crossed the path, and Aurora would have sworn the world went still.

Lorcan, self-proclaimed king of Twylia, stood before them.

He was tall and strongly built. His hair, nearly copper in color, spilled to the shoulders of his purple cloak. Jewels glinted in his crown, on his fingers. His sharply ridged face had the devil's own beauty, and so cold was the blue of his eyes that Aurora wasn't surprised to feel the queen tremble beside her.

"You dally in the garden while our guests wait? You sit and dream when you are commanded to take your place?"

"Your Majesty." Going with instinct, Aurora lowered herself to one knee at the king's feet, and used a small dash of power to draw his attention and thought to her and away from his wife. "I most humbly beg your pardon for detaining Queen Brynn with my witless chatter. Her Majesty was too kind to send me away and she sought to soothe my foolish nerves. I am to blame for the lateness of her arrival." She looked up and put what she hoped was the slightest light of flirtation in her eyes. "I was nervous, sire, to meet the king."

It was, she realized as his taut mouth relaxed, the right touch. He reached down, lifted her chin. "And who is this dark flower?"

"Sire, I am Aurora, daughter of Ute, and the foolish woman who has earned your displeasure."

"They grow them fair in the west. Rise." He drew her to her feet and studied her face so boldly she didn't have to fake a blush. Though it came more from temper than modesty. "You will sit beside me at tonight's banquet."

Luck or fate had blessed her, Aurora thought, and laid her hand on his. "I am undeserving, and grateful for the honor, sire."

"You will entertain me," he said as he led her inside, without, Aurora noted, another glance at his wife or daughter. "And perhaps show me why my son should consider you for wife."

"The prince should consider me, sire, so that I might continue to entertain you, and serve you as a daughter would, all of your days."

He glanced back at Dira now, with thinly veiled disgust. "And how might a daughter serve me?"

"To do her duty. At the king's pleasure, sire, and at her husband's. To bear strong sons and to present a pleasing face and form. To do their bidding day and . . . night."

He laughed, and when he stepped inside the crowded and brightly lit banquet hall, Aurora was at his side.

Thane watched from the spy hole in the secret chamber beside the minstrel's gallery. From there he could look down on the feasting, and the lights and the colors. At the scent of roasted meat his empty belly clutched, but he was used to hunger. Just as he was used to standing in the shadows and looking out on the color and the light.

He could hear women's laughter as the ladies vied for Owen's attention and favor, but there was only one who drew Thane's interest.

She sat beside the king, smiling, sampling the delicacies he piled on her plate, flirting with her eyes over the rim of her goblet.

How could this be the same creature who had come to him in dream and vision the whole of his life? The woman who had offered him such love, such passion, and such shining honesty? This coy miss with her sly smiles and trilling laugh could never make him burn as her light made him burn.

Yet he burned, even now, just watching her.

"Your back needs tending."

Thane didn't turn. Kern appeared when and where he chose, as faeries were wont to do. And was as much bane as blessing.

"I've been whipped before. It'll heal soon enough."

"Your flesh may." Kern waved a hand and the wall between them and the banquet hall shimmered away. "But your heart is another matter. She is very beautiful."

"A fair face is easy beauty. She isn't what I thought she was . . . would be. I don't want her."

Kern smiled. "One doesn't always want destiny."

Thane turned. Kern was old, old as time. His long gray beard covered plump cheeks and spun down to the waist of his bright red robes. But his eyes were merry as a child's, and green as the Lost Forest.

"You show me these things. This woman, this world, and you hint of changes, of restoration." Frustration edged Thane's voice and hardened his face. "You train me for battle, and you heal my hurts when Owen or Lorcan or one of their dogs beats me. But what good does it do me? My mother, my young sister, are no more than prisoners still. And Leia—"

"She is safe. Have I not told you?"

"Safe, at least." Struggling to compose himself, Thane looked back at the feasting, at little Dira. "One sister safe, and lost to me, the other trapped here until she's old enough for me to find sanctuary for her. There will never be one for my mother. She grows so thin."

"She worries for you, for her daughters."

"Leia bides with the women in the Valley of Secrets, at least for now. And Dira is yet too young for the snake to pay her mind—or to plan to marry her off to some slathering lackey. She need not worry for them. She need not think of me at all. I am nothing but a coward who hides his sword."

"It's not cowardice to hide your sword until the time comes to wield it. The time draws near."

"So you always say," Thane replied, and though he knew that Kern's magick kept those who were feasting from seeing him above them, he felt Aurora's gaze as it scanned the gallery. He knew she looked at him, just as he looked at her. "Is she a witch, then, and the visions between us an amusement to her?"

"She is many things."

Thane shook his head. "It doesn't matter. She isn't for me, nor I for her. That was fantasy and foolishness, and is done. It's Dira who concerns me now. Another two years, then Lorcan will seek to marry her off. Then she must be sent away from here, for her own safety. My mother will have no daughter to comfort her, and no son to stand for her."

"You are no good to them dead." Kern's voice went sharp as honed steel. "And no good to any when you wallow in pity."

"Easily said when your time is spent in a raft, and mine in a stable. I gave up my pride, Kern, and have lived without it since my seventh season. Is it so surprising I should be ready to give up my hope?"

"If you do, it will be the end for you."

"There are times I'd welcome the end." But he looked at Dira. She was so young. Innocent and defenseless. He thought of how she had wept to find him beaten and bleeding in the stables. It hurt her, he knew, more than the lash hurt him. Lorcan's blood might have run through her, but she had none of his cruelty.

She was, he thought, his only real pleasure since Leia's escape. So he would hold on to his hope a while longer, for her.

"I don't give up yet," Thane said quietly. "Not yet. But it had best be soon."

"Come, then, let me tend your wounds."

"No." Thane rolled his shoulders, welcomed the pain. "It reminds me. I have work."

"When it's done, meet me. It's time to practice."

Fingertip to fingertip, Aurora circled with Owen in a dance. The music was lively, and pleased her a great deal more than her partner. But he couldn't have known of her displeasure as she smiled at him and sent him a laughing glance over her shoulder when the set parted them.

When the music brought them together again, he stroked his thumb over her knuckles. "The king has favored you."

"I am honored. I see much of him in you, my lord."

"When it's my time to rule, I will outreach him." His fingers squeezed hers. "And I will demand much more of my queen than he of his."

"And what does your father demand of his queen?"

"Little more than obedience." He looked over to where Brynn sat, like a statue, with her women. "A comely face, a bowed head, and two pale daughters will not be enough for me."

"Two?"

"Dira is the youngest of Brynn's whelps. There was another, but she was killed by wild beasts in the Black Forest."

"Wild beasts!" Though she couldn't manage a squeal, Aurora clasped a hand to her breast.

"Do not fear, my lady." He smirked. "There are no beasts in the city—none that walk on four legs."

The figures of the dance parted them again, and Aurora executed her turns, her curtsies, and counted the beats impatiently until she faced Owen once more. With her head saucily angled, she stared into his eyes. "And what would be enough for you, my lord, for a queen?"

"Passion. Fire. Sons."

"There must be fire in bed to get sons." She lowered her voice, and spoke with her face close to his. "I would burn to be the mother of kings."

Then she stepped back, dipped low as the dance ended.

"Walk with me."

"With pleasure, sir. But I must have my woman with me, as is proper."

"Do you do only what is proper?"

"A queen would, when eyes are on her."

He lifted a brow in approval. "A brain as well as beauty. Bring her, then."

Aurora put her hand in his and gestured carelessly with the other so Cyra followed them out onto the terrace. "I like the sea," she began, looking out over the cliffs. "The sounds and the smells of it. It's a wall to the back, protection from enemies. But it's also passion, and possibilities. Do you believe there are worlds beyond the world, my lord prince?"

"Tales for children."

"If there were, a king could rule them all, and the sons of such a king would be gods. Even Draco would bow."

"Draco's power is weak, so he sulks in his cave. This"— Owen laid a hand on the hilt of his sword—"this is power."

"A man's power is in his sword and arm, a woman's is in her mind and womb."

"And her heart?" Now he laid a hand on her breast.

Though her skin crawled, she smiled easily. "Not if she gives that heart away." She touched her fingers lightly to his wrist, then eased away. "If I were to do so, my lord, to offer you my heart and my body, my value to you would diminish. A prize easily taken is little prize at all. So I will bid you good night, and hope you consider what I hold to be worth the winning."

"You would leave me with so many choices?" He gestured toward the women in the banquet hall as Aurora moved away.

"So you will see them . . . but think of me." She left him with a laugh, then turned to a mumbled oath when she was certain she was out of earshot.

"Empty-headed, fat-fingered *toad*! He's a man who thinks first with the lance between his legs. Well, there is little warrior in him. I've learned that much at least. Cyra, I need you to talk with the other women, find out all you can about the queen and her daughters. What are they in this puzzle?"

She cut herself off as they walked past guards and began to talk brightly of the feasting and dancing until she was back in her chambers.

"Rhiann." She let out a huge sigh. "Help me out of this gown. How do women of court bear the weight every day? I need the black tunic."

"You're going out again?"

"Yes. I felt eyes on me when I was at banquet. Eyes from above. Gwayne said there was a spy hole next to the minstrel's gallery. I want a look. Would Lorcan station guards there during a feast? He seems too sure of himself to bother."

No, it had not been guards watching her, Aurora knew. It had been the grass-green eyes of her wolf. She needed to learn why he'd been there.

"And I need to see how the castle is protected during the night." She pulled on her tunic. "I have enough magic to go unnoticed if need be. Did you learn anything of use?" she asked as she strapped on her sword.

"I learned that Owen went back and beat the stable hand after all."

Aurora's mouth tightened. "I'm sorry for it."

"And that the stable hand is Thane, son of Brynn, whom Lorcan took as queen."

Aurora's hands paused in the act of braiding her hair, and her eyes met Rhiann's in the glass. "Brynn's son is cast to the stables? And remains there? His father was a warrior who died in battle beside mine. His mother was my own mother's handmaid. Yet their son grovels at Owen's feet and grooms horses."

"He was not yet four when Lorcan took the throne. Only a child."

"He is not a child today." She swirled on her cloak, drew up the hood. "Stay inside," she ordered.

She slipped out of the chamber, moved silently down the corridors toward the stairs. She drew on her magic to bring smoke into the air, blunt the guards' senses as she hurried by them.

She dashed up to the minstrel's gallery and found the mechanism Gwayne had described for her to open the secret room beside it. Once inside, she approached the spy hole and looked down at the hall.

It was nearly empty now, and servants were beginning to clear the remnants of the feast. The queen had retired, and all but the boldest ladies had followed suit. The laughter had taken on a raucous edge. She saw one of the courtiers slide his hand under the bodice of a woman's gown and fondle her breast.

She hadn't been sheltered from the ways of men and women. The Travelers could be earthy, but there was always a respect and good nature. This, she thought, had neither.

She turned away from it, and focused instead on the essence of what had been in the room before her.

One that was human, she thought, and one that was not. Man and faerie-folk. But what had been their purpose?

To find out, she followed the trail of that essence from the room and out of the castle. Into the night.

There were guards posted on walls, at the gates, but to Aurora's eyes they looked sleepy and dull. Even two hundred good men, she calculated, could take the castle if it was done swiftly and with help from inside. As she worked her way along the wall, she heard the snores of a guard sleeping on duty.

Lorcan, she thought, took much for granted.

She looked toward the south gate. It was there that Gwayne had fled with the queen on the night of the battle. Many brave men had lost their lives so that her mother could escape, so that she could be born.

She would not forget it. And she would take nothing for granted.

Her senses drew her toward the stables. She smelled the horses, heard them shifting in their stalls as she approached. Though she scented man as well—sweat and blood—she knew she wouldn't find him there.

She stopped to stroke her horse's nose, to inspect the stall, and others. Whatever Thane was, he did his job here well. And lived poorly, she noted as she studied the tiny room that held his bedding, the stub of a candle, and a trunk of rough clothes.

Following the diagram in her mind, she searched the floor for the trapdoor that led to the tunnels below the stables. One channel ran to the sea, she remembered, the other to the forest.

It would be a good route to bring in her soldiers, to have them take the castle from the inside. If Lorcan hadn't found it and destroyed it.

But when she opened the door, she felt the air stir. Taking the candle stub, she lit the wick and let its wavery light guide her down the rough steps.

She could hear the roar of the sea, and though she was tempted to take that channel, just to stand by the water, to breathe it in, she turned toward the second path.

She would have Gwayne bring the men through the forest, split into companies. Some to take the walls, others to take the tunnels. Attack the walls first, she calculated, drawing Lorcan's forces there while the second wave came in from under—and behind.

Before he could turn and brace for the second assault, they would run him over. And it would be done.

She prayed that it could be done, and that she would not be sending good men to their deaths for nothing.

She moved slowly through the dark. The low ceiling made it impossible to stand upright, and she could imagine the strain of a man making the same trek in full armor.

And it would be done not after a night of feasting and dancing but after a hard march from the hills, through the forest, with the knowledge that death could wait at the end of the journey.

She was asking this of her people, and asking that they trust the fates that she would be worthy of their sacrifice. That she would be a worthy queen.

She stopped, bracing her back against the wall of stone and dirt as her heart ached. She would wish with every ounce of her blood that it was not so. That she was only an ordinary woman and could leap onto her horse and ride with the Travelers again, as she had always done. She would wish that she could hunt and laugh, love a man and bear his children. Live a life that she understood.

But to wish it was to wish against the fates, to diminish the sacrifices her parents had made, and to turn her back on those who prayed for the True One to come and bring them back into light.

So she lifted her candle again and headed down the tunnel to plot out her strategy.

When she heard the clash of steel, she drew her own sword. Snuffing out the candle, she set it down and moved soft as a cat toward the narrow opening.

She could see them battling in the moonlight, the young man and the old. And neither noticed as she boosted herself out of the tunnel and crouched on the floor of the forest.

5

HERE WAS HER wolf, and she thrilled to see him.

He fought with an icy focus and relentless strength that Aurora admired and respected—and envied. The skill, yes, the skill of a warrior was there, but it was enhanced by that cold-blooded, cold-eyed style that told her he would accept death or mete it out with equal dispatch.

The faerie was old, it was true, but a faerie nonetheless. Such creatures were not vanquished easily.

She could see the sweat of effort gleaming on Thane's face, and how it dampened his shirt. And she saw the blood that seeped onto the cloth from the wounds on his back, still fresh from a lashing.

How could a man wield a sword with such great talent and allow himself to be flogged?

And why had he watched the feasting through the spy hole? It was his gaze she had sensed on her. And his essence she had sensed there. His, and that of the old graybeard he battled now.

Even as she puzzled it over, two columns of smoke spiraled on either side of Thane. And became armed warriors. He blocked the sword of the one on his right and spun away from the sword of the one on his left as it whizzed through the air.

Raising her own, Aurora leapt. She cleaved her blade through one of the warriors and vanished it back to smoke. "Foul play, old one." She pivoted, and would have struck Kern down if Thane hadn't crossed swords with her.

"At your back," she snapped out, but the warrior was smoke again with a wave of Kern's hand.

"Lady," the faerie said with an undeniable chuckle, "you mistake us. I only help my young friend with his training." To prove it, Kern lowered his sword and bowed.

"Why am I dreaming?" Thane demanded. He was out of breath as he hadn't been during the bout, and the surging of his blood had nothing to do with swordplay. "What test is this?"

"You are not dreaming," Kern assured him.

"She's not real. I've seen her now, in flesh. And this is the vision, not the woman." Love, lust, longing knotted inside him so that he fought to ice his words with annoyance. "And neither holds interest for me any longer."

"I'm as real as you," Aurora tossed back, then sheathing her sword, she twisted her lips into a sneer. "You fight well. For a groveling stableboy. And your sword would be all that interests me, if I believed you'd gather the courage and wit to use it on something more than smoke."

"So, no vision, then, but the simpering, swooning female." He lifted the cape she'd tossed aside when she leapt to his defense. With a mocking bow, he held it out. "Go back to your feather bed, else you catch a chill."

"I'm chilled enough from you." She knocked his hand aside and turned on Kern. "Why haven't you treated his wounds?"

"He doesn't wish it."

"Ah, he's stupid, then." She inclined her head toward Thane again. "Whether you are stupid or not, I regret you were beaten on my account."

"It's nothing to do with you." Because the beating still shamed him, he rammed his sword back into its sheath. "It's not safe for a woman alone beyond the walls. Kern will show you the way back."

"I found my way out, I can find my way back. I'm not some helpless female," she said impatiently. "You of all men should know—"

"I do not know you," Thane said dully.

She absorbed the blow to her heart. They stood in the dappled moonlight, with only the call of an owl and the rushing of a stream over rocks to break the silence between them.

Even knowing the risk of mediation, Kern stepped up, laying a hand on Thane's shoulder, the other on Aurora's. "Children," he began brightly.

"We're not children any longer. Are we, lady? Not children splashing in rivers, running through the forest." It scored his heart to remember it, to remember the joy and pleasure, the simple comfort of those times with her. To know they were ended forever. "Not children taking innocent pleasure in each other's company."

She shook her head, and thought how she had lain with him, in love, in visions. Him and no other. "I wonder," she said after a moment, "why we need to hurt each other this way. Why we strike out where we once—where we always reached out. And I fear you're right. You don't know me, nor I you. But I know you're the son of a warrior, you have noble blood. Why do you sleep in the stables?"

"Why do you smile at Lorcan, dance with Owen, then wander the night with a sword?"

She only smiled. "It's not safe for a woman alone beyond the walls." There was, for just an instant, a glint of humor in his eyes. "You watched me dance."

He cursed himself for speaking of it. Now she knew of the spy hole as well as the tunnels. And one word to Owen . . . "If you wish to make amends for the beating, you won't speak of seeing me here."

"I have no reason to speak of you at all," she said coolly. "I was told faeries no longer bided near the city."

At her comment Kern shrugged. "We bide where we will, lady, even under Lorcan's reign. Here is my place, and he is my charge."

"I am no one's charge. Are you a witch?" Thane demanded.

"A witch is one of what I am." He looked so angry and frustrated. How she longed to stroke her finger over the lightning-bolt scar above his eye. "Do you fear witchcraft, Thane of the stables?"

Those eyes fired at the insult, as she'd hoped. "I don't fear you."

"Why should an armed man and his faerie guard fear a lone witch?"

"Leave us," Thane demanded of Kern, and his gaze stayed locked on Aurora's face.

"As you wish." Kern bowed deeply, then disappeared.

"Why are you here?"

"Prince Owen needs a wife. Why shouldn't it be me?"

He had to choke down a rage, bubbling black, at the thought of it. "Whatever you are, you're not like the others."

"Why? Because I walk alone at night in the Black Forest, where wild beasts are said to roam?"

"You're not like the others. I know you. I do know you, or what you were once." He had to curl his hand into a fist to keep from touching her. "I've seen you in my dreams. I've tasted your mouth. I'll taste it again."

"In your dreams perhaps you will. But I don't give my kisses to cowards who fight only smoke."

She turned, and was both surprised and aroused when he gripped her arm and dragged her around. "I'll taste it again," he repeated.

Even as he yanked her close, she had the point of her dagger at his throat. "You're slow." She all but purred it. "Release me. I don't wish to slit your throat for so small an offense."

He eased back and, when she lowered the dagger, moved like lightning. He wrested the dagger from her hand, kicked her feet out from under her before she could draw her sword. The force of the fall knocked the wind out of her, and she was pinned under him before she could draw a breath.

"You're rash," he told her, "to trust an enemy."

She had to swallow the joy, and the laugh. They'd wrestled like this before, when there had been only love and innocence between them. Here was her man, after all.

"You're right. The likes of you would have no honor."

With the same cold look in his eyes that she'd seen when he fought, he dragged her arms over her head. She felt the first licks of real fear, but even that she held tight. No groveling stableboy could make her fear. "I will taste you again. I will take something. There has to be something."

She didn't struggle. He'd wanted her to, wanted her to spit and buck and fight him so he wouldn't have to think. For one blessed moment, not to think but only feel. But she went still as stone when he crushed his lips to hers.

Her taste was the same, the same as he'd imagined, remembered, wished. Hot and strong and sweet. So he couldn't think, after all, but simply sank into the blessed relief of her. And all the aches and misery, the rage and the despair, washed out of him in the flood of her.

She didn't fight him, as she knew she wouldn't win with force. She remained still, knowing that a man wanted response— heat, anger or acquiescence, but not indifference.

She didn't fight him, but she began to fight herself as his mouth stirred her needs, as the weight of his body on hers brought back wisps of memories.

She'd never really been with a man, but only with him in visions, in dreams. She had wanted no man but him, for the whole of her life. But what she'd found wasn't the wolf she'd known, nor the coward she thought she'd found. It was a bitter and haunted man.

Still, her heart thundered, her skin trembled, and beneath his, her mouth opened and offered. She heard him speak, one word, in the oldest tongue of Twylia. The desperation in his voice, the pain and the longing in it made her heart weep.

The word was "Beloved."

He eased up to look at her. There was a tear on her cheek, and more in her eyes where the moonlight struck them. He closed his own eyes and rolled onto his bloody back.

"I've lived with horses too long, and forget how to be a man."

She was shaken to the bone from her feelings, from her needs, from the loss. "Yes, you forget to be a man." As she had forgotten to be a queen. "But we'll blame this on the night, on the strangeness of it." She got to her feet, walked over to pick up her dagger. "I think perhaps this is some sort of test, for both of us. I've loved you as long as I remember."

He looked at her, into her, and for one moment that was all there was, the love between them. It shimmered, wide and deep as the Sea of Wonders. But in the next moment the heavy hand of duty took over.

"If things were different . . ." Her vision blurred—not with magicks but with a woman's tears. It was the queen who forced them back, and denied herself the comfort. "But they aren't, and this can't be between us, Thane, for there's more at stake. Yet I have such longing for you, as I have always. Whatever's changed, that never will."

"We're not what we were in visions, Aurora. Don't seek me in them, for I won't come to you. We live as we live in the world."

She crouched beside him, brushed the hair from his brow. "Why won't you fight? You have a warrior's skill. You could leave this place, join the rebels and make something of yourself. Why raise a pitchfork in the stables when you can raise a sword against an enemy? I see more in you than what they've made you."

And want more of you, she thought. So much more of you.

"You speak of treason." His voice was colorless in the dark.

"I speak of hope, of right. Have you no beliefs in the world, Thane? None of yourself?"

"I do what I'm fated to do. No more, no less." He moved away from her and sat, staring into the thick shadows. "You should not be here, my lady. Owen would never select a wife bold enough to roam the forest alone, or one who would permit a stable hand to take . . . liberties."

"And if he selects me, what will you do?"

"Do you taunt me?" He sprang to his feet, and she saw what she'd hoped to see in his face. The strength and the fury. "Does it amuse you to find that I could pine for one who would offer herself to another like a sweetmeat on a platter?"

"If you were a man, you would take me—then it would be done." If you would take me, she thought, perhaps things would be different after all.

"Simply said when you have nothing to lose."

"Is your life so precious you won't risk it to take what belongs to you? To stand for yourself and your world?"

He looked at her, the beauty of her face and the purpose that lit it like a hundred candles glowing from within her. "Yes, life is precious. Precious enough that I would debase myself day after day to preserve it. Your place isn't here. Go back before you're missed."

"I'll go, but this isn't done." She reached out, touched his cheek. "You needn't worry. I won't tell Owen or Lorcan about the tunnels or the spy hole. I'll do nothing to take away your small pleasures or to bring you harm. I swear it."

His face went to stone as he stepped back, and he executed a mocking little bow. "Thank you, my lady, for your indulgence."

Her head snapped back as if he'd slapped her. "It's all I can give you." She hurried back to the tunnel and left him alone.

She slept poorly and watched the dawn rise in mists. In that half-light, Aurora took the globe out of its box, held it in the palm of her hand.

"Show me," she ordered, and waited while the sphere shimmered with colors, with shapes.

She saw the ballroom filled with people, heard the music and the gaiety of a masque. Lorcan slithered among the guests, a serpent in royal robes with his son and heir strutting in his wake. The black wolf prowled among them like a tame dog. Though his eyes were green and fierce, he kept his head lowered and kept to heel. Aurora saw the thick and bloody collar that choked his neck.

She saw Brynn chained to the throne with her daughter bound at her feet, and the ghost of another girl weeping behind a wall of glass.

And through the sounds of lutes and harps she heard the calls and cries of the people shut outside the castle. Pleas for mercy, for food, for salvation.

She was robed in regal red. the sword she raised shot hot white light from its killing point. As she whirled toward Lorcan, bent on vengeance, the world erupted. The battle raged—the clash of steel, the screams of the dying. She heard the hawk cry as an arrow pierced its heart. The dragon folded its black wings and sank into a pool of blood.

Flames sprang up at her feet, ate up her body until she was a pillar of fire.

And while she burned, Lorcan smiled, and the black wolf licked his hand.

Failure and death, she thought as the globe went black as pitch in her hand. Had she come all this way to be told her sword would not stand against Lorcan? Her friends would die, the battle would be lost, and she would be burned as a witch while Lorcan continued to rule—with the man she loved as little more than his cowed pet.

She could turn this aside, Aurora thought returning the globe to its box. She could go back to the hills and live as she always had. Free, as the Travelers were free. Content, with only her dreams to plague or stir her.

For life was precious. She rubbed the chill from her arms as she watched the last star wink out over Sorcerer's Mountain. Thane was right, life was precious. But she couldn't, wouldn't, turn away. For more precious than life was hope. And more precious than both was honor.

She woke Cyra and Rhiann to help her garb herself in the robes of a lady. She would wear the mask another day.

"Why don't you tell her?" Kern sat on a barrel eating a windfall apple while Thane fed the horses.

"There's nothing to tell."

"Don't you think the lady would be interested in what you are, what you're doing. Or more what you don't?"

"She looks for heroes and warriors, as females do. She won't find one in me."

"She . . ." With a secret little smile, Kern munched his apple. "Does not seem an ordinary female. Don't you wonder?"

Thane dumped oats in a trough. "I can't afford to wonder. I put enough at risk last night because my blood was up. If she chatters about the tunnels, or what passed between us—"

"Does the lady strike you as a chatterbox?"

"No." Thane rested his brow on a mare's neck. "She is glorious. More than my dreams of her. Full of fire and beauty— and more, of truth. She won't speak of it, as she said she wouldn't. I wish I'd never seen her, touched her. Now that I have, every hour of the rest of my life is pain. If Owen chooses her . . ."

He set his teeth against a flood of black rage. "How can I stay and watch them together? How can I go when I'm shackled here?"

"The time will come to break the shackles."

"So you always say." Thane straightened, moved to the next stall. "But the years pass, one the same as the other."

"The True One comes, Thane."

"The True One." With a mirthless laugh, he hauled up buckets of water. "A myth, a shadow, to coat the blisters of Lorcan's rule with false hope. The only truth is the sword, and one day my hand will be free to use it."

"A sword will break your shackles, Thane, but it isn't steel that will free the world. It is the midnight star." Kern hopped off the barrel and laid a hand on Thane's arm. "Take some joy before that day, or you'll never really be free."

"I'll have joy enough when Lorcan's blood is on my sword."

Kern shook his head. "There's a storm coming, and you will ride it. But it will be your choice if you ride it alone."

Kern flicked his wrist, and a glossy red apple appeared in his hand. With a merry grin, he tossed it to Thane, then vanished.

Thane bit into the apple, and the taste that flooded his mouth made him think of Aurora. He offered the rest to a greedy gelding.

Alone, he reminded himself, was best.

6

W RAPPED IN A purple cloak pinned with a jeweled brooch, Lorcan stood and watched his son practice his swordsmanship. What Owen lacked in style and form he made up for in sheer brutality, and that had his father's approval.

The soldier chosen for the practice had a good arm and a steady eye, and so made the match lively. Still, there were none in the city, or in the whole of Twylia, Lorcan knew, who could best the prince at steel against steel.

None would dare.

He had been given only one son, and that was a bitter disappointment. The wife he had taken in his youth had birthed two stillborn babes before Owen, and had died as she'd lived—without a murmur of complaint or wit—days after his birthing.

He had taken another, a young girl whose robust looks had belied a barren womb. It had been a simple matter to rid himself of her by damning her as a witch. After a month in the dungeons at the hands of his tribunal, she'd been willing enough to confess and face the purifying fires.

So he had taken Brynn. Far cousin of the one who had been queen. He'd wanted the blue of royal blood to run through the veins of his future sons—and had he got them, would have cast his firstborn aside without a qualm.

But Brynn had given him nothing but two daughters. Leia, at least, had possessed beauty, and would have been a rich bargaining chip in a marriage trade. But she'd been willful as well, and had tried to run away when he'd betrothed her.

The wild beasts of the forest had left little more than her torn and bloody cloak.

So he had no child but Dira, a pale, silent girl whose only use would be in the betrothing of her to a lord still loyal enough, still rich enough, to warrant the favor in two or three years' time.

He had planted his seed in Brynn again and again, but she lost the child each time before her term was up, and now was too sickly to breed. Even the maids and servants he took to his bed failed to give him a son.

So it was Owen who would carry his name, and his ambitions turned to the grandsons he would get. A king could not be a god without the continuity of blood.

His son must choose well.

He smiled as he watched Owen draw blood from his opponent, as he beat back his man with vicious strikes until the soldier lost his footing and fell. And Lorcan nodded with approval as Owen stabbed the sword's point into the man's shoulder.

He'd taught his son well. A fallen enemy was, after all, still an enemy.

"Enough." Lorcan's rings flashed in the sunlight as he clapped his hands. "Bear him away, bind him up." He waved off the wounded soldier and threw his arm around Owen's shoulders. "You please me."

"He was hardly worth the effort." Owen studied the stain on his blade before ramming it home. "It's tedious not to have more of a challenge."

"Come, the envoys have brought the taxes from the four points, and I would speak with you before I deal with them. There are rumbles of rebellion in the north."

"The north is a place of ignorant peasants and hill dwellers who wait for Draco to fly from his mountain." With a glance toward the high peak, Owen snorted in disgust. "A battalion of troops sent up to burn a few huts, put a few of their witches on the pyre should be enough to quiet them."

"The talk that comes down is not of Draco but of the True One."

Owen's mouth twisted as he gripped the hilt of his sword. "Tongues won't flap of what is forbidden once they are cut out. Those who speak of treason must be routed out and reminded there is only one king of Twylia."

"And so they shall be. The envoys brought six rebels, as well as the taxes. They will be tried, and executed, as an example, as part of your betrothal ceremonies. Until then, the tribunal will . . . interrogate them. If these are more than rumbles, we will silence them."

They strode through the gates of the castle and across the great hall. "Meanwhile, preparations for the rest of the ceremonies proceed. You must make your choice within the week."

Inside the throne room, Owen plucked a plum from a bowl and threw himself into a chair. "So many plums." He bit in, smiled. "All so ripe and tasty."

"There's more to your choice than a pleasing face. You may take any who stirs your blood into your bed. You are the prince, and will be king. Your bedmates may slake your lust, but your queen must do that and more. You must have sons."

Lorcan poured wine, and sat by the fire that burned even so early in the day for his comfort. "Strong sons, Owen. So you must choose a woman who will be more than a pretty vessel. Have any here found your favor?"

"One or two." Owen shrugged. "The latest arrival interests me. She has a bold look in her eye."

"Her dowry would be rich," Lorcan considered. "And her father's lands are valuable. She has beauty enough, and youth. It might do."

"The match would tie the west to us, and as Ute's land runs north along the hills, such positioning would be strategic."

"Yes, yes." Lorcan rested his chin on his fist and considered. "The Realm of Magicks still thrives in pockets of the west, and too many men run tame there who preach of Draco's spell and the True One. It's time to look to the far west and north, and smother any small embers of treason before they flare."

"The Lady Aurora's father, it seems, is unwell." Owen took another bite of his plum. "If we were wed, he might sicken and die—with a bit of help. And so his lands, his fortifications, his wealth would come to me."

"It might do," Lorcan repeated. "I'll take a closer look at this one. If I approve, your betrothal will be announced at week's end at the masque. And you will be pledged the following morning."

Owen raised a brow. "So quickly?"

"With the wedding ceremony to take place at the end of a fortnight—by which time every man in the world must render a token to mark the events—the masque and the wedding. The shepherd must render his finest rams, the farmer one quarter of his crop, the miller a quarter of his grain, and so on, so as to provide their prince and his bride with the stores for their household."

Lorcan stretched his booted feet toward the fire. "If the man has no ram, no crop, no grain, he must render his oldest son or if he has no son, his oldest daughter, to serve the royal couple. Craftsmen and artisans will bequeath a year of their time so that your home can be built on the western border and furnished as befits your rank."

"Some will not give willingly," Owen pointed out.

"No. And the business of persuading them to do their duty to their king will bury all mutterings of the True One, scatter rebellious forces, and forge our hold on the west. Yes." He lifted his goblet in toast. "I think it may do."

Under the guise of serving his mistress, Rohan walked with his head humbly bowed. His heart was full of rage edged in fear. He kept his eyes lowered as he moved past guards and into the sitting room where Aurora gathered with the women to take rose tea and chatter about gowns and the upcoming masque.

"Your pardon, my lady."

Knowing her part, Aurora spared him a single disinterested glance. "I am occupied."

"I beg your pardon, my lady, but the lace you requested has arrived."

"A full day late." She set her cup aside and shook her head at the women who sat closest to her as she rose. "It will probably be inferior, but we'll see what can be done with it. Have it sent to my chambers. I'll come now."

She walked out behind him, careful not to speak to him or to Rhiann, who followed in her wake, until they were behind doors again.

"Lace." She sighed heavily, and poured ale to rid her mouth of the oversweet taste of the rose tea. "How I am lowered."

"Lorcan's envoys returned today with taxes levied against the four points."

Aurora's mouth thinned. "He will not keep them for long."

"They brought also six prisoners."

"Prisoners? What prisoners are these?"

"They say they are rebels, but four are only farmers, and one of them is aged and near crippled, while another is no more than a boy. The other two must have been set upon and taken while scouting. One of them is Eton."

Aurora lowered herself slowly to a chair as Rhiann bit back a cry. "Our Eton? Cyra's betrothed?"

"Eton was wounded, and all are being kept in the dungeons." He curled his hands helplessly into fists. "They're to be questioned by the tribunal."

"Tortured," Aurora whispered.

"It's said they'll be executed for treason within the week. Flogged and branded, then hanged."

"Compose yourself, Rhiann," Aurora ordered when the woman began to weep. "It will not happen. Why were they taken, Rohan? How are they charged with treason?"

"I can't say. There's word among the servants that rebellion is brewing, that the True One is coming."

"So Lorcan strikes before he is struck." She pushed to her feet to pace as she brought the positioning of the dungeons into her mind. "We must get them out, and we will. We have a week."

"You can't leave them there for a week." Rhiann struggled against fresh tears. "To be tortured and starved."

"I have no choice but to leave them until we are ready to attack. If we try to free them now, we could fail, and even if we succeed, such a move would put Lorcan on alert."

"Eton may be dead in a week," Rhiann snapped. "Or worse than dead. Is this how you honor your family?"

"This is how I rule, and it is bitter to me. Eton is like my own brother. Would you have me risk all to spare him?"

"No." Rohan answered before Rhiann could speak. "It would not honor him if you spared him pain, or even his life, and Lorcan continued to rule."

"Get word to him if you can. Tell him he must hold on until we can find a way. Send a dispatch to Gwayne. It's time. They are to travel in secret. They must not be seen. How long will it take them? Three days?"

"Three—or four."

"It will take three," Aurora said firmly. "I will meet him in the forest, near the tunnel, at midnight when he arrives. I'll know what must be done."

"Cyra." Rhiann grieved for her daughter. "How will we keep this from her?"

"We won't. She has a right to know. I'll tell her. She should hear it from me."

She went out in search of her friend, hoping she would have the right words, and met Owen as she stepped into the courtyard.

"Lady Aurora." He took her hand, bowed over it. "I was about to send word for you."

"I am at your pleasure, my lord prince."

"Then you'll honor me by riding out with me. I've been busy with matters of state all morning, and wish for a brisk gallop and your lovely company."

"I would enjoy nothing more. May I meet you in an hour, my lord, so I might find my maid and change into proper attire?"

"I'll wait. Impatiently."

She curtsied, tipping her face up with a saucy smile before rising and hurrying away. She found Cyra in the kitchens, her eyes bright and round with gossip.

"I require you," Aurora said coolly, then turned away so that Cyra had to rush after her.

"I've learned all about—"

"Not now," Aurora said under her breath. "I'm riding out with the prince," she said in a clear voice. "I'll want my red riding habit, and be quick about it."

"Yes, my lady."

Only Aurora heard Cyra's muffled giggle as the girl rushed ahead to the bedchamber. And only Aurora hoped she would hear Cyra's laughter again.

"And be quick about it," Cyra mimicked with another giggle as soon as Aurora closed the door behind her. "I had to bite my lip to keep from laughing. Oh, Aurora, I've learned all manner of things. The kitchens are fertile ground."

"Cyra, sit down. I must speak with you."

The tone had Cyra stopping to look at Aurora as she lifted up the red habit. "Do you not ride out with Owen, then?"

"No. Yes, that is—yes." Aurora pushed at her hair. "Yes, within the hour."

"It'll take nearly that long to get this done. A lady of your station would have her hair dressed differently for riding. It has to suit the hat, you know. We'll get started and exchange our news. Oh, Aurora, mine is *so* romantic."

"Cyra." Aurora took the habit and tossed it aside so she could grasp Cyra's hand. "I have word of Eton."

"Eton? What of Eton? He's in the north, scouting for Gwayne." The rosy flush was dying on her cheeks as she spoke, and her fingers trembled in Aurora's. "Is he dead? Is he dead?"

"No. But he's hurt."

"I'll go to him. I have to go to him."

"You can't. Cyra." She pushed her friend into a chair, then crouched at her feet. "Eton and five others were taken by Lorcan's soldiers. He was wounded. I don't know how badly. He was brought here, to the dungeons."

"He's here, in the castle? Now? And he lives?"

"Yes. They will question him. Do you know what that means?"

"They will torture him. Oh." Cyra squeezed her eyes shut. "Oh, my love."

"I can do nothing for him yet. If I try . . . all could be lost, so I can do nothing yet. I'm sorry."

"I need to see him."

"It isn't safe."

"I need to see him. They send food down to the jailers, to the tribunal, and slop to the prisoners. One of the kitchen maids will let me take her place. If he sees me, he'll know there's hope. It will make him stronger. He would never betray you, Aurora, and neither will I. He's proud to serve you, and so am I."

Tears swam into Aurora's eyes, then she pressed her face into Cyra's lap. "It hurts to think of him there."

"Then you must not think of it." She stroked Aurora's hair and knew that she herself would think of little else. "I will pray for him. You'll be a good queen because you can cry for one man when so much depends on you."

Aurora lifted her head. "I'm so afraid. It comes close now, and I'm so afraid that I'll fail. That I'll die. That others will die for me."

"If you weren't afraid, you'd be like Lorcan."

Aurora wiped her eyes. "How?"

"He isn't afraid because he doesn't love. To cause such pain you can't love or fear, but only crave."

"Cyra, my sister." Aurora lifted Cyra's hand and pressed it to her cheek. "You've become wise."

"I believe in you, and it makes me strong. You must change or you'll be late and annoy Owen. You need to keep him happy. It will make his death at your hands all the sweeter."

Aurora's eyes widened. "You talk easily of killing."

"So will you, when I tell you what I've learned. Hurry. This will take some time."

7

"BRYNN WAS ONE of your mother's women, and her friend," Cyra began.

"I know this. Now she sits as queen. Though not happily, by all appearances." Aurora turned so Cyra could unhook her gown.

"She—Brynn—was widowed in the great battle. Thane was but three. In the year that followed, Lorcan decided to take a new wife. It's said—whispered—that she refused him but that he gave her the choice between giving herself to him and her son's life."

"He would murder a child to win a wife?"

"He wanted Brynn, because she was closest to the queen, in spirit and in blood." Cyra helped Aurora into the riding habit and began to fasten it. "I only know it's said that Brynn wept to another of the handmaidens—the mother of the kitchen girl who spoke to me. She swore her allegiance, and gave herself to Lorcan for his promise to spare her son's life."

Aurora sat at the dressing table, staring at her own face, and asked herself what she would have done. What any woman would have done. "She had no choice."

"Thane was sent to the stables, to work, and was not allowed inside the castle from that day, nor to speak a single word to his mother."

"Hard, hard and cold. He could have taken Brynn by force and killed the boy. He kept him alive, kept Thane alive and within her reach, never to touch or speak. To make them both suffer, to cause pain for the sake of it. Payment," Aurora said aloud as she let herself drift into the nightmare of Lorcan's mind. "Payment for her first refusal of him."

"This is his way," Cyra agreed. "A way of vengeance and retribution. Brynn married Lorcan, and twice miscarried his child before she gave birth to a daughter, who was Leià. Three years after, she bore Dira."

"She had no choice, but Thane . . . he's no longer a child."

"Wait, there's more." Cyra brushed out Aurora's hair and began to braid it. "When Thane was but seven, he ran away—to join the rebels, it's said. He and a young friend. They were caught and brought back. The other boy, the brother of the maid who told me, was hanged."

The horror of it cut through her heart. "By Draco, he hanged a half-grown boy?"

"And forced Thane to watch it done. Thane was beaten and told that if he insulted the king again, another would die in his place. And still he ran away, less than a year later. He was captured, brought back, beaten, and another boy his age was hanged."

"This is beyond evil." Aurora bowed her head. "Beyond madness."

"And more yet. Lorcan took the baby, Dira, his own daughter and half sister to Thane, to the stables where Thane was shackled. She was only days old. And he put his own dagger at the baby's throat. If Thane ran again, if he spoke ill of Lorcan or Owen, if he disobeyed any law or displeased the king in any way, Dira would die for it, then Leia, then Brynn herself. If he did not submit, any and all who shared his blood would be put to death."

"Could he kill his own?" Struggling to see it, Aurora rubbed a hand over her troubled heart. "Yes, yes, he could do it. She is only a female child, after all," she said bitterly. "And how could a brother, a boy, a man, risk it? He could run, and now he could escape, but he could never forfeit his sisters' lives, risk his mother's."

She thought of what she'd seen in the crystal. The wolf walking like a tame dog, while his mother and sister were chained to the throne. And the ghost of another sister stood trapped behind glass. "No, he could not run, he could not fight. Not even for his own freedom."

"He never did so again," Cyra confirmed as she rolled the braid into a thick knot at the base of Aurora's neck. "He speaks little to others, stays among the horses."

"He makes no friends," Aurora said quietly, "except a girl in a vision and an aged faerie. Because to make friends puts them at risk. So he's always alone."

"It breaks my heart." Cyra dashed a tear from her cheek. "They think he's beaten—Lorcan, Owen, everyone. But I don't believe this is so."

"No." She remembered how he'd looked in the forest with a sword in his hand and the cold fire of battle in his eyes. "It is not so. He has buried his pride and given more than half his life to the waiting, but he is not beaten." She reached back to take Cyra's hand. "Thank you for telling me."

"A man who would humble himself to save another is a great man, greater perhaps than one who fights."

"Stronger. Truer. I misjudged him because I didn't look beyond my own eyes, into my heart. This wolf is not tamed. He stalks. I have fresh hope." She got to her feet, turned. "Go see your man, but take care. Take great care. Tell him, if you can, it won't be long. Three days, no more than four, and we will bring a flood to the City of Stars. I swear on my life, Lorcan will drown in it."

She stepped in front of the looking glass, and her smile was a warrior's smile. "Now we'll go flutter and preen for the son of the devil, and see what use he is to us."

Aurora hurried to the stables, hoping for a moment alone with Thane. Her horse and Owen's were already saddled. Owen's personal guard stood at the riding gelding's head.

She moved to her own mount as if inspecting the horse and the tack.

"You, there." She approached the stables, clapped her hands imperiously. "Stableboy!"

Thane stepped out. He kept his head lowered, but his eyes lifted, and the hot resentment in them blasted her face. "My lady."

For the benefit of the guard, she crooked a finger and moved to her mount's far hind leg. She bent as if to inspect the knee, and as Thane did the same, she whispered. "I must speak with you. Tonight. I'll come to the stables."

"There is nothing more to say, and you put yourself and me at risk."

"It's urgent." Risking a touch, she brushed her fingers over the back of his hand. "Beloved."

She heard the clatter of armor and sword as the guard snapped to attention. Giving her horse a light pat, she straightened and turned to smile at Owen.

"Do you have some trouble with this . . . thing?" Owen demanded, sneering at Thane.

"Indeed, no, my lord. My mount seemed to favor this leg when we rode in. I was complimenting your boy on the care of my horse. I'm very fond of my horse." Deliberately, she reached into her purse and drew out a copper. "For your good work," she said and handed the coin to Thane.

"Thank you, my lady."

"It isn't necessary to give him coin, nor to speak to him."

"I find such small boons ensure good care." She moved, subtly, so that she stood between Thane and Owen, and sent the prince her brightest smile. "As I said, I'm very fond of my horse. Will you help me mount, my lord? I am so looking forward to a gallop."

Owen shoved the mounting block aside and set his hands on Aurora's waist. She laid hers on his shoulders and let out a flirtatious laugh as he vaulted her into the saddle.

"You're very strong, my lord." She gathered her reins. "I also have a fondness for a strong man." With another laugh, she clicked her tongue and sent her horse flying away from the stables.

Owen, she discovered, was a mediocre rider on a superior mount. She reined herself in to keep pace with him. It was good, despite the choice of company, to ride. To feel the freshness of the air on her skin and to be away from the clatter of the castle and the smells of the city.

Her men, she thought, would come from the northwest, using the forest for cover and keeping off the roads. Then the hills would ring with the battle and, when it was done, with victory.

"You look thoughtful, Aurora." Owen studied her as they slowed to a trot at the edge of field and forest.

"Only admiring the beauty of this country, my lord. And wondering how pleasant it is to know that all you see is yours."

"The woman I choose will have part in that."

"If you will it," she said carelessly, and walked her horse along the forest path. "There is rich land in the west, as well. My father tends what's his with a firm hand and a clear eye. The hills reach high there, and the cattle grow fat on them."

"The name of my bride will be announced at the masque, at week's end."

"So I am told." She slid her gaze toward his, quirked her lips. And slid her power over him like silk. "Do you know it?"

"Perhaps I do." He reached to take her reins and stop her horse, then leapt from his own. While she raised her eyebrows, he circled, then lifted his arms to pluck her from the saddle. "But a prince must take care in selecting a bride. One who will be queen."

She laid her hand on his chest. "So he must—as a woman must take care, my lord, in who takes her favors."

"I want a woman who will stir my blood." He pulled her closer and would have taken her mouth if she hadn't laid her fingers on his lips.

"A man's blood is easily stirred. And if a woman gives him what he desires before a pledge is made, the woman is a fool. What man, what king, wants a foolish wife?"

"If you give me what I desire, and it pleases me, I will make the pledge. Lie with me now, and you will be queen."

"Make me queen." She played her fingers along his jaw. "And I will lie with you. I will give you sons, and great pleasure in the making of them."

"I could take you." He dug his fingers into her hips. "You couldn't stop me." His breath came short as he lifted her to her toes. "You belong to me, as every blade of grass in the field beyond belongs to me. I am your lord. I am your god."

"You have the strength, and the power." And though she had a dagger beneath her skirts, she couldn't afford to use it, not even in defense against rape. "Why take by force today what would be given freely in a few days' time?"

"For excitement."

She only laughed, and tapped his cheek. "To hump like rabbits in the dirt? Hardly befitting you, my lord, or the woman who wishes to sit by your side, and lie by it. The waiting will, I think . . ." She traced her fingertip over his lips. "Hone appetites."

"A sample, then." He circled her throat with his hand, squeezed, then covered her lips with his in a brutal kiss. She tasted his desire, and his delight in force. With all her will she swallowed revulsion and fury, and let him take.

She thought of how he would pay for this, and for the thousands of cruelties to her people, for his part in humiliating Thane. For every lash Eton might suffer.

When his hands pawed at her, when they clamped bruisingly on her breasts, she neither struggled nor winced. For he would pay.

"My lord, I beg you." She hoped the quaver in her voice could be taken for passion rather than the rage she felt. "Indulge me and wait for the rest. You will not be disappointed, I promise."

"Would you rather I nibble some housemaid to sate my appetite?"

"Such a man as you would have great appetites. I will do my best to meet them, at the proper time." She broke free. "Your kisses make me tremble. It will break my heart if you only toy with me."

He grasped her waist and tossed her up to the saddle more roughly than necessary. "You'll know my answer at week's end."

Bastard, she thought as she gathered her reins. But she smiled, with her lashes lowered. "And you, my lord, will know mine."

She wanted to bathe, to rub her lips raw so that there was nothing left of the taste or feel of him. But she laughed and talked her way through another night of feasting. She lifted her cup to the king in toast. She danced, and pretended only feminine flusters and objections when Owen pulled her into the shadows and touched her body. As if he had the right.

Her mind was too troubled to speak of it to Rhiann as she removed the ball gown and put on her nightdress. She watched the sky, careful not to venture too close to the window, as the world quieted toward sleep.

Then, donning cloak and hood, she slid out into the night, to the stables.

She knew he wasn't there. She understood now that part of her would sense him, would always sense him. So he hadn't waited for her, as she'd asked.

Once again she took a candle and followed after him through the tunnels, and into the forest beyond.

He stood in the moonlight. It showered over his ragged shirt, his unkempt hair, the worn boots.

"I told you not to come."

"I need to speak with you." She blew the candle out, set it down. "To see you. To be with you."

He stepped back. "Are you mad, or simply sent here to ensure I will be?"

"You could have told me when I asked why you stay here."

"It's nothing to do with you."

"Everything you do, everything you are, and think and feel, all of you has to do with all of me."

"You rode with him."

"I do what needs to be done, as you do. Thane." She reached out a hand as she moved to him, but he turned away.

"Will you be wedded to him, and bedded to him? Does that need to be done?"

For the first time in days a smile that came from her heart curved her lips. "You're jealous. I'm small enough to enjoy that. He will never have me as a man has a woman. You already have."

"I haven't. I won't."

"In dreams you have." She moved in, laid her cheek on his back and felt his body go taut as a bowstring. "You've dreamed of me."

Both heart and body strained toward her. "All of my life, it seems, I've dreamed of you."

"You love me."

"All of my life." He spun back, held her at arm's length when she would have embraced him. "You kept me alive, I think, in dreaming of you. The loving of you, and being loved. Now, by the gods, you'll be the death of me."

"No one lives forever." She took off her cloak, spread it on the ground. Then, standing in the moonlight, she drew off her nightdress, let it pool at her feet. "Live now."

He reached out, wound her long, dark hair around his fist. He could walk away from this, still had the strength. Or he could take love, one precious moment of love, and have its comfort and torment with him the rest of his days.

"If hell awaits me, I'll have one night in heaven first."

"We'll have it." She waved a hand and around them cast a circle of protective fire. The light of it shimmered in golds as a thin mist covered the ground in a pure white blanket.

"I've waited for you, Thane." She touched her lips to his, fit her body to his. "Through the light, and through the dark."

"For this one night with you, I would trade a thousand nights alone. Bear a thousand lashes, die a thousand deaths."

"Midnight nears." She smiled as he lowered her to the soft and misted ground. "It's my hour."

"It will be ours. Aurora." He kissed her tenderly, very tenderly. "My light."

Sweet, so sweet, that merging of lips, the brush of fingertips over flesh. She knew his taste, his touch, so warmly familiar, and yet so gloriously new. The feel of his body, the hard muscle, the ridged scars, aroused her, as did the gleam of his eyes in the glow of witch fire.

"Thane. My wolf." With a laugh, she reared up and nipped at his chin. "So much better than a dream."

Their lips met again, a deep search that had her trembling beneath him, and shifting restlessly as needs heated in her blood. Her heart thundered under his palm—the hard callus of his labors, then under his mouth—the hot brand of his need.

And her belly began to ache as if with hunger. Her own hands became more demanding, tugging at his worn shirt. The sound of cloth ripping was only another thrill.

He wanted to go slowly, to draw this night into forever. She could vanish, he knew, when the sun struck, and he would be left with more misery than he thought he could bear.

But his need for her was impossible, enormous, and the love that stormed through him stole his breath. The urgency built with every touch, every murmur, until he was half mad.

Whatever he took, she gave, then only demanded more. She cried out his name when he drove her to peak, then clung relentlessly with her mouth like a fever on his.

The empty well of his life flooded full, and he knew for the first time something he would kill to keep.

His hands clamped on her wrists. He looked down at her with eyes fierce and gleaming green. "You'll never belong to him. He'll never touch you like this."

"No." Here was power, she realized. Another kind of female power. "Only you. It is the woman who gives herself to you, and only you." She heard the bells begin to strike the hour. "Mate with me, join with me. Love with me. We'll be more together than either can be alone."

He plunged inside her, watched the power and the pleasure of the moment rush over her face. And felt the rough magic of it whip through him.

Then she was moving under him and with him, and for him. Their fingers locked, their lips met.

Overhead, lightning flashed in the form of a dragon, and the stars flared red as blood.

8

WHEN THE WITCHING hour passed, she stayed with him. But she knew the time grew short. If they were as others, she mused, they could remain like this, wrapped warm in her cloak, and sleep until dawn broke.

But they were not as others.

"I have much to tell you," she began.

He only drew her closer to his side. "You're a witch. I know. I'm bewitched. And grateful."

"I've cast no spell on you, Thane."

He smiled and continued to study the stars. "You are the spell."

"We are the spell." She shifted so she could look down at his face. "I'll explain. You are a hero to me."

He looked away from her and started to move.

"A man who would put all he wanted, all he needed, aside to protect others? The greatest of warriors. But that time is ending." She took his hand, brought it to her lips. "Will you stand beside me? Will you pledge me your sword?"

"Aurora, I will pledge you my life. But I won't lift a sword knowing the act will bring another down on my sister. My mother. Or some poor innocent. They hanged my friend, and he was but six seasons. His only crime was in following me."

"I know." She kissed his cheek. "I know." And the other. "No harm will come to your family, or to any in your stead." She reached out, picked up her dagger, and drew it across her palm. "I swear it, on my blood."

He gripped her hand. "Aurora—"

"She is my sister now. She is my mother now. You are my husband now."

Emotion stormed across his face. "You would take me this way? I'm nothing."

"You're the bravest man I know, and you're mine. You are the most honorable, and the most true. Will you take me?"

The world, Thane thought, could change in one magic hour. "I'll get you away to safety. I know how it can be done, with Kern's help—"

"I go nowhere."

"To the Valley of Secrets, through the Realm of Magicks," he continued, ignoring her protest. "My sister is safe there, and so will you be."

"Your sister? Leia lives?"

Fury flashed onto his face. "He would have sold her, like a mare. Bartered her like a whore. She was but sixteen. With Kern's help, she was taken from the castle and away, and her cloak left torn and bloodied deep in the woods. She lives, and I will owe Kern and his kind all of my days. But she is lost to me, and I can't risk getting word of her to my mother, to give her even that much comfort."

Not a ghost, Aurora realized, but a memory. Shielded and safe—and apart. She touched her fingers to his cheeks. "What did it cost you?" she murmured.

"Kern asked for no payment."

"No—what did Lorcan and Owen take from you? What scars do you bear from their anger at the loss of so valuable a possession to them? So many times, when we came to each other in visions, I saw your sadness. But you would never tell me."

"You would always bring me joy. Beloved."

"They whipped you in her stead. Laid the lash on your back because they couldn't lay it on hers. I can see it now, and that you reached through the pain, beyond it, because your sister was saved."

"Don't look." He gripped her hands when her smoky eyes went dark with vision. "There's no pain here now. And there will be none. Kern will help me get you away. You, and my mother and sister, your women. Then I'll find the rebels, and come back to deal with Lorcan and his whelp."

"You won't have to look far for the rebels. They're on their way even now. Your mother and your sister will be safe. I've sworn it. But I stay, and I fight." She laid her hands on his shoulders to stem his protest, and looked deep into his eyes. "A queen does not sit in safety while others win the world."

She got to her feet. "I am Aurora, daughter of Gwynn and Rhys. I am the Lady of the Light. I am the True One, and my time has come. Will you stand with me, Thane the Valiant, and pledge me your sword?"

There was a light around her as she spoke, as gold as sunlight and stronger than the witch fire she'd conjured. For a moment it seemed a crown of stars sat sparkling on her head, and their brilliance was blinding.

He had to struggle to find his voice, but he knelt. "My lady. I never believed in you, and still I knew you from my first breath. All that I have, all that I am is yours. I would die for you."

"No." She dropped to her knees to take his face in her hands. "You must live for me. And for the child we made tonight." She took his hand and pressed it to her belly.

"You can't know—"

"I do. I do know." Her face, her voice, were radiant. "You gave me a child tonight, and he will be king, and rule this world after us. He will be more than either of us, more still than the sum of us. We must win it back for him, and for our people. We will take from Lorcan, in blood if we must, what he took in blood. But you must live for me, Thane. Swear it."

"I swear it." In all of his memory he'd lived with nothing. Now in one night he was given the world. "A son?"

"For the first. We will make others." With a laugh, she threw her arms around him. "They will be happy, and so well loved.

And they will serve, Thane." She drew back. "Serve the world as well as rule it. This can be. I begin to see so much of what can be. I needed you to clear my vision."

"How many come? What are their arms?"

"Now you think like a soldier." Satisfied, she sat on the ground. "I'll know more soon. Here, at midnight the night after next, we meet Gwayne. He is my hawk, and he brings the forces. Two of mine are held now in the dungeon. One is as dear as a brother to me. They must be freed, but not until the night of the masque. I pray they live to see that night, and they are not to be sacrificed."

"I can get them out. I know the tunnels and underground better than any. There are others held there who would stand with you."

"What do you need?"

"One good man and his sword would be enough."

"You shall have him. This must be done, and quietly, in the hour before the masque. The wounded, or those too weak to fight, must be taken through the tunnels and away. Men will die, Thane. There will be no choice. But I want no man's blood spilled carelessly. Some would swear allegiance if given the opportunity. From what I've seen, not all who serve Lorcan do so with a full heart."

"Some serve only in fear of their lives or the lives of their loved ones." He shrugged when she studied him. "Men often speak their mind around horses. And minions."

"You are no one's minion."

"I've been less than that." His hand curled into a fist. "By the blood, for the first time since childhood I know what it is to want, more than to live, to stretch out of this skin and be. I would have served you," he said quietly. "I have seen you wear the Crown of Stars, and I would have served you in anything you asked, servant to queen. But to have loved you, as a man loves a woman, has changed everything. I can never go back."

"Only for a short time. My wolf will conceal his fangs only for a short time. I must go now. When we move, Thane, we must move quickly." She went willingly into his arms, held close. "We'll have all of our lives for the rest."

And for the rest, he thought, as he let her go, she and the child would be protected at any and all costs.

•   •   •

Hoping to avoid Owen for the day, Aurora made plans to go into the city and there measure the feeling among the people—and the strategy of attack and defense. It was difficult to deny herself a trip to the stables and even a fleeting moment with Thane, but she sent Rohan to order the carriage, as was fitting for a lady of her station.

"Soon there will be no more need for pretense. Or the wait," she added and touched Cyra's shoulder. "The prisoners will be freed, and the wounded among them taken safely into the forest. I promise you."

"He suffers, Aurora. My Eton suffers. I could barely stand to see him so. Many held there don't even know their crime, and some are driven mad by the dark and the starvation."

"It won't be dark much longer. Men held there have fathers or sons or brothers. They'll fight with me. I saw the dragon in the sky last night, and the red stars." She laid a hand on her belly. "I've seen what can be."

She hooked her arm with Cyra's and started across the courtyard. And heard the clash of armor as guards snapped to attention.

The heat of battle flashed in her blood even as she bowed her head and curtsied to the man who called himself king.

"Majesty."

He took her hand to bring her to her feet, and didn't release it. "A pretty light on a gloomy morning."

"You are too kind, sire. But even a dank day in such a place is a joy."

"And do you ride out again today?"

"I go into the city, with your permission, my lord, in hopes to find something appropriate for the masque. I don't wish to dishonor you or the prince by arriving at such a spectacle in my country garb."

"You go unescorted, lady?"

"I have my men, sir, and my women." She fluttered up at him. "Will I not be safe enough?"

He chucked her under the chin and made her spine freeze. "Beauty is never safe enough. Do you not seek the company of the prince?"

"Always, my lord. But . . ." She offered a slow, sidelong smile. "I fear he may become bored with me if I am too accessible. Do you not think that a man desires a woman more when she is just out of reach?"

"You're a clever one, aren't you?"

"A clever mind is a valuable tool to a woman. As is amiability, so if you prefer I forgo this venture and wait upon Prince Owen's pleasure, I will do so." She glanced over as Rohan brought her carriage into the courtyard. "Shall I send it away again, sire?"

"Go, and enjoy. I look forward to seeing what catches your eye in the shops." He helped her into the carriage, and was obviously pleased when she peeked out the window and sent him one last smile.

"He makes my skin crawl," Aurora said as she flopped back against the seat.

"He would have you for himself if he could." Rhiann nodded wisely. "There's a look in a man's eye when he imagines such things. Having you for his son is his next choice."

"What he'll have is my sword at his throat. And a happy day that will be. How much have we left to spend?" she demanded.

Rhiann carefully counted out the coins in her purse, and had Aurora blowing out a breath.

"I hate to waste it on foolishness, but I have to make a showing. Lorcan will expect it now."

"You can be very particular," Cyra said, and worked up a smile. "Turning up your nose at the offerings, sniffing at materials, waving away baubles."

"I suppose. I'd rather be inside the taverns listening to the talk, but we'll leave that to Rohan." She glanced out the window of the carriage, and her heart ached at the sight of children begging for food. She thought of the taxes levied, all the coins stored inside the palace.

"I have an idea, something that might distract Lorcan and help our army move into the forest unnoticed. Chaos," she declared, "is another kind of weapon."

Furious, Owen stalked into the stables. He'd wanted Aurora, but she was off—with no word to him—to the city. He'd planned another ride, with a picnic by the river. And a seduction.

If he were to choose her, and his mind was nearly made up, he expected her to be available at his whim. It was best she learned that now.

There were others with more beauty, others with more generous attributes. If she refused to come to heel, he would take one of them as queen, and make the intriguing Aurora a consort.

He pushed his way into a stall where Thane was wrapping a foreleg for the mount of one of the soldiers.

"Saddle my horse."

Thane kept his head lowered as he continued to wrap the leg. "Yes, my lord."

"Now, you worthless nit." He struck out, slapping Thane in the face with the back of his hand.

Thane took the blow, and though he knew it was foolish, he checked his grip on the halter so that the frightened horse shied and canted, driving Owen into the wall of the stall.

"You'll pay for that, you ham-handed bastard."

There was enough satisfaction in watching Owen go white as bone and scramble out of the stall to take all the sting out of the next blow. "A thousand pardons, my lord prince."

"I'll deal with you later. Get my horse, and be quick about it."

As Owen strode out of the stables, Thane grinned and wiped the blood from his mouth.

"The mount's wasted on him." Thane turned and saw Kern leading the already saddled horse from its stall. "A lame one-eyed donkey would be wasted on him."

Thane ran a hand over the gleaming neck of Owen's stallion. "If the gods are with me, and I live, I will have this horse as my own. Thank you for saddling him."

"A simple matter, in a complicated time."

"You knew who she was. Who she is."

"The True One shines."

"She does." Thane rested his brow on the stallion's neck. "I have such love for her. Fierce and frightening love. I'll do what needs to be done, Kern, but I ask you, whatever you've given me over the years, to give it now to my family. I can go into any battle, take any risk, if I know they're protected."

"You've stood as their shield long enough. I'll stand for you when the time comes."

"Then I'll be ready." He led the horse out, and stood meekly at its head while Owen berated him.

"I'll be ready," he repeated and watched Owen spur the mount and ride off.

The sky stayed dim, but no rain fell. Aurora watched the dark clouds and prayed that the storm brewing would hold while her men marched toward the city. She used her time there to study the fortifications, to watch the changing of the guard under the guise of wandering among the shops.

The wares were rich, and the people starving.

"There is talk," Rohan told her as she stood by as if to supervise the loading of her goods into the carriage, "of portents. The dragon flew in the sky last night, and the stars bled."

"And what do the people make of these portents?"

"Some fear it's the end of the world, some hope it's the beginning."

"They're both right."

"But those who dare speak of hope do so in whispers. More were dragged from their homes in the night and charged with treason. There are murmurs, Aurora, that Lorcan will use the masque for some dark purpose, that he plans some sorcery."

"He has no such powers."

"It's said he has sought them." Rohan glanced left, right, to be certain they weren't overheard. "That he has courted the dark. Sacrifices. Human sacrifices to draw power from blood."

"Superstitious mutterings. But we won't ignore them." She climbed into the carriage and rode back to the castle with her mind circling a hundred thoughts.

There was a time for warriors, and a time for witches. When the hour was late, Aurora stirred her power. She called the hawk, and ten of his fellows. Then twenty, then a hundred. And more, until the sky teemed with them. Standing in her window, she raised the wind and, lifting her arms, threw her power into it.

Hawks screamed, circled, dove. Guards and courtiers rushed to the courtyard and the gardens, to the city, to the walls. There were cries of fear, shouts of wonder.

The great birds flew into the castle, through window and door, and sent servants scurrying under chair and bed. The beat of wings, the call of hawk, filled the air as in a golden mass they streaked into the treasury, plucking coins in their talons, streaming out again to drop them like rich rain on the city.

With cries of wonder and delight, men, women, and children rushed out of their homes and hovels to gather the bounty. When the call to arms came, many of the soldiers were as busy as the townspeople stuffing coins into pocket and purse. Before order could be restored, the cry of hawks was an echo, the beat of wings a memory.

The streets of the city glittered with coins.

An early payment, Aurora thought, watching the chaos below her window. The rest would come, very soon.

There was talk of little else the next day. Some blamed the strange raid on faeries, or witchcraft. It was said that the king's rage was black. Soldiers posted proclamations warning that any citizen found with coins would forfeit a hand.

Still, there was not a single coin left on the streets, and for the first time Aurora heard more laughter than woe when she listened to the city.

The confusion had kept her out of Lorcan's and Owen's way through the day, and given her time to have young Rhys slither into the dungeons with food for the prisoners while the guards gossiped.

But the time for giving food and coin to those in need was over, and the time for war was nearly upon her.

Distracted, she hurried toward her chamber to make final preparations for meeting Gwayne, and she didn't see Owen lurking. He had her back to the wall and his hand at her throat. She was already reaching for her dagger before caution had her fisting her hand and struggling to turn the battle light in her eye to fear.

"My lord. You frighten me."

"What game do you play?"

She shivered and turned her lips up in a tremulous smile. "Many, sir, and well. What have I done to displease you?"

"I did not give you leave to fritter off. Two days have passed, and you have not sought my company. I did not give you leave to travel into the city yesterday."

"No, my lord, but your father, the king, did so. I only sought the shops in hope that I might find something to please you for the ball. We have nothing so fine in the west as in the City of Stars. Please, my lord." She touched her hand to his. "You're hurting me."

"I've made it clear that I favor you. If you don't wish me to turn my eye toward another, take care, Aurora."

"Your favor, my lord, is all I could wish, but your passions unnerve me. I'm only a maid."

"I can make you more." He pushed his hand between her legs. "And less."

"Would you treat me so?" She wished for tears, willed them into her eyes as rage spewed through her. "Like a doxy to be fondled in doorways? Do you show your favor by dishonoring me?"

"I take what I wish. When I wish."

"My lady!" Rhiann screamed in shock and rushed down the corridor with Cyra at her heels.

Aurora broke away, to fall sobbing into Rhiann's arms and let herself be carried away into her chamber.

The minute the door was shut and secured, she stood dry-eyed. "Speak of this to no one," she ordered. "No one." She looked at the hand she held close to her side, and the dagger in it. "The prince of pigs has no idea how close he came to being gutted. I will not dine tonight. Send word that Lady Aurora is indisposed."

She sat and picked up a quill. "I have work."

9

She wore a high-necked gown to hide the bruises in a color chosen to blend with the night. There was enough anger left from her encounter with Owen to have her strapping a short sword at her side as well as the dagger on her thigh.

She threw on her cloak, with her mother's brooch pinned inside it.

She carried no lamp or candle, but slipped like a shadow through the castle. At the sound of approaching footsteps, she pressed herself against the wall, and through the veil of witch smoke watched two guards lead a serving girl toward Owen's chambers. The girl's face was pale as the moon, and her eyes dull with fear and resignation.

Aurora's hand clamped on the hilt of her sword, her knuckles white with rage and impotence against the metal. She could not interfere, could do nothing to help the poor girl, for to do so would risk all.

But he would pay. She vowed it. As his father would pay for his treatment of innocence.

She hurried down the steps, easing through doorways, and slipped out of the castle through the kitchen. Drawing up her hood, she made her way to the stables under the cover of darkness.

The instant she was inside, Thane pulled her into his arms. "I worry," he whispered even as his lips sought hers. "Every moment I can't see you, touch you, know you're safe, I worry."

"It's the same for me." She eased back, just to touch his face, and saw the bruises. "Oh, Thane."

"It's nothing. Nothing he won't pay for."

Instinctively she touched the neck of her gown, thought of the marks of Owen's hand hidden under it. "Payment will be made. I swear it. Come, and let's pray that Gwayne and our army await."

He lifted the door to the tunnels, but when he reached for a lamp, Aurora stilled his hand. "No. Tonight, we go by my light. It must be shown," she said as she drew the crystal star from the pocket of her cloak. "To give those who would fight hope, to let them see what they risk their lives for."

The star shimmered, and the light within it grew until it pulsed pure white. It beamed through the dark of the tunnels and became as bright as day.

And she was the light, burning with the power and purity of it. His throat stung, and his heart swelled with a mixture of love and wonder. "My lady. If my heart and my sword, if my life were not already yours, I would lay them before you now."

"Keep your life, beloved, for a thousand stars would never light mine without you. I need my wolf." She took his hand as they moved through the tunnels. "My lord of the stables. You know more of courtly matters than I."

At his quick laugh she shook her head. "You do," she insisted. "I was raised as a Traveler—educated, it's true, by book, by battle, by journeys and song and story, but there will come a time when I must hold court. It plays on my nerves."

"You are every inch a queen. It's a wonder men don't fall to their knees when you pass."

"You love me." And it warmed her to say it. "So it would seem so to you. It won't just be a matter of defeating Lorcan, but of convincing the people of the world that I am true. The work is just beginning."

"I'm used to work."

It was Kern who waited at the end of the tunnel. He wore light armor and his battle sword. "They come, Lady of the Light. But first, I bring you greetings from the Realm of Magicks." He bowed low. "And request to speak as envoy."

"You are welcome, sir." She glanced at Thane in confusion when Kern remained bowed.

Thane grinned, sent her a wink. He hadn't been tutored by a faerie throughout his life without learning the protocol. "You do honor to your queen, Lord of Magicks. Greetings to you from the world of men. You have leave to speak."

"Well done." Kern rose with a twinkle in his eye.

"Meaning no offense, but can we speak freely here?" Aurora gestured with her free hand. "Men and faerie folk share the forest, and the night. I am not queen until I'm crowned, and I have much yet to learn on how to be one. What word do you bring from your realm?"

"I have a lengthy and lyrical speech prepared."

"Lengthy it would be," Thane assured Aurora. "I can't promise the lyrical."

"However"—Kern shot his student a steely stare—"I'll cut it to the bone. The Realm of Magicks is at your command, Lady of the Light. We will fight with you if you'll have us."

"You haven't raised your forces or your powers against Lorcan in all these years. Why do you offer to raise them now?"

"We've raised your wolf, my lady, as it was written. I am for him, and he is for you. The hour to do more had not come."

"Faeries can die at the hand of men—and more, it's said that Lorcan courts magic. Will you and yours risk all that is to come?"

"We have died at the hands of men, hands that follow Lorcan's command. And some of us have turned from truth to embrace the lies. Some from weakness, some from fear, and some from the ambition for greater powers. Our kinds are not so different in such matters, my lady. We will follow the queen into battle. Will the queen trust my word?"

Aurora turned to Thane. "I'll trust yours."

"He's as true as any I know."

"Then thanks to you and your kind, Lord of Magicks. What you've said here tonight, and what you'll do on the morrow, will never be forgotten."

He took the hand she offered, bowed over it. "Your hawks provided fine entertainment in the night, Majesty."

"There is little entertainment in this place. I craved some. And it served to keep Lorcan and his dogs' eyes on the city, and away from the forest."

"Now your white hawk approaches."

She swung around and saw Gwayne step away from the trees, alone. Regal protocol was forgotten in the sheer joy of seeing him. She sprang toward him, threw her arms around him. "I've missed you! There's so much to say, and little time to say it." She drew back, studied his face. "You're tired."

"It was a long journey."

"How many are with you?"

"We're two hundred strong, but many of those are farmers, craftsmen. Boys." He gripped her hands, squeezed. "Some are armed with clubs, pitchforks, or simply stones from the fields, but they come."

"Then they're valued for it, every one."

"They need to see, Aurora, to believe, for they're weary, and some grow frightened. Without a stir of hope, some will scatter by morning."

"They will see, and they will believe." She reached back for Thane's hand. "This is Thane, who is my mate, the wolf of my visions. And Kern of the faeries, who is his teacher and brings us word from his realm of their loyalty to the True One. Take us to the army, Gwayne, so they can see. And pray to the gods I find the words to stir them."

Gwayne led them through the forest, calling a low signal to sentries already posted. The camp was rough, the faces of the men she saw pale with fatigue. Some were old, others much too young, and her heart began to ache with the knowledge of what she would ask of them.

She shook her head before Gwayne could speak. "I must do this myself. If I can't do this, I can't do the rest. They have followed you this far, my hawk. Now they have to follow me."

Gathering herself, she climbed onto a wide stump and stood quietly for a moment while the men shifted and murmured and studied her.

"I am Aurora." She didn't lift her voice, but kept it low so the murmuring stilled as the men strained to hear. "I am the Lady of the Light. I am the queen of Twylia. I am the True One. The woman I am weeps at what has been done to the world, to the people and the magicks of it. My father, the king, was slain through treachery, and my mother, the queen, gave her life for my birth. I am from death, and my heart bleeds knowing that more death will come from me. I am a woman, and have no shame of tears."

She let them fall silently down her face and glimmer in the moonlight filtering through the trees.

"I am Aurora." Her tone strengthened as she loosed her cape and flung it aside. As she drew her sword and raised it to the sky. "I am the Lady of the Light. I am the queen of Twylia. I am the True One. The warrior in me burns at what has been done to the world, to the people and the magicks of it. I will not rest, I will fight unto death to take back what was stolen from me and mine. My sword will sing into battle. I am a warrior, and I have no fear of death when the cause is justice."

Once more she held the crystal star in her palm and drew from it, from herself, the power of light. Men fell back, or dropped to their knees as that light grew and grew until it burned like a thousand candles. Wind whipped through the forest, sent her hair flying as she held both sword and star aloft.

"I am Aurora!" Her voice rang through the night, and the bells began their toll of midnight. "I am the Lady of the Light. I am the queen of Twylia. I am the True One. I am a witch, and my rage for what has been done to the world and my people is cold as ice, is hot as flame, is deep as the sea. My power will light the dark, and it will blind those who stand against me. I am woman and warrior, witch and queen. I will weep and fight and blaze until the world is right again. And all who follow me will be remembered and honored until the end of days."

She threw back her head and punched her power toward the sky. Light carved through the black, and spun in mad circles of golds and reds and silvers. And became a crown of stars.

"None but the True One dares to wear the Crown of Stars. None but the True One can bear its weight and its heat. None but the True One can give the world back to the people and the magicks. When next the moon rises, I will fight for the world and take my crown. Will you follow me?"

They roared for her and cheered. The soldier and the farmer, the old and the young.

She sheathed her sword and passed her hand over the star so that its light slowly dimmed. "Rest now," she called out. "Rest and gather your courage and your might. I go with my hawk, my wolf, and he who serves the dragon to prepare for the battle."

When she would have leapt down, Thane circled her waist with his hands and lifted her to the ground. "A queen shouldn't jump from a tree stump after so stirring a speech."

"I need you to remind me of those small details." Her lips curved at the smile in his eyes. "And to look at me just like that, as often as possible."

"I am at your service."

"And now we need to gather our forces, and our brains. Gwayne? A quiet place where we four can speak?"

"May I serve here, my lady?" Kern asked, and at her nod, he flicked both wrists.

They stood now in a brightly lit chamber with a fire snapping in the hearth. Kern gestured toward a table and the chairs that surrounded it. "This is my rath, and a good private place for plots and plans. Be comfortable. Would you have wine?"

"By the gods, I would," Gwayne said, with feeling. "It's been a dry march."

"And food?" Platters of meat, bread, cheese, and fruit appeared on the table.

"No warrior eats until all eat," Aurora said and earned a proud look from Gwayne.

"Your men will be fed, Majesty. We are pleased to offer our hospitality tonight."

"Then eat." She slapped Gwayne on the back. "While I tell you what I know."

She told him of the masque, of the dungeons, of the threat to Brynn and Dira, and with Thane's help she drew diagrams of the fortifications and the locations of guards.

"Your father was a good friend," Gwayne said to Thane, "a brave warrior with a true heart. He would be proud to know what you have done, and will do."

"Most of my life I've felt he would be ashamed I hadn't lifted my hand."

"He loved your mother and you above all things. You have each sacrificed self for the life of the other. A man would be proud of such a wife, and such a son."

"I don't want those sacrifices to be in vain," Aurora added. "Brynn and Dira must be protected, and Leia kept safe until the castle and city are back in our hands. Brynn and Dira's presence will be required at the masque. I want at least one man each by their side, to shield them, then to escort them to safety with Rhiann and Cyra."

"There's an anteroom here." Thane pointed to the drawings. "With a passage gained by opening this panel by a mechanism in the hearth. My mother knows of it. Either she or Dira could lead the way from there."

"It must be done quickly, before Lorcan thinks to use them as a bargaining tool. Just as freeing those in the dungeons must be done quickly. And quietly. We strike there first, while the company is gathered in the great hall for the masque. When it's done, we divide our troops. Into the tunnels to strike at the castle from the inside, to the walls—here and here?" She glanced at Thane for approval.

"The weakest points," he agreed. "A breach could be made, and from those three attacks, confining Lorcan and his personal guard between."

She rose as Gwayne and Thane debated battle strategy, and she moved to the fire to study the images she saw in the flames.

She could hear the beat of her own heart, and knew it beat for revenge. There was a lust in her belly for blood—Lorcan's blood.

When she looked down at her hands, they were wet with it, and in her head were the agonized screams of the dying as her sword cut viciously through flesh and bone.

And in the flames she saw the Crown of Stars go black.

"Blood and death," she declared when she sensed Kern behind her. "If I hunger for this, what manner of queen am I?"

"Having hunger and sating appetite are different matters, lady."

"I want this, for myself. His blood on my hands." She held them up, knowing Kern could see as she saw. "But it isn't for the good of the world, is it? To seek to take a life, even such a life as his, this is not light. It is not why I was made. Not why I am here."

"To see that is power, and truth."

"And still, I know there will be blood, there will be death. Of those I love, of those who follow me. I send them into battle and to the grave. This is the weight of power. Tonight, I turned my back on a young girl, knowing she would be ill used. Because if I had intervened, I might have betrayed the greater cause. But is there a greater cause, Kern, than the fate of a single innocent?"

"I don't rule. Such questions are part of a crown."

"Yes, they are. I could do nothing else then. But now . . . It can be done another way. Am I strong enough to trust the crown instead of the sword? I've tested so little of my power to put such matters to it. To call the wind, a flock of birds . . ." She wrapped her arms around herself. "That's a game, not battle."

"And you know what your sword can do."

"Yes. I spoke the truth. I don't fear death in battle, but I fear the lives that will be lost on my account. And I fear what will become of me, and the world, if I take one if there's a choice. Thane trusts you. So will I." She closed her eyes. "Do you know what is in my mind?"

"I do, my lady."

"And you'll help me."

"I will."

"Then we will plan for battle this way." She glanced back at her teacher, and her lover. "And hope for victory in another."

10

THE CASTLE, THE city, the countryside made ready for the masque. The prettiest maids were gathered up and brought in to serve and to decorate—and, Aurora noted, to serve *as* decoration. Farmers were ordered to offer their finest crops or livestock to the king in tribute. Wine and ale were hauled in on wagons, and without payment, so that the king and his guests could revel.

Portents were spoken of only in whispers. Lights, such great lights, seen in the forest at midnight. The stars that had circled into a crown in the night sky.

Open talk of such matters could lose a man his tongue.

Lords and ladies from all reaches of Twylia traveled to the City of Stars for the celebrations rather than displease the king who held them under his merciless thumb. Some with eligible daughters sent them to the hills or into caves, or into the Valley of Secrets, risking death or poverty. Others brought the maidens and prayed that the prince would pass their daughters over for others.

There were whispers, too, of rebellion, but the king ignored such foolishness and basked in the glory of the feast to come.

The dark glass showed no man who would claim his crown. And when he drank the blood of a sorcerer to bring visions, he saw only the shape of a wolf and the delicate hand of a woman who held the world in her palm.

He ordered his best hunters into the woods and the hills to track and kill any wolf. And garbed himself in his richest robes.

Time was short, and the risk worth taking. Armed, Thane hurried through the tunnels and chanced the daylight to find Gwayne.

"This isn't your place, or your time," Gwayne told him. "We are moving at sunset and still have much to prepare."

"Lorcan sent six hunters out nearly an hour ago. They'll come this way. If they find you and even one escapes, you'll fight your battle here rather than on your chosen ground."

"Are these men loyal to Lorcan?"

"Loyalty is cheap here."

Gwayne fingered the hilt of his sword. "Then we'd best offer them a dearer coin."

Aurora chose white, the color of truth, for her gown. In her vision she had worn red, the color of blood. So she made this change deliberately, and hopefully. But not foolishly. The long, flowing sleeves hid the dagger she strapped to her wrist. Over Cyra's objections, she left her hair down, falling straight to her waist and unadorned. And in a gesture of pride and defiance, she pinned her mother's brooch to the gown between her breasts.

"He might recognize it," Rhiann objected.

"If he does, it will be too late." She took the globe and the star. "I'll need these." she slipped them into a white velvet purse. Turning from the looking glass, she held out her hands, one to Cyra, one to Rhiann. "You've been mother and sister to me. Whatever changes tonight, nothing changes that. I ask that you see my beloved's mother and sister safe. If the light doesn't shine for the midnight hour, you're to take them to the Valley of Secrets, where Leia bides, and seek sanctuary. Your vow on it."

"Aurora," Rhiann began.

"Your vow on it," Aurora insisted. "I can only do what I must do with a clear heart and mind."

"Then you have it. But the light will shine."

Thane waited until the mounted hunter was directly below the bough, then leapt upon him. The force sent them both tumbling to the ground, and the alarmed horse shied.

Before a breath could be taken, Thane had his sword at the man's throat. "Call out," he said quietly, "and it will be the last sound you make."

"Thane of the stables?" There was as much shock as fear in the tone; "What recklessness is this? I am on king's business."

"It is a new day," Thane said, then hauled the man to his feet. "Take him off with the others." He shoved the hunter toward two of the rebels who waited in the shelter of the trees. "His bow and quiver will be useful. Tell Gwayne I've gone back. I will be listening."

With a sense of purpose in every stride, he hurried back to the stables. Whatever happened, he would not pass another night there, sleeping on the floor like an animal. Tonight his family would be free, and he would live—or die—in the service of his lady.

"You're late," Kern complained the moment Thane climbed through the passage.

"I had business."

"You've had considerable here as well, which I've seen to. Guests are still arriving, and their horses require care. You might have been missed if I hadn't been here to deal with it."

"I'll tend the horses, then I am done with this. I swear if I have any say over what's done, whoever takes my place here will have decent quarters and payment for his labors."

With some reluctance Thane unstrapped his sheath.

"I said I tended the horses. You've no need to labor over them again." Lips pursed, Kern circled Thane. "It will be considerable labor to tend to you."

"What? What's wrong with me?"

Kern pinched one of Thane's ragged sleeves between his fingers. "Nothing a bath and a barber and a tailor of some skill can't fix. But we've no time for all of that. I'll just have to see to it myself."

"I don't need a bloody barber before a battle."

"You need one before a masque. But the bath first. Believe me, you can use one."

Kern snapped his fingers twice and conjured a copper tub full of steaming water.

"I'm not going to the masque, but to the dungeons to help free the prisoners. I don't think they'll care if I smell sweet or not."

"The prisoners are being freed even now."

"Now?" Even as Thane reached for his sword, Kern waved a hand. And Thane was naked.

"For the sake of the gods!"

"You're not needed. My kind are adept at getting into locked places." Kern grinned. "We enjoy it. You'll be needed at the masque, and you won't get past the guards unless you're bathed, groomed, and properly attired. The tub, boy."

"I'll stand with Gwayne, lead—" He found himself in the tub, immersed. He came up sputtering.

"You waste breath arguing. Are you afraid to go to a ball?"

"I'm not going to dance, thundering hell. I'm going to fight."

"And so you may. But if and when, you fight by her side. To get to her side, you need what I'll give you. Wash." Kern circled the tub while Thane sulked and scrubbed.

"Is this the queen's bidding?"

"No. But she will be pleased enough. It is her wish and her will to take the throne with as little blood as possible. The magicks have agreed to aid her in this," he added as Thane's head came up sharply. "We will enchant the guards to sleep, and the walls will be breached without sword. No man will die in the city or outside the keep. But inside, Lorcan's power must be faced and vanquished, or she cannot rule. There is the battle. Dark against light. The pure against the corrupt. And there you must be."

Kern tapped his finger to his lips, considering as Thane hauled himself out of the tub. "Simplicity, I think," he stated and, wagging his finger, garbed Thane in royal blue with tiny flecks of gold. "No, no, not quite."

Thane scowled at the lace spilling over his wrists. "I feel like a fool."

"As long as you don't behave as one, we'll have no problem." He changed the blue to black, the gold to silver, and nodding, drew Thane's hair back in a short queue. "Dress swords only." He snapped and had a jeweled-handled sword in the silver sheath.

Pleased for the first time by the turn of events, Thane drew the sword. "A fine weapon. Good balance."

"It was your father's."

Thane lowered the sword and stared into the eyes of his teacher. "Thank you. I fail, too often, to thank you."

"Meet your destiny, and that is thanks enough. One last touch." Kern waved a hand and covered the top of Thane's face with a black domino.

"Take your place," Kern said quietly. "Stay true to your blood and your heart. The world rests on what passes tonight."

Aurora held herself straight, fixed a flirtatious smile on her face, and stepped into the great hall. Music was playing, and already lines were set for dancing. Tables groaned with platters of food, and hundreds of candles streamed light.

Dress was elaborate, with feathers and furs, high headdresses and flowing trains. She saw Lorcan drinking deeply of wine, with his queen pale and silent beside him.

The first order, she thought, was to separate them so Brynn and Dira could be spirited away to safety. Despite the masks and costumes, she had little trouble in locating Owen and staying out of his line of sight. She walked directly to the king, curtsied.

"Majesty, my humble thanks for the invitation to so lively a celebration."

"The voice is familiar, as is . . . the form." He tapped a finger under his chin, studied her smile and the eyes that looked out of a sparkling silver mask. "What is the name?"

"Sire, the guessing is the game." She trailed a finger down his arm in a daring move. "At least until the hour strikes twelve and we are unmasked. Might I beg for a cup of wine?"

"Asking is enough." He snapped his fingers and a servant hurryied over. Deliberately, Aurora shifted to look back at the dancing, and had Lorcan turning his back on his wife. "Would you care to take a turn of the room with me?"

"Delighted and charmed." He offered her his arm. "I believe I have guessed this game, Lady Aurora. You are, I believe, the most daring of the maidens here."

"One expects a king to be wise and clever, and you are, sire." She lifted her glass as they walked, and saw Rhiann nod. The first move would be made.

She chattered, commenting on the costumes, complimenting the music, knowing that she would soon circle toward Owen. But while she did, Brynn and Dira would be safely away. As would her own women.

"Lovely lady." Aurora's heart stopped at the voice when the courtier in black bowed in front of her. "Might I steal you away for a dance?"

Struggling to gather her scattered wits, she inclined her head. "If His Majesty permits."

"Yes, yes, go." He waved her away and held out his cup for more wine.

"Are you mad?" Aurora said under her breath.

"If love is madness, I am so afflicted." Thane led her across the room, and hoped it was far enough away. "But the fact is, I don't dance. Would that I did. You are so beautiful tonight."

"Do something," she hissed.

"I'll feed you." He began to pile a plate with delicacies. "It's something flirtatious courtiers do for ladies at balls—so I've seen when I've spied on them. Sugarplum?" Grinning, he held one up to her lips.

She bit in and laughed. "You are mad. I'm so glad to see you. I want to touch you, and dare not. Your mother and sister are being taken to safety."

"I saw them go. I can never repay you."

"Learn to dance, then one day promise to dance with me."

"On my oath. If I could, I would whisk you out on the terrace, kiss your lips in the light of the rising moon. And there would only be music and moonlight for us." He took her hand, brushed a kiss over it. "I know what you've planned with the magicks. You should have told me."

"I was afraid you and Gwayne would never agree. You wish for blood—both of you, and you've earned it—both of you. I'm denying you your right."

"I would not have agreed." His eyes lifted to hers with a sudden shock of power. "I do not agree. There are bruises on your throat, beloved. You didn't quite cover them."

"Have they any more import than those he put on you?"

"Yes. Oh, yes."

"Find another kitten to stroke." Owen snapped out the order, shoving Thane aside. Even as Thane's hand gripped the hilt of his sword, Aurora stepped between them. "Sir," she said lightly to Owen, "I am no kitten."

"A cat, more like, rubbing herself against any willing leg."

"If you think so of me, I'm surprised you would spend a moment in my company." She started to turn away, resisted when Owen took her arm. With her back to him she mouthed *Not yet* to Thane, then faced Owen once more. "You make a spectacle of us, my lord. The king will not approve."

Owen took her hand, squeezing until her fingers ground bone to bone. He leaned close and spoke in a voice like silk. "I will not choose you. But I will have you. Had you been more agreeable, you would have been queen."

She saw two of the king's personal guards rush into the hall, heard the clamor, and knew the rebels were over the walls and through the tunnels.

She stepped back and, over the shouts, spoke clearly. "I am queen."

11

"YOU WILL HAVE nothing," she said. "For nothing is what you have earned. Your time is ended, and mine begins. The hour is about to strike."

"No woman speaks so to me." Owen drew back his hand. And Thane's sword was out and at his throat.

"Touch her, and I will slice your hand off at the wrist." With his free hand Thane pulled off his mask. "Don't interfere," he said to Aurora. "I'm not a man if I don't stand for myself and my lady, at long last."

"Your lady," Owen spat.

"My lady, and my queen." Thane stepped back a pace. "Draw your sword."

Chaos was already reigning as guards battled the rebels who charged into the hall. Lords and courtiers dragged screaming women away from the fray, or simply left them and scrambled for cover themselves. Aurora cast aside her own mask and called out for a sword. She would have no choice now but to fight her way to Lorcan and cut off any chance of escape.

Owen pulled his sword. "Stableboy, I will cut you apart, piece by piece, and feed you to my dogs."

With a thin smile, Thane made a mocking salute with his sword. "Will you fight, you tedious braggart, or simply talk me to death?"

Owen came in fast, striking, thrusting, and Thane felt his blood sing. Their swords crossed, slid hilt to hilt, and he grinned between the lethal vee. "I have dreamed of this."

"You dream your own death."

They broke apart, and steel flashed against steel.

Wielding a sword of her own, Aurora slashed blades aside, shoved a swooning woman into a courtier's arms, then whirled to fight back to back with Gwayne.

"Outside?" she shouted. "The walls, the tunnels."

"It's done. This is all that's left. The faeries hold them fast, and the dungeons are clear."

"Then we end this." She looked toward Lorcan and saw his sword was bright with blood. "We take him."

With Gwayne, she fought her way to the king. They battled through the panicked guests, leaping over the fallen and the fainting to be joined by others as she called them to arms. They pressed the outnumbered guards to the walls, and Aurora locked swords with Lorcan.

"You may take me," she said calmly. "I think you won't, but you may. If you do, these men will cut you down. You will not live through this night unless you lay down your sword."

"You will be hanged." His eyes burned black. There was blood on his hands, she saw. As there was on hers. "You will be drawn, quartered, and hanged."

"Lay down your sword, Lorcan the usurper, or I will end this in death after all."

"There will be death." But he threw down his sword. "It will be yours."

"Tell your guards to lay down their weapons. You're outnumbered here. Tell them to lay down their weapons so you might hear my terms."

"Enough!" He shouted it with Aurora's sword to his throat. "Lay down your swords. Your king commands you."

The sounds of clashing steel dimmed until there was only Thane's blade against Owen's.

"Let him finish," she said to Gwayne. "The hour has not yet struck. This is his time, not mine, and he must live it. Put Lorcan on the throne he values so much, and hold him there."

Across the hall the two men fought like demons. Winded, Owen hacked and cleaved, and cursed when Thane's sword flicked his away. Enraged, he grabbed a candlestand and heaved it, following with vicious sweeps as Thane dodged aside and spun back into attack.

"You are too used to sparring with soldiers who are beaten or banished if they dare best you," Thane taunted. "Now that it's your life—"Thane slashed, and cut neatly through Owen's silk doublet to score the flesh—"You're clumsy."

"You are *nothing*! Coward, whipping boy."

"I carry your scars." Thane sliced the point of his sword down Owen's cheek. "Now you carry mine. And that is enough."

With two quick thrusts, he knocked Owen's sword out of his hand, then pressed his own to his enemy's belly. "I won't kill you, as I wish you many years of life. Years of misery and humiliation. On your knees before your Majesty."

"I will not kneel to you."

"It is not to me you kneel. But to her." He stepped aside, shifting his sword point to the back of Owen's neck so the man could see Aurora standing among the fallen and the frightened.

"You are," she said to Thane, "what I have always wished for. What I will always prize. In the midst of battle, when vengeance was your right, you chose honor."

"Whore!" Owen shrieked it. "Drab. She lay on her back for me. She—"

Thane shifted his grip on the sword and slammed the hilt into the side of Owen's head. When Owen fell unconscious, Thane booted him carelessly aside. "I'm not perfect," he said with a flashing smile, and Aurora laughed.

"I believe you may be. The hour comes." She could feel the power rising in her. "I almost wish it wouldn't. That we could walk away, and live in a cottage in the woods or ramble across the world in a wagon. I almost wish it, but it comes and I have no choice."

"A cottage, a world, a crown. It's all the same to me, if I'm with you."

"Stand with me, then." She turned and faced Lorcan as he sprawled on the throne under the swords of her men. "Lower your swords, step back. Open the doors, the windows. Let the people in, let them know what happens here at the witching hour, at my hour. Lorcan, stand and face me as you did not face my father or my mother. I am Aurora. I am the Lady of the Light. I am the True One."

She walked toward him as she spoke and flung out her arms. "Are there any here in this company, any here in the City of Stars, in the world, who will not pledge their loyalty to the True One? For they are free to leave this place, and to go in peace. There will not be blood or death."

"You're nothing but a woman, a whore, as my son has said. I am king. The True One is a myth babbled by madmen."

"Behold the dragon!" She pointed toward the window, and the fire that lit the sky in the shape of a dragon.

"A witch's trick." He rose and, pushing out with his hand, shot a fierce wind through the hall. It blew her hair back, set her gown to billowing. The sharpness of it sliced her hand and drew blood. But she stood against it.

"You would match your power to mine?" She arched her brows. "Here is the world, stained by my blood, and the blood of my people." She drew the crystal globe from her purse, threw it high so it spun near the ceiling and showered light and spilled out voices raised in song. "Take it if you dare. And here is the crown, the Crown of Stars."

She reached in her purse again and flung the star. It flew in dizzying circles and exploded with light.

She stood, draped in billowing white, unarmed, and waited while the bells began to strike midnight. "And this is my hour, the hour of my birth and beginnings. The hour of life and death, of power and portent. The time between time when day meets day and night meets night."

The crown circled, beamed light, and descended toward her head.

Lifting her arms, she accepted her destiny. "And in this hour, the reign of dark is ended and the reign of light begins. I am the True One, and this is my world to protect."

The crown settled on her head, and every man and woman, every soldier and servant, fell to their knees.

Outside, the people who massed could be heard chanting her name like a prayer.

"I am Aurora, descendant of Draco, daughter of Gwynn and Rhys. I am queen of Twylia."

On a roar, Lorcan grabbed the sword from a dazzled rebel and, raising it high, lunged toward Aurora. Murder was in his cry, madness was in his eyes.

And springing like a wolf, Thane leapt forward, spinning to shield her, and ran Lorcan through.

He fell at her feet with his blood splashing the white hem of her gown. With the stars still gleaming on her head, she looked down on him with a pity that was cold as winter.

"So . . . So it ends in death after all. He made his choice. The debt is paid. My father and yours." She turned to Thane, held out her hand. "My mother and yours."

The last bell struck, and the wind died. Her crown sparkled like stars.

"What was taken in blood is restored. In blood. Now let there be peace. Open the larders," she ordered. "Feed the people of the city. No one goes hungry tonight."

"My lady." Gwayne knelt before her. "The people call for you. They call for their queen. Will you go out so they can see you?"

"I will. Only a moment first. A moment," she repeated and turned to Thane. "It will be hard. After the joy, it will be hard. There will be work and sweat and time to restore faith, to bring order, to renew trust. There will be so much to do. I need you beside me."

"I am the queen's man, my lady." He brought her hand to his lips. Then with a laugh born of freedom, he lifted her off her feet, and high above his head. "Beloved. Woman of my visions, mother of my son. My light. My life."

She wrapped her arms around him, tipped her mouth to his for the warmth and power of his kiss as he spun her in circles. "Then there's nothing I can't do. Nothing we can't be."

"We'll be happy."

"Yes. Till the end of days."

With her hand linked with his, she walked out to the cheers of the people of the world.

And they raised her up to be queen, Aurora, the Light.

MIRROR, MIRROR

☾

Jill Gregory

To my mom and dad,
always in my memory and in my heart

Prologue

Dovenbyre Castle,
Grithain

As a full moon swam high in a midnight sky above the castle, the king of Grithain lay dying. He had survived countless battles and wars, two attempted poisonings, and a stabbing. All had been endured with stalwart strength. But now his heart beat faintly, and his shrewd, deep-set eyes were closed. In a velvet chair near his bed of ermine pelts and silk linens, the old witch, Ariel, huddled in a forest-green cloak, nearly as weak as the king she had served most of her days.

"The boy, Ariel . . . what will become of . . . the boy?" he managed to gasp, though his eyes remained shut.

"He will be king—or not," the witch answered in a hissing whisper.

"All this time . . . I kept him far from me all this time . . . so that he might live . . ."

"He might yet. But danger draws near. Too near," Ariel muttered. She would not lie to the king, nor to herself.

At this moment the danger to Branden, Prince of Grithain, was greater than it had been at any other time since he had first been smuggled in secret away from the castle only two days following his birth. And her powers, needed now more than ever, had never been weaker.

She was old and drained, beaten by an unseen foe, a faraway demon-wizard who had somehow poisoned her with a slow-acting spell, one so rare it went beyond her power or knowledge to counter. Drop by drop he had stolen her powers, nearly all of them, attacking her from some distant, unknown place. He had found a way to tap them, draw them from her, and yet leave her alive to know what was happening, to feel the power ebbing, the weakness overtaking her. It had been a slow, cruel, torturous death. The only thing she retained was her mind, her thoughts. Those he could not breach. But now she feared that he and his master were closing in on the prince—and only one man could save him. One mortal man . . .

"No!" A shudder wracked the old witch in her chair, and King Mortimer's eyes painfully opened upon the candlelit chamber. He ignored the servants hovering about his bed with medicinal draughts and golden goblets of wine and frightened faces, and directed his words to Ariel.

"What, witch? What makes you cry out? Is my boy dead?"

"No . . . not dead . . . but they are coming . . . lying in wait . . . Conor!" The witch screeched.

"Tell me what you see—is all lost?"

"Help . . . he needs help . . . Conor, no!" The witch hugged her spindly arms around herself, rocking her withered body in the chair as the visions, faint but certain, hammered in her head.

Suddenly her gaze flew to the window, and she stared at the full pearl of a moon.

"Midnight . . . 'tis nearly midnight . . ."

"Ariel!" The king's voice was weaker now, his breathing ragged. "Can you . . . save my boy . . ."

"Hynda, yes, I hear you," Ariel whispered, as if she was no longer aware of the king. She rocked harder in her chair, her voice low, desperate. "I hear you, my sister, but . . . she is only a girl, a mortal girl . . . yes, the mirror. The Midnight Mirror.

If I can only . . . summon the strength. . . . He has taken it, all of it . . . almost all . . ."

She rocked, back and forth, back and forth, muttering words under her breath, gathering the last frayed threads of what had once been a great blanketing power.

Ashwer quinkling sep moregose. Can argg hana swey.

The mirror. The girl. The moon. *Midnight.*

She felt a spark, one last spark—of light, of power, of magic. It splashed through her like the dizzying surge of a cool mountain spring as the king's eyes closed again and her body twitched and shuddered.

The mirror, she thought on a gasp of final effort. *Let your power awaken, mirror . . . mirror . . .*

The seconds crept closer to the hour of midnight. All of her energy flowed across Grithain to a distant cottage on the border of an ancient forest—to a girl and a cat and a mirror . . .

> *Let what was hidden be seen.*
> *Let what was dark glow with light.*
> *Let the mirror speak, its silence end.*
> *At the stroke of this midnight.*

Ariel sank back, spent and gasping, as King Mortimer of Grithain drew one final breath.

"There is hope for your son, my king," she whispered as the flames of the candles fluttered and the king's heart at last set him free. "Hope for Branden, within the mirror. We shall see . . . Majesty, we shall see . . ."

1

THE COLD SEEPED ruthlessly, like an intrepid enemy, through the walls of Bitterbloom Cottage that dark winter's night. Despite the brave blaze of the fire and the winking candles Fiona had lighted and set upon the table and upon Hynda's old bronze chest, it squeezed through the cracks and chinks, whistled across the floor, and chilled the air like puffs of snow.

Seated on the bench before the hearth, searching through the old wooden box Tidbit had just discovered and dived into with a screech, Fiona shivered in her unadorned gown of blue wool. This was one of the coldest nights she remembered since coming to live at the cottage twelve years ago. Icicles dripped from the trees beyond the window, and though there was little snow to be seen, all was blanketed in a deep, frigid silence—but for the desperate rush of the wind and the occasional howl of wolves from the bowels of the Dark Forest.

The cold was strong and bitter, like a living thing—powerful and relentless, an icy force that commanded notice in all surroundings—including this otherwise cozy parlor.

"Here, Tidbit, settle before the fire. It's too cold for your wanderings tonight," Fiona advised the dainty black cat whom she'd lifted from the box and who now prowled the room, displaying the same restlessness that Fiona felt within herself.

Tidbit had slipped out earlier this evening and returned nearly frozen, yet she couldn't seem to settle down. Almost as if she sensed something in the air, something . . . or someone . . . coming . . .

But that couldn't be, Fiona told herself as she picked up an old tangled nest of wool from the wooden box the cat had climbed into—a box Fiona hadn't noticed in ages, hidden as it was in a dark corner beneath a low bench.

No one would venture forth tonight, she told herself, *not in this cold.* Even the duke would not leave the castle on such a night. For once, she need not fear to find him at her door.

She was lonely, had been lonely ever since Hynda had died, but she wasn't *that* lonely. If she never saw the duke again, it would most certainly be too soon.

She pushed away the sense of aloneness that was almost as oppressive as the cold and concentrated on unraveling the tangles of wool, on turning them into something useful. She would knit mittens for Gilroyd. The boy was constantly losing his, and she suspected that he gave them away to the poor children of the village, those whose parents had barely enough wool to fashion tunics for their children, much less cloaks and shoes and mittens.

The Duke of Urbagran kept his villagers poor and dependent upon his good graces. While he, who was born noble, had no heart that Fiona had ever glimpsed, Sir Henry's youngest son, Gilroyd, small and straight and only ten, seemed to have more than his fair share, certainly more than any other child she had ever seen. It was only one of the things she loved about him, and only one of the reasons she would stay alone at Bitterbloom Cottage for as long as was necessary, making sure to do all she could to protect his life.

She bent her attention to the wool, but she'd scarcely succeeded in unsnarling the first few strands when the entire tangled ball suddenly slipped from her icy fingers as if by its own will and dropped back into the wooden box. She reached for it with a sigh, and that was when she spotted something shiny at the very bottom of the box.

It was a mirror.

It lay face-down, half hidden by another skein of wool, some tattered remnants of silk, and several musty leather pouches, no doubt containing old herbs and powders. Hynda had given her this box shortly after she'd first come to live at the cottage.

"For your treasures," Hynda had informed her solemnly. At one time Fiona had kept in this box every odd and end and bauble she'd received or found, including the little packets of healing herbs and powders Hynda had first shown her, the most elemental stuff of healing. And somehow the mirror must have ended up in here, too, a trinket from her childhood, forgotten, abandoned—until now.

With a small smile, Fiona reached for the small golden mirror whose handle and oval frame were studded with bits of amber. Hynda had given it to her within her first months at Bitterbloom Cottage, telling her that it was a magic mirror, a gift she herself had received from her sister, Ariel, a witch of legendary power.

She'd told Fiona, "It holds powerful magic."

Captivated, and a little afraid, Fiona had asked, "What sort of magic?"

"If you gaze into it at midnight on the night of a full moon, it might show, when it chooses, some event of great joy or great evil or great import, from past or present or even future. It has the gift of sight bestowed upon it by its maker, Ariel. She gave it to me, and I give it now to you."

If you gaze into it at midnight. It was nearly midnight now. And the moon was full tonight.

"But you never showed me much of anything, did you?" Fiona chided as she held the mirror aloft, seeing only her own heart-shaped face and even features, the gray eyes she considered unremarkable and the smooth sweep of dark hair that tumbled past her shoulders. She frowned at her reflection as memories floated back to her, memories of many nights when as a child she'd kept herself awake until midnight when the full moon shone above, and had held the mirror high, staring into it as she did now. But only once had she ever seen anything other than her own reflection.

One time, just as she lifted the mirror, she'd thought she glimpsed an image there, but it was fleeting, vanishing even as she had more tightly grasped the delicate golden handle. It was an image of a servant, it seemed, a woman of middle years, with gingery red hair and a necklace of blue stones around her throat, and a babe in her arms. She was fleeing with the babe, flanked by two soldiers—fleeing in the dark, in the cold, in the night.

But in a blink she was gone. If it had been a vision, Fiona suspected she'd missed it somehow—or perhaps, she'd mused at the time, she'd only been dreaming.

It wasn't until years later that she'd guessed what it was she had seen—the newborn Prince of Grithain and his wet nurse being smuggled from the castle.

She had no way of knowing it then—no way of knowing how intimately her own life was entwined with that of the endangered young prince. She'd stared and stared into the mirror, on six, seven full moons following that, and never seen the woman and babe again, never seen anything again other than her own face, which she found not nearly as interesting as a potential glimpse of Destiny.

"Perhaps you can show me," she murmured wistfully, "one more glimpse of Hynda, somewhere, wherever she might be now. I would so like to say good-bye."

Hynda had died a few months ago in the night, after having sent Fiona off to help with the birthing of the baker's son in the village. There had been a storm, and when Fiona had finally been able to reach home the next morning, she'd found Hynda still and cold in her bed, with the faintest of smiles upon her lifeless blue lips. She had been old, it was true, and had grown weak in the past years, but her death was still a shock. And not being able to say good-bye had left Fiona feeling even more bereft.

Hynda had been the only family she'd known since the night her parents had been taken from her when she was only nine, the night they'd been robbed and then murdered by highwaymen. And now, though she was no longer a child but a capable and sensible young woman almost as skilled in the arts of healing as the witch who had taught her, she still felt deeply the loss of her dear friend and teacher, who had taken her in and shared with her the secret of Gilroyd, and by so doing had given her life a purpose and a duty—and transferred the obligation of ensuring his safety to Fiona's slender shoulders.

She was determined to stay and keep this cottage and watch over him until the boy was safely ensconced in his rightful place, with his rightful title—and under the full and watchful guard that was his due and his burden. But it might be years before that day would come, despite the swirling rumors that of late had even reached the duke's court here in Urbagran.

The mirror flashed.

Fiona stared.

A cloud was passing across the full moon beyond the window. As it scudded clear and the cool silver light spilled down once more upon the earth and glimmered through the cottage window, the mirror blurred and flashed again, and Fiona's reflection suddenly vanished. Then, in a wink, another image took its place—an image so vibrant and clear it might have been a scene right there in the cottage—but it was an image of another place, one that Fiona recognized instantly.

It was the Dark Forest. Or, more correctly, that nearly hidden clearing within the heart of the forest where the giant oak had been sliced in two by lightning. Within the mirror, the oak's charred limbs dangled at grotesque angles, and beneath them a man on horseback was being hacked down by five others who surrounded him.

The attackers were masked and on horseback as well. As Fiona watched, her eyes widening in shock and horror, the five closed in on the tall man in the great black cloak, and all of them struck at once with their swords and cudgels.

He went down in a flurry of hooves and steel. A massive wolf-hound snarled and charged into the fray. A sword struck the animal, the fallen man shouted, and the beast bounded away into the night.

Fiona saw the glitter of a jeweled brooch at the man's shoulder as he tried to rise, even as his horse reared above him, its great legs flailing. The horse was grabbed, pulled aside, and the attackers all leapt from their steeds, descending in a wild melee upon the fallen man even as he attempted once more to spring to his feet.

Blood. Fiona saw blood. She saw the man's face as he fought, slicing deftly with his sword. His face was grim and desperate, as her father's had been when he had been attacked—and then she could see him no more as the others swarmed in for the kill and the blood flowed crimson and the blows rained down in a tempest.

This is happening. Right now. In the Dark Forest at the clearing of the great oak . . .

The mirror slipped from her fingers, falling onto the bench, but the vision stayed in her head. Fiona's heart pounded. She had to do something. *Something.*

Her mouth was dry with fear as she raced to the door. She grabbed her sapphire-blue cloak from its hook and snatched the tin of freezing powder Hynda had long ago prepared for her from its shelf, dropping it into her pocket with shaking fingers. Flinging the cloak around her, she darted out of the cottage and into the icy moonlit night. Her feet flew over the stony ground as she dashed toward the shed where her brown pony munched on straw, and in no time she was clinging to his back and urging him into a gallop, straight into the heart of the Dark Forest.

The cold attacked her with biting fingers as she rode, the wind whipped her cheeks and blew her unbound hair in every direction, but she leaned low over the pony's mane and dug in her heels. Faster, faster.

The naked trees went by in a blur, but the moonlight illuminated every root and rock and twig in the pony's path as, with pounding hooves, the beast raced toward the clearing.

Fiona braced herself as the mangled oak loomed into view, but then she gasped—the clearing held no men, no horses, no swords.

It was empty.

Then she saw it. *Him.* The fallen man, alone, lying in a pool of blood, his face cut, his cloak ripped, his eyes open, glazed with pain.

They had gone, taking his horse and his sword, leaving him for dead.

Not yet, Fiona thought grimly, yanking the pony to a halt and sliding down from the saddle in the mere beat of a heart. *Not if I can help it.*

2

HE STIRRED. PAIN cut through him, hot as stones drawn from a fire. He groaned and stared up, teeth gritted, and found himself looking into the face of an angel.

He didn't believe in angels, or in ghosts, or in much of anything but his own cunning and prowess, but that didn't stop him from seeing an angel in the woman who stood over him, gazing down at him with silver-flecked eyes. Her hair was dark as night, her skin creamy, and a light dusting of freckles graced her straight little nose. Black eyelashes, delicate as lace, framed those incredible, light-infused eyes with an ethereal beauty straight out of heaven.

"You're going to live." Her voice was soft, quiet, and pretty, too. Every bit as pretty as the small, shapely beauty to whom it belonged. "Rest now, and don't try to move. I'll bring you some broth in a while."

"Who . . . are you?" He defied her command not to move by reaching out, grasping her wrist as she began to drift away from the bed in which he found himself. All of his senses were flooding back, and with them, along with the pain wracking every inch of his body, came memory. Memory of the attack—of the men sent to kill him—and of the mission still before him, the mission that must succeed.

Everything depended upon its success.

"Tell me . . . where we are—and who knows I'm here," he ordered. His grip on her wrist tightened without his even realizing it.

Fiona went still. She stared down at the big hand that held her, a look of surprise upon her face.

Such strength in his grip. She hadn't expected that, not after he'd hovered on the brink of death all through the night. He apparently wasn't as weak as might be expected, despite the magnitude of his injuries.

"Tell me . . . who you are . . . and how I came to be here," he said with an effort.

"I am Fiona. This is Bitterbloom Cottage in Urbagran. I brought you here from the Dark Forest last night—"

"You . . . brought me? How? You're a slip of a girl. You must . . . have had help."

"I managed to get you across my pony, and then I led him home. I might be small, but I can be very determined."

Fiona couldn't suppress a smile as his eyes narrowed, studying her in disbelief. *Men. They think women are frail, helpless creatures. Little do they know of the strength or courage of women when the need is great.*

"You really shouldn't be exerting yourself," she pointed out. She wriggled free of his grasp, and he let her, his strength visibly ebbing before her eyes.

"Rest now." She spoke with quiet authority. "It's important that you gather your strength. You're not completely out of danger yet—"

"That's true." He gave a harsh laugh, and his eyes, green and cool as the richest leaves of summer beneath a shock of tousled black hair, flicked toward the window. "You'd best keep those shutters bolted tight if you value your life. They might come looking for me."

"Who might?"

"Who do you think?" He grunted suddenly as he shifted his weight and the wounds across his body burned. "The men who set upon me last night," he bit out. "And more like them."

"What do they want with you?"

"They want me dead." His eyes closed as weariness and pain overtook him and the blackness of sleep rushed upon him once more. "If they find me . . . and you . . . they will . . . kill us both . . ."

His voice trailed off, and he sank back into oblivion, his lean, chiseled face more ashen than before—as ashen as Hynda's face had been, Fiona reflected in apprehension, during the days just before her death.

Fiona hurried to the window and bolted the heavy shutters. Then she went to the hearth in the main room of the cottage, where an iron pot bubbled with the healing brew she'd mixed while the wounded man slept. It smelled strongly of sweet herbs and dark spices. She dipped a clean cloth into the murky liquid, wrung it out, then returned to the bed that had once belonged to Hynda. The man hadn't moved. His breathing seemed even shallower than before.

He has fever, she realized in alarm, touching his skin, staring at the film of sweat that had begun to glisten at his temples. She had cleaned and bandaged his wounds, and stopped the bleeding, but the danger was far from over. Infection might set in. If that happened, the poison would spread through his body, through his blood—unless she managed to cure it in time.

She began to bathe his face, his neck, and those broad, powerful shoulders with the cloth, letting the potion seep into his skin. He groaned when she touched the cloth to the cut on his cheek, and once or twice more as the potion soaked into his flesh, but he didn't open his eyes again. She dipped the cloth again and again and massaged him with it, gently swabbing the dark, crisp chest hair that was still matted and rough with dried blood.

Fiona had helped Hynda tend to wounded men before, but none, not even the duke's soldiers, had ever possessed a chest as wide and well muscled and bronzed as this stranger who lay ill and feverish in her care.

Fiona couldn't help but stare as she stroked his powerful forearms, ropy with muscle and sinew. He was darkly handsome, this near-death stranger, with his firm jaw and lean nose and those cool green eyes. Something inside her responded to him in a way that startled her. She felt a strange fluttering in her heart, not unlike the wings of a butterfly beating against her rib cage.

Yet at the same time uneasiness crept through her. Her action in saving this man last night had been both pure impulse and a reflection of her training under Hynda. Healers had a bound duty to help all those who were hurt. It was that which had driven her from the cottage out into the forest, that which had compelled her to bring this man into her home and tend him.

But now, in the cold, brisk light of the winter morning, she wondered just who he was and what he'd done to bring those men down upon him with such savagery.

She shivered at the memory of his words. They would both be killed if the men found him here. Had they been the duke's men? she wondered, biting her lip. If so, why? Or had the attackers been simple bandits, cutthroats in search of lone victims to rob and kill?

She had found no brooch upon the man's cloak—but she was almost certain she'd seen a jewel in the mirror. It had looked to be a ruby, glittering where his cloak would clasp. Perhaps the attackers *had* been thieves and had snatched it from him as they attacked. If the dark-haired man had possessed a pouch containing money, or a flask, or a dagger, they had also taken that. As well as his sword. There had been no sign of his weapon when Fiona reached the clearing. Nor of the wolf-dog she'd glimpsed in the mirror.

Her throat tightened with worry. There had been more rumors than usual swirling through Urbagran of late—dark, dangerous rumors. High King Mortimer was ailing, some said dying, in his castle at Dovenbyre. The hunt had begun in earnest for his long-hidden son, Branden, the boy-prince who would succeed him as ruler of all Grithain. Those who wanted to see the boy dead were at large, swarming Grithain and all the small outlying kingdoms, hunting the young prince even more intensively than they had these past ten years since his birth. Four young men in kingdoms as far distant as Coer Daine and Plordeddan had been murdered, all because they bore a

resemblance to Mortimer and were of the age that the young
prince would now be.

The high king's enemies were numerous, and many wore
two faces. Most dangerous of all was Conor, the outcast Duke
of Wor-thane. He was the king's older, bastard son, who had
sworn vengeance upon his father years ago when Mortimer
made it clear that Branden would be his successor to the throne.
He was rumored to have been behind the king's stabbing two
summers ago, though the whisper had never been proven.

And then there was Plodius, king of the fiefdom of Ril. It
was said he had offered a bounty for the young prince's head,
as had several other warlords who had their eye on Grithain
and could scarcely wait for Mortimer to die so that the free-
for-all could begin.

And begin it would. The moment Mortimer passed on, the
heir to the throne would be revealed and returned to Dovenbyre
for his coronation. From then on he would live well guarded
but always in danger. He would be compelled to watch cease-
lessly for his enemies, even among friends, as his father had
done before him.

But first he would have to survive the journey back to Dovenbyre. No one knew quite how that would be accomplished.
The soldiers and spies and counselors of his enemies still
combed the land, as they had for years—every land from the
Runpeldd Mountains to the Serpentine Sea—even more so now
that King Mortimer lay so gravely ill.

*And what if this stranger is one of those bent on harming
the prince?* Fiona wondered, her throat dry with fear. *What if
you have saved the life of a man who would slit Gilroyd's
throat if given the chance?*

She felt ill. Sick with worry. Yet she'd had no choice. She'd
had to help the man—it had been as natural an impulse as
breathing. But now—now she must be careful. She must watch
this man and give nothing away. Her loyalty must lie only with
Gil. With the boy she had vowed to protect, the boy who in
truth was not Gilroyd of Urbagran, foster son of Sir Henry, but
Branden, the next high king of Grithain—though he had no
notion of it yet. This boy who would be king was like a little
brother to her, and she knew with foreboding that he would

need her and every true friend he could muster if he was to fulfill his destiny and live to rule Grithain.

The man in her care slept. His sleep was fitful, and she watched him closely as the fever raged through his body. She knew what she must do—give him broth mixed with bats' feet. He would not care for the taste, but it would help to drive the fever from him. He must take it. For the sooner he recovered, the sooner he could be on his way.

On his way, yes. To wherever he was going, so long as it was far from Urbagran and from Gil.

A knock at the door of the cottage startled her, and she jumped off the stool at the side of the bed. Hurrying from the chamber, she closed the thick wooden door behind her and forced herself to remain calm as she opened the cottage door.

"My lady Fiona. You'll forgive the intrusion, I'm sure. I have come with a special invitation—" Duke Borlis of Urbagran, accompanied by four soldiers who stood some little distance behind him, broke off his speech to stare long and hard at the skirt of her gown.

"Is that blood?" he asked in his thin, sharp voice.

Fiona shifted her glance from Reynaud, who was one of the soldiers riding with the duke this morning, and looked down, startled. Indeed, blood—the stranger's blood—had spread and dried into the faded wool of her skirt.

"Yes. Yes, it is. It is deer blood, my lord. I found an injured deer in my garden this morning and tended it. Please forgive me for greeting you thus—I did not expect any guests on such a cold winter's day."

"I should think not. Only the intrepid would dare venture forth on such a day as this, eh?" His lips curved in his wide, careful smile. Duke Borlis was a stout, brown-haired man, with a thick neck and a sliver of a nose, and a pair of shrewd eyes the color of dung. He ruled his people with a whip and a sword, and prided himself on the richness of his coffers and the ruthless proficiency of his soldiers in battle.

There was cruelty in him, and no gentleness or compassion, not so far as Fiona had ever seen. She loathed the attention he paid her, and always felt an unpleasant shudder when he kissed her hand or paid her a compliment.

He certainly looked royal and elegant in his crimson velvet cloak trimmed with the silver fur of the north country foxes, but she struggled to keep her skin from crawling as his eyes bored into her face. She knew it was impossible to turn him away without an offer of hospitality.

He was a distant cousin of the high king, and considered one of Mortimer's oldest friends and allies, but Fiona—and Hynda—had never quite trusted him.

When the king had insisted that his son be hidden here in Urbagran within the kingdom of his trusted cousin, it was Hynda who had persuaded her sister, Ariel, to convince the king that no one should know of it, no one except Sir Henry, who had been chosen as the boy-prince's guardian. Even Duke Borlis himself should not know the boy was here, Hynda had argued, unless the secret were to get out and Gilroyd were to need the duke's sudden and massive protection. And so it had been arranged: only Sir Henry's wife and himself, Hynda, and—when she was old enough—Fiona, were to be privy to the secret. And, trusting Ariel's judgment, the king had finally agreed.

Fiona had never been able to explain her distrust of the duke. Hynda had advised her, though, to always take into account her instincts. Magic is often an intensification of instinct, she had told the girl often enough. Mind it as you would a spell or a potion.

"I've noticed, though, that these villagers don't seem to care how often or at what hours they disturb you," the duke added, leaning his shoulder against the doorframe since Fiona had not yet invited him inside. "It concerns me that your door is always open to the common folk and their animals, to the wild beasts that seem to find you. Especially since you now live here alone, with no chaperone or protector. May I come in?" the duke asked abruptly, and Fiona stifled a grimace at the irony of his words. She felt he was the only man in the village from whom she might need protection, and yet he was the one man to whom she could not refuse admittance.

"Of course, my lord. Forgive my thoughtlessness."

Fiona stepped aside, praying that the injured man would not cry out in his sleep, or waken and call for her. But she could hardly refuse the duke. He tended to turn churlish when anyone—and particularly she—failed to treat him with what he deemed the proper respect.

"May I offer you some refreshment? I have wine, and there is cheese—"

"I am not here for refreshment." The duke shut the door on his entourage and followed her into the cottage, glancing at the bench near the fire, the small wooden chairs beneath the window, the shelves filled with jars and bottles of medicines and herbs. There were sweet-smelling rushes upon the floor and a pot simmering over the flames. Everything was neat and tidy, just like the stunning young woman before him—save for the blood on her skirt.

"First, I would like to personally issue you an invitation to the ball I am holding in a week's time. It is in honor of an esteemed visitor—King Plodius of Ril."

Fiona struggled to keep her expression neutral. King Plodius of the small kingdom of Ril was one of those rumored to have plotted against King Mortimer in the first and second attempts upon his life. Like the accusations against Conor of Wor-thane, nothing had ever been proven, and these days Plodius was received by many who were allegedly loyal to Mortimer, but it struck her as odd—and alarming—that Mortimer's own cousin would give a ball in honor of the man.

"Thank you, my lord. It shall be my pleasure to attend." Fiona hadn't the faintest idea what she would wear for such an occasion, but she couldn't blatantly offend the duke by refusing. And she wanted to observe Plodius and the duke together and see just how close the two of them might be.

She must speak to Sir Henry and warn him to be on the alert. Perhaps it would be wise for Gilroyd to leave the district, to spend some time in a friendly kingdom when Plodius came to Raven Castle.

"Ah, good. That was easy enough." The duke's smile held satisfaction. "Now I would like you to consider a proposition," he added, stepping closer to her. "It has occurred to me that with Hynda no longer here, it is foolhardy for you to live alone so near to the forest. I've decided you must come live within the village proper—at Raven Castle. You were gently born, my lady—Hynda told me that much, and it is clear from your speech and your bearing. You shall live in more proper quarters within the castle and serve my wife as a lady-in-waiting. There is no reason you should have to deal with every sick and injured peasant who comes to your door."

"I thank you, my lord duke." *For interfering in my life.* It took all of her willpower to keep her anger hidden, and indeed, she couldn't keep a trace of stiffness from her voice, though she struggled to avoid it. "But I am trained as a healer, and a healer I shall remain. Though I am honored by your kind offer."

"It is more than an offer. I want you inside the castle gates within a fortnight."

Her blood chilled, but she kept her voice steady. "Is that an order?"

"My dear woman," he said with a broad smile, which did nothing to dim the arrogant glint in his eyes, "it is an earnest and most admiring request."

"One that I must refuse. I doubt, my lord, that your wife would wish me as a lady-in-waiting. It is customary that she choose her own, is it not? And indeed, I am certain the duchess has no lack of fine ladies to serve her—"

"My wife is obedient and wise, and does my bidding," he countered, closing the last of the distance between them. "As you ought to do. I have only your best interests at heart."

Fiona had to force herself to hold her ground, when she wanted to back up, to put distance between the two of them. She knew better than to believe the duke's silken words. The duke wanted her in his bed, as his mistress. That had been clear for some time. He had held his advances in check while Hynda still lived—but ever since her death he had become increasingly bold.

He was a man who could certainly take what he wanted, and Fiona knew the day was coming when she would have to fight or flee to escape his attentions—and neither would bode well for her. She couldn't afford to get herself locked up or banished. Gilroyd needed her close. Now there were only she and Sir Henry to protect him, to see to his care and education, and to prepare him for a future that was coming all too quickly.

"I will consider your request," she conceded, trying once more to keep the anger from showing in her eyes or her voice. She had to buy time. Perhaps Gilroyd would be summoned to Dovenbyre soon, and she could follow him there, leaving the cottage and the Duke of Urbagran behind. *And leaving Reynaud and the others too,* she thought ruefully, thinking of the young knights and village boys who had often enough declared their wish to court her but had been too fearful of the duke's wrath to do so.

"You'll *consider* it? That is less than I hoped for." The duke's eyes narrowed on her face. The next moment a small smile curled his lips. "But I will accept your answer for now. And hope that I can persuade you to see the advantages."

He stood directly before her, so close she could feel his breath on her cheeks. It smelled of fish and onions. Fiona stepped back apace. The duke advanced the same distance, laughed, then caught her in his burly arms.

"Don't be afraid, little Fiona. I would never harm you. I admire you. I only wish I could show you how very much— *What was that?*"

Fiona froze. There had been a sound from Hynda's chamber. A sound like that of some object crashing to the floor.

"Is someone in there?" the duke said in a harsh tone. He released her, staring at the closed door. He took a step toward the chamber, but Fiona caught at his velvet cloak.

"No, no, it is only Tidbit. I locked her in Hynda's room so she couldn't slip out the door. If she goes wandering in this frigid weather, she might freeze to death. She must have knocked over one of Hynda's jars or vials." Her heart pounded even as she spoke the lie. She could only pray that Tidbit wouldn't suddenly appear from wherever in the cottage she was napping and prove the falsehood. If the duke discovered the wounded man—

Why should it matter? she asked herself. Surely it wasn't the duke's men who had attacked him. It must have been thieves— he had been robbed of his brooch and his sword and money pouch. There was no reason to think the duke would wish him harm.

And yet as she stared at the nobleman before her she suddenly saw something more than the suspicion and arrogance that were stamped upon his face. She saw for the first time the small gold brooch fastening his fur-trimmed cloak. It was smaller than the brooches the duke usually wore—he was a man who liked to flaunt his wealth and possessions. And she had never seen it before. It was simple, bands of gold worked into the shape of a falcon. Two rubies glinted from the golden eyes.

Was that what she had glimpsed in the mirror—this very brooch? Had it been taken from the stranger during the attack?

"My lord, much as I have enjoyed your visit, I must not keep you any longer," she said hurriedly. "A man as important as you must have many pressing matters to attend to."

"If I didn't know better, I'd think you were trying to be rid of me." She had at least distracted him from the noise in Hynda's room. But there was a trace of anger in his tone.

Fiona offered a smile, even letting the dimples show in her cheeks. "Of course not. Your visit has been a welcome reprieve from my chores. But now, just as you have matters to attend to, so do I. I promised to look in upon the miller's wife today. She suffered a fall and can barely walk. And Simon the farmer has been unable to rise from his bed for two days. There is much for me to do."

She needn't have worried that the duke would know she had fabricated both of these excuses. He was a man totally disconnected from the people he ruled—Fiona doubted that he even knew that the miller's wife had died six months earlier, or that the farmer was as hale and hearty as a bear. He let himself be ushered to the door and and at last took his leave, but not before lingering over his good-byes and raising her hand to his lips.

Uck, Fiona thought, scrubbing the moist spot on her hand where his mouth had touched. *The man grows more detestable by the day.*

But the duke was forgotten as she rushed to Hynda's room. When she burst inside, she saw that the injured man was awake, his face and neck soaked with sweat from the fever. The brass box of dried herbs she'd left on the table beside his bed had been knocked over, and its contents scattered across the floor.

"Sorry—I was trying . . . to get up. Fell back. My arm hit that . . . box," he muttered as she went to him and placed a hand on his brow.

"Never mind, it's all right."

"I heard you . . . talking. That was . . . the duke . . ."

"Unfortunately," she responded at once without thinking, then bit her lip as his feverish gaze fastened upon her face.

"He desires you . . . in the castle . . . and . . . in his bed."

"Even a duke doesn't always get what he desires. Now stop talking and go back to sleep. You need—"

"To rest," he finished for her grimly. "I know." His hand stretched out toward her, and she realized suddenly that he wanted her to take it. She did, and a blaze of heat seemed to sear her palm. Male vitality—or was it only the fever?—burned from his long fingers to her daintier ones.

"If I'd . . . had the strength . . . to get out of this damned bed, I'd have . . . knocked him down. He insulted you—"

"It doesn't matter. Don't upset yourself." But she was stunned by his words, by his instant offer of protection. Who was this man? No one she'd ever met, even Sir Henry, had dared speak so openly against the duke, much less threaten to lay a hand on him. Especially not in her defense.

"He'll never touch you," he went on weakly. "I promise you, angel . . ."

"I appreciate your offer of protection, but I can take care of myself. I'm not frightened of the duke, not for my sake—"

She broke off, and his hand suddenly tightened on hers.

"For someone else's? Whose, then?" Those feverish eyes searched her face as he waited for her answer.

"Yours," she said quickly, appalled that she had even indirectly referred to Gilroyd, though thank heaven she hadn't named the boy. "The duke was wearing a brooch like the one I saw—" She broke off, hardly prepared to tell him about the magic mirror either.

"It was a brooch I had never seen him wear before," she added hastily, "and I thought it might be yours. That it was perhaps stolen from you by his men. *Was* it the duke's men, then, who tried to kill you?"

"A gold falcon . . . with ruby eyes," he murmured.

"Yes!"

His own eyes closed, and his hand fell away from hers. "Mine. I will take it back from him and give it to you . . . when I am . . . stronger."

With that he dropped into sleep once more.

Fiona stood at the bedside, stunned. So the duke's men *had* been behind the attack. Not outlaws. *The duke.*

She swallowed. Why was this man Duke Borlis's enemy? And was he also Gil's?

"I need to know your name. And what you're doing here," she whispered. But he didn't hear her. The fever burned in him, and he slept on.

She turned her attention to the dried herbs that lay scattered on the floor and began carefully placing them back in the box. They were fragrant with the warm blackberry and myrtle scent that she associated with Hynda herself, and for a moment as she breathed in the scent that flooded the room she could almost feel the old witch in the chamber with her.

If only you were here, Hynda. You would know what to do, how to nurse this man so that he might live, and whether or not he is an enemy.

But Hynda was gone, and as Fiona touched a soothing hand to the dark-haired man's brow, she knew that she must find a way to save his life herself.

For that day and night, and all of the next two days, she fought the fever and the wounds and the vicious fire that seemed to burn through him as he tossed upon the bed like a ship on a tumultuous sea.

And then on the fourth day, when the icy grip of cold outside the cottage finally broke and the sun peeked through to thaw the icicles in the trees, he stopped his thrashing and the fever vanished. But he did not awaken, and she couldn't rouse him. His sleep deepened, as if drawing him further away.

Before, she'd been able at least to force a few sips of broth now and then between his lips, but now he slept like one who was already dead, only his chest rising shallowly and falling with every breath.

Fiona huddled wearily at his bedside, her own limbs aching with fatigue. He would either awaken again or not. There was nothing more she could do.

Staring at him, she felt nearly as spent and weak and sick as he looked. Night and day she had tended him. She had tried draughts and potions and herbs and rubs, she had tried talking to him, urging him to come back, and she had tried prayer.

Now there was nothing more to try. She must wait. And hope.

The hours crept by. Midnight came in the vast, cold stillness beyond the cottage window. Ravens flapped their wings overhead, wheeling into the forest. Tidbit flicked her tail, back and forth, back and forth—then leapt from the chest of drawers to the foot of the injured man's bed.

And the man's eyelids fluttered.

Fiona went still.

They fluttered again. "Yes, wake up," she whispered, slipping from her stool, edging to the bed, and closing her hand around his. She needed to reach him somehow, to encourage him to pull himself up from the abyss, toward wakefulness and all the offerings of life.

Her fingers wrapped around his as with all of her body and mind she willed him to live.

His hand was much larger than hers, and his palm felt warm and reassuringly alive.

He has so much vitality, she thought, for even now, though he was ill and asleep and struggling for life, strength seemed to emanate from him, stirring something inside her.

"You can do it," she urged, staring into his lean, handsome face. "I don't even know your name, but I know you can do it. All I ask is that you wake up."

He groaned and a moment later stirred. Fiona held her breath.

Then, slowly, his eyes opened and focused upon her.

"It's you. My . . . angel." His voice was deep, raspy. Though not as weak as it had been the first time he'd awakened. "You're still . . . here," he whispered.

"Yes, but I'm not an angel. I'm the one who found you. Save your strength, though. Don't talk. I'll be right back with—"

"Don't leave." Again, somehow, he had hold of her, his fingers tightening around hers with that burst of surprising strength. "Stay."

Fiona shook her head. "Not this again. Lie still. I am only fetching you some broth. It will make you stronger."

His hand dropped. His eyes closed. But the moment she returned with the broth and set it down on the small chest beside the bed, he came wide awake again, those cool green eyes locking on her face.

"How long . . . have I been here?"

"Four days."

"My sword . . . where . . . is my sword?"

"Gone. There was no sword in the clearing when I found you. I—"

"And my . . . horse?"

"He was gone too." Fiona regarded him worriedly as his eyes closed yet again. "Don't waste your strength with questions. You're fortunate to be alive. But now I must try to lift you up so that you can eat. Can you help me a little?"

He began to struggle upward, and she slipped an arm beneath his shoulder, using all her strength to help him to a sitting position, then shoving several pillows behind his broad back.

"This broth will help to restore you. You must take it all." But as she lifted the steaming spoonful of broth toward his lips, he looked aghast.

"What is that? It smells . . . like rotting meat." He eyed the spoon she held warily, and Fiona gave him an encouraging smile.

"It is a special herb broth. It will make you stronger and help your wounds to heal much more quickly than they otherwise would." He frowned, and she saw he was going to protest, so she rushed on imploringly.

"If you can get down one bowlful of it, it will speed your recovery, and I promise that your next meal will be much more enjoyable. I will cook you an entire pot of real beef broth then, and you shall have mutton, and barley bread—"

"I don't . . . want this rot. Take it away."

She tilted her head to one side. "My goodness, I've cared for tiny children who are better patients than you." She sighed and once more brought the spoon toward his lips. "Don't be childish now. Open your mouth and—"

"By the gods . . . bring me real food, woman, or I'll—"

"Don't tell me you're afraid?" she chided softly. "A strapping man like you, who fought five men at once and lived to tell about it—and you're afraid of a bowl of broth simply because it contains bats' feet—"

"Bats' feet! By all the devils in hell—" he broke off suddenly. "How do you know . . . about the five men?"

"Eat your broth," Fiona said sweetly, "and perhaps I shall tell you."

There was a long pause. He stared at her with open dislike and intense distrust, then shifted his gaze to the bowl of dark broth, which Fiona had to admit did smell most foul. He shuddered. Then he clamped his lips together.

"For a woman who looks like an angel . . . I half suspect you are the devil's own daughter," he grunted out between clenched teeth. "Very well, I will drink your damned broth. But only if you answer *all* of my questions."

"I shall—as soon as every drop of this broth is gone."

Fiona kept her expression neutral, though she couldn't help but feel sorry for him as she watched him swallow spoonful after spoonful of the broth. It did have powerful healing properties, but the taste was enough to make any man moan. This man, however, drank it in silence—stiff, furious, resigned silence—and when he was finished and the bowl was empty he slumped back against the pillows and eyed her with the same ruthless determination with which he'd swallowed the broth.

"Now tell me. Quickly. Who are you, how do you know about the men who attacked me? Tell me . . . everything."

3

FIONA SAW THAT the exertion of eating the broth and of speaking had wearied him. But he looked so serious and so intent that she knew there was no hope of persuading him to rest before exerting himself more. She drew the stool nearer to the bed, perched on it, and spoke quietly.

"I am called Fiona. I told you once. Do you remember?"

Slowly, he nodded. "Bitterbloom Cottage," he muttered after a moment.

"Yes, at the edge of the Dark Forest. I found you in the clearing, left for dead by the men who attacked you. They were Duke Borlis's men, I gather, since they stole your brooch. Why does the duke want you dead?"

"I'm the one asking the questions, angel." He forced out the words despite his fatigue. "Who else knows I'm here?"

"No one."

"You're sure?"

"Yes, but—"

"How far are we from Raven Castle?" he interrupted with a frown.

"Not far." She fought to keep her voice steady. "I would like to know why I am harboring a man sought by the Duke of Urbagran."

At that he looked into her eyes. "Because you have a kind heart."

"That isn't what I mean. Why does the duke want you dead?"

"Let's just say he and I are at . . . cross-purposes. And you and I—" He broke off wearily, his head sagging back against the pillow. Frustration showed in his face. "How long . . . until I am stronger? Strong enough to get out of this bed—to ride, to fight?"

"The broth you drank will do you good in very short time. It is an especially potent brew. Perhaps by tomorrow, or the next day, you can rise and begin to move about, but as for fighting—" She shook her head. "I would advise you to wait."

"Some things can't wait." His mouth was a thin line. He wasn't usually an indecisive man, but at this moment, stuck in this damned bed, too weary to even lift his head, and with the wound in his chest beginning to throb anew, he hesitated to tell this lovely girl the whole truth. He knew that she was beautiful, and brave, and that she'd saved his life, but that was all he knew—other than that she'd vowed to protect Branden.

If he told her the truth, right now, how would she react? Would she panic, run away to give warning? Or would she wait to hear him out? Could she possibly believe the fantastic tale he was going to tell her? If not, she could cause great harm.

And he was too weak to follow or stop her.

No, he couldn't risk it. Not yet. Not until he had more strength, enough to handle her, to control the situation, no matter how she received his words.

He turned his face toward the ceiling, and she saw his shoulders and the muscles in his neck relax, as if he were willing himself to do so. "I am Cade of the Hill Country beyond Nevendale. I was sent here . . . to help you. Not that I can do a very good job of it at the moment," he added bitterly.

Fiona's eyes widened in astonishment. "Sent here to help me do what?"

"To do what you have pledged." He looked at her directly now, that sharp gaze of his seeming to penetrate her very soul. "To protect the boy who is the next high king of Grithain."

Fiona went perfectly still, as if his words were a spell, turning her to stone. *Be careful*, a tiny voice inside her warned. *It might be a trick.*

"I don't know what you're talking about—" she began, but he interrupted her roughly.

"The high king himself sent me—and so did Ariel. They instructed me to come here, to find you and Sir Henry and to take charge of Branden's protection. I have a troop at my back—they should reach Urbagran within the next days—and soon the army of Grithain will be headed here as well. Until then, we three must keep Prince Branden safe."

Fiona went pale, staring at him. Despite what he'd said, she needed to be cautious. "I . . . don't know anyone named Branden. I believe you have fallen victim to rumor. There is no one here by that name, no one who could possibly be the high king's son, not in Urbagran—"

His arm flashed out and seized hers, dragging her closer, practically down atop him on the bed. Her face was only a breath away from his.

"Think it through, angel. I know about you. I know about Sir Henry. And I know about Gilroyd. How would I know, if not for being told by King Mortimer himself? No secret has been so closely guarded as this one."

He heard her sharp intake of breath, and saw her cheeks go pale as moondust. Something tightened inside his gut as those exquisite silver-gray eyes searched his, desperately, frantically, trying to read truth or falsehood in their depths.

"I am a friend to the boy—and to you," he said grimly. "You need not fear me."

Fiona's head was spinning. Hope flickered in her heart. Was it true, he was here to help? An ally? How else would he know so much, if he didn't have the trust of the king?

There was one way, she thought with a gulp. If the spies of Duke Conor or King Plodius or some other petty king had broken the secret at last and sent him to murder Gil.

"Ariel is the sister of Hynda, the witch who raised you," he continued in a steady tone, still imprisoning her arm. "She instructed me to tell you that she has spoken to her sister in the afterworld, where she has gone. Hynda wishes you to know that she watches over you still—"

Fiona gasped. Tears filled her eyes. *Could it be true?* she wondered, caught halfway between hope and grief.

"I can see you loved her." He gave a slight nod. "That is as Ariel said."

He was a man who, beyond all else, knew how to rein in his passions, but he found himself unexpectedly touched by the emotions rushing across the girl's face. He let go of her arm and with his finger dried the single tear that slipped down her cheek.

"I am glad I could bring you word of her."

Her eyes shimmered, wonderingly, and again he fought against unfamiliar sensations. *There is no time for this,* he told himself sternly. *No time for gentle talk, for sympathy or softness.*

And yet, for a moment, he found himself fascinated by the woman who had saved his life. He almost . . . envied her. All that she felt was betrayed now in those striking eyes. Sorrow, pain, hope, joy. *Love.* How strange. He had never loved anyone. Nor had anyone loved him. For a fleeting moment, he wondered how it would feel—to love.

Then he steeled himself. In his world, in his life, he had no time for such things. Nor did he have the inclination for them.

"What else did Ariel say?" she whispered.

Weariness was dragging at him. He fought it as he'd fought everything in his path for the past ten years.

"She said that it is time now for you and Sir Henry to join forces with me. All that you two have done for Branden in the past has served him well, but now he needs a defender—a champion. Someone who would fight to the death for him."

"You've almost fought to the death already, only a few days ago," she murmured, thinking of how courageously and desperately he had fought against the five men in the clearing.

"And I'll do it again, if need be. But I'd rather escort him to safety without the need for a fight. Things are coming to a head. The king is dying—he may be dead already."

"Oh, no. Not yet—"

"Duke Borlis is Branden's enemy." It was becoming more difficult to talk. His chest hurt. He tried to take a deep breath, to push on, but the exertion of both eating and talking was taking its toll.

"That is one thing I have recently learned on my own. He and Plodius of Ril are plotting together, though I don't know exactly what they intend. You must get word to Sir Henry. He must come here, meet with me, and we can decide how best to protect the boy until—" He paused, took a deep breath, and she could see the fatigue passing across his face, turning his skin a pasty gray.

"We've lost . . . too much time . . . all these days when the fever raged . . . and . . . I don't even have a sword. But the danger, it's growing . . ."

"You'll be better able to face it if you sleep now." Fiona drew the blanket up around his shoulders, hoping he couldn't see that her hands were shaking. "Rest. Let the healing broth do its work. Tomorrow you'll be better, and I'll bring Sir Henry to hear . . . what you have to say."

He was watching her, clearly struggling against the weariness that engulfed him. "In the morning . . . early . . . *you must bring him.*"

"Yes. Sleep now." She took a deep breath and hoped he couldn't see how shaken she was by all he had told her. If it was true, by the stars and the moon, the danger to Gilroyd was great and all too imminent.

If it was a lie, then this man was Gilroyd's enemy, and that spelled danger too. "Whatever awaits, Cade of the Hill Country, you cannot face it yet," she said as calmly as she could. "First, you must rest."

"It doesn't seem . . . I can do much of . . . anything else . . . for the time being," he muttered, and she sensed the frustration edging his words. But even as he spoke them his eyes closed, and she saw him drifting, drifting into sleep, no longer able to resist the exhaustion dragging at him.

Fiona stood back, studying him as he slept, frantically trying to decide if he was telling the truth. Her instinct told her yes, but she didn't completely trust her feelings. Something about him drew her in a way she couldn't explain, a way that had nothing to do with reason or with proof. She liked him. He seemed . . . decent.

No, more than decent. And it wasn't merely because he was dark and strong and handsome as a knight out of some wonderful romantic legend, she told herself, though he was all three. It wasn't because of that intriguing black stubble along his jaw, or because of the keen intelligence that gleamed from his eyes, or because he had wiped her tear from her cheek with such gentleness. She sensed something in him, something solitary and cool and, yes, decent.

There is more in him than he would have anyone know, even himself, she thought suddenly.

She prayed she was right about him. Prayed she wouldn't rue the day she'd saved this man's life, bringing him to the cottage, working night and day to heal him—only so he could threaten Gil.

Her stomach clenched painfully at that possibility, and for a moment she felt so ill she nearly swayed. She grasped at the wall, bit her lip to steady herself, and at last stole off to her own bed.

But it was a long while before she slept, for her thoughts were full of fears. She sensed that she'd found the Midnight Mirror again *now* for a reason—that it was playing some role in her destiny, perhaps in Grithain's destiny, finally, after all these years. She sensed that danger was creeping closer to Gilroyd with each passing day and that events were about to change forever the happy, peaceful days she and Hynda and Sir Henry had known with the boy for these many years.

These events had already begun. They'd started on the night she'd seen the vision in the mirror. And now she could only wonder where they would lead—and what part the stranger would play in them.

She must not trust him, she warned herself, as the moon drifted through a misty purple sky toward morning. She must watch him closely. And do whatever was necessary to protect the boy.

Tomorrow I will get word to Sir Henry that I must speak to him. I'll have him come to the cottage and meet this Cade of the Hill Country, see if he knows him, if he can help me question him. We need to know if this man is who he claims to be.

When she finally slipped into sleep, her dreams were restless. She awoke three times in the night, bolting straight up in her bed, thinking someone had called her name. It sounded like Hynda.

But there was only silence in the cottage—except for the steady rush of the wind at the windows and her own hurried breathing.

4

Fiona rose shortly after dawn, weary of tossing in her bed. She washed, donned a fresh gown of deep amber wool, and brushed her hair, then with quick, nimble fingers bound her waterfall of curls into a smooth black braid that swung down her back nearly to her waist. She rushed through her morning chores and was setting dark bread and apples and cheese on a plate for Cade's breakfast when she heard the sound she usually loved and craved to hear. But today it filled her with a mixture of emotions. Happiness, yes—but also anxiety.

Gilroyd and Wynndom—Sir Henry's true son, and for all intents and purposes Gil's older brother—were rapping on the door to the cottage, and she could hear their laughter and bright chatter through the walls.

Hurriedly she closed the door to Hynda's room and ran to welcome them. As she opened the cottage door, the bitter winter wind rushed in, and with it tumbled Gil and Wynn, both red-cheeked and grinning at her beneath their cloaks and hoods.

But that was where all similarity between the two boys ended. Wynn was tall and gangly for his fourteen years, already taking on the look of the man he would soon become. His hair was the same reddish brown as Sir Henry's, and always looked unkempt, falling across his brow and into eyes that were brown as walnuts. Gilroyd was only ten, still a boy not yet on the cusp of manhood.

He was stocky and capable-looking, with long eyelashes, serious eyes that were more gray than blue, a straight nose and solemn mouth, and a sensible manner that made him seem older than his years.

Straight brown hair, with no hint of red in its thick strands, framed a youthful face that promised to become both strong and handsome. While Wynn had an easygoing assurance and good-natured grin, Gilroyd was quieter, his expression more thoughtful, and he seemed to think long and hard over matters that others simply dismissed.

"Father's servant is coming later today with venison and fowls—and some spices, goat cheese, and milled flour for you," Wynn announced.

"And Father sent you this note," Gil added, digging in the pocket of his brown cloak and at last fishing out a much-folded sheet of parchment.

"Thank you for both. I must give you a note for him too," Fiona said hurriedly, hoping the stranger was still sound asleep. Despite her uneasiness at their arrival, she was glad, as always, to see the camaraderie and friendship between these two who had been raised as brothers. She only hoped they would feel the same when the truth came out, when Wynn discovered that the younger boy, the one who would *not* inherit their father's title and lands, would instead become the high king of all Grithain, a king with unimaginable riches to whom every noble in the land would be obliged to vow fealty.

She quickly unfolded the note and glanced down at it.

My dear child, I have been called away on business but have urgent matters to discuss with you. I shall call upon you when I return. While I am gone, watch over all in your care.

*My seneschal, Desmond, is, as always, at the ready to be
of service for your good causes, if you shall need him.*

It was signed *Sir Henry.*

Dismay filled her, but she quickly hid her distress as she saw
Gil watching her. "Father went to Aardmore—he ought only
to be gone a day or two," the boy said, as Wynn hungrily eyed
the plate of food.

"He left me in charge," Wynn bragged, still staring at the
apples and bread and cheese. "The servants and his men-at-
arms must report to me while he is gone."

"I don't mind," Gil said quickly, with his ready smile, as if
he feared Fiona would feel sorry for him because his brother
had the greater honor. "One day Father and Wynn will both be
away, and then it will be my turn to be in charge. All that is
good comes to those who wait patiently for their turn at great-
ness, that is what Father told me once—"

"He did? He never said any such thing to me." Wynn
shrugged dismissively, then turned to Fiona with an eager,
hopeful smile. "You don't happen to have any apples and
cheese to spare, do you, Lady Fiona? I'm starving."

"I am too," Gil piped up. "We had breakfast, of course, but
Cook served us gruel and Wynn and I both hate gruel. Still,
twice in a week she insists we must eat it, but when she isn't
looking we sneak it to the side door and toss it out for the
chickens and geese."

Fiona smiled and hesitated, with a quick glance at the door
to Hynda's room. "Sit down, then. I'm afraid I don't have time
for a long visit this morning, but you may have this—and then
be on your way."

She moved the plate of apples, cheese, and bread to where
Wynn was taking his seat and then touched Gil's shoulder
lightly. "I'll bring you another in the blink of an eye."

In Hynda's chamber, Conor clung to the wall near the door,
intent on not falling down. He'd heard the arrival of the boys,
and he'd heard the angel's laughter, and had managed to work
his way toward the door. His legs felt like mush, and his
strength was quickly ebbing, but he had to see the two boys—
he had to see for himself the prince he'd been hunting for these
past two years.

He inched open the door. The angel was there, serving them. The taller boy was too old, and had no look of Mortimer about him. The smaller one was half hidden by the woman, but . . .

Conor felt every muscle in his body tighten. It must be he. He wished he could get closer, get a clear glance.

"Remember the falcon whose wing was broken?" The young boy was looking up at the woman. Seeing the serious expression on his face, Conor drew in his breath.

So had Mortimer looked at him ten years ago, when he was but eighteen—piercing him with the same fierce, serious eyes, the color of the gray stone by the sea, and telling him never to set foot in Dovenbyre again.

"He returned yesterday," the boy said. "You mended his wing and made him well, and he had flown into the woods, but then, he came back."

"Did he?" Fiona saw that the boys had eaten every crumb on their plates, and she brought two wedges of spice cake to the table. "He must have wanted to thank you for taking such good care of him. Did he stay?"

"No. He brought me a black stone in his beak. And then he flew away."

"A . . . stone?" Fiona stiffened, her smile slowly fading. Only once had Hynda's sister, Ariel, who had formed the Magic Mirror, visited them at the cottage, but she had made an unforgettable impression. Her powers were great and far more varied than Hynda's, and she had taught Fiona several things during her stay. *A bird that brings a branch in its mouth signals life and hope,* Ariel had said. *Perhaps a child on its way, or a time of plenty to come. A bird that flies into a home signals death. And one that brings a stone warns of danger.*

"What's wrong?" Gil asked, his brow furrowing in worry. He was always quick to notice the moods and sense the feelings of those around him. "You look as if you're going to weep."

"No, no, don't be silly. It is only that I have much to do today. I'm afraid it is time for you to return home for your lessons—"

"We practice jousting today, in the fields!" Wynn announced. He threw his brother a laughing glance. "I am much better at it than Gil."

"Because you are taller," the younger boy pointed out indignantly. "But Kenovan says I have a gift with a lance—and for riding destriers. When I am grown taller I think I shall knock you off every time!"

"We'll see about that, sprout." Wynn playfully punched the other boy in the arm. "Race you home!"

They rushed to the door, shouting their thanks to Fiona for the meal, and as she followed them she glanced anxiously toward the door of Hynda's room, worried that their shouting and chatter might have awakened her patient.

To her shock, the hard green eyes of Cade of the Hill Country met hers through a crack in the door. He had seen. He had heard.

Her blood froze. No sooner had the boys darted up the hill toward the manor than she slammed the cottage door and flew to Hynda's chamber. She found Cade only a few inches from where she had glimpsed him, trying to make his way along the wall back to his narrow bed. His mouth was grim, and sweat covered his face as he tried not to collapse.

"What do you think you're doing? You shouldn't be out of bed—it's too soon!" She caught his arm, anger pumping through her as she tried to hold him up. "Put your arm around me. Lean on me."

"No, I'll pull you down." He was breathing hard, and his face was flushed.

"No, I'm strong. Lean on me, damn you."

If he hadn't been so exhausted, his eyebrows would have shot up. This slight, gentle girl with her midnight hair and glorious eyes had a temper. Despite everything, he chuckled, though it hurt the wound in his chest.

"Do as I say," she snapped. "We have to get you back into bed."

"That's what I like . . . a woman trying . . . to get me into her bed . . ." He slid his arm around her and let her take some of his weight. Concentrating hard, he took a step toward the bed. Then another. He was very aware of her small form close against his side, supporting him, her breath coming hard, her face tightened with resolve, though he could feel her struggling with the effort of holding him upright.

"Almost there," he muttered, unsure of whether he was trying to encourage her or himself.

"Do stop wasting your breath," she gasped.

It seemed to take forever, but at last he was lying across the bed once more. Every muscle in his body seemed to have the consistency of the gruel the boys had disliked so.

Not just boys, he reminded himself, his jaw clenching. *One of them was the boy-prince, Mortimer's heir. The boy he had vowed long ago would never live to take the throne.*

The angel bent toward him, and he felt her hand on his brow. Such a soft, slender hand, and she smelled like flowers, though it was not yet spring.

"I shouldn't be surprised if the fever comes back." She was scowling at him, stern as his old nurse when he was a boy and had been hauled back to the solar by the grooms after stealing his uncle's destrier for a midnight ride.

"And just what did you think you were doing getting out of bed in your condition?" Despite the gravity of the situation, it was amusing to see such severity in the face of such a young and beautiful woman.

"I heard . . . voices. Wanted to see who it was."

"It was only neighbor children. You needn't have bothered."

He turned his head to better study her face. "So you didn't believe me, then?" A trace of anger steeled his voice. "You didn't believe a word I told you yesterday. I *know* that the younger child was Prince Branden—the boy you call Gilroyd." He frowned, looking so cold, so determined suddenly that fear struck her heart. "Why do you deny it?"

Fiona felt the blood pounding in her temples. Despite being slumped across the bed, ill and injured, he still looked every inch a warrior, a fierce one at that. The kind of man who could well be a danger to Gil, if he so chose.

Yet she wanted to believe him. Wanted to know that she had saved him for a reason, that he was here to help. Heaven knew she needed help, what with Hynda gone and Sir Henry suddenly away. It was all on her shoulders, and, if he was telling her the truth, the danger was close.

But what did she know, really, about this man, about any man?

When Reynaud had begun courting her—polite, handsome, pale-haired Reynaud—she'd been happy and excited, she'd thought his feelings were deep and true, but he'd been frightened off easily enough by a frown and a word from the duke. One word, that's all it had taken. And no other man in the village had ever dared even so much as he.

She had little knowledge of men, except that their bodies, for all their strength, could be felled by illness or injury as easily as any child's. But of their minds and hearts and characters—she knew only that aside from Sir Henry, there were none she could trust.

Not when it came to protecting Gil.

So, this man, who had nearly been killed beneath a midnight moon, this man, who had called her angel and looked at her with such steady strength in his eyes, could well be one of Mortimer's enemies, a man who, unable to kill the king by poison or dagger or battle all these years, was now set upon murdering his son.

A small voice inside her whispered *no*. The same small voice that wanted to trust him. That was drawn to him.

But how could she take a chance with Gilroyd's life?

Still, he had mentioned Ariel, and Hynda. She felt to the bottom of her soul that his words had borne the ring of truth.

"I'm sorry. I . . . have to be careful," she said, biting her lip. "Don't you understand?"

"To a point. But if we're going to keep the boy safe, you need to trust me."

She nodded uncertainly, her hands nervously smoothing the folds of her skirt. "I know," she whispered, and swallowed hard.

Some corner of his heart softened. Despite her best efforts, her emotions showed in her face. That beautiful, vivid, changeable face. She was torn between trust and doubt, and who could blame her?

It was apparent to him that her commitment to the boy was as solid and unyielding as stone.

All the more reason not to tell her the truth . . . not yet. If he did, she would scamper out of here faster than a rabbit fleeing a cabbage patch, and he was in no shape to run her down.

One more day, he thought, *and I'll be stronger, able to take control. Of her, of the boy. My men will no doubt be here . . . one more day.*

"I heard Branden say that Sir Henry is gone to Aardmore. Did his note mention what took him from Urbagran?"

"No, only that he has urgent matters to discuss with me when he returns."

"Well, we have urgent matters to attend to right now." He shifted on the bed, wincing at the fire that licked through his wounds. "I'm going to need a sword. And a horse. You don't happen to have either one of those, do you?"

She shook her head. "I believe my pony, Star, would be much too small for you."

"No doubt." He grimaced, with weariness or frustration, she couldn't tell which. "What about a sword? Or any manner of weapon?"

Her lips trembled. "Do you really think it will come to violence—so soon—before Sir Henry comes back? You must know you're in no condition to fight—even to ride. You could barely get back to this bed."

"I'll do what I need to do!" he said curtly, then checked himself at the wariness in her eyes, the way she stepped back a pace. Her teeth worried her bottom lip.

"Sorry." He gritted his teeth. "I didn't mean to chop your head off, but I'm not accustomed to lying around, weak as a damned puppy."

He tried to sit up, then fell back wearily, raking a hand through his hair. "Look, would you happen to have any more food to spare for a weak, hungry man who feels like he could devour a dragon?"

"Well . . . I'm fresh out of dragons, but I believe I might find something edible in my pantry."

"Just so long as you don't bring me any more of that vile broth."

She almost smiled.

"What you served those boys would be more to my liking," he added, eyeing her hopefully.

"I'm sure it would be." With a noncommittal shrug, she turned and walked out of the room.

He shifted again, studying her retreating figure, all too aware of the sensual sway of her hips, and of that dark braid swinging down her slender back. She was lovely—petite and elegant— and the most unusual female he'd ever met. And he'd met more than a few.

He remembered having kissed and seduced and tumbled into bed with more women than he could count since he'd reached manhood, but not one of the proper ladies he'd danced with or tavern wenches he'd dallied with had ever affected him quite like this small, capable female whose eyes reflected every emotion, who had saved his life at risk to her own and pledged her loyalty to a boy being hunted in every corner of the earth.

Keep your wits about you, he admonished himself. *This is no time to be distracted by a woman, any woman. There is too much at stake.*

Yet, when she brought him a silver tray bearing sausage and barley bread, apples and jellied eggs, sliced cheese and olives and spice cake, he could have kissed her.

But he refrained. First, because he didn't think she'd like the idea and second, because this time tomorrow she would probably want to drive a stake through his heart. Whatever trust and solicitousness she was showing him at this moment would vanish like mist in sunlight as soon as he dropped the Cade of the Hill Country tale and told her his true name.

The goal to which he had committed his life was now before him. He had one chance to accomplish what he had long ago made up his mind to do. And if he failed, there would be no other.

Nothing—and no one—must get in his way.

5

Raven Castle

"MY LORD DUKE!" The breathless servant skidded to a halt before Duke Borlis in his private chamber and bowed low. "The messenger from Dovenbyre has arrived!"

The duke, seated on a velvet chair drawn up before an ornate gilded table, continued to glare into the murky crystal ball before him—the crystal ball that showed him nothing, absolutely nothing, of what he wished to see.

"The man says it is urgent," the servant continued rapidly, his hands clasped before him. "He must speak with you and begs you to admit him to—"

"Send him in, you fool!" The duke frowned after the man as he spun around and raced back into the hall. *Idiots. Idiots and incompetents, that's what I'm surrounded by*, Duke Borlis thought angrily as he shoved back his chair. He began to pace back and forth across the chamber, a muscle twitching in his neck as he tried to contain his impatience. He'd been waiting forever, it seemed, for Mortimer to die, for his chance at last— and for confirmation of what he had suspected for months to be true—that Mortimer's legitimate son and sole heir to the throne was living right under his nose in the home of Sir Blubbery-Dud Henry.

It would be simple to grab the boy and slit his throat. There was no need to rush—still, his blood was racing hot and quick in his veins, pumping wildly through his heart. Now that it was so close, he could not wait. All that he'd dreamed of, all that he'd yearned for, was now within his reach.

He only needed to hear those words—

He wheeled around as the messenger, filthy with travel, his gaunt, homely face red and half frozen, staggered into the room. The man glanced once, longingly, at the fire blazing heartily in the hearth, then settled his gaze rigidly upon the duke.

"My lord, I rode as fast as humanly possible. I have come straight from Dovenbyre—"

"Don't waste words, you imbecile, just tell me," the duke snapped. "Is my cousin dead or not?"

"He is dead, my lord."

Ah. Borlis caught his breath. At last. *At last.* He closed his eyes, picturing the castle at Dovenbyre, so much grander, more splendid, more luxurious than his own Raven Castle. He pictured himself seated upon the high king's throne, ruling over all of Grithain. With all the riches of the land in his coffers. And all of the soldiers under his command.

His way was almost clear, except . . .

"The boy." Borlis spat the words. "What have you heard about the boy?"

"It is as you thought, my lord duke. Your spy managed to get word to me the moment the news spread through the castle. The prince indeed is in your own realm. The boy known as Gilroyd, younger son of Sir Henry, is in fact the true son of King Mortimer. Dovenbyre is sending an army to retrieve him, so that he can attend the high king's funeral and so that the coronation can take place as soon as possible. Sir Henry himself is to ride at the head of the troops that bring the boy back to Dovenbyre."

"Exactly as I prophesied, my lord duke." The duke's counselor, Kilvorn, a crafty old magician of druid ancestry, fairly purred. He rose from his deep tufted chair in the darkened corner of the room and paced quickly toward his master. "All goes according to my plan. The troops of the high king will be too late. Sir Henry is away—there is nothing to stop us from seizing the boy this very day—"

"Yes, sir—there is. I . . . I have more news, and it is troublesome, my lord." The messenger's voice quivered.

Both the duke and Kilvorn glared at him, and the man began to quake. He was covered with mud, exhausted, and now he was weak with fear. This duke was not one to greet ill news with composure.

"Speak, then!" the duke bit out. "Be quick about it, or I'll have your tongue."

"A troop of soldiers has entered Urbagran." The man's words tumbled out in a frightened rush. "I caught a glimpse of them— they rode full speed, like creatures flying from the depths of hell. Twenty men, well armed and astride horses larger, stronger than any I've ever seen. A wolf-hound bounded alongside them. I doubled back to an inn along their route and questioned the owner. He told me he recognized the leader, a fearsome warrior named Dagnur, who is . . . he is . . ."

"He is who?" The duke shouted, stamping toward the man in rage. "Speak or I'll have you thrown in the dungeon for a fortnight."

"He is the chief lieutenant of Duke Conor of Wor-thane," the messenger babbled, his lips quivering.

"Conor?" The duke stared at the man, then suddenly chuckled. He turned to the old soldier standing with feet apart near the window. The old soldier nodded at him.

"Conor of Wor-thane is dead," the duke said smugly. "He is no longer a threat. Isn't that right, Carien?"

"He is dead, my lord duke. Hacked to bits, and left for the wolves," the old soldier replied with satisfaction.

The duke turned back toward the messenger and waved a hand dismissively. "Conor's pathetic little troop will be dealt with. Without him, they are no threat to me. He is the only one who might have had a better claim than I to the soon-to-be-empty throne. If you have nothing more to report, you may go."

The messenger bowed low and fled the chamber as if his cloak were on fire, and the duke addressed his counselor. "So, Conor had a troop behind him. We will find them and dispose of them as we did their leader. They have twenty men, we shall send forty."

"It took five to one to slay Conor of Wor-thane," the counselor pointed out thoughtfully, stroking his scraggly gray beard.

"But few men of our age are known to be as fierce a fighter as Conor. I daresay being twice outnumbered will be sufficient to defeat them. And I need the rest of my troops to gather for the coming larger battle."

The duke spun around and began pacing the rich chamber, with its carpet of rushes and its golden sconces and velvet chairs. "I want the boy taken today—now. There is no longer any reason to wait."

He glanced at the old soldier. "See to it. Find him. *Now.*"

"As you wish, my lord." Carien nodded and stalked from the room, the jeweled handle of his sword glinting in the sunlight that poured through the castle windows.

"If you please, my lord, may I ask . . . what then?" The black-eyed counselor gave a cough. "Will you hold the prince until the arrival of King Plodius?"

"Perhaps. Or perhaps I will kill him immediately and move my army toward Dovenbyre at once."

"You would be wise, my lord, to honor your agreement with King Plodius. Seize the boy, but keep him alive until the ball. Then, with Plodius's men and your own people gathered as witnesses that very night, have the boy publicly abdicate the throne to you. So what if Plodius gets all of Urbagran and the southern tip of Dovenbyre for his help? As high king, you can afford to part with some land. The strength of his army combined with yours will assure your capture of the throne, and that is the true goal—"

"This can all be decided later. The agreement with Plodius of Ril is mine to keep or to dissolve," the duke snarled. "I will decide when I have seen the boy."

He turned back to the murky crystal ball and gazed at it once again, as if expecting it to show him something he much desired to see. "Why is it you cannot make this blasted ball show me the future? Show me all of Grithain kneeling at my feet?"

The counselor's pasty white skin tightened and turned even pastier. "It was made by Ariel. And though her power has diminished, it still seems to haunt this ornament. It will not show you or me anything. Nor will her magic mirror, if we were to find it, or any of the wands she created for opening the mists of time. Her secrets and the last of her powers are dying with her in Dovenbyre. Perhaps if she still lives when we reach the castle, we can force her to submit their power to our wills."

The duke picked up the crystal ball, stared at it a moment in contempt, and hurled it across the room. It smashed into the stone hearth and splintered into a thousand glittering fragments.

"I don't need Ariel any longer. Or her magic toys. I will have Grithain, all of it, and the future will be mine. I no longer need a crystal ball to show me that."

And he paced to the window, watching for his men to ride out, to hunt down the boy who would make all his ambitions come true. A moment later, there was a flurry in the courtyard—horses, men, shouts, the flapping of banners and the glint of swords. Then the portcullis lifted and the gates opened and the men charged out into the fields to find the boy-prince of Grithain.

The duke watched them, smiling with anticipation.

Soon. Very, very soon . . .

6

W E'RE ALMOST THERE, Fiona thought, nudging her heels into her pony's sides with a growing sense of urgency. Her stomach was knotted with worry. She had to get back to the cottage—and quickly. She had to see if Gil had gone there.

Her throat tightened at the thought, and she prayed he hadn't. *Please, no. Please don't let him be there with Cade. I'm not sure . . . Until I speak with Sir Henry I can't be sure . . .*

She'd spent the day at the hut of a farmer whose wife was enduring a difficult labor, and after six brutal hours, she had managed to help the woman survive the breach birth of a bawling baby boy.

His soft cries, and the weak smiles of the woman and her husband, had filled her with relief as she began the ride home— until she'd ridden to Sir Henry's manor to check on Gil and see if Sir Henry had returned, only to learn that he had not. He was now gone two days longer than he'd expected. That was not so great a time, but Fiona was uneasy. She desperately

needed to consult with him. Her distress grew when the seneschal, Desmond, informed her that young master Wynn had the
sniffles and had been confined to his bed by the orders of the
boys' old nurse, who was feeding him a diet of hot broth and
honeyed wine. Gil had apparently slipped away on foot when
no one was looking, and had most likely gone exploring in the
woods as he liked to do. Though Desmond had dispatched a
groom to find the boy and keep an eye on him, so far neither
Gil nor the groom had returned.

What if he's at the cottage? she wondered, her heart in her
throat. *What if he's visiting at this very moment with Cade of
the Hill Country beyond Nevendale?*

Smoke-gray clouds were drifting in, blotting out the sun,
giving the sky an overcast hue that added to her sense of foreboding.

Gil's fine, she told herself, trying to stay calm. *Cade would
not harm him. Ariel sent him—she must have . . .*

Yet the small inkling of doubt was enough to make her heart
thud as she rode. Today the healing broth had already begun
to show its good effects on her patient. Cade had seemed much
stronger when she left the cottage this morning, and by now
he must feel even more restored. The broth had done its work—
though he was still in some pain, he was no longer an invalid,
and it would be no trial for him to overpower a boy if that
were his intent.

Oh, why hadn't she taken Gil with her to the village today?
Why hadn't she warned him to stay at home? But what excuse
could she possibly have given that wouldn't have made the
young scamp even more eager to head outside?

By the time the cottage came into view, Star was racing
along at a full gallop. They flew over the ridge, past the twin
oak trees and the furze bushes and the winter grass. Fiona slid
from the saddle almost before the pony had reached a complete
halt.

"Gil!" she cried, running toward the cottage, her cloak billowing behind her. "Gil, are you—?"

She broke off as she pushed the door wide and saw Gil and
Cade of the Hill Country sitting opposite each other on the
floor. Before them, placed at odd spots, was spread an assort-
ment of spoons and small jars of herbs and some twigs and

stones. As Fiona stared, Gil lifted his smiling, eager young face to her, scooping a spoon into his hand.

"Lady Fiona, look! We are planning a great battle. This stone here is Conor's castle, and the spoon is me leading my troops. We come from the north and Conor said if I am to station five hundred men here where this jar is, at the ford—"

"C-Conor?" Fiona interrupted his words, her gaze swinging in fear to the man she had rescued in the forest. *Not that Conor, please God, not him,* she thought, terror surging through her as her former patient came all too steadily to his feet, looming above her at his full height of well more than six feet. His gaze pierced her, grim and watchful and entirely too purposeful for her peace of mind.

"I thought . . . your name is Cade—"

"He is Conor of Wor-thane, a great duke, of a kingdom even larger than Urbagran," the boy piped up, pride and excitement shining on his face. "He is my friend. He wants to know Wynn, too, and Father—when he returns, of course. He came here looking for the lost prince of Grithain, and I'm going to help him find him—"

"Gil—go home! This very moment, go. Run!"

She dashed forward, pulling the boy to his feet in one swift motion, pushing him toward the door.

"Fiona, don't do this. Listen—" The man who'd called himself Cade began.

But she planted herself between him and the boy and shrieked, "Wynn needs you, Gil—his life is in danger. Run home to him *now*! Run!"

But even as her words rang in the air, another sound, a low roaring sound, made everyone in the cottage turn toward the open door behind her.

In the distance, a troop of men could be seen riding hard across the gray rock ridge. Their horses thundered down toward the open land—straight toward the cottage.

"Those are my men, Gil." Conor spoke quickly. His tone was firm and commanding. At the same time, he moved forward with stunning speed for a man still suffering from injuries. Though pain shadowed his face, he lost no time in planting himself between Gil and the door. "You must stay now and meet them. I will explain—"

"No, Gil, run! Wynn needs you. Go to him—run!"

Snatching up a poker from the hearth, Fiona swung it wildly toward Conor. He ducked adroitly aside and grabbed it, but in that moment of distraction the boy leapt past him and bolted out the door.

"Run, Gil!" she shouted, and grabbed for another poker. Conor seized this one in midswing and yanked it from her grasp, tossing it aside with the first.

"Damn it, what the hell are you doing?" he shouted, anger darkening his lean face. He dashed toward the door and bolted outside to see Gil streaking like a young deer toward the two trees and the furze. His men were galloping in from the opposite direction, coming fast, with Tor bounding behind the horses' heels, and he waved an arm, signaling them to turn toward the trees. But just then another sound made his jaw clench.

He whipped around toward the trees at the same instant that Fiona dashed out beside him.

Together they saw the troop of men, forty strong, emerging from the wood. They bore directly down upon the small boy running toward them.

"*No.*" Fiona breathed the word in horror and agony as she recognized the black-and-scarlet banners of the Duke of Urbagran. "The duke's men. Oh, no . . ."

Before her anguished eyes, Gil froze. Then he spun around, glancing back uncertainly toward her and Conor, then toward the troops closing in from the north, and finally once more toward those bearing down on him from the wood. He went perfectly still. But even from a distance, Fiona could see the fear and confusion on his pale young face.

Conor charged toward the boy, sprinting headlong, and she took off after him, but she couldn't keep up with him, even hampered as he was by his injuries. She tried desperately to catch him, but he widened the distance between them, running straight for Gil.

But the boy veered east, trying to dodge both sets of troops chasing him. It was a clever move, but it was not enough. The foremost of the duke's riders reached him.

It was Reynaud, Fiona saw, a sob catching in her throat. He leaned from the saddle and scooped Gil up before him like a rabbit, then wheeled his horse with a shout. Taking up the cry, the rest of the duke's men followed him, turning their horses and thundering back toward Raven Castle.

"What the hell have you done?" Cade—no, Conor—rounded on her, fury in his eyes. There was no pain on his face now, only anger and a fierce frustration as he seized her by the shoulders, his hands clamping tight.

"You've killed him, you know. Are you satisfied now? If my men don't catch him, the duke will butcher him without a moment's thought."

"And your men wouldn't?" she cried, her eyes brimming with tears of grief. "Do you think me a fool? Everyone knows Conor of Wor-thane covets the throne himself, has always coveted it. Maybe the duke's men seek only to protect him." This idea brought a sliver of hope. "They must have known you came here planning to kill him yourself!"

"The hell I did." He swore savagely then, a string of oaths that she'd never heard all together before. Then he shook his head, took a breath, and let her go. He stepped back a pace from her, very deliberately. She had the impression he was exercising utmost self-control.

The man who faced her now was nothing like the patient she had nursed from death's door. If he felt pain, he didn't show it. A roaring power seemed to infuse him, and fury vied with reason as he raked a hand through his hair. He turned from her then as if she wasn't even there, addressing his troop of riders as they swarmed around them.

"After them!" he ordered the men before they could even completely halt their horses. "They have the prince—try to overtake them before they reach the castle gates. Tor, *stay*," he commanded the enormous wolf-hound whose hind leg was roughly bandaged with blood leaking through. The animal limped to his side and sank down onto the ground, panting, laying his head upon his master's boot even as Conor's soldiers galloped off in pursuit of the duke's forces.

"Here's a patient for you—you'd best take as good care of him as you did of me, for he was wounded at the same time," he told her in a more level tone, as one hand dropped to rest upon the dog's shaggy head.

"I wish I'd never touched you!" Fiona's voice shook as she gazed at him in helpless rage. "I wish I'd never gone out to rescue you. I should have let you die in the snow."

He scowled, and his green eyes glinted hard and bright as marbles in the sunlight. "If you want to see Gil alive again, you'd better thank your lucky stars you saved my life. Because I'm going to get him out of Raven Castle alive and see him crowned king. Yes, Mortimer is dead, and Gil is my half brother. But I don't want to take his place, and I damn well don't want him dead. I haven't for a long time now. I've spent the past five years of my life trying to assure his safety. And now," he said, his gaze nailing her with icy clarity, "in a matter of moments, you've ruined everything. Now he is in more danger than ever before."

As his words penetrated her anguished mind, a fresh horror struck her. "No! No, it can't be true."

"Believe what you want." He turned away from her and spoke to the wolf-hound, a word of command in a tongue she didn't understand. The beast clambered to his feet and limped along at his master's heels, as Conor of Wor-thane headed back toward the cottage.

Fiona stood alone in the cold, fading light, watching the two troops of riders retreating into the gray distance and the man and wolf-hound making their way back toward her home. Her home, where only a short time ago Gil had sat upon the floor, amid spoons and jars, his eyes eager, happy.

"What have I done?" she whispered into the thin, icy air. "Oh, Hynda, by the stars and moon, what have I done?"

7

TWILIGHT STOLE ACROSS the sky. Soon the ancient forest and all of Urbagran would be cloaked in darkness.

In Bitterbloom Cottage, a golden fire blazed in the hearth as Fiona sliced potatoes into a pot of water and set out thick slabs of dark rye bread. The wild goose Conor's men had killed roasted on a spit over the flames, filling the cottage with the savory aroma of meat. Conor's great wolf-hound lay sprawled on a horse blanket in the corner, resting from his journey, his wound freshly tended and bandaged. Though the dog appeared exhausted, his ears perked up at the merest rustle of branches outside the cottage, or at the low murmur of Conor's voice as he and his lieutenant, a thick-necked man named Dagnur, conferred in the corner.

"So that's all of it. We must go in tonight. He may well wait for Plodius to arrive, but we can't take that chance." Conor's eyes narrowed. "From what I know of Borlis, he won't kill the boy instantly. He is like a cat—he likes to torment his prey, to savor the anticipation of the kill. But he may not be able to control himself for any length of time, and he may choose to double-cross Plodius."

Dagnur grunted in contempt. "He has betrayed his own cousin, and he's intent on murdering a boy no bigger than a gnat. There's not a rotten thing I'd put past him, not if it'll gain him the throne."

"That's why we'll find a way in. Tonight."

"I know a way in." Fiona turned from the pot of potatoes and met his eyes, her own filled with anguish—and desperate hope. "Let me help you," she demanded.

Conor's cool green gaze studied her briefly, but Dagnur couldn't hold his tongue.

"We don't want any plan *you* have to offer," he snarled. "You're the one who sent the prince running away from us and straight into the duke's clutches."

Conor saw Fiona flinch as if the hurled words were a blow. "Dagnur, that's enough."

"But—"

"I won't have you speaking to her in that tone."

"Even though it's all her fault? You know it as well as I," the red-haired man said roughly. "If it weren't for her, we'd have him safe—"

"Enough." Quiet steel rang through Conor's tone as he sent the other man a warning glance. "The lady Fiona meant no harm. She has saved my life, against all odds. And she protected Prince Branden for years."

"Until today," the lieutenant muttered, with a dark look, but Conor's arm shot out and gripped his shoulder, and Fiona saw a flicker of surprise and pain in the burly man's face at the powerful grip.

"It was my fault, Dagnur. Mine. Not hers. Do you understand?"

The lieutenant glared back at him, then winced again as Conor continued the pressure on his shoulder. "I understand," Dagnur grunted, and Conor's arm dropped.

"Leave me your sword, then," Conor ordered in a milder tone. "Arm yourself with another when you set up camp in the forest. And stay on guard for a surprise attack," he added.

"Now that they know we're here, they might decide to root us out."

Dagnur nodded as he handed over his sword. "We'll be ready."

"Good. Return here an hour after sundown. By then I'll have your orders." His gaze flicked to Fiona, his eyes unreadable. "And a plan of attack."

The moment Dagnur was gone, Fiona turned back to the potatoes and began to stir the bubbling pot. Yet she heard Conor set down the sword and cross the floor to her. She sensed his lean, powerful frame behind her even before he touched her shoulders and turned her around.

His hands, she noted, with a wrench of her heart, were unexpectedly gentle on her flesh, yet they seemed to burn right through her amber gown.

"This is more important than the meal. Tell me the way in."

"First you tell me something, *Cade of the Hill Country*. Why did you lie to me?"

"If I'd told you I was Conor of Wor-thane, you'd either have let me die or gone running to hide the boy from me, and I was too weak then to stop you. I needed you, needed your help, your trust, until my men arrived or my strength returned, whichever came first. It wasn't such a bad lie. Only my name. The rest is true. What I told you about the king, about Ariel, all true."

Could she believe him? Heaven help her, she wanted to. She needed to. She searched his face.

"Even what Ariel said about . . . Hynda? That was the truth as well?"

He nodded. "I swear as I stand here before you."

A tremor ran through her. "But how can this be, that you are here to protect Gil? Everyone knows you hate the king. You swore ten years ago that Prince Branden would never sit on the throne. We heard the story even here—how Mortimer ordered you from Grithain, how you shouted that as eldest son of the high king you should have Grithain—"

"I don't deny my words. I am the eldest son of the high king. But I was born a bastard, and a bastard I remain to this day."

Silence fell but for the crackle of the fire, the bubbling of the pot.

"Because King Mortimer never . . . married your mother," she said softly, prepared for his fury at her statement of this widely known truth, but to her surprise he continued to regard her calmly.

"No, he did not. She was a widowed noblewoman when they met—and when they lay together. And he had been pledged to another already, to Branden's mother. It had been agreed upon by both families, for political reasons, and my father was a political man. Oh, he provided for me, and for my mother, until she died—though we didn't need much. My uncle came to live at our keep and he helped her to govern, and Wor-thane prospered, even without the high king's 'gifts.' But Mortimer never thought of marriage to her. He kept his promise to wed the princess of Albanon, thus ensuring the larger expansion of his kingdom—and a legitimate heir."

"You were . . . are . . . bitter?"

"I've left bitterness behind me, along with my childhood."

Shadows played across his face. Or were they merely the flickering reflections of the fire? "When I was young I was angry and hotheaded. I was eighteen when I had that famous fight with my father, when I said those things—about Branden never sitting on the throne. I came to regret them. Even," he said, his voice rueful, "to feel great shame about them. It wasn't long before I realized that Mortimer had not really wronged my mother or insulted me. He was behaving . . . like a king, thinking of his kingdom first and foremost. And I realized something else—I had no real desire to be a king, especially one unsanctioned by his own father. I have no taste for politics. My abilities, my instincts, lie on the battlefield."

He met her gaze steadily. "I decided I could put them to good use by helping my brother rule Grithain rather than tearing him and the kingdom apart."

Fiona searched his face, that leanly handsome, dark-stubbled face she'd come to know so well these past days, the face of the man who had called her "angel" and promised to protect her from the duke, the face of the man who had played games with spoons and rocks on the floor with Gil while she was gone, instead of killing him. It suddenly struck her that if he'd wanted his half brother dead, he would have seen to it and disappeared long before her return to the cottage.

So—it was true, all true. Conor of Wor-thane had come here to protect Gilroyd, and she had instead sent the boy running blindly from him—and straight into danger.

Her throat ached, and her heart had never felt so heavy in her chest. "I . . . misjudged you. I've ruined everything!" she choked out.

"You had help. My lie pushed you to the wrong conclusion. I meant what I said. We're both to blame. But don't despair. We're going to get the boy back. I won't let the duke harm him even if I have to burn down Raven Castle and everyone in it. Now will you tell me the way in?"

"On one condition."

He made a sound of impatience, and his hands suddenly tightened on her shoulders. "Egad, you're a stubborn woman. What now? What more can I do to prove myself? You are wasting time—I need to get to the prince—"

"Let me help you. Let me go with you."

His jaw tightened. But his tone was even as his hands fell from her shoulders and dropped to his sides. "Impossible. It's too dangerous."

"I know the castle, and you don't. Hynda and I have been called there to tend to injured servants, wounded knights, and noble visitors who fell ill. I know the staircases and the corridors and the private chambers. I even know where the staircase to the dungeon lies," she breathed, although she shuddered inwardly at the thought that Borlis might have imprisoned Gil in that dreadful place. "And I know the secret tunnels that allow you to bypass the guards and the gates," she finished quickly. "We have been ushered quietly inside more than once. And I know both of the secret ways."

His gaze sharpened. "You little minx." A wicked grin split his face. "Out with it, then. Tell me all you know—everything about the castle. I'll use it to find Branden . . . your Gilroyd—and bring him to safety. I swear it."

"He is in there because of me, Conor. I'm going too." Her delicate jaw locked. Looking down into her eyes, which glowed like warm polished silver in the firelight, he saw that her expression was resolute. More resolute than any he'd ever encountered, even considering all the men he'd seen fighting for their lives and families on the battlefield.

How could anyone so small and fragile-looking possess so much courage?

And suddenly he realized that her knowledge of the castle could well prove invaluable and it made perfect sense to bring her. If only it wouldn't bring her to danger—

Yet that shouldn't weigh with him. The prince was the only one who mattered now. His well-being came before all others in the land. Still . . .

Conor's chest ached at the thought that something might happen to her. That she could be injured, perhaps even slain in the perilous mission that lay ahead. Gazing at her, at the way her dark hair shone in the firelight, the way her vivid eyes gazed determinedly into his, he knew an almost overwhelming urge to take her in his arms and kiss her, to vow to her that he would keep her safe.

But he refrained from doing either. This was no time for softness, for sweet words, or promises he might not be able to fulfill. No time for even a friendly kiss, much less a dalliance with this woman who would fit so lushly in his arms.

Dalliance? Where had that come from? He obviously wasn't thinking straight. It wasn't even as if that word described what he was feeling now. It didn't, but he couldn't explain what word might. He didn't understand the heated emotions surging through him as he stood so near to her, the heaviness in his loins, in his very heart. It wasn't simple lust—that much he knew. Lust was part of it, but not all. He wanted more than that sumptuously feminine body. He wanted—

Enough. Forcing such strange—and thoroughly inconvenient—thoughts away, he cleared his head, then took a deep breath.

"You may come along, but you'll follow my orders, every one of them, instantly and with no arguments."

"I will. Unless you tell me to do something utterly stupid and against my better judgment—"

"Damn it, Fiona!" He seized her arms and yanked her toward him, intending to give her a little shake—he swore he intended merely to shake some sense into her. But instead he pulled her close and found her sweet rosebud mouth no more than a breath away from his and her lovely breasts jammed up against his chest.

"My men follow my orders to the letter, and if you go on this mission with us, I expect you to do the same," he told her angrily, trying not to be distracted by the smooth creaminess of her skin, by the way she fit against his body.

She was peering up at him, her eyes flashing, stubborn as always. "Your men are *required* to follow your orders," she pointed out breathlessly. "But you see, I am my own person. I am Gilroyd's protector and . . . and a healer and I'm *not* one of your men—"

"No, you're *not*—you're not a man at all, damn it—and that's the problem," he growled, then wished he could bite off his tongue.

"What do you mean—problem? What problem might that be?"

Suddenly, staring into her eyes, all too aware of the delicate warmth of her body pressed against his, he saw something more than stubbornness, more than wonder and that slight flash of alarm. He saw hope. Hope of . . . what?

"I'm not going to kiss you," he heard himself saying thickly. Thunder and lightning, why had he said that? Surely she had bewitched him.

"I don't want you to," he heard her murmur, her voice soft as angel's wings. But that look of hope, of excitement and— was it *invitation*?—still glistened there in her beautiful silver eyes.

Her lips were parted, trembling a little. He could almost swear she *wanted* him to kiss her.

"It wouldn't mean anything even if I did," he added darkly, and she gave a tiny nod.

"I . . . don't suppose it would. So . . . if you're not going to kiss me, you really ought to let me go."

Yes. He ought to let her go. He ought never to have drawn her this close. She was too beautiful, and damn it, she smelled like flowers. Like rare, exquisite summer flowers, the kind he'd found only at the highest peaks of Moryian on the Island of Dome.

He wondered how she would taste, how she would feel . . .

Suddenly, the urgency of the mission before him somehow became mixed up with the urgency he felt to taste those innocent pink lips, and he heard himself say in a hoarse voice he didn't even recognize, "I'll let you go. Soon . . ."

Then Conor of Wor-thane did something he never did. He acted on impulse. He kissed the woman in his arms before either one of them could think about it or do anything to stop it.

He'd meant it to be a quick kiss, one which would merely satisfy his curiosity about how those lips would feel, how they'd taste. But instead the kiss changed, exploded, becoming long and hot and deep, igniting an even more powerful hunger within him.

Her mouth burned against his. Her arms twined around his neck as he took the kiss deeper, and she gave a moan, a moan of pleasure and surprise so sensual it sent desire roaring through him. Their hearts slammed against one another, frantically, wildly, pounding in unison.

The desire that surged through him was more potent than a jug of spiced wine, and Conor, for all his worldly experience, had to struggle to keep himself from tearing at her gown, from throwing her down on the rug before the fire. Her slender arms tightened around his neck, drawing him ever closer, and the eager wildness of her mouth as she kissed him back made him burn with a savage need for more. His hands moved over her, quickly, hungrily, and time stood still.

Amazement pounded through him. Kissing her felt far better, far more powerful than anything he'd expected. Anything he'd known. He lost himself in the softness of her, in the flowery perfume of her skin, the sweep of her throat. Everything about her stunned him, from the strawberry taste of her mouth to the willing way she opened herself to him, heart and soul, in that simple cottage lit by firelight and candle flame in the shadow of the ancient forest.

Then a sound tore their lips apart—the sound of the wolf-hound growling, roaring.

In a flash Conor pushed her away and spun around at the same moment that the beast sprang toward the cottage door. At the exact same instant the door burst open and four armed soldiers rushed inside.

Fiona screamed. Reynaud was in the lead, charging toward Conor, his sword leveled, but with a flying leap Tor crashed into his chest and knocked him backward into the man behind him, and they both went down.

In the next moment everything happened at once.

Conor swept up the sword Dagnur had left for him, and steel rang against steel as two soldiers thrust their weapons toward him simultaneously. From the corner of her eye, Fiona saw Tidbit sail in a blur of black fur past the fallen men in the doorway and disappear into the twilight. But she had no time even to call out to the fleeing cat. She grabbed the poker she'd raised only hours before against Conor and ran toward one of the men attacking Conor, striking him across the back. He yelped in pain and wheeled toward her, but Conor leapt between them, blocking the man's advance with his own body.

"Get back, Fiona. Stay out of this," Conor ordered her crisply. She had no time to argue, for both men moved in against him once more, and the three engaged in a vicious thrust and parry, just as Reynaud hurled himself to his feet. Leaving his companion to wrestle with the growling wolfhound, he seized Fiona's arm and spun her around. Harsh anger blazed across his face.

"You—you are helping this swine? You've betrayed the duke!"

"You've betrayed the high king!" Fiona countered even as her heart leapt into her throat, for Conor had narrowly escaped a cut, and in the next instant his sword grazed his opponent's chest.

"The Duke of Urbagran will soon be the high king," Reynaud retorted and made a move to drag her toward the door, but she flinched away from him and braced her feet, raising the poker.

"Stand back!" she warned.

His eyes narrowed to slits. "You little fool, as if that will stop me!" The words had barely left his mouth before he launched himself at her.

Heart pounding, Fiona swung the poker at him, but he dodged the blow and then seized her arm, wresting the poker from her grasp. She screamed as he raised his arm to strike her, but the next instant he collapsed like a sack of rocks as Conor's fist slammed into his face.

Trembling, Fiona met Conor's eyes. They seemed to burn into hers, but she couldn't read them. Couldn't see beyond the hard green blaze of ruthlessness that had wiped all trace of gentleness from his face. Dazedly, she looked past him and saw that the men he'd been fighting lay dead on the cottage floor, crimson blood pooling beneath them.

"Tor—*down!*" Conor ordered, as the bloodied man the wolfhound had attacked tried to crawl away.

Suddenly Dagnur and a handful of other men appeared at the cottage door and hauled the wounded man on the ground to his feet.

But when they started toward Reynaud, Conor stopped them.

"Leave this one to me." He glanced over his shoulder at the dead men. "Bury them, and take the Lady Fiona back to your camp. Guard her well while I question the prisoner."

"I'm not going anywhere." Fiona pushed past Dagnur to Conor's side. "This is my home, and I want to speak to Reynaud as much as you do."

"Fiona—" Conor broke off. He recognized that set look in her eyes. He was learning better than to waste his breath arguing with this particular woman.

"Stay, then," he said grimly. "But don't interfere."

In a very short time Reynaud's arms were bound with rope and he had been thrust onto a bench. Dagnur and the others had left the cottage, and only Fiona, Conor, and Tor remained, each of them staring at the handsome, pale-haired prisoner, who peered from one to the other with trepidation.

"You're going to stand by and let him beat me—torture me?" Reynaud demanded at last, fixing his gaze accusingly upon Fiona. "There was a time when I thought you cared for me. As I cared for you."

"You didn't care very much, did you? Not enough to defy the duke." She stepped closer to him. "Once you knew the duke didn't approve of your courting me, you disappeared like a rabbit down a hole."

He had the grace to flush. "Fiona, please—"

She held up a hand. "None of that is important now, Reynaud, and I'm not going to hold it against you," she said softly. "If you tell me this instant where Gilroyd is, where the duke is holding him, I won't let Conor lay a hand on you."

"I don't know, Fiona, and that's the truth. But even if I did, I wouldn't tell this bastard—"

Conor's fist crashed into his face once more, and he crumpled onto the bench. Fiona gasped, and felt the color draining from her own face, but she managed to refrain from crying out in protest.

"Where's the prince?" Conor demanded, his tone hard as iron. "If you want to live, you'd best answer me quick."

"I told you, I don't know—"

Conor hit him again, and Fiona's stomach twisted. She hated this. She was a healer. Her instinct was to protect Reynaud from injury, to heal his bruises. She had to stop this. She couldn't just stand by and let Conor hit him again. But what about Gilroyd?

"Tell me, Reynaud." She jumped between the two men and put her hand soothingly on the soldier's sweat-soaked brow, as blood oozed from a bruise on his face. "He won't touch you again if you tell me the truth. I promise. But if you don't tell me . . ."

She took a deep breath. "I'll leave now and let him do what he will."

Reynaud stared at her in shock.

"Please, Reynaud—tell me now, for your sake and for Gil's. He's only a boy, and the duke wants to kill him. If you don't tell me, I'll walk away and Conor"—she glanced over her shoulder at the tall Duke of Wor-thane—"well, we both know Conor will kill you."

Silence fell in the cottage, but for the low growl of the wolfhound and the crackle of the fire's dying flames.

Reynaud stared blearily into her eyes. Tor snarled. Reynaud blanched as Conor took a step forward and loomed over him.

"Leave now, Fiona. He won't talk unless it's beaten out of him."

As if in approval, Tor growled again.

"Reynaud . . . this is your last chance!" Fiona whispered, and he suddenly turned to her imploringly.

"The boy is locked in a secret room off the duke's private chamber. Now tell him to let me go."

"Has he been hurt?" Fiona asked.

"No. He doesn't understand what's happening, but he's unharmed. At least he was when I left," he added, the words pouring out of him as if he couldn't unload them quickly enough. "Duke Borlis is following Lord Kilvorn's advice. They are waiting for King Plodius to arrive. Now you tell him, Fiona! Tell him how to let me go. Now!"

"How do we get into this secret room?" Conor demanded, grabbing Reynaud's shoulder, glaring down into his panicked face.

"I don't know. That's the truth. Only the duke knows—and Kilvorn. I saw the door open, saw the boy inside for an instant, then they sent me away."

"You're lying," Conor muttered, and the dog stood up, a low snarl in his throat.

"No, I swear, 'tis the truth. Fiona—"

"I believe him." She turned to Conor. "Duke Borlis would not share such a secret with a soldier. Reynaud is not a chief lieutenant, he is not the duke's confidant."

Conor nodded. "Agreed." He took her arm and led her away from Reynaud, to the opposite corner of the cottage. "Pack up what food you can. We must start for the castle at once. We'll have to hide and wait for our opportunity to get in. Do you know where the duke's private chamber is?"

"I have never been there, but Sir Henry has, and he told me about it. I'm sure I can find it."

"Good girl."

"Do you think Gilroyd is safe? At least for now? That the duke is indeed waiting for Plodius before he—before he—"

"I think that the Duke of Urbagran is capable of anything—including changing his mind." Conor's face was more grave than she had ever seen it. "And I think we need to get Gil out of there tonight. If you've changed your mind, if you don't want to come, my men will keep you safely guarded at the camp. You need only tell me exactly what you know of the castle's layout and passages and—"

"I am going, and that is that."

The simply spoken words, the quiet determination in her eyes, filled him with a surge of admiration. He fought the urge to take her into his arms, to hold her for only a moment more before they left the relative safety and shelter of the cottage. He had to think of Branden—to ride swiftly, move secretly, and fight without mistakes. He couldn't afford a moment's distraction, including giving in to these damn feelings churning inside him—these feelings that were surfacing at the most unexpected times and in the most unexpected ways. For a most unexpected woman.

He steered his thoughts to the matter at hand and turned from her, trying not to think about the kiss they'd shared, the sweetness of holding her in his arms.

"Reynaud will live—for now—as my prisoner," he said curtly. "Dagnur will take charge of him. And Tor will stay to guard him," he added. As if he understood, the wolf-hound let out a low, quick bark.

Conor dropped a swift, friendly hand to stroke the beast's head, then turned toward her again as the man on the bench sagged in defeat. "I'll saddle the horses, Fiona. You gather what you will. We leave at once."

"I am ready," the angel who had saved his life said simply. "Ready for whatever must be done."

8

FIONA AND CONOR rode in silence through the mist-shadowed night. A silver slice of moon and a spattering of diamond stars faintly revealed their path, which skirted south of the stony hill upon which Raven Castle perched. With every step of her pony, every crunch of a branch and breath of the wind, Fiona stiffened, imagining the duke's men in hiding, about to pounce.

But the night was still and cold and empty, save for the naked trees, the wild creatures that rustled unseen in the brush, and the careening thoughts that raced through her mind.

She thought of Gil, locked in a hidden room high in the castle. How frightened he must feel, how alone. Her heart clenched painfully. They'd get him out, they *had* to get him out.

She thought of Ariel and the magic mirror, of Hynda and Sir Henry, of the life she had lived at Bitterbloom Cottage—all of it now in jeopardy, everything she and Hynda and Sir Henry had worked for all these years—and a desperate determination swept over her.

She thought of something else too—the man riding behind her in the opalescent moonlight. Conor of Wor-thane, who had stormed into her life only a short time ago, and who now dominated it. Her destiny and his were bound together, their fates and Gilroyd's linked. He had become a part of her life in so many ways in such a short time and now . . . there was that kiss. That powerful, soul-shaking, impossibly tender kiss, which she would never forget to the end of her days.

She had kissed only Reynaud before tonight, and at the time it had all been new and exciting and flattering, and she had thought the kiss wonderful.

But this kiss had been more than wonderful. More than exciting. It was like dancing where before one had merely walked. It was like tasting the sun and the moon when one had only eaten dust.

This man who had kissed her in the cottage had stirred her as Reynaud never had. Somehow or other, without her ever realizing it, he had laid siege to her heart.

But she was certain that for him the kiss had been only an impulse, a moment's pleasure. He was a worldly man, a brilliant warrior, the duke of a thriving kingdom, and when this mission tonight was over, if they were triumphant, he and Gil would ride away to Grithain and she would go on without them. Without both of them.

So she had better learn to live with that knowledge and to deal with the challenge before her. Gil's life and future were all that mattered, she told herself. If she allowed herself to be distracted by foolish thoughts and romantic wishes, she would be putting Gil's life and her own in even graver danger.

She rode on, chilled and agitated, as the night wind rose like a great transparent ghost, whipping about her. She and Conor didn't speak a word until they had ridden a mile beyond the castle and found the secret cave along the cliffs of Urbagran, the cave Hynda had shown her long ago. They left their horses at its mouth, and as Conor lit a torch, she whispered to him to follow her.

But even as she turned her head to warn him that the cave roof was low, her foot slipped on the slick rock. He grabbed her arm just in time to keep her from falling.

"Careful." His arm slid around her waist. "Are you all right?"

"Yes—thank you. I'm not usually so clumsy—I'm just so worried. What if we're too late?" she gulped. "What if the duke has already—?"

"Don't think about it. Never consider failure. When you look ahead, think only of success."

His words steadied her. He was a soldier above all else, she remembered, gazing up at the strong contours of his face. Conor of Wor-thane, the fiercest warrior in five kingdoms. And he was speaking as one now.

You would do well to listen, Fiona told herself, and forced all her doubts and fears from her mind.

"I'll remember that," she said softly, and stepped deeper into the cave.

The rock floor was damp and uneven beneath their feet, the air dank as they followed the winding tunnel in silence. Fiona thought of Conor's troop of men, led by Dagnur. They were traveling a different route, more than a mile to the north of the castle. It was a more circuitous route to a hidden passage Fiona had described that was wide enough for them to lead their horses into and that would enable them to emerge within the bailey, bypassing the castle moat and gate.

Hynda had learned all the secret routes years ago when she'd been brought in to tend to dungeon prisoners without the duke's knowledge. The passageway was guarded, it was true, and while Hynda had used a sleep-and-forget potion to get past them, today Dagnur and the soldiers would overcome the guards by a combination of force and surprise, and fight their way inside the castle.

Fiona had to stoop as she passed beneath the low roof of the tunnel and glancing back, she saw that Conor, much taller than she, was bent nearly double. But he made no complaint and moved not only with swiftness but with surprising stealth for a man of his size. She knew he must still be in pain—the healing broth could not yet have perfectly restored him from all of his injuries—but in the golden light of the torch he looked fit and grim and resolute as they went deeper and deeper into the cave tunnel, following it for an entire mile back to the castle, beneath the gate and the moat and the courtyard, into the heart of the hill itself, emerging at last into an even smaller tunnel, which ended at a thick iron door.

"Beyond this is the storeroom. It is alongside the dungeon," she whispered. Just then, voices boomed from the other side of the door, and she pressed her hands to her lips. Conor froze for an instant, then his free hand shot downward to the hilt of his sword.

From the other side, a voice could be heard barking orders, but she could not hear what was said. Another voice, harsh and guttural, replied.

"It could be the guards changing places, or something being carried from the storeroom," Conor whispered in her ear. "Move back where it's wider. We'll wait until they're gone."

So they edged back fifty paces. Conor spread his cloak on the ground, and they sat, side by side, listening to the faint voices ahead, as the torchlight danced over the glinting rock walls.

Once Fiona saw, to her dismay, the tail of a rat disappearing back the way they had come. The rat made her think of Tidbit, who had disappeared during the fight in the cottage. She wondered if she would ever see her again, if she would ever go home to Bitterbloom Cottage. Then she reminded herself to think of victory, to think of Gil being rescued and taken to Grithain, to safety.

"Did you care greatly for him?"

Conor's voice was low but clear in the darkness.

"You mean Gil?" she whispered. "Yes, I care for him with all my—"

"Not Gil. Reynaud." He spoke shortly. "You were most concerned about his welfare."

Startled, she met his gaze in the flickering darkness. Flames seemed to flash in the cool green depths of his eyes. His mouth looked tense. Could it be he was *jealous*? Of *Reynaud*?

Dazedly, she shook her head. "N-no, I don't care for Reynaud at all. Why should I? He was among those who helped to capture Gil, he is a traitor to Grithain—"

"But he courted you at one time. And you apparently received his attentions willingly." His eyes were shuttered now. Unfathomable. "So you must have cared for him. You also made me spare him."

This was true. Since Reynaud had been sent as a prisoner to the camp Dagnur had set up, if the mission to free Gil succeeded, it was the new king of Grithain who would decide his fate.

"I am a healer, Conor. I don't like to see anyone hurt, much less killed. I know violence is necessary in times of war—which perhaps this is, but . . ."

"It was more than that. There was once something between you. Do you still have those feelings for him?"

"No." Amazingly, it was true. She had felt nothing toward Reynaud but bitterness and disappointment for a long time. And now she felt only contempt.

"I thought I cared for him once—or, at least, that I might *come* to care for him. But he wasn't the man I thought he was. And he didn't care for me. Not enough, anyway," she added darkly. "The moment Duke Borlis flicked his little finger at Reynaud and instructed him to stay away from me, Reynaud obeyed without a second thought."

"He's an undeserving bootlicker," Conor muttered. "An idiotic fool. You deserve far better, angel—a man who is worthy of you, who will take care of you."

"I've never needed a man to take care of me," she replied with dignity. "I only want a man who will love me." Her words were quietly spoken in the dank tunnel. "A man I can love. And one day," she added, as lightly as she could, "I hope to find him."

Conor stared at her in the darkness, as the flickering torchlight illuminated her creamy skin and the silver glow of her eyes. There was that word again. *Love.* He pitied her for wishing for something so elusive, something he didn't believe in any more than he believed that snakes could fly. Beyond the door, the sound of raised voices continued, and he spoke softly, feeling obligated to warn her.

"I learned a long time ago not to wish for the impossible, angel. Finding love in this world is more than any sensible human being should hope for," he said.

She looked stunned. Dismayed. "You don't believe . . . in love?" she gasped.

He laughed. "Love is nothing but a myth—a made-up tale like those describing the unicorns of old—or sea monsters or moon-elves." He shook his head. "I saw nothing resembling love in the keep where I grew up, and certainly not upon any battlefield, or in any home or castle I have visited. I have seen people scraping by, tolerating one another, conspiring against each other, and fighting one another to the death—but love—"

He leaned back against the wall of the tunnel. "Never have I seen love."

Suddenly he became aware of the stricken expression in her eyes. "Don't get me wrong," he said hastily. "If that's what you want, I hope you find it someday."

"I . . . wish the same for you."

"Thanks, but don't waste your wishes on me. Love was never in my past, and it's not a part of my future. Battle, perhaps, and power, maybe, and a great deal of hard work to make the kingdoms one under the new king, but love—no."

"You'll . . . never marry, then?" Fiona asked in a low tone.

"I didn't say that." He shrugged. "Marriage is different. It's something that is arranged, a practical matter. That I can understand. When the proper time comes, I'll take a wife, a convenient one, as my father did before me—as my mother did when she married the third Duke of Wor-thane—"

He broke off, holding up a hand. "Wait. Listen."

She did as he asked, hearing the faint drip of water somewhere and . . . nothing else. The voices beyond the door had ceased. It was time, time to find Gil and get him out of Raven Castle.

But she wanted to hear more, to know why Conor didn't believe in love, never sought it, never even hoped for it. She was ashamed that at a moment like this she was remembering the gentleness of his kiss and realizing there must never be another between them.

Enough, she thought, swallowing her sadness, though her heart felt like it had been sliced in two. *The time has come to think of Gil. Only of Gil.*

"We must go now," she whispered and scrambled to her knees.

He helped her up, and they made their way quickly back down the corridor to the iron door.

"I don't hear anything," Fiona breathed as she leaned close to the door. But in her head she still heard his words. *Don't waste your wishes on me.*

He nodded and held the torch aloft as she searched for the key concealed in a crevice of rock beside the door. Finding it, she brushed her fingertips methodically back and forth across the door until she felt the small indentation where the hidden key fit.

A moment later, Conor put his shoulder to the door and eased it forward. It gave a slight creak, which made Fiona's heart stop. But only darkness greeted them. The storeroom was deserted.

"The stairs are this way," Fiona whispered as they slipped out of the small room packed with sacks of grain and wheat, but Conor moved instead toward the doorway leading to the dungeon.

"A moment," he said. "There is something I need to see."

Mystified and uneasy, she followed him into the dungeon corridor, her skin prickling in horror as the smells and sounds and putrid dankness of the place assailed her senses. The rows of cells, the moans of men—if only she could bring her medicines and tend to them.

Suddenly she realized that Conor was striding along the corridor, glancing quickly into each cell.

There were no guards at this time of night, thank heavens, what with the prisoners securely locked in, but what was he doing?

"Badger."

"My lord!"

A man in a cell halfway down the corridor stuck his bony arm through the bars, and Conor grasped it in warm greeting.

"Now to get you out of here," he muttered.

"There, near the staircase—a hook. The keys to all the cells are on it, my lord—"

Even before he'd finished speaking, Fiona spotted the thick ring of keys and snatched it from the hook. She hurried down the corridor to Conor and watched in silence as he used the key to unlock the cell.

"This is one of my most trusted men-at-arms. He had been sending me reports on Borlis for months, and then suddenly they stopped. I knew he'd either been caught and killed, or imprisoned."

A gaunt man whose face was almost completely obscured by a dirty brown beard nodded at her, then slipped out of the cell as Conor pushed the door open.

"The duke holds Prince Branden prisoner in this castle." Conor spoke quickly and in a low tone. "We're going to free him now. Unlock all the cells and lead these men out of here. Fight with whatever you can. These men deserve a chance at freedom and whatever distraction they cause in escaping will aid us."

"Right." Badger nodded. He looked weak and frail, and Fiona could only wonder if he would even have the strength to climb the stairs. But when she saw the determined gleam in his hooded eyes, she knew that he, like Conor, would find the strength.

"Before you go, my lord, you should know that the duchess has been confined to her chamber for months now," he said in a wheezy voice. "She discovered that Borlis planned to betray King Mortimer and she tried to get word to the high king. There's no love in that marriage—matter of fact, I think the duchess hates Borlis almost as much as she fears him. He stopped her message from going through, and she has been a prisoner of her husband since that day."

"Soon she will be a widow and will no longer have to fear him," Conor said darkly, handing Badger the torch.

Fiona touched his arm. "We must hurry. I am afraid for Gil. Please—"

He turned to her. "We're going now. Are you prepared for whatever will come?"

She nodded, her stomach churning. There would be bloodshed, suffering, fighting—but at the end of it, she prayed, they would find Gil, unharmed. And Conor would still be alive at her side.

"Yes, let us go," she whispered urgently.

Conor took her arm and they ran for the stairs, even as the freed prisoner began moving from cell to cell, unlocking the doors as the inmates stirred and cried and shouted.

They ran up the stairs, knowing that at any moment a horde of others would follow.

Fiona's heart leapt into her throat as a heavyset guard who'd been lifting a mug of ale to his lips saw them and set down his mug with a clang, even as with his other arm he drew his sword.

Before he could swing it, or shout, Conor ran him through.

"Don't look," he ordered Fiona as he pulled her past the falling man.

They pounded along the corridor and reached an alcove leading to the great hall. "The staircase going to the upper chambers is that way!" she gasped, pointing to their left, and they hurried past the great hall, swarming with soldiers and servants, and started up a narrow torchlit stair.

Halfway up, they met another guard—at the same instant that a commotion sounded below. Fiona pressed herself against the wall as Conor and the guard met in a clash of swords and bodies. The guard let out a shout, others answered, and then she closed her eyes as Conor's sword plunged into his chest and the man tumbled past both of them, down the steps. Dead.

"Hurry!" Conor seized her arm and dragged her with him, even as the sound of boots thumping and swords ringing and men's frantic shouts filled the castle, top to bottom.

When they reached the landing, Fiona dashed toward a curtained alcove. "Quick—in here."

He disappeared behind the curtain just as the landing swarmed with men.

Someone was giving orders. "You three check above, the rest of you search belowstairs. Find them now—or the duke will have all our heads!" the harsh voice shouted.

Trembling, she held her breath as the sounds of men running thundered past, seeming perilously close beyond the curtain. At her side, Conor towered over her, one arm around her shoulder as he too waited for the rushing guards to pass. Where his hand touched her shoulder, she felt a tingling heat. What was wrong with her? Even in these dire circumstances, she was so intensely aware of him, when she should have been aware only of their danger.

Yet danger or no, his hand upon her, his strong body next to hers, comforted her. She wasn't alone in her quest to save Gil—Conor was with her, and together they could do anything.

Where that thought came from, she had no explanation—and no time to ponder, for the sounds of shouting and fighting grew more distant and Conor pushed the curtain aside and stepped out.

In the dim light she saw his face—and for the first time she saw the strain beginning to show. By all rights the man ought to be still resting in bed, healing broth or no. Much as it had helped him, it was not a complete cure, and he had no business fighting at this stage of his recovery. And yet, gazing worriedly into that hard, handsome face, she knew that through sheer will he would allow no injury to slow him down.

"Which way?" he asked, and she drew him toward another small corridor, even narrower than the others.

"The private staircase to the upper chambers of the duke and duchess are at the end of this corridor," she whispered, pointing. "Hynda and I tended to the duchess once when she had a fainting spell and the seneschal brought us this way."

The staircase widened unexpectedly at the end of the narrow corridor and was lit with torches. Quickly, they ran up the steps and found themselves outside the private apartments of the duke and duchess.

"There—that's the duke's chamber."

Conor entered first, his sword at the ready, but the vast and ornate chamber was empty save for the silk-draped bed, the velvet chairs and golden candlesticks, the blazing hearth and intricate tapestries adorning the walls.

Fiona dashed to the wall opposite the hearth, and her fingers flew over the stone, searching for a lever or an indentation, however small, something that would hint as to the location of the hidden chamber. Conor joined her, and together they inspected the wall, scanning and touching the smooth blocks, lifting the jewel-colored tapestry, looking for the way to open the wall of stone.

"If Reynaud was lying—" Conor growled.

"Here!" Fiona's hand paused on the wall just at the edge of the tapestry. "There is a notch here, very small. It's in the shape of a star—"

But before she could explore further, or press the star shape, a voice behind her made both of them freeze.

"Ah, intruders in the duke's apartment. He will be most displeased. Turn around, and touch nothing, or these guards will cut you down."

Slowly, Conor and Fiona turned to face two brawny guards wearing the crimson and gold of Urbagran. Their swords were drawn, ready to strike, but they were waiting, waiting for orders from the scraggly-bearded figure who had spoken, a squat, slit-eyed creature that Fiona recognized with a chill of dread.

"Kilvorn, counselor to the duke," she said in a low tone to Conor, and the old magician with the blood of the druids in his veins smiled malevolently through thin gray lips.

"Duke Borlis will be especially pleased to entertain *you* in his chamber, lady. But not so this man. I know who you are, trespasser, you are the bastard of Wor-thane. So you are not dead after all."

"No, but you will be soon." Conor's voice was colder, calmer than a winter sea. "Take us to Prince Branden if you wish a chance to spare your pathetic life."

"Threatening a magician whose powers could turn you into dust is most unwise."

"Wait, Kilvorn. Do not strike him down just yet," a new voice broke in. The Duke of Borlis himself strode into the chamber. "I want to know how this comes to be, that the Duke of Wor-thane still lives."

Despite the fact that shouts and commotion still rang through the castle, Duke Borlis and his counselor both appeared unruffled and focused only on the intruders. From their expressions, Fiona realized with a sinking heart that they felt no threat to the success of their plans, despite the uprising from the dungeon, despite finding Conor alive.

And why should they? she thought in despair. *We are only two and we are trapped.*

"I live because your soldiers did not finish the job." Conor met the duke's stare with deadly calm. "There was still life and breath in me when they left me to die in the snow."

"And dear Fiona, our own healer, used her skills to save you," the duke sneered, and now his gaze shifted, boring solely into Fiona. The glint in his eyes filled her with fear.

But she spoke steadily. "Yes, I saved his life. And I would do it again."

"You disappoint me, Fiona," he said softly. "And worse, you lied to me. When I visited you at your cottage and heard that sound, it wasn't your stupid cat at all, was it? It was this man hiding in the other room, recovering from his injuries. You lied to me, and you betrayed me. And not only me—you have betrayed Urbagran. You're going to regret that."

"You are the betrayer. You betrayed your own cousin—the high king."

"The high king is dead." Borlis smiled. "And now Grithain's fate is in my hands."

"Open this door and release the prince, or you'll bring down the wrath not only of Grithain but of Wor-thane and its allies against you." Conor started toward him, but the two soldiers instantly jumped before the duke and Kilvorn, crossing their swords to bar Conor's path.

"You want the boy dead as much as I do," Borlis snarled. "Only you wish to be the one to step into his place. That will never happen." He spoke to his men, his words sharp and rapid. "Leave the woman be, for now. But kill the man—here, now, before my eyes. It's time to be rid of Conor of Wor-thane once and for all."

"No!" Fiona cried, as the men advanced. She darted forward, arms outstretched, to bar them from Conor, but he swiftly grabbed her and thrust her behind him, then sprang to meet the challenge. There was a blur of bodies and a clash of swords as Conor parried their dual thrusts, and in a lightning stroke his sword drew blood from the arm of one man, even as he sent the other's sword skidding across the floor.

As another soldier burst into the room to help, Fiona plunged her hand into the pocket of her cloak and seized the packet of freezing powder still hidden there from the night she'd rescued Conor. An instant later she was flinging a fine thimbleful of the stuff over the soldiers and then over the duke and his counselor. The moment the powder touched their skin, each of them froze in place, unable to move even a muscle, not even to twitch their eyes to one side or the other.

"Quick, we must get Gil out," she cried as Conor spun toward her. "The effects of the powder last only a few moments!"

She reached the stone wall an instant before Conor and swiftly found the star-shaped indentation again. Pressing it, she held her breath. Suddenly an invisible door within the wall shifted, splitting free of the stone, rolling inward with a resounding creak.

And there in a narrow chamber lit by a single torch, Gil sat upon a pallet on the floor, looking scared.

The moment the door opened and he saw Fiona and Conor, he scrambled to his feet, relief flooding his serious young face.

"I knew you'd come, Lady Fiona! But how did you ever find me?" he cried, rushing toward them.

Fiona seized his hands, knelt and risked a precious few seconds in a hug. "I'll explain later, Gil. Come, we must run! Follow Conor!"

But as they bolted from the hidden chamber back into the duke's bedroom, Fiona suddenly doubled over. Pain ripped through her like a thousand blades driving through her flesh, slicing her bones. Bright red spots swam before her eyes, and she sank to her knees with a cry of agony that pierced Conor like an arrow.

"What is it? What's wrong?" He knelt beside her, his arms enfolding her as she looked at him in stricken silence, her eyes glazed with the pain.

She couldn't speak, couldn't move, could only gasp as agony slashed through her, tearing at her insides, consuming her in a blast of fire. Red-hot torment engulfed her, ate at her, and the world was a sickly black maze made up of pain and more pain . . .

"Take Gil . . . go," she finally managed to gasp aloud, her face whiter than a skeleton's bones. "There's no . . . time . . . Get him . . . away . . ."

"We're not leaving you." Conor cradled her close, terror and helplessness engulfing him. Her suffering was horrible to behold. And he didn't know how to help her. There was no mark on her, nothing he could see, but he was losing her. She was slipping away.

"Don't leave us," Gil shouted, and Conor knew he too saw the life being squeezed from her. His voice quavered, "Tell us how to help you!"

Her body trembled and she could no longer speak, for the pain had paralyzed her tongue.

"We have to help her," Gil cried in panic, grabbing Conor's arm. "Please! How do we help her?"

"You cannot help her, either of you." They both looked up to see Kilvorn struggling to emerge from the freezing spell. His powers aided him in defying it. For even as the duke remained frozen, the magician was able to move his lips and his wand, and Conor saw him tilting it ever so slightly in Fiona's direction, casting the spell. Then as Conor watched, the wand shifted toward Gil.

"It's a death spell," the old magician hissed. "Too late. It cannot be broken."

Conor dove for him like a hawk and grabbed the wand, tossing it to the floor with one hand, while with the other he seized the magician by the throat.

"Gilroyd, are you all right?" he called, glancing over his shoulder.

"Yes," the boy shouted, "But Lady Fiona . . . I think she's dying!"

Conor's hands shook. "Reverse the spell!"

Rage and fear surged through him as the duke and the guards began to stir, some of them now able to blink, to flex their shoulders, wiggle their fingertips. It would be only a matter of moments before the effects of the freezing powder wore off. Before Fiona lay dead . . .

"Reverse it!"

"I won't," the magician croaked out as Conor tightened his grip on the man's throat. "I can't . . . only magic can break the spell . . . even if you kill me, it won't . . . reverse . . ."

"Then you reverse it!"

"Never . . . never . . . *Guards, seize this man!*" the magician shouted as his arms suddenly regained their power and he began trying to push Conor away.

Suddenly two more soldiers charged into the room, and Conor saw that they were his own men. But instead of relief he felt only despair. Fiona was dying—dying a horrible death filled with pain—and there was nothing he could do for her.

He wasn't accustomed to feeling helpless. Or to feeling . . . what? This deep, terrifying fear, this sense of loss. He couldn't lose her—not this gentle, sensuous beauty with the spirit of a warrior and the touch of a healer.

Her face was frozen in torment, her skin waxy and cold, whiter than the snow within the Dark Forest. His heart wrenched, and something broke, something he'd never felt before snapped inside him.

No! a voice deep in his soul shouted. *No, she can't die. I can't lose her.*

"Put the spell on me instead," he demanded hoarsely. "Damn you, transfer it to me!"

Kilvorn's eyes glittered black. "Her death will hurt you far more than your own!" he chortled, even as Conor's hands tightened like chains around his throat.

I'm going to lose her, Conor thought in raging black despair. He couldn't stop this, any more than he could stop his own heart from rending in two. She was going to die.

At that moment a black cat darted into the chamber in a blur of gleaming dark fur. Its eyes glistened in the torchlight as it circled wildly through the chamber now filled with people, dashing among Borlis's guards and Conor's men, and the boy who knelt by Fiona, watching her agonized face in despair.

"Tidbit," the boy gasped as the cat rushed past him, running in circles, darting here and there.

Suddenly, without warning, the cat sprang straight at the magician. Conor flinched backward as the cat's claws embedded themselves in Kilvorn's face, and a moment later the cat dropped to the ground and dashed toward Fiona and the boy, its tail swishing.

Blood dripped from the magician's flesh and he shrieked in agony. "No—no!"

It was then that Conor saw the glitter of a crystal shard in the magician's lined and sunken cheek. Black blood poured from the tiny wound the shard had caused.

And even as the blood poured from the scratch, Fiona's pain began to ebb. She caught her breath, and a shudder went through her.

Within the blackness that still claimed her, she saw a beam of golden light, shimmering like a torch at the mouth of a cave. And an image—no, two images, side by side, blurred together. Ariel, all silver and sheer, and Hynda, in flowing robes brown as the earth.

Her heart leapt toward them.

"No, child. Not yet. Go back," Ariel murmured.

"It isn't your time, Fiona." Hynda shook her head.

Fiona felt herself floating toward them. Leaving the pain behind. But as she went closer, they retreated, their hands before them, as if pushing her away.

"Go back," they insisted. "Back, back," they chanted in unison.

The light disappeared as suddenly as it had come. With a moan, Fiona opened her eyes. Her vision cleared almost instantly, and the pain seemed to drain from her in a whoosh.

She saw Gil peering frantically into her face, then she saw Conor, stooping to lift her, his skin ashen with fear. She spoke in a hoarse whisper.

"It's gone. Whatever it was . . . it's gone."

The magician, however, sank to his knees, even as Duke Borlis regained the full use of his limbs—and his voice.

"Get up!" Borlis ordered the slit-eyed old man, who reached up to the crystal and plucked it from his cheek. "What is that? What is wrong with you?"

"The crystal . . . ball. Ariel's damned crystal ball . . ."

"I smashed it—it's gone."

"One shard remained. The cat . . . has found it . . . magic . . . Ariel . . . has killed me."

"Are you telling me that there was enough of Ariel's magic in that one shard of glass from the ball to do this to you?" the duke roared. "Kilvorn, for years you drained her of her power. How could one shard do this?"

"She made the crystal when she was young . . . strong . . . now she must have some power left . . . if only a little. How . . . I don't know . . . she ignited it . . . the power in the ball . . . it is destroying me."

The duke turned furiously to his guards, now fully recovered, and watching the magician fade into nothing but a thin, gray, mistlike specter before their eyes.

"Forget him! Seize *them*! Kill them all now—all three, the woman, the boy, and the bastard of Wor-thane!"

But even as Conor's men leapt forward to protect their duke, Dagnur and several others of his troop rushed into the chamber. Seeing his men outnumbered and about to be outfought, the duke suddenly shoved his own soldiers toward the enemy and used the opportunity to bolt from the room.

"Dagnur, after the duke!" Conor commanded, and the red-haired warrior charged from the chamber in pursuit.

"He must be caught . . ." Fiona whispered, her voice weak. "If he escapes he will always be a danger . . . to Gil . . . Don't stay . . . on my account . . . Go . . ."

"I'm not leaving you—either one of you," Conor vowed. He gathered her closer, cradling her against his chest. The battle erupting between his men and the duke's shifted to the corridor as Urbagran's soldiers also sought to escape, and the three of them found themselves suddenly alone in the duke's chamber, save for the slowly shrinking, fading specter of the magician.

"Can we go home now?" Gil asked, drawing a deep breath. "I want to see if Wynn is all right."

"Wynn will be fine . . . and so will you," Fiona murmured. "Gil, there's something we have to tell you. Something you need to know . . . now." But suddenly she felt very tired. Kilvorn's spell had nearly killed her . . . and though the pain was now gone, it was difficult to keep her eyes open. She felt weak, so very weak.

She felt herself slipping away, as if she were going under in a deep, endless blue sea.

Peaceful. Very peaceful. The last thing she saw as she sank beneath the surface of still water was Conor. He was speaking to her, but she couldn't hear him any longer. His lips were moving, his eyes intense and frantic, but she couldn't hear . . . couldn't see . . . couldn't speak . . .

"*Nooooo!*" His voice reached her from a long way off . . . and then she was gone, sinking, sinking, to the place where the moon dropped off the end of the earth, to the sea of silence at the farthest, deepest corners of midnight.

And the world above was no more.

9

"Wait, my dear. Where are you going? Is something wrong?"

Sir Henry's voice halted Fiona in midstride. She'd been trying to escape the crowded great hall at Dovenbyre as quickly as her jeweled shoes would carry her, but when Sir Henry called out to her, she sighed, pasted a smile on her face, and turned to face him.

"Gilroyd and Wynn and I have scarcely seen you all evening," he huffed, out of breath from hurrying to catch her. "Come, my dear, join us. The singer from Amelonia is bringing his harp into the great hall even as we speak. Gil very much wishes you to enjoy the festivities with him."

Enjoy the festivities? Fiona thought bleakly. How she wished she could—but she had never felt less festive.

All around her, people were laughing and chattering, sipping wine from golden goblets and proposing boisterous toasts to Prince Branden's health. The great hall was bursting with candlelight and incense, with ladies in finely embroidered silk gowns and lords and knights in velvet tunics. The pre-coronation feast had been more sumptuous than anything she could have imagined.

But she had never felt more heavyhearted. And she didn't want to hamper anyone else's enjoyment of the evening—particularly Gil's—with her own troubles.

For Gil's sake, she knew she ought to go back and try to pretend some more. She ought to sit beside him and clap her hands and chat with Wynn and laugh and seem happy. She *was* happy that Gil was safe and ensconced in the castle, happy that both Duke Borlis and Plodius of Ril had surrendered in a battle on the outskirts of Grithain, and that their men had all pledged allegiance to Prince Branden, who would be crowned king on the morrow.

But she needed a few moments in her own room, a few moments where she could let the pretense slip. A few moments to think, to *feel*, in private. A few moments to grieve.

"I have a slight headache," she said quietly. Then as Sir Henry's kind, pink face furrowed in worry, she forced a smile. "It will be better soon, I think. I walked in the garden to get some air, thinking it might help, but . . . no. Perhaps I drank too much wine."

"Ah, I'm sorry." His shaggy brown-and-silver brows drew together in concern, and he patted her arm. "You should rest, then—you want to be able to fully enjoy the coronation tomorrow. I'll explain to Gil. He would be sadly disappointed if you were unable to be present for *that*."

"I'll be there, Sir Henry, never fear." She touched his arm. "Nothing would keep me from Gil on such an important day."

"Of course not. And you above all else deserve to be there, my dear. If not for you and for Conor of Wor-thane, Gil would not be alive to be crowned king at all. And where was *I* when all the trouble broke out?" he asked ruefully, shaking his head, as behind them in the hall the notes of a harp stirred the incense-rich air.

"Off on a wild-goose chase, in Aardmore, that's where I was. Waiting for a message about the health of the king, a message that came nearly too late. Little did I know my delay there could have been disastrous."

His mouth twisted in dismay. "I wish I could have been of help to you, child, but thanks to our lucky stars, we had Duke Conor on our side—who would ever have thought it would turn out like that? He has proven himself a true brother to the boy, after all. And speaking of Conor"—he stopped short, caught up in his own thoughts and oblivious of the sudden pallor that had sucked all color from Fiona's cheeks—"have you heard the news?"

"N-news?"

"Conor is here—he arrived at the castle only a short while ago. He'd ridden half the night. And he's put down the last bit of unrest in the eastern valleys of Ril—just in time for the coronation."

"How very . . . fortunate," Fiona managed, hoping he couldn't see the panic surging through her. "Sir Henry, please excuse me. I must go to my chambers."

"Of course, my dear, of course."

He watched in concern as she hurried away, one hand gripping her pale-blue velvet skirt as she fairly bolted up the staircase, fleeing as if demons pursued her.

The poor girl. She hasn't been quite the same since all of that business at Raven Castle, he reflected. Oh, she'd recovered within a week from the aftereffects of that monstrous spell the druid magician had cast upon her—and with no ill effects that anyone could see—but something was different about her. Wynn and Gil had remarked upon it too.

Her smile had lost some of its radiance, her skin looked paler than he'd ever noticed it being before. She laughed less. And she often seemed preoccupied, even sad.

Perhaps she misses Bitterbloom Cottage, he reflected. *After all, it is the only home she remembers.* Well, even though he would prefer that he and Wynn stay on a bit longer with Gil to see him properly settled, if Fiona was truly homesick, he would arrange an escort to take her back to Urbagran at once. She could leave right after the coronation, if that was what she wanted. *Perhaps,* Sir Henry thought, *her spirits will bloom again when she reaches home.*

Fiona had to struggle to keep from racing like a thief through the castle as she flew up the staircase and down the corridor to her chamber. The knowledge that Conor was here within these very walls filled her with such a riot of emotions that she couldn't sort them all out. She only knew that she wasn't ready to see him again—and she didn't know if she ever would be.

But she must see him again—tomorrow, at the coronation. And she'd better have herself under control by then.

Reaching her bedchamber, she rushed in and closed the door, startling Tidbit, who'd been dozing by the fire. The cat lifted her head and gazed at Fiona with shining amber eyes. But Fiona scarcely noticed the cat, or the fire, or the grand furnishings of the chamber. Her heart pounded as she sank down upon the rose satin-draped bed and buried her face in her hands.

Conor's image swam into her mind's eye and her heart trembled. She hadn't seen him since she'd slipped into that unnatural slumber following Kilvorn's spell. The aftereffects of the failed death curse had lingered for nearly a week, and when she'd awakened, she'd found herself at Grithain Castle. Conor's troop and the army of men sent from Dovenbyre to escort Gil to safety had carried her there on a litter.

But Conor had not stayed on in Grithain.

In fact, Sir Henry had told her, Conor had left Grithain the same day that she awakened here in this bedchamber, finally free of the magician's spell. He'd ridden off that very hour at the head of a sizable army to put down a rebellion rumored to be brewing in the eastern valleys of Ril.

It was important work, Fiona knew, and she was grateful for Gil's sake that Conor was defending him from enemies the boy couldn't possibly yet be expected to counter. But . . .

He'd left without seeing her. He'd not even left her a note, a message for when she awakened. And in all these weeks, though he'd sent reports to Grithain, he'd never once sent word to her, or as far as she knew, inquired about her.

He has more important matters to deal with now, she told herself, as she pushed herself off the bed and stalked to the window. *Things like battles, and prisoners, and treaties.*

He probably never again has thought about that kiss—our kiss—the only one, she reflected, tears suddenly burning her eyelids, *that we will ever have.*

Taking a deep breath, she brushed the tears away with the back of her hand. She had to come to grips with that. He'd warned her in the tunnel that he didn't believe in love. He didn't want it, didn't seek it, didn't regard it.

And didn't feel it, she realized with a painful knot in her throat.

The problem was, she did. She loved Conor of Wor-thane.

They were different, as different as spring and winter, night and day, sun and shadow. And she'd been a fool ever to think there could be anything more than a meaningless, dallying kiss between them.

Clouds shifted suddenly in the darkened sky, revealing the full March moon. She stared at it, remembering one month earlier when the moon had glowed full on another night: the night of the Midnight Mirror, when she'd been shown the man fighting for his life in the Dark Forest—the night she'd saved Conor's life.

She whirled from the window and hurried to the gilt table where the Midnight Mirror rested amid her brush and combs and baubles. Sir Henry had directed the men who'd brought her to Grithain to bring her garments and every item a woman might want, and someone had included the Midnight Mirror with its amber-studded handle.

Fiona lifted it, peered into the glass, and saw her own reflection. Nothing more. The mirror's face was as blank as her own future.

It isn't yet midnight, she reminded herself. At that moment there was a rapping at the door.

Fiona set the mirror down, her heart beginning to hammer. *No, that couldn't be Conor. He'd left without a word of farewell. Why would he come to see her the moment he returned? It was probably Wynn or Gil, come to urge her to rejoin the others in the great hall.*

Yet somehow she knew, even as she opened the door, before she saw him, she knew.

"There you are." Conor's eyes lit at the sight of her. His tall frame seemed to fill the doorway as he took a step forward, past the threshold, into the room. Fully recovered from his injuries now, he looked stronger, larger, tougher than she'd ever seen him. And certainly every bit as handsome. Behind him she saw Tor, sitting on his haunches, guarding the corridor.

"Aren't you going to invite me in?"

"It seems a little late for that." She stepped back further, aware that her knees were trembling beneath the skirt of her gown and that her voice was unsteady. She struggled to regain her composure, but it wasn't easy, not now that she was seeing him again. He looked more striking than ever in a rich plum tunic that encased his wide shoulders. His face was clean-shaven and lean, his eyes sharp as green spikes beneath his thick-curled black hair.

And her heart ached at the sight of him.

She fought back the joy and the yearning, the desire to throw her arms around him and kiss him one more time, a kiss that would have to last her forever.

Instead she inclined her head gracefully and spoke with just a shade of breathlessness. "Of course you are welcome. After all you've done for Gil—for Grithain—you are no doubt welcome everywhere in Dovenbyre Castle."

"Everywhere but here, is that it? You're angry with me."

She didn't respond. Conor closed the door and followed her into the room as she turned and walked away from him, crossing to the window, where she stood in profile, gazing out at the night.

There was something different about her, he noticed. She was stiff, restrained. Cold. His angel, his Fiona, the girl he had dreamed about every night since he'd left Grithain, was warm, vibrant, giving. This woman, beautiful as a crystal statue in her pale blue gown, her midnight hair flowing loosely past her shoulders, had herself under rigid self-control—the same sort of self-control, he realized, that *he* had exercised on the day he left her, when his first instinct had been to crush her in his arms.

"Angry with you?" she responded at last, her tone so cool it made him flinch. "No, I'm not angry. Why would I be? You did all you promised to do, you helped me to save Gil, you defeated his enemies, you have helped to make the kingdom of Grithain whole and safe—"

"I let that druid magician cast a death spell on you. You nearly died and I couldn't stop it," he said tersely, and at the words, she met his eyes and shook her head.

"No, that wasn't your fault. I knew there was danger when I insisted on going to Raven Castle with you. No one could have stopped Kilvorn. Except Ariel." She took a deep breath. "They say she died that night. I think it must have been her final burst of power that brought Tidbit there to find the crystal shard—to kill the magician and break his spell."

"Thank the stars and the moon for that. Fiona . . ." He seized her then and pulled her up against his chest, his blood surging at the warm, lush feel of her close against him. "When I thought you were dying, I wanted to die. You probably don't know this, but I offered to die in your place—I would *gladly* have died in your place. But that wicked old bastard wouldn't hear of it—"

"I know. I heard. Thank you," she murmured very quietly. His arms were around her, and she was dying again. Of want, of need. Tears filled her eyes. "I appreciate all you did—"

"Damn it, stop thanking me and stop placating me. Tell me why you're treating me like this! As if I am a stranger, someone you must accord civility and nothing more! Don't you know I would have given my life for you? I would now. I will forever. I protected you as best I could, and though it wasn't good enough—"

"You left me." Tears filled her eyes as she lifted her face to his. She struggled a moment in his arms, and then gave up, her shoulders slumping forward, her voice breaking.

"Without a word, before I even awakened to see your face . . . you left me."

He went stock-still. In her eyes he saw pain, distress. And a heartbreaking sadness that pierced him more deeply than any arrow or blade ever had.

"I never meant to hurt you." He touched her cheek, brushed his thumb along the smooth, pale skin. "Never. I didn't leave until I knew you were waking up. I was there, watching you, listening to you breathe, and all I wanted was to see you open your eyes, to hold you in my arms. Then—you said my name. And that . . . scared me. Strange, isn't it? A soldier who's never faltered on the battlefield, scared by a woman speaking his name."

His mouth twisted. "I was a coward. And I ran away."

"You could never be a coward—" she began, but he cut her off.

"Oh, yes. I was afraid of *you*." He shook his head, his green eyes darkening. "Afraid of what I feel for you."

"And—what is that?" she breathed, searching his eyes, as a tiny beam of hope sparked inside her.

"L-l-love." He stumbled over the word, cleared his throat, and repeated it, more firmly, looking dazed. "Love."

"You . . . ran away because you . . . *love* me?"

"Cowardly, I know." A sheepish grin split his face, then he yanked her closer still and brushed a kiss across the tip of her nose. "But it's all your fault. It hit me suddenly . . . and hard. All these feelings—I needed to see if I could fight them, conquer them, or forget them. If I could forget *you*. But I couldn't, not for a single moment. And more than that, I didn't want to," he said softly, almost wonderingly, and then he crushed her to him, wrapped his arms around her and kissed the single teardrop sliding down her cheek.

"Now I'm going to try to make you forgive me."

"H-how are you going to—"

"Like this," he said in a most determined way, and he slowly, gently, and thoroughly kissed her.

It was a long, deeply possessive kiss—and it left her trembling in his arms. When it was over, before she'd scarcely drawn breath, he buried his hands in her hair and kissed her again.

This time the kiss was hotter, fiercer, awakening a fire within her. It sent flames licking through her blood, tingling down to her toes. Her breasts ached, and a wild craving began deep in her core. She could feel his heart pounding against hers, beat for beat, she could feel his strength and his passion and his need. Her own soared to meet it, and a dizzying heat burst through her.

"Tell me again, tell me you love me," she urged, when he lifted his lips, and his lightning grin seared her soul.

"I love you. With all my heart, I love you."

"I love you too—and I forgive you," she breathed.

"Too easy, angel." He shook his head and laughed low and deep. His lips whispered against her ear. "I haven't yet begun to prove myself to you."

"You . . . haven't? What else . . . do you have in mind?" Her lips curved, her breath caught with delight. And answering laughter sprang softly from her throat.

"I'll show you. It's only midnight. I have all night to show you. But first—"

He reached into his pocket and pulled out a green velvet pouch, then withdrew a brooch—the same brooch she'd glimpsed in the mirror, the one Duke Borlis had stolen and worn.

"I promised I would recover this and give it to you."

"There's no need—"

He closed her palm around it firmly. "Accept."

She tingled with infinite pleasure at his air of authority, and her eyes shone into his. "It's beautiful—and I thank you."

Reaching over, she set the brooch upon a table of inlaid silver and then pulled him toward her. "Now what about convincing me some more of how much you love me?" she invited softly.

"What do you think I'm trying to do, woman? I've never had experience with this and you're not making things easier."

To her astonishment, he dropped to one knee and reached into the pouch again. This time he pulled out something that glimmered wildly in the candlelight. Clasping her hand, he placed a ring in the center of her palm—a delicate golden ring alight with a circle of amethysts surrounding a cool, glittering emerald.

Fiona caught her breath. It was the most beautiful thing she'd ever seen.

"Marry me, angel. Marry me, and be my bride, my wife, my love, for all of our days."

Wordlessly, Fiona stared at the ring. And at the man who'd given it to her. He was gazing at her with a warmth and passion in his eyes that filled her with joy. Yet . . . she had to be sure . . .

"You said marriage was a practical thing, that it had nothing to do with love—"

"What did I know? I didn't know anything, Fiona, until I nearly lost you. Until that spell nearly took you from me—"

His voice shook, and for a moment he bowed his head. Then he lifted it, and there was no mistaking the raw emotion in his eyes. Tenderly he pulled her down upon his knee, cupped her

hand in his. Slowly, he kissed her palm and then slid the ring
onto her finger.

"I was right about it being practical, Fiona. Marrying the
woman you love—the woman you need—is eminently practical. Otherwise a man can't think of anything else, can't get
anything done. Can't know a moment's peace."

He stared for a moment at the emerald shining upon her
slender finger, then looked into her eyes again. "I want a life
with you, angel, a life of peace and happiness, a home like you
made at Bitterbloom Cottage. We can live at Wor-thane, at
Grithain, at Bitterbloom Cottage—wherever you wish, it
doesn't matter. But I need you at my side. In my bed. And
always, in my arms."

The last of her doubts melted like snow in May. What else
was a girl to do? She leaned over and kissed him, her heart
opening to him fully even as her lips parted beneath his.

"Yes," she whispered against his mouth as she felt the passion rush through both of them, powerful as a coursing river.

"Yes, yes, and yes."

The next thing she knew, he had swept her up in his arms
and was carrying her to the bed. Her blue gown fell like a
cloud to the floor, and his dark tunic was gone in a flash, leaving hot skin against hot skin, muscle and sinew against softness
and silk, whispers and laughter and promises in the dark. Midnight came and they were swept away.

On the gilt table, the Midnight Mirror began to shimmer. An
image flickered in the glass—Fiona and Conor, in the courtyard
of the white keep of Wor-thane—a young boy laughing on a
pony before them, twin girls of four twirling at their feet, and
Fiona's belly gently swelling with another child. Sunlight dappled the courtyard . . . a teen-aged King Branden with an entourage of thirty arrived at the gate, and . . .

What was that? Two silvery shadows flickered in the upper
corner of the mirror—perhaps ghosts or angels or witches, who
knew? It might have been two misty-robed sisters looking on
in silent approval.

Then midnight was past. The images vanished. And the mirror's magic was no more.

But the future could still be glimpsed. It shone in the eyes
and the souls of the lovers on the satin-draped bed, as deeply

entwined in each other's arms as they were in each other's hearts.

Somehow they both knew that their duty to the new young king was only beginning, that his happiness and safety would be part of their lives for years to come, but they also knew that tonight was just for them, a celebration of love found, held dear, and cherished.

Theirs was a night of promises, of passion, and as dawn approached . . . of wedding plans.

Fiona and Conor were married at Dovenbyre Castle one month later—at the stroke of midnight beneath a full and glowing moon.

The End

Dream Lover

Ruth Ryan Langan

1

"MEN." ALLISON KERR stormed around the living room of her cramped Manhattan apartment, wishing she could kick something. She'd been running on pure nerves for hours, as hurt and anger warred within her.

She looked up at the gray-and-white tabby watching with wise old eyes from his perch on top of the television. He belonged to her next-door neighbor Iris, a flight attendant, who left him with Ally whenever she was away overnight. Ally was fond of saying that because of her transient lifestyle, Mactavish was the closest thing she had to a pet.

"They're all jerks, Mactavish. You can't trust any of them."

At her outburst the cat jumped down from the TV and began weaving in and out between her ankles as though to console her. "Oh, I didn't mean you, you sweet old thing." She lifted him into her arms, burying her face in the soft fur, and fought the temptation to weep. "Tedious Ted isn't worth my tears. No man is." Her voice lowered with temper. "I should have known

199

he was a phony right from the start. He was too good to be true. Sending me dozens of roses at work so my boss would be impressed. Picking me up in a limo for that black-tie dinner dance and dazzling all my neighbors. None of it meant a thing. It was all just so much theater, and he was the leading man."

From the TV set came a familiar voice, heard around the world every New Year's Eve. "Will you look at this crowd in Times Square, waiting to usher in the New Year!"

Ally glanced over in time to see the camera panning the happy celebrants. Slowly it zoomed in on a young couple locked in a passionate kiss, oblivious to the pushing and shoving going on around them by strangers watching the giant globe suspended high above.

Ally set the cat on the floor. "Look at that, Mactavish."

The cat obediently turned toward the television.

"Honey, you'd better wake up and smell the coffee," she shouted to the young woman on the screen. She planted her hands on her hips. "The minute you admit you love him, the thrill of the chase will be over. Then honesty will set in. He'll move on to greener pastures. He'll hurt you and humiliate you, and even"—she absorbed a sudden rush of pain—"take your best friend to bed."

"Just a little while to go until the beginning of another year," the voice on the TV intoned, "and the celebration will begin."

"That does it. This pity party is over." Ally stomped into her tiny kitchen and opened the refrigerator. She filled a bowl with milk before tucking a bottle of bubbly under her arm and snagging a champagne flute.

With the cat at her heels, she stalked back to the living room and set the bowl on the coffee table, next to the documents spilling out of her attaché case. She intended to spend her holiday lost in work. It would be the perfect antidote for her pain, especially since it had been her dedication to her work that Ted had blamed for all their troubles.

Ally moved aside the framed photograph of a handsome man in uniform with his arm around a pretty young woman holding an infant in her arms, and paused as a flood of memories washed over her. Of her mother making a game out of their move from military base to military base, until her long battle with illness ended. Of her father's loving care of the woman he adored, despite the demands of his career. But not even a father's love could ease the pain of a young girl's loss of her mother. Each time they piled their meager belongings into a rented trailer and moved on to another town, another school filled with strangers, Ally would convince herself that this move would be their last, that they would finally put down roots. Of course, it never happened.

Was that why she'd ignored all the warning signs with Ted? Had she been so determined to belong somewhere, to find the perfect mate, that she'd overlooked his obvious flaws?

Her father's words of warning played through her mind.

"Don't be taken in by phonies, Ally girl. Wait for the real deal. No matter how fancy the package, look inside, and get to the heart. You deserve only the best in your life."

Now that he'd joined her mother in death, Ally was feeling miserably alone, especially after this stinging betrayal by a man she'd thought she could trust with her heart. It was, she realized, the lowest point of her twenty-nine years.

"Oh, Dad. I really let myself get taken." She sniffled as she set the portrait aside. "But never again. From now on I'll pour all my energy into my career. I've had enough of looking for love in all the wrong places."

Hearing the way her voice was trembling, she took a deep breath. "I don't care if we're alone on New Year's Eve, Mactavish. We're going to celebrate. Come on."

At once the cat leaped up to the table and began lapping milk.

Ally popped the cork and filled the flute, watching the bubbles foam up and over the edge. "Here's to us, Mactavish. You and me." She lifted her glass. "From now on I'm through with men." She blinked hard, refusing to give in to tears. Still, it hurt to realize how blind she'd been. After Ted had complained bitterly about the hours she'd been spending away from him, she'd hurried back to town early to surprise him, but it was she who was surprised. It may have been a story as old as time, but the pain was as new, as unexpected, as if she'd been the first woman ever betrayed by a man.

"No more putting up with fools." She filled the flute again and slumped down on the sofa. "I've got my work. It's all I need. The only man I'd settle for now is a dream lover."

Mactavish licked first one paw, then the other, all the while watching her as she propped her feet on the coffee table.

"Someone tall, dark, and handsome." Warming to her subject, she took another sip of champagne and closed her eyes. "A man with wit and charm who would care more about me than about himself." She gave a dry laugh. "Now that would be a switch."

Mactavish jumped from the table to the sofa and curled up beside her.

"You think I'll be unable to resist petting you, don't you?" She took a long drink while running her other hand down the length of Mactavish's back. "You know me so well. I've always been a sucker for a sad face." She sat absently petting the cat. After a long silence she could feel her normally sunny nature returning. "As long as I'm fantasizing, I may as well make it good. I think my dream lover should live in a castle and be disgustingly rich. But of course, he doesn't give a hoot about that. He's unimpressed by wealth or title. All he really wants is a woman who will love him for himself. And there I'll be, the one he's been waiting for all his life." She scratched behind the cat's ears, eliciting a series of contented purrs. "From the moment he meets me, he'll know without a doubt that I'm the only woman for him."

As she reached for the bottle and poured another glass, she felt her head swim. "I've never cared all that much for champagne, but tonight is special." Her voice thickened. "Tonight Ally Kerr has decided to grow up and face reality. And the reality of my life is this. The only man worthy of my heart is a dream lover. From now on I'll save my energy for the really important things, like my career. It's all I need. Isn't that right, Mactavish?"

She looked down as the cat ran his tongue over the back of her hand. "Of course you agree with me." Her lips quivered just a bit, but she managed a shaky smile. "If only people were as wise as cats."

She set her glass aside and tucked her feet under her. On TV the crowd began chanting, counting down the seconds to midnight. Ally was too tired to care. Pillowing her head on the arm of the sofa, she closed her eyes. As she drifted into sleep, the throng erupted into chaos, just as she found herself in the throes of the most amazing dream.

She was seated in the back of an ancient Rolls, chauffeured by an imp of a man who looked suspiciously like Mactavish. Those same wise old yellow-green eyes watching her in the rearview mirror. That same salt-and-pepper fur, only now it had turned into tufts of wiry hair curling around a rosy-cheeked face that could have belonged to a gnome. He spoke not a word, but drove along a narrow road that climbed steadily upward through heavily forested countryside. The view from the car's window was breathtaking, with craggy mountain peaks hovering over mist-shrouded glens and streams rushing over rugged boulders to spill into a lake far below.

Though she'd never been here before, she knew this land.

When the car came up over a rise they were in a verdant meadow. In the distance was a fabulous manor house that resembled a castle, set amid rolling hills. On either side of the road leading to it was a series of formal gardens, with well-placed statuary and fountains. They drove past a crystal-clear pond where two white swans glided in circles, looking too perfect to be real.

They came to a stop, and the driver hurried around to open her door. Ally started up the massive granite steps. The front door opened, and she knew instinctively that her lover was there on the threshold, eagerly awaiting her arrival.

There was such a feeling of peace here. A sense that after a lifetime of traveling the world in search of roots, she was finally home.

With a little laugh she quickened her pace, her heart pounding at the knowledge that she would soon see the face of the one with whom she would spend the rest of her life. "Oh, my darling . . ."

The dream dissolved as she was abruptly yanked from sleep by the shrill ringing of a telephone.

Ally sat up, shoving her hair from her eyes. The smile that had touched her mouth in sleep was replaced by a frown as she realized what had disturbed her.

The phone rang a second time, and then a third, before she managed to get to her feet and cross the room.

"Yes. Hello." She glanced at a clock. It read two in the morning. That added to her frustration. She didn't know which was more annoying—the fact that she had been denied the satisfying ending to her dream or the fact that anybody would phone at such an hour on New Year's Day.

"Hey, Ally."

The voice of her boss, David Harkness, swept the last cobwebs of sleep from her mind. "Do you know what time it is?"

"Yeah. Can't be helped." He cleared his throat. "I need you to fly to Edinburgh today."

"Scotland? You want me to fly to Scotland on New Year's Day? Have you been drinking?"

"No time for jokes." She could tell by the muffled voice that he was running his hand over his face. She knew David Harkness well enough to know his every mannerism. This one was used to cover frustration.

"I wouldn't bother you on a holiday . . ." More muffled words that had her sighing. Whenever David was about to assign her an unpleasant chore, he would make this gesture, then massage the pulse at his right temple. "But this is an emergency, Ally."

She was suddenly tense. Though she secretly disdained David's work ethic, she genuinely liked his young wife, who was carrying their first child. "Is it Tara?"

"Yeah. We're at Manhattan General. The doctor tried to stop the labor, but he said it's too late. Ready or not, that baby's coming today."

"A month early?"

"Yeah." He sighed. "Look, Ally, I got word that Hamilton Hall is available. If we get there first with the best offer, it's ours. You know I'd be there if I could. But I can't, and now it's up to you."

At the mention of the bed-and-breakfast in the Scottish Highlands, Ally's tone changed. Now she was all business. Harkness and Crewel was a New York–based conglomerate that bought old buildings around the world at bargain prices, stripped them of anything valuable that could be sold for a profit, and then tore them down or renovated them for use as modern retail or office space.

"You've been after Hamilton Hall for ages. Why did they decide to sell now?"

"I don't know and I don't care. I just know I want it."

"Any complications I ought to know about?"

With the bark of a hospital loudspeaker in the background, David's voice grew louder. "Not that I've heard. Just get there as soon as possible to nail down the offer to purchase. Make a list of the antiques that will bring the best price. We'll get our legal department on the rest of the details as the deal progresses."

"I suppose there's no chance of putting me up somewhere else while I do this deal?"

He gave a mirthless laugh. "I'm sure it would endear us to the sellers if they were to learn that our representative wasn't even willing to stay under their roof."

"Yeah. I guess you're right. But you've seen how shabby . . ."

"You don't have to stay overnight. Just get a signature on the document, check out the antiques, and take the next flight out. If you need to freshen up, I'm sure they'll let you use one of their rooms. You can sleep on the flight home. Just remember to make a point of mentioning any and all apparent flaws, since we're coming in with the lowest figure we can manage without being insulting."

"I'll remember," she said tiredly. "I just hope when bonus time rolls around you'll remember that I spent my entire New Year's Day traveling to a seedy hovel in the middle of Nowhere, Scotland."

"If it's any comfort, it's only for one day. By nightfall you'll be on your way home. And to soften the blow I've ordered first-class air tickets. Will that make it a little easier?"

She was pleasantly surprised. It wasn't like David to spend a cent more than necessary, especially on one of his employees. "You're too good to me, David." She gave an exaggerated sigh. "All right. Kiss Tara. And that new baby. Tell them both I'll see them tomorrow." She gave a quick laugh. "Just think. By the time I land in Scotland, you'll be a proud papa."

His tone suddenly changed from cool businessman to concerned husband. "Ally, I'm scared stiff."

"Don't be, David. Tara's going to be just fine. Now get back to her and hold her hand. And, David?"

"Yeah?"

"Try not to faint. That way the hospital staff can concentrate on the new mother and baby instead of the father lying on the floor."

At her laughter he gave a lōng, deep sigh. "Got to go, Ally. Bring us home that deal."

As she replaced the receiver and turned, she caught sight of Mactavish dozing on the sofa. How she wished she could join him just long enough to finish her dream. There was no time for foolishness now. She had packing to deal with. Thank heavens Iris had a key to her apartment and would be coming back later today to pick up her pet. With this crazy lifestyle, Ally thought, it was just as well that she had no one depending on her.

"Scotland." She was shaking her head as she started toward her bedroom, her mind suddenly swimming with a million details she needed to see to before leaving the country. "In the dead of winter. Where did I go wrong?"

2

Heath Stewart was in no mood to celebrate. His head was splitting, though he couldn't decide if it was from the alcohol he'd consumed or the drugs the doctors had given him after the accident. His body ached in a dozen different places. His mouth was so dry his tongue seemed too big for it, and every time he blinked, his eyes felt scraped by sandpaper.

"Happy New Year, sir."

At the flight attendant's chipper greeting, he could barely keep from snarling. If he heard one more cheerful voice, he'd really have to punch something.

He leaned a hand against the wall and waited for the dizziness to pass. Cursing through gritted teeth, he took another step. He was getting aboard this plane if he had to crawl.

His life had taken an ugly turn. He'd had his fill of so-called friends and party animals. For a little while at least, he was looking forward to something he'd never expected to want again in his lifetime. Peace and quiet. All he wanted was to be left alone to lick his wounds.

He put one foot in front of the other and moved doggedly along.

Ally settled herself in the first-class section of the plane and, because she was almost the last to board, considered the empty seat beside her a good omen. Maybe she would be lucky enough to have this space to herself so she could really get some work done. She flipped open her palm notebook and began transferring information from it to her laptop.

"Here you are, sir."

Ally nearly groaned as a flight attendant directed a late-arriving passenger to the seat beside hers just as the plane's doors were slammed shut.

"Thanks." His movements were shuffling and awkward as he stowed a duffel in the overhead compartment, then slipped out of a well-worn backpack and jammed it in as well, before taking his seat. "Oh. Sorry." He folded his long legs into the cramped space, bumping Ally in the process.

She moved her feet and shrank back against the window, all the while keeping her attention glued to the screen of her laptop. There would be only a few minutes more before she'd have to stow her equipment until after takeoff, and she still had a dozen or more things she wanted to transfer to her hard drive.

After several muttered oaths while he struggled to fasten his seat belt her seatmate turned to her. "I hate to bother you, but would you mind giving me a hand with this?" He rubbed his shoulder. "This arm just doesn't want to cooperate."

His voice had the burr of Scotland.

As she reached over to help him with the seat belt, she had a quick impression of shaggy coal-black hair badly in need of a trim, a stubble of beard darkening his chin, and a world-weary expression in the bluest eyes she'd ever seen.

"Broken?"

He shook his head. "Just bloody sore. The doctor gave me some pain medication, but all it's done is make me fuzzy-headed."

"That's not the worst thing. It'll help you sleep." She turned away and concentrated on her laptop.

When the flight attendant paused beside his seat to ask if he needed some help, he seemed to have trouble rousing himself from his medicated fog to answer. "Thanks, but you're a bit late. My seatmate was kind enough to lend a hand. If you don't mind, though, I'll take a pillow."

The attendant placed it behind his head. "If you need anything else, just let me know."

"I will. Thanks." He closed his eyes.

Ally studied the way he was sprawled all over her space as well as his own. Once they were airborne she kicked off her shoes and touched the speed-dial button of her cell phone. "Marti? Ally. By the time you get this message at your office I'll be in Scotland. I'd like you to fax me a list of clients interested in antiques, along with their wish lists. Underline anything specific that might fetch a higher price for the firm. As soon as I get to my destination I'll start faxing you a list of what I've found. I'm sure, from my research, that some of them will be one-of-a-kind family heirlooms. Scottish, mostly. Others will probably be French, English, Italian."

Beside her, Heath listened to her rapid-fire delivery. Did she never stop? As soon as she finished leaving one message, she was off and running to the next, and the next, without bothering to catch a breath.

She wiggled in her seat, and he opened one eye to watch as she adjusted it to the most comfortable position. If he'd heard that voice on his telephone, he would have thought he was talking to a human dynamo. A dynamo with attitude. Nothing shy or hesitant about her as she plowed through a list of business details that would have had most executives reeling. But the voice didn't seem to fit the slender woman who was busily tapping a pen on the armrest as she left yet another message, this time to someone named Armand.

"Ally Kerr here. I may have just the sort of treasures you've been looking for since last December. As soon as I have a chance to catalog the pieces, I'll fax you a copy."

A cap of fiery curls framed her small heart-shaped face. Her fair skin was that amazing porcelain trademark of a true redhead. She wore oatmeal-colored woolen slacks and a matching turtleneck. Her only adornment was a pair of small gold studs in her ears. Heath had already checked her fingers for rings and had noted none. Not that he was interested, but when a guy had reached thirty-five without falling into the marriage trap, it was an automatic reaction.

As her voice droned on, he found himself drifting into the first restful sleep he'd had in days.

Ally set aside her phone to enjoy a quick meal, while indulging herself for a few minutes with her favorite mystery author. It wasn't exactly the way she'd imagined spending New Year's Day, but it could have been worse. Her smile slipped a notch. She could have been watching football with Tedious Ted and some of the professional athletes he claimed as close personal friends. Come to think of it, Ted surrounded himself with celebrities. To make himself feel important? Why hadn't that occurred to her when they'd first met? Because, she thought with a sense of shame, she'd allowed him to dazzle her with his lavish lifestyle.

As the attendant removed her tray it occurred to Ally that although her ego had been badly bruised, she had escaped that relationship relatively unscathed. It hurt to think that Ted had been cheating with her best friend. Ex–best friend, she mentally corrected. But at least she'd learned the painful truth about him before it was too late. Though she had enjoyed his shameless pursuit, and the expensive gifts he'd lavished on her, she hadn't lost her heart to him.

It was easy to see in retrospect that he'd been all flash and no substance. That's what hurt the most. That she had been so blind to what should have been so painfully obvious.

"Looks ominous." The sleep-roughened voice beside her brought her out of her reverie.

Ally managed to compose her features, annoyed that this stranger had caught her wallowing in misery.

"It can't be that bad." He nodded toward the book in her hand. "Grizzly murder, though. The butler did it."

"There is no butler."

"The cook, then. I always get those two mixed up."

"No cook either."

"Ah, well, it's not worth fretting about. Old fool deserved to die. He'd been mistreating everyone in the book."

She bit back a smile. "The victim is young and beautiful."

"Now I remember. It's all this medication. The brain's muddled, and I—"

Hearing his quick intake of breath, she leaned a bit closer. "Are you hurting?"

"Some. Probably time for another pain pill." He released his seat belt and started to get up, but quickly slumped back into his seat, overcome by waves of pain. "Not a good idea, I guess."

Ally could see the pallor even that small effort had caused. "I'll get your medicine. Where do you keep it?"

"There's a bottle in my backpack."

She eased past him and stood in the aisle, opening the overhead bin and removing his backpack.

As she did, he indulged himself in the view of softly rounded hips and long, long legs. This was way better than the nurse he'd had to endure in the emergency room, who'd been built like a fullback and had barked orders like a drill sergeant.

Because Ally didn't feel comfortable rummaging around in his belongings, she set the backpack on his lap. With his good hand he dug in and came up with the prescription bottle.

Ally shook a pill into his hand and returned the bag to the overhead compartment, then slid past him to her seat. "The label said you should take that with food."

"Did it?" He wondered how she would react if she knew how much he'd just enjoyed the press of her backside brushing across his knees. "No wonder I'm feeling so loopy. Right now, even without a plane, I'd be flying."

That flash of droll humor had her grinning despite herself.

Minutes later, after Ally pressed the call button for him, an attendant arrived with water and a dinner tray.

Ally dialed her cell phone and watched as her seatmate downed the pill, then struggled with his knife and fork. After a few attempts, he set them aside and simply stared morosely at the food.

Cradling the phone between her ear and shoulder, Ally picked up his knife and fork and began cutting his food into bite-size pieces, all the while chatting away to a message machine somewhere in Manhattan.

"Thanks." Heath couldn't figure out what surprised him more—the fact that she would offer help without being asked or the fact that she did so without even pausing for a breath. "Sorry to be such a slug."

Ally put a hand over the mouthpiece of her phone. "You can't help it if you're hurting."

"But I'm not used to causing so much trouble."

"No problem." She put the fork in his good hand and continued her conversation. "Caroline? Ally Kerr here. You can expect a fax from me no later than tomorrow with a list of available antiques. I'd appreciate it if you'd get back to me by the end of the week. There's going to be quite a rush on these things, since they're all one of a kind and have been held by the same family for generations."

When she disconnected, her seatmate shot her a long look before proceeding to eat. When he finished, he leaned back and sighed, as though exhausted by the effort. "That's the first food I've had in more than twenty-four hours."

Ally looked up from her laptop computer. "Why?"

He shrugged. "No time. I was airlifted off the slopes and—"

"Slopes?"

He nodded. "I was skiing in Montreal."

That brought a jolt of surprise. For some strange reason, she'd imagined him being mugged on the streets of New York, not skiing in Canada. In that frayed sweater and ski pants with the tear in the knee, he didn't so much resemble a ski bum as a real bum, or a down-on-his-luck visitor, eager to escape the big city before anything worse happened to him. "Your first time skiing?"

He shook his head. "Far from it. But I've never done anything like this before. A stupid mistake. I misjudged a turn. One moment of carelessness, and the next thing I knew, I woke up just as I was being hauled down the mountain and loaded onto a copter for a flight to the local hospital. From there I decided to fly to New York and return home."

"Where is home?"

"It's a wee bit of a place in the Highlands that no one has ever heard of. What about you? What would bring a lovely lady to Scotland this time of year?"

"A business trip."

"Business? On New Year's Day?"

Ally laughed. "I wasn't supposed to be here. But my boss is about to become a father for the first time, and I'm taking his place." Without thinking, she reached up and adjusted the pillow behind his head. "Once that pill kicks in, you should probably think about getting some more sleep. Would you like a blanket?"

He nodded, pleasantly surprised by her concern. "That would be nice."

Again Ally slid past him and opened the overhead compartment. By the time she'd draped a blanket around him, his eyes were closing.

"You may not look like it, but you're definitely an angel of mercy." His voice was thick with sleep.

Ally squeezed back into her seat and watched as he drifted off. Judging by the curve of his lips, he was having a pleasant dream.

Ignoring the words on her computer screen, she turned to stare out the window at the night sky, wishing she could escape with as much ease. She needed to be fresh when she arrived. But between business and these negative thoughts that kept flitting through her mind, she couldn't seem to settle. If she had so badly misjudged Ted, what made her think she could trust her judgment in other things? Where was her life headed? She'd worked her way up from a low-level job at an auction house to a position as assistant to one of the executives at Harkness and Crewel. She was the hardest worker on the company's payroll. She knew that if she just stayed the course, she would soon join the ranks of the executives. But though the work was satisfying, she wasn't certain it was something she wanted to do for the rest of her life.

So what did she want?

The answer came instantly. Her own business, where she could call the shots. It would have to do with antiques, she knew. She had become something of an expert, as she'd always been attracted to the old and the odd.

She stifled a yawn. For now she would settle for a satisfying ending to that dream. She struggled to remember everything about it, but the thing that stayed in her mind wasn't just the primitive landscape, or the lush gardens, or even the beauty of the manor house itself. It was that feeling of coming home.

She closed her eyes. If she concentrated hard enough, she might just be able to slip back there and finally meet her dream lover. She hovered on the edge, waiting for sleep to claim her, desperately craving the feeling of peace she'd sensed in her dream.

Something heavy brushed her, and she jerked awake to find that her seatmate had shifted until his head rested beside hers. Before she could shove him away, he moaned and she felt the warmth of his breath on her cheek.

At the sound of his own voice, he sat bolt upright, which only caused him to suck in a breath at the sudden, wrenching pain.

He swore softly and rubbed his aching shoulder. "Sorry. I seem determined to inflict myself on you even when I'm asleep."

"It's all right. I know how hard it is to get comfortable when you're in pain."

"I'm not sure I'd be as understanding if I were in your place. Tell me, have you ever been in this sort of pain?"

"No. But I watched my mother suffer, and saw the way my father was able to ease her pain with nothing more than a little tenderness." She had a sudden thought. "Are you a doctor?"

"Afraid not. Why do you ask?" Despite the drugs, his eyes seemed clearer now. Cool blue, they peered into hers with such intensity that she flushed and looked down at her hands.

"I've heard that doctors who've had to suffer become more tolerant of their patients. It makes you more aware of another person's pain."

His smile was quick and sly as a rogue, and she felt it go straight to her heart. "So you're saying that some good will come out of all this, and all my suffering will actually make me a better person?"

She couldn't help laughing. "I didn't realize I was preaching. But my mother used to say that a certain amount of suffering builds character."

"I'll remember that in the days to come when I'm gritting my teeth and swearing as I try to button my shirt."

That only made Ally laugh harder. "I don't think swearing comes under the heading of building character."

He sat back, studying her with a bemused expression. "You really ought to laugh more often. You go from lovely to beautiful in the blink of an eye."

At his unexpected compliment she could feel a sudden flush stealing over her cheeks.

Seeing that he'd caught her by surprise, he offered his good hand. "We've not been formally introduced. My name is Heath Stewart."

"Allison Kerr." The moment she placed her hand in his, she felt the most amazing rush of heat. It started in her fingertips and shot along her arm before settling deep in her core. "My friends call me Ally."

" 'Allison' is far too lovely a name to ever be reduced to 'Ally.' "

She withdrew her hand, wondering if she'd just imagined that jolt. Still, the tremors continued to shudder along her spine, leaving her feeling oddly off balance.

He merely smiled. "Kerr. You've a bit of Scots blood in you."

"Some. It was my father's dream to visit the home of his ancestors."

"Did he like it?"

"He never made it."

"I'm sorry. And your mother?"

She ducked her head. "They're both gone."

"And now their daughter is fulfilling their dream."

Ally shook her head. "I wish I could. But this trip is strictly business. After a few hours in your country, I'll be on a plane heading home."

"A pity to come all this way and see nothing of the place."

"It is." She sighed and clasped her hands, turning to look out at the darkened sky. "Maybe next time."

Beside her his voice took on a low growl of anger. "I consider those three words to be the cruelest ever spoken."

She glanced over and saw that his eyes had already closed, shutting her out. Perhaps she'd only imagined the edge to his tone. Or perhaps it was a combination of pain and sleep. Whatever the reason, it caused a tiny ripple of unease along her spine.

Maybe next time. How many times had she used that phrase? It ranked right up there with *If only . . .*

Annoyed with the direction of her thoughts, she snapped open her laptop and forced her mind back to her work. But every so often she found herself glancing at the sleeping man beside her and wondering what had set off that sudden flash of emotion. The depth of it seemed at odds with this quick wit and droll humor.

At some other time, in some other place, she might have enjoyed getting to know Heath Stewart better. Unfortunately, right now there just wasn't time for anything more than the business that had brought her here.

3

"DON'T YOU EVER sleep?" Heath blinked against the single overhead light illuminating Ally's head as she bent over her paperwork. "What time is it?"

She checked her watch. "Almost four in the morning in New York." She managed a smile as she adjusted her watch to European time. "You had enough sleep for both of us."

"I hope I didn't snore. I'm told I sound like a foghorn."

She laughed. "Oh. That was you. I thought we'd gone down somewhere over the Atlantic."

He pretended to be horrified as he leaned close to whisper, "Did the other passengers ask you to muzzle me?"

"Well, I was getting some dirty looks from them, and I thought about putting a pillow over your head, but I was afraid you'd fight back and get that shoulder aching again." She set down her notebook with a look of concern. "How are you feeling? Ready for another pain pill?"

Heath nodded his head as he gingerly touched his shoulder. "In a little while. I'd like to keep a clear head for a few minutes." He kneaded his flesh and managed a smile. "Want to join me for some coffee?"

Ally thought about the work she'd hoped to finish during this flight. But a few minutes wouldn't hurt. Almost regretfully, she set her work aside. Minutes later she and Heath were munching pastries and sipping steaming coffee.

"I'm starting to feel human again." Heath stroked the stubble that darkened his chin. "Well, almost human. I can't wait for a hot shower and a shave."

"A nice soft bed sounds good to me. Of course, when I get to my destination, there won't be time for anything except to get down to some serious work if I'm going to make it back to the airport in time for my flight home."

"What is it you do?"

"My firm buys old buildings and resells them."

"Where's the profit in that?"

She shrugged. "There are the furnishings. We work with dealers who have clients eager for collectibles. But it's the antiques that offer the best avenue for serious profit."

"Sounds almost ghoulish."

Her smile faded a bit. "I suppose it is in a way. It's the part I dislike most about my work. It means going into a place that someone once loved and stripping it of everything of value."

"Are you an expert on antiques?"

She nodded. "I used to work at an auction house. I've always been intrigued by them. I love thinking about people who've lived in one place for generations, all using the same articles and feeling so familiar and comfortable with those who came before them." She couldn't help laughing as she added, "Of course, I have nothing against new things as well. Especially new bed linens and new towels." She wrinkled her nose. "Not that it matters what I like. I won't be sleeping on bed linens anyway. I'll be lucky if I get more than a quick glimpse of the rooms."

"You aren't staying over?"

She shook her head. "My job is to make a rather quick judgment on whether or not there are enough valuable art objects and collectibles to make the purchase worthwhile, and if so, to present the firm's offer to purchase. Once the client signs, I'll catalog the items I think we should include in the sale and leave the rest for our legal department to handle."

"Sounds easy enough."

"It couldn't be simpler." Seeing the way he flinched as he lifted the cup to his lips, she set aside her tray. "I think it's time for that pain pill."

This time he didn't argue as she retrieved his bag and handed him a pill. Minutes later he drifted back to sleep.

Ally was in the middle of yet another phone message when the flight attendant began preparing the passengers for landing at London's Heathrow Airport.

A short time later their plane touched down and began its taxi to the terminal. When at last they came to a stop, Heath scrambled to his feet and opened the overhead bin. Ally stepped into the aisle beside him. When their shoulders brushed, she was surprised by the sudden rush of adrenaline that she felt.

With her attaché case in hand she took hold of his scuffed bag. "I'd better give you a hand with this. Otherwise, I'm afraid, you might overdo it and find yourself right back where you started."

The look he gave her was probing. "I'm grateful, Allison Kerr. Do you always take such good care of strangers?"

"Old habits are hard to break." She found herself blushing before she looked away.

He carefully shrugged into his backpack, then held out his hand. "I think I can manage."

"All right." She handed over the duffel and saw him wince with pain. "You may want me to take that duffel off your hands, though."

He reluctantly agreed and followed her along the aisle. Even in his drug-fogged state, he couldn't help admiring the view from this angle as he exited the plane behind her.

There was little time to do more than give him his bag before Ally was swallowed up by the line at Customs. She produced her passport and answered questions while her luggage was inspected. Afterward she made her way toward yet another terminal and the plane that would take her to Edinburgh. It was much less crowded here, and she was glad to see that the passengers were already boarding. She took her seat and glanced idly around, but Heath was nowhere to be seen.

Just as the doors were about to close, he stepped inside. Despite the pain etched in his eyes he managed a slight grin as he took the seat across the aisle.

She wasn't fooled by that smile. "Did you forget to take your pain pill?"

"No time."

"You have time now." Before he could refuse, she was up and handing him his bag.

He arched a brow. "You're beginning to remind me of a certain overbearing nurse in the hospital in Montreal. I think she was the reason I decided to head to New York."

"There are those of us who take our medicine, and those who can find a hundred reasons why they shouldn't."

"I see you've figured out which one I am." After rummaging around, he came up with the pills and swallowed one.

Satisfied, she stowed his bag and took her seat. A short time later she was pleased to see him asleep.

When they landed at Edinburgh, Heath insisted on carrying his own luggage. As Ally stepped outside the terminal, she caught a glimpse of him talking to someone. Just then several people shoved past her, blocking her view. When the crowd cleared, Heath was standing alone beside an ancient car idling at the curb.

He opened the door. "I've snagged a car and driver. Climb in. I'll see you to your destination."

Ally was already shaking her head. "You don't have to do this. It's probably miles out of your way."

"It's the least I can do after all you did for me on the plane."

"Heath. No."

He was already taking the overnight bag from her hand. "I insist."

She gave a sigh. "All right." She allowed herself to be helped into the backseat.

Heath unceremoniously tossed his bags on the floor and climbed in beside her.

The driver turned. "Where to, miss?"

"The name of the place is Hamilton Hall. I'm told it's in the Highlands. Do you know of it?"

As they started away Heath seemed surprised by her destination. "That's not far from my home. I haven't seen that old place in years. It was originally a hunting lodge. It's been in the Hamilton family for eight or nine generations. They turned it into a bed-and-breakfast some years ago, but I've heard that it's become pretty run-down. I'm afraid you're in for a bit of a drive. Why don't you try to rest until we get there?"

"I can sleep on the plane later. Right now I'm too keyed up to even close my eyes." She glanced around at the lovely old buildings of the city as they sped along a narrow street. "I wish I had time to really see your country."

"So do I. Seeing Scotland is like falling in love."

Ally turned her head to study his profile. There had been a different tone to his voice just now. Soft. Seductive.

"You're glad to be home, aren't you?"

"Is it so obvious?" He sighed. "When I left, I was convinced that I really needed to get away. Too many responsibilities. Too little time for my own pleasures. Poor me. I'm sure you know the story. But here I am, just days later, so relieved to be back. Something happened to me in that hospital."

"Well, you said it was a nasty fall."

He shrugged and braced himself as the driver suddenly turned the wheel and started down a narrow lane that led past a country kirk where the ringing of bells filled the air. "It was more than that. I felt as though something monumental was about to happen, and if I didn't get home at once, I'd miss it."

As they sped through a tiny village Ally couldn't help sighing at the row of pretty houses. When they left the village behind and entered a modern highway she picked up the thread of conversation again. "Maybe you're about to win a lottery."

That had him laughing. "In order to do that, I'd have to buy a ticket."

She watched the passing scenery with more than a little interest, wishing they could slow down so she could fill her mind with the lovely images of trees and rocks, and swollen streams tumbling into deep gorges. "You're not interested in gambling?"

"I suppose we're all willing to gamble on some things. In my case, it just isn't on the lottery." He turned to her. "What about you, Allison? What would you gamble on? Love? Or money?"

She took a moment to consider. "Certainly not love."

"Really? Why?"

"You know what they say. Once burned."

"I see. A love affair gone bad?"

She winced. "Something like that. Though it wasn't really love. Just . . . a foolish heart, I guess." Eager to change the subject, she said, "I've never been much of a gambler. I've always liked having everything laid out in logical order."

He quirked an eyebrow. "Don't we all? So, what do you do when life throws you a curve?"

She gave him an impish grin. "I duck. Or curl up in a fetal position and whimper."

He was shaking his head. "I doubt that. We may have only met, but I think I know a thing or two about you already. You don't seem the type to whimper."

"Okay, maybe I don't whine, but I do stomp around and mutter. And kick the furniture. It's not a pretty sight."

Despite his pain he found himself laughing with her as the car turned off the highway to follow a narrow lane for several miles. After passing through another picturesque village, they came to a stop in front of a four-story building of faded gray stone, with a weathered sign that read HAMILTON HALL. Though it was midday, there seemed to be no one about.

When the car rolled to a halt, Heath shoved open the door and stepped out, then offered his hand to Ally.

She ignored the little curl of heat at the touch of his hand. "I really want to thank you, Heath. This was very generous of you."

He glanced at her hand, then up into her eyes. "No more generous than you were."

She saw something flicker in his eyes a moment before he lowered his head. The kiss was the merest brush of mouth to mouth, as soft as a butterfly's wings. But it had them going very still before drawing apart a little too quickly.

His eyes were focused on her with an intensity that made the breath back up in her throat.

"I'll get my bag." Ally was surprised at how difficult it was to speak.

Before she could turn away he touched her shoulder. Again she absorbed the most amazing jolt.

"The driver will see to it." Heath spoke to the driver, then turned to her. "I'll go inside with you."

"There's no need. I'm sure you want to get home."

"In a few minutes. But I haven't been here since I was a lad. I'm curious to see if it's as I remember it."

As they neared the door he sniffed the air. "Odd. Shouldn't the cook be preparing something in the kitchen?" He shot her a conspiratorial grin. "This is an inn, after all. What guests there are may be out and about, but any staff worth their wages should be getting things ready for the patrons' return. Come on." He surprised her by catching her hand. "Are you up for some of Scotland's finest beef and biscuits?"

Ignoring the quick flutter of heat, Ally pressed a hand to her stomach. "You just had to plant that thought in my mind, didn't you? How am I supposed to survive on stale coffee and a granola bar now?"

He paused. "Is that what you usually eat?"

"No." Her grin widened. "It's usually just the stale coffee. The granola bar is a bonus when my schedule isn't quite so hectic."

He was shaking his head as he led her up the steps and through the front entrance. "I can see that you really need someone to take you in hand."

"This from the man who couldn't even cut his own food on the plane."

"That's right." He brought his mouth to her ear so he wouldn't be overheard by the dour old man standing at attention behind the front desk, watching their approach with interest. "But I'm feeling much stronger now. I want you to promise me that you'll insist on the staff feeding you, Ms. Kerr."

She struggled to ignore the little curls of pleasure as his warm breath feathered the hair at her temple. "I believe I can do that."

"Indeed you can. No more stale coffee and sawdust in a paper wrapper. I'm talking about real food." He escorted her to the front desk.

Ally studied the faded name tag pinned to the old man's lapel. "Good afternoon, Duncan. My name is Allison Kerr, with

Harkness and Crewel. I have an appointment with Sir Malcolm Hamilton."

The old man never changed expression, but his blackbird eyes stared holes through her. "Sir Malcolm is expecting you. He asked that I take you to his office. If you'll follow me."

"Would you mind if I come along?" Seeing Ally's look of surprise, Heath was quick to explain. "I met Sir Malcolm when I was just a lad. He was quite kind to me. I'd like to take a moment to say hello before I leave."

When Duncan gave a slight nod of his head, Ally and Heath hurried along behind the old man and were ushered into an office that had seen better days. In fact, Ally thought with regret, everything in this place had seen better days.

When they were alone Ally studied the faded carpet and furnishings, the shabby draperies. "No wonder the Hamilton family has decided to sell. It would take a fortune to restore this poor old hunting lodge to its former beauty."

Heath nodded. "It's far shabbier than I'd remembered it. Still, it manages to exude a certain charm, don't you think?"

"I'm not sure 'charm' is a word I'd use to describe this place. But . . ." She looked around. "There are enough antiques in this room alone to recover the deposit I'm prepared to hand over when Sir Malcolm accepts my company's offer."

She walked closer to examine a family crest hanging above the mantel. "This is three hundred years old, at least."

The glint of crystal caught her eye, and she reached out to touch a many-faceted crystal bowl that had probably been new during the reign of James I. She couldn't help sighing. "Such treasures."

"I see you're as good as your word. You do know your antiques."

Ally nodded. "Such a pity that Sir Malcolm's family will no longer be able to enjoy them."

She and Heath fell silent.

Agitated, Ally perched on the edge of a chair across from the scarred wooden desk, watching the minutes tick by. Finally she got to her feet and walked to the window, where gold-tipped clouds seemed to open up, spilling light across the gardens. Though the winter landscape was as faded as the room in which she was standing, it looked enchanting.

She glanced at her watch. "Where could Sir Malcolm be?"

Heath shrugged. "I'm sure he's just busy with other guests."

"I suppose." She pressed a hand to her stomach. "I know it's afternoon here in Scotland, but my body is still on New York time, and I'm desperate for some coffee."

The thought had her pacing back and forth, from the desk to the window, then back again.

Watching her struggling to contain all that energy, Heath couldn't help grinning. "If you'd like, I'll check at the . . ."

They both looked up to see a tall, distinguished gentleman standing on the threshold.

"Miss Kerr. Malcolm Hamilton. I'm sorry I kept you waiting."

"That's not a problem." She decided she liked his smile. "I hope you don't mind, but I've brought a friend along."

Heath crossed the room. "Heath Stewart. I'm sure you don't remember me. We met when I was just a lad."

"I haven't forgotten. You were fishing on the banks of the loch, and I joined you."

"You did much more than join me. You stayed the day, as I recall, and rowed me across the loch at day's end. Afterward, I spent the summer making a pest of myself, showing up on your doorstep whenever I was feeling alone. I've never forgotten your kindness."

"It was a memorable summer for me as well, Heath. I was feeling lonely and useless until you came along. In fact, I have a photograph that was taken of us that first day." The old man opened a cabinet and removed a small black-and-white photo of a solemn little boy and an unsmiling man holding fishing poles and standing awkwardly beside each other. "Perhaps you'd like to have this as a reminder of that day."

"Thank you. That's very kind of you, Sir Malcolm." Heath tucked it into his pocket and turned to Ally. "I've kept the driver waiting long enough. Thank you for looking out for such an annoying seatmate."

"I didn't mind. Really. Thank you for seeing me to my destination. I've enjoyed meeting you."

"The pleasure was all mine."

Sir Malcolm cleared his throat, and the two of them looked over at him.

"Were you two sharing the same car and driver?"

They nodded.

"Then I'm afraid your plans will be somewhat altered." At their puzzled frowns he explained. "When I was passing through the lobby I noticed the luggage by the door. The car was just leaving."

Heath arched a brow. "You mean the driver left without collecting his fare?"

"So it seems. And rather abruptly. Perhaps there was an emergency."

"Is there another car available to take Heath home?"

The older man turned to her. "I'll try to arrange something, Miss Kerr. But our village is a small one, and we usually have to summon a car and driver from one of the bigger towns." He smiled at Heath. "Perhaps you'd like to use one of our rooms here at Hamilton Hall to refresh yourself."

"Thank you, Sir Malcolm. That's very kind of you." Heath turned toward the door. "I'll leave the two of you to discuss your business."

Ally stared after him. When she realized Sir Malcolm was watching her, she tore her gaze from the doorway.

He smiled and indicated a chair beside his desk. "Please make yourself comfortable, Miss Kerr. Did you have a good trip?"

"It was fine, thank you." Ally settled herself on the edge of the chair. She was already thinking about the drive back to the airport and wishing she had carved out a bit of time to see some of the countryside before heading home.

When Sir Malcolm was seated at his desk, she opened her attaché case and withdrew a sheaf of documents. "As you know, I'm here to make an offer on Hamilton Hall on behalf of my company, Harkness and Crewel. I was told to warn you that the condition of this building will certainly limit the amount we're willing to pay. But I've been authorized to make you a fair price, as long as you agree to include the furnishings, especially any antiques, in my company's offer to purchase. Once you sign this document, our legal department can handle the rest of the details."

"Yes. Well." Instead of accepting the papers from her, he steepled his fingers and regarded her. "I'm afraid something's come up, Miss Kerr."

"Something?" She felt a flash of unease. "I don't understand."

"I'm sorry that you were under the assumption that your company is the only one interested in buying Hamilton Hall. It was never my intention to mislead you. We've had another offer. A good one, I might add, which we intend to study before we make any decisions."

So much for David's insistence that this would be a cookie-cutter deal.

"I see." She glanced at the documents in her hand. "Would you care to look these over?"

"Of course, Miss Kerr." He accepted the papers and set them on his desk without even glancing at them.

She was already pulling her cell phone from her pocket. "You realize that I'll have to call New York with the news, and await instructions. They may ask to know the offer made by their competitor, so that they can match it."

"Indeed." He got to his feet. "In the event that your employer asks you to stay on, may I offer you the hospitality of Hamilton Hall while you're in Scotland, Miss Kerr?"

If the public rooms were this unkempt, she was certain the sleeping quarters would be much sadder. But she couldn't allow her personal feelings to spoil a business deal. Besides, this would give her more time to catalog the contents.

"Thank you. That's very kind of you, Sir Malcolm."

"Not at all." He smiled, and she was reminded of the Cheshire cat. Not so strange, when she considered that she was feeling a bit like Alice in Wonderland. "Perhaps your friend, Heath Stewart, would like to stay overnight as well."

"I'm sure he'll be gone soon. He told me that his home is somewhere nearby."

"I can see that you're not very familiar with our Highlands. The land is forbidding. Not easily traversed. In the event that a car is not easily summoned, I hope you'll let him know that he's welcome to stay here at Hamilton Hall as long as he pleases."

Ally thought about it a moment before saying, "Only if you would be good enough to charge his room to my company." She'd noticed the shabby sweater, the well-worn bags. She flushed and had a sudden need to explain. "After all, he was kind enough to drive me here. I'm not sure he can handle the additional expense of a room. It's the least I can do in return for his kindness."

Sir Malcolm gave a slight bow of his head. "That's most generous of you, Miss Kerr. Of course I'll do as you wish."

When the older man took his leave, Ally flipped her cell phone on and punched in a series of numbers while she tapped her foot in annoyance.

Some days, she thought with a sigh, it just didn't pay to get out of bed.

Still, if she wanted to be brutally honest, the trip hadn't been completely wasted. There was the matter of that kiss. She hadn't experienced a rush like that in a very long time.

Of course, considering her luck with men, maybe it was just as well it had been shared with a man she would never see again after today.

4

ALLY SEARCHED THE rooms of the inn until she stumbled upon Heath in the kitchen. As she stepped into the cavernous space, she looked around in surprise. He'd pushed the sleeves of his sweater above the elbows and was busy stirring something on the stove. "What in the world are you doing?"

"Cooking."

"I can see that. But why?"

"Duncan told me their cook left with the rest of the staff two weeks ago."

"Two weeks ago?"

"Apparently they were no longer able to pay the help, so they closed their doors to guests and sent the employees home. From the looks of Duncan, I think he wishes he'd done the same."

That had Ally chuckling.

"So I decided to take matters into my own hands. Since I'm stuck here until a car and driver arrive, I thought we'd celebrate the conclusion of your deal."

"A bit premature, I'm afraid." Ally studied the room. Despite the clutter of pots and pans, there was a trace of faded elegance. Ornate plaster walls and scarred wooden floors bore the patina of age. Ancient tapestries fluttered from beams high overhead. A table had been set for two in front of a cozy fire.

"What's happened?" Heath walked closer and caught her hand.

At his touch she was forced to absorb the most amazing rush of fire and ice snaking along her spine. Though she thought about removing her hand, she found she didn't want to.

She stared down at their joined hands. "Sir Malcolm told me that my firm isn't the only one interested. He's considering another offer as well. I had to phone my boss with the unhappy news that we aren't home free."

"How did he take it?"

She shrugged. "How do you think? He's not happy, of course. Because it's New Year's Day and he's still at the hospital, scrambling to get all the partners together for a conference call to determine how to proceed. They may counter with more money, or they may step aside. For now, I've been told to stay here until I hear from them."

"Relax, Allison. This isn't the end of the world." Heath's smile grew wider. "Think of it this way. You won't have to get back on a plane tonight. And now you've been given the opportunity to see something of Scotland."

She struggled to ignore the flutter of unsettling feelings deep inside. "I doubt I can see much in what's left of this day."

"You never know." He glanced up as a timer sounded. "Ah, lunch."

When he turned away Ally clasped her hands together, wondering at the effect this man was having on her nerves. Each time he touched her she had to steel herself against giving in to the desire to sigh like a love-struck teen.

With an economy of movement Heath began setting things on a serving cart, which he wheeled up to their table. He then uncovered the silver trays on it to reveal thin slices of cheese and perfectly browned biscuits, as well as a little pot of jam and cups of steaming tea.

She gave him a look of surprise. "You fixed all this?" When

he nodded, Ally gave a shake of her head. "How in the world did you manage?"

He shot her a roguish grin. "Cooking relaxes me."

"Is that what you do for a living?"

"I suppose you think we should all be high-powered wheelers and dealers." He arched a brow. "Do I detect a note of disapproval?"

"Of course not. Especially not right now, when the mere smell of that food is reminding me just how hungry I am."

He held her chair and took a seat across from her, then served both their plates and watched as she bit into a biscuit.

"This is wonderful, Heath. So. Does cooking pay the bills?"

His smile was slow and lazy. "Not exactly. That's why I also have to fill endless ledgers with endless columns of figures."

"An accountant? Now that I can understand. My life is a continuous flow of paperwork." She helped herself to jam.

"So I've noticed. What do you do for relaxation?"

She shrugged. "I'll let you know when it happens." While he refilled his plate she glanced around and lowered her voice. "Where's Duncan?"

"Probably down in the village frightening little children."

She put a hand over her mouth to hide the giggles. "He does look pretty glum." She gave a mock shudder. "Not that I blame him. It probably comes from spending time in this place."

"Oh, I don't know." Heath gave her an easy smile. "I find it rather charming."

"You're joking."

He saw the way she narrowed her gaze on his shabby sweater, the rough stubble of beard that darkened his chin. His grin widened. "You can save your pity, Allison. I realize I look quite at home in this sad little place, but then, I'm not looking my best."

"You look fine." At his smug smile she couldn't help adding, "For a man who took a nasty spill on the slopes and is only now coming out of a drug-induced haze."

"That's more like it. Stick to honesty, Allison. Despite whatever coaching you've been given by your boss, you don't have the knack for lying."

She gave an embarrassed laugh. "David says it's one of my shortcomings."

"It's not a flaw. I find your honesty quite endearing."

Ally tucked into her food with a hunger that surprised her. She looked over at him with new respect. "Have I told you what a good cook you are?"

"Thank you. It's nice to know I haven't lost my touch."

She glanced around the faded old kitchen. "I think I've been a little hard on this place. There's a nice feeling here."

He nodded. "I was thinking the same thing." He gave her a sly wink. "Even if it is deserted, and more than a bit shabby."

They shared a laugh.

When at last they sat back sipping the hot tea, Ally said casually, "By the way, Sir Malcolm offered you a room. I told him to bill it to my company."

Heath's head came up sharply. "You what?"

Seeing his disapproving look, she was quick to add, "I told my boss about your kindness in driving me here, and he agreed that it was only right that you shouldn't have to pick up your expenses. Of course, he's feeling so mellow about the birth of his healthy, beautiful baby girl that he would have agreed to anything right now." She decided to keep to herself the fact that David had told her that the cost of the extra room would come out of her wages.

"There's no need for that, Allison."

"I insist." Now it was Ally's turn to place a hand lightly over his. This time she blamed the rush of heat on the log blazing on the hearth. "It's the least I can do to repay you. After all, if it weren't for me, you'd already be home."

His quick, disarming smile did strange things to her heart. "But it wouldn't be nearly as much fun as spending time at the beautiful, charming Hamilton Hall. At your company's expense."

"You did say you were eager for a shower and shave. It's just what you need to feel fresh before you head home."

He looked down at her hand, resting lightly on his, then up into her eyes. "That efficient businesswoman you show to the world really is a disguise. My first impression of you was right. You're an angel of mercy, aren't you?"

There was that flush again. She hadn't blushed like this in years. But there was just something about the way he looked at her. Or rather through her, in a way that was most disconcerting. "I'm just being practical."

"Of course you are." That rogue's smile of his was growing wider by the minute.

She picked up a spoon and began to tap it nervously on the linen-clad table. "How is your shoulder feeling?"

Heath reached across the table and took the spoon from her hand. When she looked up in surprise he merely took her hand in his and smiled. "I like the way you worry over me, Allison."

"I'm not worrying over you." Seeing the way he was studying her, she flushed. "All right. I suppose I am. A little. After all, you've been on medication and you've gone without sleep. And now you've missed your car and driver. I'd worry about anyone after all that." She withdrew her hand and stared into her tea, then picked up the cup and drained it. When she looked up again she was all business. "This was a wonderful beginning. Now I think that after a shower I might be ready to face what's left of the day." She glanced at the dirty dishes and began rummaging around for a dishtowel. "Since you cooked, I'll clean up."

He winked as he began filling the sink with hot soapy water. "We'll clean up together. I'll wash. You dry."

"You should be resting. You never answered me. How does your shoulder feel?"

He gave a quick roll of his shoulders and smiled. "I feel like a new man. In fact, as soon as I stepped inside Hamilton Hall, I noticed that the pain had faded. Probably because of that last pill I took on the plane."

Half an hour later Ally hung the damp towel to dry and trailed Heath out of the kitchen. They found Duncan at the front desk. He informed them that a car had been located, but it was now on a run to the airport and wouldn't be available for several hours. While Ally picked up their room keys, Heath walked outside and retrieved their bags from the front stoop, where the driver had hastily deposited them before driving off in a rush.

Minutes later they were following Duncan along the hallway toward their rooms.

The old man opened the first door and stood aside. "Sir Malcolm suggested that the gentleman might take this one."

Ally could see why. The room was decidedly masculine, with a massive fireplace along one wall and a huge bed that dominated the center. Off to one side was a wardrobe, and just beyond she could see a tiled bath. Though the furnishings were ancient, and faded to muddy brown, there was a feeling of solid comfort about them.

With nothing more than a glance around, Heath tossed his backpack and duffel on the bed, then followed Ally and Duncan to the room next door.

"Sir Malcolm recommended this one for the lady."

When Duncan stood aside, Ally stepped into the room.

"Oh." The word came out on a sigh.

She'd expected it to be like the one they'd just seen. But this room was completely different, with an airy feminine feel to it. The fireplace was gold-veined white marble, and the canopied bed was covered in faded white satin. The draperies had been drawn to reveal French doors that looked out over a neglected garden. Just outside her door was a marble bench strewn with falling leaves from a gnarled chestnut tree.

Like the other rooms they'd seen in Hamilton Hall, it was old and dusty, and would have been improved by a thorough scrubbing.

"Thank you, Duncan. This is just fine." Ally accepted the keys from his hand before he walked away.

Heath strolled across the room and stood with his hands behind his back. "A pity it isn't summer so you could open the doors and really enjoy the view."

"It doesn't matter. It's a much prettier sight than the one I had from my apartment window in New York just before I left."

Heath thought of the slushy streets and piles of snow that had already turned the color of coal dust. "You're right. New York wasn't a pretty sight. Speaking of which—" He ran a hand over the stubble at his chin. "I must be quite a sight myself. Time for that shower. I wish I had a change of clothes as well, but I had them shipped home."

Ally nodded. "I never thought I'd be here long enough to change."

When he was gone Ally hurried into the bathroom and

looked around in surprise. Like the bedroom, it was done in white and gold, the marble shower and tub piled with faded gold towels bearing the monogram of the Hamilton family. Despite the dust and neglect, it was easy to see what it must once have looked like.

She felt a momentary twinge at the thought of Sir Malcolm allowing this legacy to fall into the hands of strangers. Still, Harkness and Crewel had the resources to restore it to its former glory. That ought to give the old man a measure of comfort in his retirement years.

She put all thoughts of business out of her mind as she stripped off her clothes. But instead of turning on the shower taps as she'd planned, she decided to fill the tub and treat herself to a long, luxurious bath, something she hadn't had time for in weeks.

Heath stepped out of the shower and draped a towel around his hips before reaching for his cell phone. After listening to his voice-mail messages, he tossed the phone aside and crossed the room to stare morosely out the window.

He'd been in the strangest mood since his fall on the slopes. First there'd been that sense of urgency to return to Scotland. And now that he was back on his home turf, the urgency had been replaced with a kind of lethargy. He didn't care if he ever completed the journey to his home.

Why this abrupt change of heart?

The answer came instantly. Allison Kerr. From the moment he'd seen her, he'd felt the most compelling urge to know her better. Not that such a thing should surprise him. She certainly wasn't the first pretty face to snag his interest. But there was something more than a mild flirtation going on here. It had him just a bit concerned. Each time she did something uncommonly kind or sweet, he found himself dealing with feelings that made him extremely uncomfortable.

He sank down on the edge of the bed, deep in thought. He'd always considered himself a practical man. Hadn't it been bred deep into his bones? He winced at the thought. And yet, ever since that drug-induced dream at the hospital, he'd become aware of another side to his nature. One he hadn't thought about, and certainly hadn't acknowledged, in years.

Maybe it was just his body's way of telling him to slow down. After all, he'd been on a treadmill of hard work and even harder play for years now, and he saw no end in sight.

Then again, this might be the result of an overactive imagination. Or a case of simple lust. Allison was certainly different from the kind of woman that usually attracted him. But that kiss had been a revelation. He couldn't recall the last time he'd been so staggered by nothing more than a brush of mouth on mouth.

Such a sweet mouth.

Intrigued, he reached for his clothes and dressed hurriedly. As long as he was here, he may as well see how all this played out. Soon enough he'd have to leave this fantasy behind and return to reality. Until then, he would just relax and enjoy the ride with the fascinating Allison Kerr.

With her hair curling damply around her face from the bath, Ally found herself irresistibly drawn to the garden. Pulling on a warm jacket, she stepped outside and was surprised to find Heath standing in a patch of thin winter sunlight.

"Well." He turned to give her a long, assessing appraisal. "Don't you look fresh."

"I might say the same." She couldn't hide her surprise. "You look . . . different."

"It's the beard." He grinned. "Or I should say the lack of it."

"No. It isn't that." She shook her head, trying to figure out why the sight of him should have caused such a reaction. All hot and cold in the space of a single moment.

Could a shower and shave change a man so completely?

His clothes were the same he'd been wearing since she first saw him. Denims with a tear at the knee, probably from his fall on the slopes. A dark green sweater with traces of blood at the shoulder. But now, instead of looking pale and pained, he seemed energized.

He had a wide brow, across which a lock of dark hair tumbled, causing him to sweep it aside with the back of his hand. His eyes were a deep, dark blue, the color of the sky at midnight. His nose was perfectly chiseled, his mouth gently curved with a smile. Though not handsome in the classic sense, he had a distinct air of authority about him that hadn't been evident when she'd first met him. He seemed to be a man completely comfortable in his own skin. But then, she argued, why not? He was back in his own country.

"How does your shoulder feel?"

He idly rubbed it. "Odd. Not even a twinge. Why don't we take a stroll around the hills?"

Ally couldn't hide her surprise. "I thought you'd be eager to get home."

"So did I. But now that I'm here, I want to show you some of the sights. If the car arrives, the driver can wait. Do you have time?"

"I have nothing but time right now." She touched the pocket of her slacks. "I have my cell phone, so I won't miss any calls from the firm."

"What did we do without our modern conveniences? I left my number with Duncan, so he can phone me the minute the car and driver arrive." He placed a hand beneath her elbow and walked with her along an overgrown path in the garden. When they came to a rusty gate he opened it and waited for her to step through, then closed it behind them and fell into step beside her.

"Just beyond this hill is a lovely clear loch that has always been one of my favorites."

"Why?" She turned to him with a smile.

"I suppose because I sensed a kindness in Sir Malcolm that I didn't find in most adults. The first time he found me fishing in his loch, instead of sending me away, he joined me."

"Why do you call it his loch?"

"It sits on his family's property. That makes it his."

Ally made a mental note to convey this information to her boss. It just might justify an increase in their offer, if such a thing were needed.

"Didn't you have any other adults who would take you fishing?"

He shook his head. "My mother was . . . gone. And my father had no time for such activities." He fell silent a moment before saying, "Sir Malcolm told me stories about a fire-breathing creature that guarded the loch. As big as a ship it was, with a long snakelike tail and claws that could snag a man with but a single swipe of its mighty foreleg." He paused. "Odd. I haven't thought about that in years."

Ally couldn't help laughing at the seriousness of his tone. "How did such legends spring up? Your land seems to have more than its share."

"That's true." Heath shrugged. "Perhaps because we're such a fanciful people. We love our monsters and mysterious creatures. Our spells and enchantments. And there've been just enough reports of them throughout the ages to keep the stories alive for centuries."

She swiveled her head to study him. "Don't tell me you believe them."

"All right, I won't tell you." He caught her hand, easily linking his fingers with hers. "But I'm afraid it's so. All true Scotsmen believe."

There it was again. That strange reaction to his touch. He'd done nothing more than take her hand, but her head was swimming as though she'd been caught in some passionate embrace. She decided that a lecture to herself was in order. Had she learned nothing from the episode with Tedious Ted? Still, she didn't see the harm in a little flirting. "I think you're just having fun with me, Heath."

"You could be right." He stared down at their joined hands. "Is it working?"

"I'll let you know."

"Fair enough. Look." As they crested a ridge he pointed to the lake far below, where sunlight was burning off the last of the mist that danced in little clouds just above the water. "Sir Malcolm had a name for those tufts of fog. He called them fairy smoke."

"Oh." She went very still. "It's beautiful."

"You should see it in summer, with the heather growing along the ridge." His tone softened. "And in the spring, when the sheep are turned out to pasture and cover the hillsides, eager for tender young grass. And in the fall, when the rains come and the streams overflow their banks and roar down from the Highlands as they rush to join the river."

For a moment she could see it. All of it, just as he'd described.

She turned to him with a teasing smile. "Are you sure you aren't employed by the government to entice tourists to come here?"

"Is it that bad?"

"Worse. You should hear your voice, Heath, when you speak about this place. You could be describing heaven."

He gave her a slow, assessing look that had her heart leaping to her throat. "Maybe I am." Without warning he cupped a hand to the back of her head and drew her close. "Speaking of heaven, I've been wanting to do this again."

The kiss wasn't nearly as tentative this time. As soon as his mouth covered hers she had to reach out and clutch at his waist for fear of falling. There hadn't been time to prepare herself for the quick, jittery jolt to her system. Her pulse was throbbing at her temples. She took in a shaky breath. Had the earth tilted just a bit? She waited until the sky stopped revolving ever so slowly.

He rested his hands lightly on her shoulders as he lifted his head and stared down into her eyes. "I'm not sure even heaven could compare with that."

Seeing the surprise in her eyes, he caught her hand and continued toward the lake.

Though Ally managed to keep up with his long strides, her breath was coming hard and fast, as though she'd been running for miles. In her whole life, she'd never known a simple kiss to affect her like this. She wasn't at all certain she liked these feelings. Especially coming on the heels of the scene with Ted.

Time to slow down, she cautioned herself, and remember that she was here on business, not pleasure. She had to admit though, that kissing Heath Stewart had just given the word "pleasure" a whole new meaning.

5

"LOOKING FOR MONSTERS?"

Heath's words brought Ally out of her reverie as she stood beside him on the banks of the lake. "Just enjoying the peace of this place. It seems odd to hear no traffic sounds."

He nodded. "It's one of the things I miss most about my home in Scotland whenever I leave."

"It would be hard to leave something this beautiful. Why would you ever want to leave?"

He shrugged. "Sometimes the very isolation of this place gets to me. I think I'll be better off surrounded by people." His tone lowered. Hardened. "But then, when I'm with them, I realize it isn't what I wanted at all. Maybe we're all fooled into thinking we'll find happiness somewhere else, when it's actually right in front of our noses all along."

That made Ally smile. "My father used to say that. We traveled a lot, and he used to tell me that we carry home in our hearts. I'm afraid that wasn't exactly what a thirteen-year-old girl wanted to hear when she was about to start yet another year in another new school filled with strangers."

Before Heath could ask more about her childhood, she pointed to some tumbled stones on a distant hill above them. "What are those?"

"Remnants of an ancient keep."

"A castle?" She couldn't hide her excitement. "Can we go there?"

"If you'd like." He took her hand in his as they climbed to a high meadow and made their way toward the ruins.

Ally paused to run her fingers over the stones, made smooth by the forces of nature. "Think how long these have stood guard here."

"They're said to be from the eleventh century."

"And still they stand." That drew a sigh from her lips. "Don't you ever wonder about the people who built this fortress? How they lived? How they died?"

"I have indeed. As a lad I often came here and I swore I heard their voices." He realized he'd never before admitted this to anyone since growing to adulthood.

"What did they say?"

He shrugged, sensing at once that he could trust her with something this intimate. "They talked about their lives. About the joy of living, the sorrow of dying in battle. Still others spoke in an ancient tongue that I couldn't understand. When I told my father, he said it was just the wind sighing through the rocks. But Sir Malcolm told me that he'd heard them too, when he was just a lad. He warned me that the voices would stop when I grew to manhood."

"Why?"

"Because, he said, men lose the ability to converse with the spirits. Only the pure, untarnished heart of a child can do so."

"Maybe you should try to engage them now, to prove him wrong."

Heath shook his head. "I'm afraid I would only prove him right." His tone changed, deepened with feeling. "This heart was tarnished a long time ago."

At a sudden gust of chill wind Heath caught her hand and led her away from the ruins. "Our winters may not produce the snow that you get in New York, but you can't deny that the wind carries the same bite." He tucked her hand in the crook of his arm and drew her close. "I've an idea that'll warm us both."

"Where are we going?"

He merely smiled. "You'll see."

They slipped into a forest of towering evergreens, sheltered from the wind, and followed an overgrown path. Huddled deep in the woods was a tiny cottage, its walls nearly obscured by a tangle of vines. Heath gave a push on the door, and led her inside out of the wind.

She glanced around in surprise. "What is this place?"

"Just a deserted cottage." He closed the door and crossed the room to rub away the dirt and cobwebs that coated the many-paned little window. "When I was a wee lad there was an old woman who'd taken up residence here. She could do anything. Mend a bird's broken wing. Coax a deer to take food from her hand. In my innocence I thought of her as a witch, and I always called this the witch's cottage."

"Did she know what you thought of her?"

He nodded. "She seemed to find it amusing."

"Did she ever talk to you?"

"Oh, yes. Looking back, I realize she enjoyed my company and was absolutely delighted by my questions." He turned and leaned against the windowsill. "Funny, I haven't thought about her in years. She was a tiny woman, no bigger than a child. She had long silver hair that fell in wild tangles. I'm sure she never bothered to comb it. And yet this little cottage was neat as a pin. She would invite me in for tea and scones. And we'd talk and talk. She never seemed annoyed by my endless questions the way other adults were. She answered everything, no matter how trivial it may have seemed to her. And she took the time to walk with me through the forest and show me the plants that could heal, and the ones that could nourish, and those to avoid because they might cause harm."

Ally glanced around, loving the feeling of peace in this place. "What happened to her?"

Heath shook his head. "I was tramping through these woods one spring after my stay at university and found the cottage abandoned. When I inquired, I learned that she had passed away the previous winter. It turned out she didn't live here all year, but only in the summer months. In the winter she lived at Hamilton Hall. She was Sir Malcolm's mother."

"His mother? Don't you think that odd that she would live way out here by herself?"

"Not at all. This was part of their family land, and it was a place that called to her. It had been her grandmother's cottage."

"How did you come to spend so much time here? Did you grow up nearby?"

He shrugged. "Not so far."

Ally sensed that he was uneasy talking about his home. Was he ashamed of it? He'd admitted to being a sad little boy. Was his sadness due to neglect or poverty? Or was it something deeper?

He shoved away from the sill. "You must be getting cold. Would you like to go back to Hamilton Hall?"

"Not particularly."

As they stepped back into the woods he nodded toward the cell phone in her pocket. "No word from New York?"

She shook her head. "I know what they say about no news. But in this case it seems ominous. I'd be willing to bet the partners have everyone scrambling to find out just who's bidding against them and how high they have to go to close the deal without paying more than absolutely necessary." She paused a beat before saying almost apologetically, "I reported the fact that there are no guests. I hope that won't be a strike against Sir Malcolm."

"Be careful." Heath chuckled. "I may start to believe you're rooting for Hamilton Hall to win out over your company."

"Not at all. I think it would be a nice addition to our holdings. But it pains me to think that all those beautiful antiques that have been in the Hamilton family for generations will fall into the hands of strangers."

"There is that," Heath agreed. "But how else can Hamilton Hall be saved? I doubt there are many willing to provide an infusion of money on something that may never show a return on their investment."

Ally arched a brow. "Are you sure you're not an investor? Just now you sounded exactly like my boss."

He kept her hand in his as they continued walking. "Tell me about him. Is he also your mentor?"

"I suppose he is. David taught me everything I know about the business. When I first started working for him, he made it clear that I couldn't afford to have any personal feelings for a client. Our goal is to buy the client's property for the best price we can negotiate. Sentiment will only get in the way." She lowered her voice, as though revealing a dangerous secret. "I know what our competitors call us. Instead of Harkness and Crewel, they refer to us as Heartless and Cruel."

If she expected him to laugh, she was surprised to see him studying her closely. "Tell me." Heath paused a moment as she took out her cell phone and punched in a series of numbers. "Just how good a pupil do you think you've become?"

"Good enough to be trusted with this assignment. And I intend to prove it."

"Even if it means living up to the title of Heartless and Cruel?"

She flinched. "Maybe I won't go that far. But I intend to purchase Hamilton Hall for my company. It will be another notch on my belt and get me another step up that ladder to corporate executive."

She listened to a voice on the phone, then disconnected with a sigh.

"Now what?"

She shrugged. "Nobody is answering the phones. I keep getting their voice mail. It's so frustrating to be kept in the dark like this. I feel like I've been dropped down a well and everything is going on somewhere high above."

He couldn't help chuckling. "Who knows? Maybe you're the lucky one. While they're scrambling, you can just relax and let it all happen."

"I'm not much good at sitting idly by and doing nothing."

"Who says you'll be idle?" He caught her hand. "Come on. I know just the thing to take your mind off work. I say it's time to play before this day gets away from us."

"But what about your car? What happens if your driver refuses to wait until you return to Hamilton Hall?"

"Then he'll just have to come back for me in the morning."

She stopped to stare at him. "You're planning to stay the night?"

"Maybe I am." He realized that though he hadn't given it any thought, he wasn't surprised by his decision. At the moment, wild horses couldn't drag him away from this intriguing woman.

As he started forward she held back. "Where are we going?"

Heath pointed. "I spotted a boat. Come on."

When they reached the banks of the loch he helped her inside the small rowboat bearing the name of Hamilton Hall. "This is the same one Sir Malcolm used all those years ago. They keep this for their guests."

The minute Ally was seated he shoved away from shore, then jumped in and picked up the oars.

"Where are we headed?"

He gave a pull on the oars, and the little boat headed into the breeze. "To the other side, of course."

"But why?"

"Because it's there."

There was that smile again, grabbing her heart and squeezing until she couldn't help but return it with one of her own.

At her little peal of laughter he paused in his rowing. "What's so funny?"

"You. Us." She laughed again, the sound as clear as a bell on the silent air. "Whatever are we doing in a boat on a lake in the dead of winter?"

"Can you think of a better place to be than here?"

She watched the play of muscles in his upper arms as he leaned into the oars, then dragged her attention back to his question. "It's odd, but I can't think of anywhere else I'd rather be."

"You see? Neither can I. So sit back and enjoy the ride, Allison Kerr. This day is for your father, who never got to see the home of his heart."

She ducked her head and pretended to study the water, in order to hide the quick rush of tears that threatened. How could he possibly know what his words meant to her? They were quite simply the sweetest thing she'd ever heard. And yet it had taken this man, practically a stranger, to remind her that she could choose to see as much of her father's country as possible before returning to the harsh reality of her life and her career.

"Maybe, if you're very blessed, you'll see the creature that's said to inhabit this loch."

At Heath's words Ally studied the water. For a few minutes she couldn't see anything but rolling waves. But as her eyes adjusted, she caught sight of something murky moving ever so slowly just beyond the boat.

"Heath, I see it." Her tone was breathless as she strained to see more. "Look." She pointed to where his left oar hovered and grabbed his arm. "Stop rowing or you'll frighten it away."

He lifted the oars, and the little boat drifted. They watched in silence as the shadowy figure hovered just below the surface, as though watching them, then disappeared from view.

Heath wondered at the magic of the moment. Was it seeing the creature? Or was it the touch of her hand on his arm? In his mind, one seemed as monumental as the other.

He closed his hand over hers. "You should feel very good about yourself. It isn't every visitor to our land that gets to glimpse, up close and personal, our resident monster of the loch."

She shook her head, for the moment too awed to speak. When she found her voice she managed to say, "Of course, I don't really believe in monsters. It was a fish. Or an eel." She looked to him for confirmation.

He merely smiled. "A very large fish or eel, since it could have toppled our boat with one swish of that tail."

She'd already thought of that, and had felt a quick moment of panic. "Have you ever seen it before, Heath?"

She thought his smile faded a bit. "Not since I was a lad. Though I've looked for it often enough through the years. It would seem you have those magical qualities that cause the beast to trust you."

He released her hand and took up the oars again.

As they rowed toward shore, they both fell silent, lost in private thoughts.

It occurred to Ally that the day had suddenly taken on a whole new air of excitement.

In a single day she was in a new country, seeing things she'd only read about in travel magazines. Best of all, she was experiencing it all with a man who, though a bit mysterious, was proving to be a charming companion.

It didn't hurt, she thought in a moment of honesty, that he was easy on the eye and had the ability to rock her world with nothing more than a simple kiss.

Simple?

She found herself laughing aloud, then ducking her head to hide her emotions.

There was nothing simple about the man or his kiss. And to be completely honest, she wanted desperately to kiss him again.

6

"CAREFUL." HEATH BEACHED the boat and held out his hand, helping Ally to shore.

Together they scrambled up the banks of the loch and paused to look around.

She lifted a hand to shield her eyes from the sun. "It looks so different from this side of the lake."

He nodded. "Odd, isn't it? I've always thought they seemed like two different worlds."

At the thoughtful, almost sad tone of his voice she turned to study him, but he was already focused on something in the distance.

"Come on." He beckoned. "I know the perfect spot to show you a bit more of your heritage."

"You mean my father's heritage."

"That makes it yours, too, Allison."

At his words she went still, considering. The smile was slow in coming, but when it did, it reached her eyes, lighting them with the most amazing fire. "It's true. I'd never thought of it like that before. This land is my heritage, isn't it?"

He found himself mesmerized by the way she looked, her cheeks pink from the chill breeze, her eyes dancing with unconcealed delight. "It's time you and Scotland got acquainted. Who knows? Maybe it could be your future."

"My future is with Harkness and Crewel."

"Oh, yes." He grinned. "I forgot for a moment how driven you are."

She slapped his arm playfully. "Well, don't you forget it again."

They hiked across a meadow where cattle grazed. The cows took no notice of them as they threaded their way through the herd. By the time they'd climbed higher, the air had gentled and the sun was warm enough that they shed their jackets.

"Tired?" Heath turned to catch her hand in his.

"You're talking to a city girl, remember?" She struggled to ignore the quick skitter along her spine, but it was impossible to deny the attraction any longer. She decided to simply relax and enjoy it. After all, she hadn't sworn off liking men. She just had no intention of losing her heart to one. Older and wiser, thanks to Tedious Ted. That was her new mantra. "I'm used to walking miles in the dead of winter when I can't catch a cab."

"Then another kilometer shouldn't make much difference to you."

She laughed, effortlessly keeping up with his loose, easy strides. "It might, if I were wearing high heels and slogging through ice and snow." She scrambled beside him over a low fence of tumbled stones and continued walking across a meadow of faded heather. "But here in the Highlands, with these proper sturdy shoes, it's a walk in the park."

"Speaking of parks—" He paused to watch her reaction as they reached the highest point in their climb. "I thought this might impress you."

Ally stared around in amazement. It appeared to be a child's playground, set in the middle of a high, deserted field. "What is this?"

"Exactly what it appears to be. A park. And a child's playground."

"But who could ever find it, let alone enjoy it, way out here in the middle of nowhere?"

"We found it, didn't we? That must mean it isn't completely isolated."

She laughed. "Only because you knew where to look." She studied him more closely. "How did you know about this?"

He gave a negligent shrug of his shoulders. "Would you believe me if I said it was just a lucky guess?"

"Not a chance. You knew exactly where you were taking me."

He cleared his throat. "It was built by a father to assuage his guilt about having no time for fatherhood, to amuse a lonely little boy who was being raised by a series of indifferent nannies."

"How sad." Ally looked around. "I wonder if it brought the little boy any pleasure."

"What little boy wouldn't adore his own private paradise?"

At the note of sarcasm in his tone Ally glanced at him in surprise. So much anger there.

And then the truth dawned. "You were that little boy?"

When he said nothing she decided not to pursue it further. She turned away and started running. Over her shoulder she called, "Come on. I'll race you."

Heath started after her. She reached a swing hanging from a tall wooden crossbar, just steps ahead of him. When she sat down, he caught the rope and gave it a shove, sending her soaring. Within minutes she was pumping her legs and swinging as high as the top of the bar.

Heath leaned against the brace, crossing his arms over his chest to watch her. She was such a delight. As carefree as any child, sailing back and forth, her hair streaming out behind her, her voice trilling with laughter.

"Come on, Heath. Jump on the other swing and we'll race."

He couldn't resist the challenge. Before long they were both sailing high, feeling the bite of the winter air on their faces.

"Look at us, Heath!" Ally glanced over at him with a laugh of pure delight. "We're flying."

"So we are. Where are your wings?"

"I keep them hidden under my jacket."

That had him chuckling.

When he slowed down and stepped away, Ally gave another delighted laugh. "Afraid of the competition, are you?"

"I much prefer the view from here." He was grinning up at her.

Holding on by one hand, she lifted the other toward him. "If I jump, will you catch me?"

"I can't believe you even feel the need to ask."

Without a thought to what she was doing she let go of the rope. "Here I come."

Giddy with laughter, she sailed through the air and felt strong arms wrap around her, keeping her feet just off the ground. She was held so close she could feel the strong, steady beat of his heart inside her own chest.

"You did it!" With a joyful shout she lifted her face to his. "You caught me."

She saw his eyes narrow slightly as he regarded her. Against her mouth he muttered, "I told you I would. I couldn't bear to ever let you fall, Allison."

This time his kiss wasn't like the others. His lips moved over hers with a possessiveness that had the blood roaring in her temples. This was all heat and fire and a wild rush of needs that had her clinging as he took the kiss deeper, then deeper still. On a sigh she wrapped her arms around his neck and offered him more.

He took, feasting on her mouth until they were both breathless. When he lifted his head she nearly moaned in distress. He lowered her ever so slowly until her feet touched the ground and pressed his lips to the soft curve of her neck.

Against her throat he muttered, "Oh, Allison. What am I to do about you?"

She pushed away a little, forcing air into her parched lungs. "You're going to have to stop doing what you're doing before I lose my last thread of common sense."

"Promise?" He ran nibbling kisses from her throat to her chin, until his mouth hovered just above hers. "Are you saying that if I kiss you senseless I can have my way with you?"

"When you kiss me like that, you muddle my brain. Now just hold on to me for a minute while I wait for the world to settle."

He framed her face with his hands and stared down into her eyes. "It's nice to know I wasn't the only one to feel the earth move just now."

At that she laughed. "I think kissing you is definitely dangerous." She looked over his shoulder toward the child's merry-go-round. "Come on. I see another way to get dizzy."

"Maybe. But it won't be half as much fun as the way I just did it."

"You have a very inflated opinion of yourself, Heath Stewart."

Laughing, they crossed the play area hand in hand. When Ally climbed aboard, Heath began pushing. After a series of creaking protests, the merry-go-round began turning easily. When it was spinning, he jumped aboard and and grinned at the expression of pure joy on Ally's face.

"Oh, this is wonderful." Ally shrieked with laughter. "I haven't been on one of these since grade school."

When it started to slow, Heath stepped off and spun it again. This time he leaped on beside Ally and wrapped his arms around her, pressing his lips to a tangle of hair at her temple. They remained that way, locked in an embrace, while the chill wind whistled past them, and the gentle motion of the merry-go-round soothed.

When it came to a stop Heath tilted her chin up, forcing her to meet his eyes. "Now tell me the truth. Are you as dizzy as when we kissed?"

"Absolutely."

He kissed the tip of her nose. "I warned you once before, Allison. You're a terrible liar." He glanced up at the sun, which was quickly fading behind the peaks of the mountains. "I think it's time we get back to Hamilton Hall before we both turn into icicles."

"I wish we could stay here always and play."

"Do you?" He went very still as he stared down into her eyes. "I believe you mean it."

"I do. I can't think of anything sweeter than having our very own playground."

He dropped his arm around her shoulders. As they made their way back to the banks of the loch, it seemed the most natural thing in the world for Ally to put an arm around his waist and match her steps to his.

They felt good together, she realized. They felt . . . right.

She quickly dismissed such foolishness. Had she learned nothing from her recent disaster?

As Heath settled her in the boat he leaned close to press a kiss to her temple. "Cold?"

"No." It was true, she realized. Despite the chilled air, all she could feel was the warmth that still lingered from his touch.

"We'll be seated in front of a cozy fire in no time." He leaned into the oars, and the boat skimmed the surface of the loch.

Ally couldn't tear her gaze from the muscles of his arms. She wanted those arms around her. Wanted desperately to feel his mouth on hers again.

When they reached the far shore Heath beached the boat, then helped her out. Instead of turning away he drew her into the circle of his arms and held her close against him.

Her mouth skimmed his cheek as she lifted her head. "Were you reading my mind again?"

"Hmmm?" He turned slightly and their lips met.

"I was just wishing you would do this."

"Your wish is my command." He spoke the words against her mouth, then inside as her lips parted.

"Ah." There was the sound of someone clearing his throat. "Here you are."

At Duncan's raspy voice, they stepped apart like guilty children and stared in surprise.

The old man was holding a flashlight. "Sir Malcolm sent me to find you. He was worried that something might have happened to you."

"We're . . . fine." Ally could feel herself blushing at his scrutiny, and she was grateful when he lowered the flashlight and turned away.

Heath shot her a roguish grin as he asked, "Has the car come for me, Duncan?"

"I'm afraid not." The old man picked his way carefully through the darkness and led the way to the inn. "Sir Malcolm said it appears you'll have to wait until morning."

In the darkness Ally could see the curve of Heath's lips. "You don't seem too upset about the news."

"Not at all." He caught her hand, and together they followed the old man. "In fact," he whispered against her cheek, "I'm looking forward to it."

When they stepped through the back door into the kitchen, they were delighted to find a cozy fire on the hearth.

"What's this?" Heath glanced at the table set for two.

"Sir Malcolm thought the two of you might enjoy a quiet supper. He arranged for a meal to be sent up from the village."

"How thoughtful of him." Ally hurried across the room and was surprised and pleased to see a snowy linen cloth, fine china and crystal, and even candles gleaming in an ornate silver container. "Please thank Sir Malcolm. Will he be joining us?"

"I'm afraid not."

Ally clasped her hands together. "I was hoping to speak with him. I really need to report something back to my firm."

"Perhaps in the morning." The old man gave a slight nod of his head, then walked away.

When they were alone Heath opened the ancient oven and breathed deeply. "Something smells wonderful." Using an oven mitt he lifted the lid of a roasting pan. "Roast goose with stuffing, in honor of the New Year." His smile grew. "And tiny roasted potatoes and little pearl onions." He looked over at Ally. "What's your choice? Shower first, and then feast? Or are you too hungry to wait?"

She couldn't help laughing as she patted her middle. Business was quickly forgotten. "That wonderful aroma just reminded me how hungry I am. But I crave a hot shower even more."

"All right." Heath replaced the lid and closed the oven. "Let's get to it."

He caught her hand and they hurried from the room.

When they stopped outside her door he gave her a quick, dangerous smile. "We could save time if we showered together. Not to mention soap and hot water."

"Hmmm." She pretended to consider it as she opened her door. When he started to follow her inside she laughingly closed the door in his face. "Sorry. Did I mention that I shower alone?"

"Spoilsport." She heard his laughter as he continued on to his room next door.

Within minutes she had stripped and was under the warm spray. Afterward she dressed and ran a brush through the tangles of her hair before stepping into the hallway. At the same moment Heath's door opened. He shot her an admiring glance as he walked toward her.

"That was fast." He caught her hand. "Afraid I'd beat you to dinner?"

"Not a chance. I had my ear to the door." She felt the quick flutter of nerves at his simple touch, and had to take several breaths to calm her racing pulse.

"Such a lovely ear." He leaned close and brushed a tickling kiss to her lobe, sending another rush of heat along her spine. As he led her toward the kitchen, he lifted her hand to his mouth. "I hate to say this, but I'm glad Sir Malcolm isn't joining us for supper. I much prefer having you all to myself."

"All right. As long as it's truth time, I have to admit that I feel the same way." Though Ally had been cautioning herself to play it cool, she found it so easy to be open and honest with Heath. There was just something about him that invited her trust.

In the kitchen they worked in companionable silence. While Heath opened the oven and removed the roasting pan, Ally lifted a bottle of wine from a crystal ice bucket.

She studied the label, admiring the vintage. "It looks like our host has thought of everything."

"So it seems." Heath arranged their food on a platter, then unwrapped the linen nestled in a silver basket to reveal fresh rolls.

Ally handed him a crystal goblet of pale amber wine.

He touched the rim of the glass to hers. "It's been a memorable day, Allison. Here's to an equally memorable night."

Though he spoke the words lightly, she couldn't help shivering at the look in his eyes. Without a word she sipped, then set the goblet on the table.

Heath held her chair, and his hand lingered a moment at her shoulder before he took the seat across from her. He served her plate, and then his own.

After one taste her smile grew. "Oh, this is wonderful."

He tasted and nodded his agreement. "I couldn't have done better myself."

"Are you telling me you could make a meal this delicious?"

"You don't believe me?" He touched a hand to his heart. "I'm wounded."

She was laughing as she bent to her food. In truth, she'd never tasted anything this grand. The vegetables were done to perfection. Even the rolls were so fresh, they tasted as though they'd just come out of the oven. And the wine. One sip and it went straight to her head.

Or was it this man?

He was looking at her over the rim of his glass as though she were dessert. The thought had her grinning wildly.

"What's so funny?"

"Just a thought."

"Care to share it?"

She shook her head, sending red curls tumbling.

He reached across the table and caught a strand, allowing it to sift through his fingers while he studied her with a look so intense that she felt the heat rush to her cheeks again.

"Care to share what you're thinking?"

"Why don't I show you?" He stood and rounded the table, caught her hand and helped her to her feet. He lifted both her hands to his lips, kissing first one, then the other, then looked into her eyes. "You have to know what I want, Allison. More than food, more than wine. I want you as I've never wanted anything in this world."

He drew her close and nuzzled her temple, breathing her in. And then his mouth moved over her eyes, her cheek, the tip of her nose, and hovered just above her lips. "Tell me you want this too."

She was a sensible woman. Hadn't she always been ruled by her head instead of her heart? It was the one thing that had given her such pride. And yet, at this moment she couldn't think of a single thing except the need to feel his mouth on hers. She craved it as desperately as her lungs craved air.

Wrapping her arms around his neck, she lifted her face to his. "Kiss me, Heath. Right now."

His eyes were grave, as was his tone. "If I do, I won't be able to stop."

In a voice that she hardly recognized as her own, she whispered, "I won't ask you to stop."

7

THIS WAS WHAT she'd been craving. She could feel the heat, the strength, the barely controlled passion in Heath's kiss. Even though her first instinct was to step back from it, she found she couldn't. For, in truth, that same heat, those same emotions, had taken over her reason. She felt her body go fluid at his first touch.

Without any thought to the consequences, she leaned into him, letting the passion take her. It seemed so right to be here, with this man. In his arms. Though she knew almost nothing about him, she felt no fear. Only this terrible need. A need that had her returning his kisses with a desperation that caught her by surprise. This was madness. They'd known each other only a few hours. But if it was madness, at least she wasn't alone in it. She could feel the way his heart thundered, with such fury it seemed to be beating inside her own chest. Could feel the warmth of his breath as his mouth burned a path of fiery kisses down her throat. It thrilled her to know that he was as staggered by these feelings as she was.

"Heath." Needing to slow things down, she put a hand on his chest. "We ought to think about what we're doing."

"Too late." His mouth curved into that dangerous rogue smile she'd learned to love, then lowered to hers, drawing out the kiss until she had to wrap her arms around his waist or risk falling.

She could feel her blood roaring in her temples. Could feel her bones begin to melt as he changed the angle of the kiss and took it deeper.

She opened herself to him, wanting to give more. And he fed, like a man starved for the taste of her. The need between them excited her even as it frightened her.

While he explored the wonders of her mouth, she drank him in. Here was a man of secrets, dark and mysterious. And she was determined to learn all of them. Who he was, and why he'd stayed here with her instead of returning to his home. But for now she would put aside her curiosity, and any lingering fear, for she tasted goodness in him as well. Though he kept much to himself, she knew without a doubt that he would never hurt her.

When he tugged her sweater over her head, her mind emptied of everything except the knowledge that she wanted him. Desperately. It was her last coherent thought.

Heath ran a finger along the bit of lace covering her breasts, until, annoyed with even that thin barrier, he nearly tore it in his haste. The sight of all that smooth skin, as pale as milk, held him enthralled. For a moment all he could do was stare.

"So bonny, Allison." His burr deepened, until she thought for one brief moment that she was hearing a voice from another time, another place. "You're so perfect." It was Heath's voice again, softer, with the tones of his homeland less evident.

He leaned forward to run his tongue down the sleek column of her throat.

A little sigh escaped her lips. She could do no more than arch her neck and cling to him as he trailed soft, feathery kisses along her throat to her collarbone. When he dipped his mouth lower to capture one erect nipple, she felt her knees buckle.

Without a word he lifted her in his arms and strode down the hallway toward their rooms. Because his was closer, he stopped and nudged the door open with his hip.

The room smelled of woodsmoke. Someone had prepared a fire on the hearth. The bed linens had been turned down, in anticipation of the night, and candles flickered in crystal hurricanes set on night tables on either side of the bed. A lovely old tapestry rug before the hearth, faded and worn, glowed with the reflected light of the fire.

Heath kicked the door shut and headed toward the bed, with his precious treasure still in his arms. Because he couldn't wait a moment longer to taste her lips, he paused to kiss her. He realized at once that it was a mistake. The blaze of heat nearly consumed them both. He set her on her feet and covered her mouth with his, while his hands, those strong, clever hands, moved down her back to her waist, where his fingers worked at the fastener of her slacks.

Impatience had her tugging on his sweater, tossing it aside, then skimming her hands across his chest.

"You're beautiful, too, Heath. So bonny." The unfamiliar word flowed easily from her mouth. He was, she realized, a feast for her eyes. His body was sculpted, the muscles taut.

At last she was free to run her fingertips over the ripple of muscles that before she'd only glimpsed. The thundering beat of his heart added to her excitement, and she boldly trailed her fingers across the flat planes of his stomach before reaching for the snaps at his waist.

With one quick tug his clothes joined hers on the floor at their feet. They came together in a kiss that spoke of hunger, of need, of wild desperation. All of the things that had occupied her attention for so many years no longer mattered. Not the company in New York, not the important deal that had brought her here. Certainly not the man who had betrayed her with her friend, or the pain they'd inflicted on her heart. At this moment she couldn't even recall their names. All that mattered was this man, and the pleasure she found in his touch.

"Allison. My sweet, bonny Allison." He whispered her name like a prayer.

No man had ever touched her like this before. One moment as gently as if she were a fragile flower. The next with all the fury of a firestorm, creating a need so desperate it had her pulse pounding and her breath burning her lungs. Now all she could do was hang on as, with hands and mouth, he took her for the wildest ride of her life.

Though the bed was mere steps away, it may as well have been miles. Neither of them was willing to slow the passion that was sweeping them along in its tide. Too weak to stand, they dropped to their knees.

He found her, hot and moist, and drove her to the first breathless peak while she clung to him, dazed and breathless. Before she could recover her senses he lay down and drew her into his arms.

The thought of taking her, hard and fast, had him trembling with need. He was desperate for the release that only she could give him. But he wanted so much more. Calling on all his willpower, he slowed the pace, hoping to draw out the pleasure as long as possible.

He kissed her, long and slow and deep, while his hands moved over her, exploring, arousing. And all the while he watched her in the flickering firelight, loving the way she looked, her eyes focused on his, her lips parted as she struggled for each ragged breath.

With lips and fingertips he teased her breasts until she moaned in pleasure and opened her arms, inviting him to join with her. But still he held back, wanting to take her and himself to the very edge of madness.

He loved the way she looked, her body damp with sheen, her eyes heavy-lidded with passion.

"Heath." His name was a hoarse whisper, torn from her lips as she shuddered once more with pleasure.

They came together in a kiss that nearly shattered both their hearts. A kiss that spoke of a driving, desperate hunger.

Heath knew he could wait no longer. The need had become a wild and raging beast inside him, taking over his will.

He entered her with a fierceness that startled him. But when he tried to slow the pace, she surprised him by wrapping herself around him, urging him to move with her, matching her strength to his as they began to climb.

"Allison." He hadn't expected this explosion of need between them. It caught him by surprise as he framed her face with his hands and found himself drowning in her eyes. Eyes that were wide and focused on him with an intensity that touched a chord deep in his heart.

Their breathing was shallow as they continued to climb higher and higher to the very pinnacle. For a heartbeat they seemed to tremble and pause, pierced by the most exquisite jolt of pleasure. They stared into each other's eyes with matching looks of wonderment. Then together they stepped over the edge. And shattered into a shower of stars.

"Are you all right?" Heath lifted his face from her neck to brush a finger over her cheek. Just the slightest touch, but she moved against it like a kitten.

"Ummm." It was all she could manage.

They lay, still joined, cushioned only by the rug.

"I didn't mean to be so rough." He muttered an oath. "I took you like a savage on the floor." He started to pull away, but she stopped him.

"We took each other, as I recall." Now it was her turn to touch a hand to his cheek.

His quick grin went straight to her heart. "We did, didn't we?"

"Ummm." Again that purr of pleasure.

"A woman of many words, I see."

That had them both laughing.

He shifted, rolling to one side and drawing her into the circle of his arms. "You're amazing, you know." He traced the outline of her lips with his fingertip.

She bit it lightly. "You're not half bad yourself, Heath Stewart."

He brushed his lips over hers. "I was inspired by the dazzling woman in my arms."

She pulled away a little to look into his eyes. "Are you hoping to flatter me?"

"Is it working?"

"Maybe just a little."

His smile grew. "Good. Sorry about the floor."

"Well, next time we might want to try the bed."

He tipped up her chin. "So, you're saying you wouldn't object to a next time?"

She met his look with just a hint of a grin. "I think I could be persuaded."

"Maybe this will help." He ran his hand along her side until his thumb encountered the swell of her breast, sending the most amazing jolts through her system. As he caressed her, he covered her mouth with his in a kiss that had the breath backing up in her throat.

"Oh, yes." When he lifted his head she wrapped her arms around his neck and drew him back for another. Against his lips she whispered, "I could definitely be persuaded."

"Ah, Allison. You're so sweet. So generous. So . . ."

At the unexpected rush of heat they came together in a kiss so hot, so searing, they wondered that the floor beneath them didn't begin to smolder.

Once again the bed was forgotten as, with soft sighs and moans of pleasure, they were carried away by the storm raging between them.

Heath's voice was muffled against her throat. "Tell me more about your childhood."

Sometime during the night they'd finally made it to the bed, where they'd fallen into an exhausted sleep. Now, with the only light coming from the gleaming coals on the hearth, they lay together, talking softly, as comfortable as old lovers.

Ally had told him about Ted's betrayal with her friend, and realized that it no longer mattered to her in the least.

"I want to know everything about you. What you were like as a girl. Where you lived. How you spent your time."

"I told you. I was an Army brat. We lived in half a dozen different countries, and all over the U.S."

He lifted his head to study her. "I know you moved a lot. But did you like it?"

"I didn't dislike it. That was just our life." There was a long moment of silence before she added, "I tried to like it for the sake of my parents. Every time I started to make friends in my neighborhood, or in my new school, it was time to move on. And because my mother was sick a lot, I didn't want to burden her with my problems. But every time the order came to move on, I dreaded it."

"Was your father any help?"

"He tried. But the Army was his life. What energy he had left was saved for my mother. With her, he was patient and gentle."

"That's nice to hear. It explains why you're so patient and gentle."

"Am I?" She seemed genuinely surprised.

"I suppose you think you're one tough cookie." Heath played with a strand of her hair. Before she could object he touched a finger to her lips. "So you kept it all inside and dealt with moving on the best way you could."

At her little nod he smiled. "Maybe that's what all kids do. Make the best of their lives, and try not to burden those they love."

"Is that what you did?"

"I wasn't as successful at keeping my unhappiness a secret as you."

"Why were you unhappy, Heath?"

When he offered no words she turned to him, studying the gleam of firelight in his eyes. "It's time for the truth, Heath. You've ducked and dodged and very cleverly changed the subject whenever I got too close to it. I've trusted you with my truths. Now you have to trust me with yours."

After several long moments of silence he nodded. "That's only fair."

Deep in thought, he stood and crossed to the window, keeping his face averted. "My mother walked out of my life when I was five. I never saw her again."

For a moment Ally was speechless. She'd thought his problems, like hers, were with a former lover. "How awful. What about your father?"

He gave a dry laugh. "My father couldn't handle being dumped. To prove something to himself, and to her, I suppose, he chased so many women, it became something of a joke. Let's see. There was a faded French actress. An over-the-hill London model. The wife of a well-known politician. The only time I saw my father was on the front page of the tabloids."

Hearing the pain in his voice, Ally slipped out of bed and hurried across the room to take his hands in hers. "I wish I could change what happened to you, but I can't. But there is something you can do."

Heath stared at their joined hands. "What's that?"

"You can forgive your father and mother."

When he opened his mouth to protest, she touched a finger to his lips to silence him. "I know it isn't easy to forgive something so deep, so painful. But it's necessary if your poor heart is ever going to heal." She looked up at him. "My father once told me something I've never forgotten. He said that most of us do the best we can with what we have." Ally lifted his hands to her lips and kissed each palm. Closing them, she pressed them to her heart. "I know this can't ease your childhood pain, but whenever you need a kiss, Heath, here is mine, ready to soothe you."

At the sweetness of the gesture he drew her close and pressed his lips to her temple. "I've never known anyone like you, Allison. You're the sweetest, most generous woman I've ever met. I think you truly are an angel. It's funny. I've seen the terrible things love can do to people. But it wasn't until now, until you, that I realized it can also do wonderful things. I believe that somehow in this place we're being touched by magic."

She pushed a little away. "Heath—"

He stopped her protest with his lips on hers. "You realize that something special is happening here, don't you?"

"I don't know what to think." She rested her hand on his chest and found the strong, steady beat of his heart oddly comforting. "You know I don't really believe in such things as monsters in the lake, or magic spells."

When he offered no argument she gave a long, satisfied sigh. One of them had to be sensible. "That's better. I have no doubt that very soon now Sir Malcolm will come to a decision. Whether my firm buys Hamilton Hall or he sells to our competitor, I'll be on a plane back to New York within the next day or two, and this wonderful idyll will be over."

For a moment he merely looked at her. Then the smile returned to his eyes, and his voice roughened with passion. "Then we'd better put whatever time we have left to the best possible use."

He gathered her close and ran hot, wet kisses along the column of her throat, while his hands moved over her, starting fires wherever they touched.

Everything that had happened before was forgotten as they tumbled into a world of breathless sighs and whispered secrets. A world of unbridled passion and the most exquisite pleasure Ally had ever experienced.

8

ALLY WAS CAUGHT in the dream. Spectacular scenery was rushing past the windows of her car. Once again she felt that thrill of anticipation, as though she knew exactly where she was headed.

Something heavy closed over her shoulders, pressing her to the mattress. She awoke with a start and struggled to sort out where she was.

It came to her in an instant. Hamilton Hall. In Heath's room. Heath's bed. In his sleep, he'd dropped an arm possessively around her shoulders, drawing her close.

She lay very still, watching him as he slept. A lock of dark hair had fallen over his forehead, and she thought about brushing it aside, but she didn't want to wake him. Not just yet.

He'd been the most amazing lover. With him she'd found passion, excitement, laughter. She smiled. Especially laughter. Just being with him made her happy. He was so easy to be with. With Heath she felt cherished. Special. As though she was a birthday gift and he was a little boy who couldn't wait to unwrap her.

That thought had her smiling. Allison Kerr unwrapped. Or maybe unplugged. Ever since stepping off that plane, she'd been behaving like a different person.

She was a smart, sensible woman. She'd survived the loss of her parents and endured, on a daily basis, the trials and tribulations of making a living in one of the toughest cities in the world. So she was wise enough to realize that Heath Stewart was far from the lover of her dreams. He was, by his own admission, a sometimes cook and accountant who, despite the fun they'd had together, needed to get back to his home and his job. Furthermore, Hamilton Hall could never be mistaken for a luxurious castle. But these few precious hours with him had been the most memorable time of her life. And though she knew it would soon end, she would have no regrets. In fact, she would spend the rest of her life remembering this as a very special, magical time.

"Uh-oh. Looks serious. Having regrets?"

At those whispered words she looked up to find Heath watching her, and wondered how long he'd been awake. "Of course not." She brushed aside the lock of hair from his forehead. "I was just thinking about how much fun we've had together."

"It has been grand, hasn't it? I've been thinking about what you said to me about forgiving my parents." He shook his head. "I don't know why it never occurred to me. But I think it's time I let go of the past and get on with my life."

"I'm glad."

When she started to pull away, he tipped up her chin and smiled. "You're always in such a hurry. Where are you thinking of going now?"

"I thought I'd slip out to the kitchen and see about making some coffee."

"Why don't you leave that for the cook?"

"Because he's become lazy. The last time I checked, he was lying in his bed looking extremely satisfied."

"The word is 'sated.' And I ought to be, after the night we shared. But the truth is"—he drew her close for a long, lingering kiss—"I've been thinking I'd like to try again."

"You're a glutton, Heath Stewart." She shivered as his hands moved over her. The moment he touched her, she could feel her body respond to him in a way it never had before.

"Only where you're concerned." In one quick move he rolled, pinning her beneath him. With his mouth to her throat he murmured, "We could just stay here and make mad, passionate love." He moved his mouth lower, causing her to clutch the sheets beneath her. "Or I could just forget about it and make you coffee."

Her words came out in a long, deep sigh. "Don't you dare."

"Hmm. Seems we're of the same mind on this."

They came together in a searing kiss. And then everything else was forgotten as they lost themselves in the exquisite pleasure that only lovers know.

An hour later Ally sat up and stared in dismay at the sunlight peeking through a gap in the draperies.

"Your coffee." Heath paused beside the bed and handed Ally a steaming cup from a seventeenth-century antique tea trolley.

She practically inhaled the liquid, draining the cup in several long swallows before setting it aside. "Oh, thank you. I needed that." She eyed the covered dishes. Eighteenth-century French. Hammered silver. There was a time when she would have given anything just to touch such a dish. Now she was more intrigued by the man holding it. "Something smells wonderful."

"Just a bit of eggs and cheese and thin slices of roast goose to tide us over until I can make something more substantial."

"More substantial?" That had her laughing. "At home I'd call that breakfast, lunch, and dinner."

"I can see that you need someone to see to your needs." He sat down on the edge of the bed and touched her cheek. His voice lowered. "I'm applying for the job."

"Really? Just what are your qualifications?"

His smile was quick and dangerous. "I believe you've already seen my résumé. And had a chance to . . . sample my skills."

She managed a straight face. "You are extraordinarily skilled, Mr. Stewart. I suppose I could consider your application. You realize, of course, there may be others interested in the position."

"None of them count."

"That's true. At least not anymore."

"I'm glad. I want to be the only one who matters to you, Allison." He nibbled her lips until they warmed and softened under his. He kept the kiss gentle as his hands moved over her, skimming lightly until she sighed from the pure pleasure of it.

Now they had all the time in the world to taste, to touch, to explore. And as they fed each other's hunger, they found a new depth of passion. As sharp and compelling as though it was their first time, even while they felt somehow as though they'd been together their whole lives.

"Did you see Sir Malcolm?" Heath looked up when Ally stepped into the kitchen.

She breathed in the most wonderful fragrance coming from the oven. "He's nowhere to be found. I checked his office, the hallways, the front lobby. Not a sign of him. And Duncan's missing as well. What do you make of it?"

Heath couldn't help grinning. "I'd say they really know how to give their guests what they want. Are you complaining?"

She shook her head. "That's just it. I'm grateful for every hour I get to spend here. But this just doesn't make any sense. It's morning. Sir Malcolm has to know that there are people anxiously awaiting his decision."

"Maybe he enjoys the drama."

Ally shrugged. "If that's the case, he's having himself a grand old time." She glanced at the handwritten list of antiques that she'd faxed to prospective customers. "At least my time walking through the rooms wasn't in vain."

"Always thinking of business, aren't you?"

"One of us has to." She looked down at her wrinkled slacks. "I'm thinking about walking down to the village for a change of clothes. Want to come?"

He nodded toward the oven. "I don't think I'd better trust this ancient equipment to keep running while I'm away. Why don't you go along? By the time you get back, I'll have a fine big breakfast ready."

"You're spoiling me." She walked close and brushed a kiss onto his cheek. "What more could a girl ask for than that?"

Before she could turn away he drew her back and kissed her until she sighed and wrapped her arms around his neck. "I'd say she should ask for much more." His words were muffled against her mouth. "And after we eat, I'd be only too happy to oblige."

Though her heart was stuttering, she managed to step back. "My work has never been this much fun. I intend to hold you to that."

As she walked along the lane that led to the village, her smile was as brilliant as the sunshine. The day was as much of a surprise as this entire trip was proving to be. Though it was winter, the air had gentled, and the rain that had washed the cobbled streets overnight had now blown away, leaving the entire countryside looking fresh and new.

The buildings in the village looked to be as old as Hamilton Hall, but the walkways in front of each shop had been swept scrupulously clean. A glimpse in the windows showed that they offered a wonderful array of goods, from fresh scones at a tiny bakery to gorgeous handmade woolen goods.

Ally stepped into a clothing shop and was greeted warmly by the owner. When she left an hour later she was wearing new slacks and a beautiful hooded sweater in soft heather tones. In her hands were several shopping bags bulging with more purchases. A lovely hand-embroidered pink blanket for David and Tara's new baby girl. A bright scarf for her friend Iris. She'd even picked up a crocheted mouse for Mactavish.

She hurried along the lane, eager to get back to Hamilton Hall, her thoughts centered on Heath. Now that she'd heard of his childhood, she understood the sadness that she'd sensed in him. Losing a mother to death was far different from losing one to abandonment. That was beyond her comprehension. It broke her heart to think of that lonely boy raised by a succession of nannies while his father sought diversions from his own pain.

No wonder he'd kept his secrets to himself. She wondered if there were other secrets he was keeping as well.

He was a charming companion and an inspired lover. Yet he was willing to remain at this run-down inn in the middle of nowhere. Was he hiding from something? From someone?

What foolishness. She struggled to push aside the thought. Still, the closer she got to Hamilton Hall, the more her doubts grew. She quickened her pace. The moment she stepped through the door, all her fears scattered and were forgotten. She nearly ran in her haste to reach the kitchen.

Heath was just lifting a roasting pan from the oven. He looked up with that heart-stopping smile that never failed to stir her emotions.

"New clothes." He gave her an admiring look that had the blood rushing to her cheeks. "I hope it hasn't changed the woman wearing them."

She did a quick twirl. "Same old me. See?"

"You look grand." He drew her close. "The walk has added a bloom to your cheeks."

"And here I thought you did that."

He laughed. "Thank you. I'd like to think I helped."

She set the bags on the floor and rummaged through them. When she stood, she was holding something out to him. "I bought you this. I hope it fits."

He was looking at her with a bemused expression. "You bought me a sweater?"

"Oh, don't worry. I didn't put it on the company's bill. I paid for it myself."

"You . . ." His smile grew. "You paid for it yourself? Why?"

"Because I wanted to." She was studying him closely. "I hope you're not offended. It's not a big deal."

"But it is." He tore his old sweater aside and shrugged into the one she offered. "It's a very big deal, Allison. Nobody ever bought me clothes." He smoothed it down. "How do I look?"

"Wonderful." And he did, she realized. The charcoal wool was the perfect choice to set off his dark hair and rugged good looks.

Something flickered in his eyes. Something she couldn't quite fathom.

Suddenly embarrassed, she stooped to pick up her packages. "I'll just put these away before we eat."

"No need." He took them from her and dropped an arm around her shoulders.

She paused and arched a brow. "Where are you going?"

"With you." His lips nuzzled her ear, causing a rush of heat that nearly staggered her. "Breakfast will stay warm while I thank you properly for my gift."

"There's no need . . ."

"Oh, but there is. It will be my pleasure, my love."

My love.

She shivered at the passion in his tone and hugged the endearment to her heart, even while she reminded herself that she was in way over her head. Her intention had been to simply enjoy herself. Losing her heart hadn't been part of the plan.

9

"Now to see about breakfast." Heath drew Ally close and wrapped her in a snug embrace.

She breathed him in and closed her eyes, loving the feel of his strong arms around her. "It's bound to be cold."

"That's all right." He mumbled the words against a tangle of hair at her temple. "At least there was a very good reason for it. Where are you going to begin your search for Sir Malcolm?"

She shrugged. "I'll be able to think more clearly after a hot shower."

He flashed her that killer smile and held out his hand, and she slid out of bed. "Great idea. I'll join you."

"If you do, we'll just end up back in bed."

"That's not the worst thing in the world, is it?"

She was laughing. "Not at all. But at this rate we'll never get anything done."

He turned on the taps and steam began rolling around the bathroom. "Of course," he deadpanned, "if we're sidetracked along the way, I won't take all the blame."

"An hour-long shower. I think that's one for the record books."

"Um-hmm." Heath hauled her close for a quick kiss. "Is that a complaint, Miss Kerr, or a compliment?"

They were both laughing when they stepped apart.

Heath lifted Ally's hand to his lips. "Go find Sir Malcolm and finish your business while I see about heating our breakfast."

A short time later he looked up as Ally hurried into the kitchen looking grim. "What's wrong?"

"I still haven't found Sir Malcolm. There's no trace of him."

"What did your office say?"

"It's too early to reach anybody at the office, and I'm reluctant to phone David on his cell. With a new baby, he probably isn't getting much sleep anyway."

"So you've bought a few more hours." He gathered her close. "As soon as we're finished, I'm sure we can find something to occupy our time."

Ally couldn't help laughing. "There's that gleam I've come to recognize."

"Why not? Every hour is a gift, and I'm . . ." His head came up as he caught sight of a young woman in the garden, a bouquet of flowers in her hand.

"Company." Heath pointed. "Maybe she'll be able to tell you where to find Sir Malcolm."

He caught Ally's hand and led her out the door. As they approached, the young woman greeted them with a smile.

"Hello." Heath stuck out his hand. "I'm Heath Stewart, and this is Allison Kerr."

"I'm Beth Campbell." The young woman returned their handshakes. "There was talk of a stranger shopping in the village. Where are you staying?"

Ally gave her a smile. "We've been staying here at Hamilton Hall."

"Really?" The young woman studied her with a puzzled frown. "How in the world did you arrange that?"

"My company made the arrangements. They're interested in buying it."

"I see." Beth's smile faded. "There were some in the village who were afraid this might happen."

"Afraid? Why?"

"Sir Malcolm has been the lifeblood of our village. He realized that the few visitors who came here simply weren't enough to keep our shopkeepers in business. For years he has quietly gone about helping those who couldn't pay their bills, even though it meant a terrible drain on his own finances. If it weren't for him, there would be no way for any of us to remain here. Our poor village would have been deserted for the lure of the bigger cities."

Ally eyed her suspiciously. "Did Sir Malcolm send you here to tell me this so my company would fatten its offer?"

Now it was Beth's turn to stare. "What in the world are you talking about? Surely you know there's no way Sir Malcolm could do anything of the kind, Miss Kerr."

"And why is that?"

"If your company sent you here, they must have told you why Hamilton Hall is being offered for sale." She paused to swallow, and tears filled her eyes. "When Sir Malcolm died, he left no heirs."

"Died?" Ally went rigid with shock and struggled to shake off the chill that ran down her spine. "What are you talking about?"

"Sir Malcolm died two weeks ago, Miss Kerr. Isn't that why you're here?"

"But that can't be so. Sir Malcolm met with me right after I arrived."

Beth's tone was incredulous. "Are you saying you've been here more than two weeks now?"

"I arrived yesterday."

Beth gave Ally the sort of smile she might give an addled child. "I don't know who you thought you were meeting, but it couldn't have been Sir Malcolm. It must have been one of his solicitors."

"I know the man I met. He introduced himself when he entered his office." Ally turned to Heath. "You saw him as well."

Heath nodded. "I did."

Ally arched a brow. "Is he the man you knew as a child?"

"He certainly is." Heath held up a hand. "And don't forget Duncan."

"Duncan?" Beth's eyes widened. "Duncan was Sir Malcolm's trusted manager for more than thirty years. I suppose that would be easy enough to learn if you questioned anyone in the village. After the funeral of his old friend, his poor heart simply stopped."

At their sudden silence, Beth studied the two of them, then turned away. "I see you need convincing. If you'll follow me, I'll take you to Sir Malcolm's grave. I was just on my way there with flowers."

Ally was vaguely aware of Heath's hand holding hers as they made their way across the garden and stopped before a small fenced enclosure that held several Hamilton family headstones.

Beth opened the gate and led the way, pausing to kneel and place her bouquet of flowers before stepping back. "Sir Malcolm's grave is the fresh one. He shares a grave marker with his parents, since he never married."

Heath laid a hand on the young woman's arm. "Why did Sir Malcolm never marry?"

At his obvious agitation Beth stepped back with a look of alarm. At once he removed his hand and held it stiffly at his side.

"There were whispers of a broken heart when he was young. Something about a young woman who wanted more than the quiet life a genteel innkeeper could offer. I'm not certain of the details, but he never got over it when she married a titled Highlander. Now if you'll excuse me, I'm needed back in the village."

As the young woman hurried away, Ally and Heath stared at the mound of earth and read with disbelief the freshly inscribed name and date on the marble slab.

Ally turned terrified eyes to Heath. "How can this be? What could anyone hope to gain by playing such a cruel trick?"

Heath took both of her hands in his. They were cold as ice. She was trembling, and he could see the battle she was waging with herself.

Though his own heart was none too steady, he kept his voice soft and measured. "I'm the wrong person to ask, Allison. I've already admitted to believing in monsters and spirits and magic when I was a lad. It wouldn't be much of a stretch for me to believe that Sir Malcolm had something so important to share with us that he refused to let death stop him."

She was shaking her head in denial. "Don't do this, Heath. Don't try to trick me with some nonsense about Sir Malcolm coming back from the grave. Why? What would be the point?"

"I guess that's up to us to figure out."

But she was already backing away. "It had to be one of his lawyers, hoping to force our firm to offer more. Well, it isn't going to work. I'm going inside right now to call David and have our legal department take charge of this mess."

Pulling her hands free, she made her way firmly through the garden without once looking back.

Heath remained where he was, locked in his own private thoughts as he studied the grave marker through narrowed eyes.

Later he walked along the silent halls and stepped into Sir Malcolm's office. Ally was standing beside the big desk, a document in her hand.

When she caught sight of Heath she turned on him with a look of fury. "You said it was up to us to understand. Now, finally, it's beginning to make sense to me."

"Good." He was puzzled by her apparent anger. "I hope you'll enlighten me."

"This was all a game, wasn't it, Heath?"

"A game? I'm afraid I don't—"

She held up a hand to stop him. "I thought I knew every dirty trick in the book, but this is a new one. Why didn't you just tell me you wanted Hamilton Hall for yourself, instead of pretending to be interested in me?"

"Allison, you're not making any sense."

She shook her head. "No more lies. I can't take any more. You could have waited until my company made its final bid, and then you could have bid higher. That's what reputable companies do to get what they want. But you saw how vulnerable I was, and you just couldn't resist taking advantage of the situation, could you, Heath? All that nonsense about your mother leaving you, and about a sad, lonely little boy with no one to love him. You knew exactly which buttons to push, didn't you?" She closed her eyes against the pain.

"Do you think so little of me that you believe I could reveal all the secrets of my heart just to . . . buy a run-down inn?" His smile was gone, his tone incredulous. "You can't really believe this was all some sort of act."

"Can't I?" She thrust the document into his hands. "Then maybe you can explain why your name is on this offer to purchase Hamilton Hall."

Heath could do nothing more than stare in stunned surprise as he read the words of the purchase offer.

Ally confronted him, hands on her hips. "Is that your signature?"

He nodded.

"Was it forged?"

He studied the last line. "It appears to be mine, but I swear to you, I never signed this paper. I never saw it before in my life."

"So you're denying that you want Hamilton Hall?"

"Until this moment, I had no desire to own it. But now I'm not so certain."

Her tone rang with sarcasm. "And what brought about this sudden monumental change of heart?"

"I'm not sure. Maybe it was hearing that Sir Malcolm was keeping an entire village afloat at the expense of his own inheritance. It's so like him. I think about the man who neglected his own work to ease a lonely lad's pain. He took me fishing. He walked with me around the ancient ruins and encouraged me to listen to the voices that spoke to me of their history. I sensed that we shared something deeper than our mutual unhappiness. We were soul mates who found solace in one another."

"And you think you can somehow repay his kindness by buying his inn? Why?"

"It was something Beth told us at the gravesite. She said that Sir Malcolm never married, because the woman he loved married someone else. I went to his private rooms and found this." He held out a framed photograph of a very young Sir Malcolm and a beautiful dark-haired woman who bore an uncanny resemblance to Heath.

As the realization dawned, Ally could only stare. "You think he was in love with your mother?"

"It makes perfect sense. She had no conscience about leaving a man she loved because he was a humble innkeeper, or leaving a man she didn't love, even though it meant leaving behind her own son. Like a storm she blew in and out of lives, leaving a path of destruction in her wake, without so much as a twinge of regret."

"And now you're willing to do the same. Will you have even a hint of regret at betraying me?"

"I never betrayed you, Allison. On that I give you my solemn word. If your company still desires to buy Hamilton Hall, I'll destroy this document, and no one need ever see it."

"Sorry, I don't believe you. I was a fool to ever believe you, Heath Stewart. Blame it on a moment of weakness by this foolish, tender heart."

Before he could offer a protest, Ally turned and fled.

Long after the sound of her footsteps receded, Heath remained in Sir Malcolm's office, studying the photo of the man who had been kinder than his own father, standing arm in arm with the woman who had later broken his young heart and left him unwilling to trust for a lifetime.

How ironic that now, when he'd found a woman he could trust, she was convinced that he had been the one to betray her.

Ally was still trembling as she set her overnight bag near the front door and stood waiting for the arrival of the car and driver. After phoning New York and learning from David Harkness that their company had withdrawn its offer to purchase Hamilton Hall, she'd booked the next available flight home.

Sensing someone behind her, she turned, expecting to see Heath, and braced herself for another ugly scene. Instead, she sucked in a breath at the sight of Sir Malcolm.

Seeing the way she shrank from him, he held out a hand to stop her from bolting. "Forgive me, my dear. It was never my intention to frighten you."

"Who are you? And why are you doing this?"

"I am who I've always been. Malcolm Hamilton."

"Beth, the girl from the village, showed me your grave."

He gave a slight nod of his head. "My body rests there, alongside my ancestors. But my spirit cannot rest yet."

"Why?"

"I saw that lonely lad who'd been so coldly betrayed, and I felt responsible for what had happened to him."

"You? Weren't you also betrayed?"

"I was. But, I reasoned, if my pain was so great, how much worse must his have been? He was just a wee lad, deserted by the one who ought to love him more than anything in this world. What was worse, his father deserted him in pursuit of his own pleasures."

For the first time Ally could see the great kindness in those gray eyes, and she was reminded of the things he'd done for the villagers. "If you wanted Heath to have Hamilton Hall, why did you bring me into this?"

"Because I saw your pain, as well, and was moved by it."

"I don't understand."

"You were betrayed, just as Heath had been. As I had been. I could see the goodness in your heart. All you wanted was a man who would love you more than himself. All Heath has ever wanted was a woman who would love him just for himself." He gave her a gentle smile. "Don't you see? This is about much more than determining who will care for my ancestral home. It's about two lonely hearts. The two of you are perfectly suited." He looked up. "Ah, here's the car now." He took her hand between both of his. His touch was light as air, and so cold she felt it clear to her soul. "He has just come from taking Heath to his home. If you but ask, the driver will take you there, as well. His home is called Cluny Court, just around the loch and deep in the Highlands."

She shook her head. "I'm sorry, Sir Malcolm, but this is all too . . . overwhelming. I need to get back to New York." Back to reality, she thought, though she didn't say it aloud.

"Think about what you're doing, my dear. You could be throwing away your best chance for happiness."

Ally backed away, breaking contact. "Good-bye, Sir Malcolm."

She nearly ran in her haste to escape. Opening the car door, she tossed her bag on the floor, then sank back against the faded leather and closed her eyes, feeling such a wave of sadness that she could barely hold back the tears.

Pressing a hand to her temple, she called out to the driver, "Take me to the airport, please."

10

ALLY COULD BARELY stand the pain. It hurt so much to realize that she had once again put her trust in a man who had betrayed her.

Of course, Heath had denied the betrayal. As had Sir Malcolm. But then, he wasn't real. None of this was.

There was no logical accounting for what had just transpired, in the space of a day. Certainly she'd been working too hard lately. That, combined with the shock of Ted's betrayal, had caused some sort of mental breakdown.

As for Heath, maybe he was a figment of her imagination as well. That would explain why he'd been so relaxed, so attentive to her every need. He certainly hadn't been like any man she'd ever known. But if she'd only imagined him, why had it all ended so badly?

Her pain turned to anger. Oh, he was real, all right. A real jerk, just like all the others. He'd been playful and charming, had amused himself with her, and now, with their little playtime over, he'd managed to sneak in a bid on her property.

When would she learn?

Sir Malcolm, or the ghost of her imagination, had certainly talked a good game. He'd been most convincing, especially when he'd talked about the sad, lonely lad he'd befriended.

She tried to imagine Heath standing alone on the banks of the loch, looking toward the inn and the village across the way. How had he described it? Like another world. She supposed that to a boy who'd lost everything that mattered most in his life, that would be true.

The car moved slowly through the village, then out onto a modern highway. Before long Ally could see traffic, people, shops, and knew that they were leaving the Highlands behind.

So much for her grand tour of Scotland. So much for seeing her father's legacy.

Because it hurt too much, she swallowed and muttered defiantly, "Maybe next time."

The moment the words were out of her mouth she could see in her mind the darkness that had come into Heath's eyes. Could hear the anger in his tone as he'd said gruffly, "I consider those three words to be the cruelest ever spoken."

Had the frightened little boy heard his mother hurl those words at his father? Had he begged his father to stay with him, only to hear those words? How many times had he whispered a prayer in the night, only to have a distracted nanny speak those words?

Not her business, she reminded herself. Heath Stewart's childhood pain had nothing to do with her. And if he suffered a twinge of guilt now, it served him right.

I never betrayed you, Allison. On that I give you my solemn word. If your company still desires to buy Hamilton Hall, I'll destroy this document, and no one need ever see it.

With Heath's words washing over her, Ally called out sharply, "Driver, I've changed my mind. I want to return to the Highlands. To a place called Cluny Court. I believe you know of it?"

The car rolled to a halt, then turned around and started back the way they'd just come.

Ally glanced toward the driver. All she could see were his eyes, watching her in the rearview mirror. Cat's eyes, she thought with a tiny shiver. His salt-and-pepper hair curled in tufts around a rosy-cheeked face that could have belonged to a gnome.

Sweet heaven, she thought, closing her eyes against a wave of pure terror. She had completely lost it. Now she was hallucinating. Just what did it take for her to learn her lesson? With a little moan of despair she buried her face in her hands, knowing that she had finally completely lost her senses.

Or had she?

She opened her eyes to see the most amazing scenery moving past her line of vision. High, craggy mountain peaks hovering over mist-shrouded glens, and streams rushing over rugged boulders to spill into a lake far below.

"Is this the way to Cluny Court?"

The driver made no response. He simply turned the car off the road and headed along a narrow, curving ribbon of driveway.

When they came up over a rise, they were in a verdant meadow. Ahead was a manor house that resembled a castle, set amid the rolling hills. On either side of the road leading to it was a series of formal gardens, with statuary and fountains. They drove past a crystal-clear pond where two white swans glided in circles, looking too perfect to be real.

When they came to a stop, the driver hurried around to open her door.

Ally couldn't move. She was paralyzed with fear. She pressed the heels of her hands to her eyes, knowing she had finally crossed a line. Somehow fantasy and reality had merged so completely that she could no longer tell one from the other. She was lost in some sort of crazy dream.

The driver gave her a little cat smile as he gently pried her hands loose and helped her from the car.

On trembling legs she started up the massive granite steps. The front door opened, and she feared her poor heart would simply stop. It no longer mattered if she'd lost her mind. There was such a feeling of peace here. A sense that after a lifetime of traveling the world she was coming home.

With a nervous laugh she quickened her pace, her heart pounding at the certain knowledge that she would soon see the face of her dream lover. "Oh, my darling, I—"

Heath stood in the doorway, the sleeves of a crisp white shirt rolled to his elbows. "I was afraid you wouldn't come."

"I tried not to. But I had to know. I asked the driver if he knew of Cluny Court."

"Mactavish knows it well."

"Mac—"

"It doesn't matter. Nothing matters except that you've come."

When he reached for her, she shrank back, determined not to let him off the hook so easily. "You let me run."

"I could see that you were confused."

"And you weren't?"

"I was, at first. I believe I've figured it all out. Soon enough you will too, Allison." He took her hands and led her inside.

She looked around in astonishment. The foyer was magnificent, with what seemed acres of white marble and a crystal chandelier that would have cost more than her annual rent. "This is where you cook?"

"Sometimes."

She gave a little laugh. "The dinner parties must be quite something."

"They are." He led her past the foyer and into a sumptuous room with the most amazing collection of antiques she'd ever seen gathered in one place.

"Do you also keep the books for this place?"

He nodded. "There are a great many tenant farms that are part of the property." He was looking at her with that bemused expression she'd come to know. "Think you could stand to live here with me?"

"You're asking me to stay? But I thought— When I left—"

"Allison." He led her toward a chaise positioned in front of a roaring fire. "Do you love me?"

"I've only known you for a day."

"That isn't what I asked. Despite the little time we've had together, I think it's possible to know what's in your heart." He knelt down in front of her and caught her hands again. "Do you love me?"

She swallowed and nodded, feeling the sting of tears at such a shameful admission.

His smile was radiant. "There, now. That wasn't so hard, was it?"

"What about you?" She hated the fact that her voice was trembling, but she couldn't help it. There was too much at stake here.

"I think I knew from the moment you took care of me on the plane that I'd met the woman of my dreams. The way you managed to care for me while attending to your own business. The way you laughed with me. Played on my playground. And when you bought me that sweater—" He touched a hand to his heart.

She blinked at the moisture that was clouding her eyes and managed to glance around at the opulent surroundings. "What will I do here while you cook and keep the books?"

"You'll do whatever pleases you."

"Can we live on your salary? Not that it matters. I have some money saved. I suppose I could set up a little shop in the village to sell antiques."

"Would that make you happy?"

"It's something I've been thinking about for a long time."

"Then I think it would be splendid. But there's something more you need to know about me." He sat down next to her on the chaise. "I'm more than the cook and bookkeeper here. This is all mine."

Because it was too much to take in, she shook her head. "I don't understand."

"To my friends I'm Heath Stewart. But I'm also the ninth Earl of Cluny. This has been in my family for more than three hundred years. And because of my family history, I truly believed that I would never meet a woman who would love me for myself and not for my inheritance. In order to avoid the same fate as my father, I was determined to live my life alone, rather than be trapped in a loveless marriage. But Fate stepped in. In the form of Sir Malcolm."

"But why? Why would he throw us together? And why summon me all the way from New York? Besides, I wasn't supposed to be here. David was."

"You don't really believe that, Allison."

"Are you saying you don't think it was an accident?"

"I believe that nothing happens by accident. I believe that everything in life has a reason. I'm an accomplished skier, yet I fell on the slopes for a reason. You came in place of David for a reason. We were fated to meet."

"But why? Why us?"

"Why not us? Maybe Sir Malcolm, having no family, saw in us the means to an end. Even in death he wanted to assure himself that someone would buy Hamilton Hall and carry on his kindness to the villagers."

"And so he just"—she struggled for the words—"came back from the grave to throw us together?"

Heath gave her a gentle smile. "Who's to say? I'm sure there are some who would call this mere coincidence." He stood and gathered her into his arms, pressing a kiss to her cheek, her nose, the corner of her mouth. "As for me, I'll always believe we were brought together by the kindness of a lonely old man."

Against her temple he whispered, "Will you marry me, Allison, and stay with me always?"

"Marry you?" She couldn't stop the sigh that welled up from deep within. "If I marry the ninth Earl of Cluny, what will that make me?"

"My wife," he whispered against her lips. "The woman I love more than anything in this world. Loving you will make my life complete. And I give you my word that I'll do everything in my power to make you the happiest woman in all of Scotland."

As he took the kiss deeper, they felt a sudden rush of air that caused the flames to leap in the fireplace.

"What was that?" Ally looked around uneasily.

"Just the wind."

On the mantel a framed picture tumbled to the floor, shattering the glass. Heath hurried over to pick it up. He brushed aside the shards, then stared in surprise before handing it to Ally.

It was the faded photo of a very young Sir Malcolm standing beside a wee lad on the banks of the loch. Only now that the glass was missing, Ally could see a slight stain around the two of them, that exactly resembled a glow of light. Inside the light was an angel with its wings encompassing them. And instead of the somber looks she'd noted in Sir Malcolm's office, these two were now smiling.

Ally set the photo back on the mantel and reached out to touch Heath's cheek. It was only a touch, but he closed his hand around hers and gave her a smile that erased the last of her doubts.

"Do you believe now?"

She nodded.

"Welcome home, Allison," he whispered against her mouth.

Home.

She had to blink back tears, but they were tears of joy.

The journey had been long and often disappointing, but it ended here, in the arms of this man. Not a dream lover, but a flesh-and-blood man who would love her, cherish her, and keep her trust always. Not just in a dream but for a lifetime—and beyond.

The Midnight Country

Marianne Willman

For Nora, Ruth, and Jan—
And for our readers who bring
the magic to life!

Prologue

NIGHT FELL OVER Beaumont Foret with a swift and prodigal beauty. One moment the château's turrets glowed copper and gold, the next they were black silhouettes against a glittering extravagance of stars.

Inside the tallest turret, light shone on glass-fronted shelves that lined most of the room from floor to ceiling. They were filled with leather-bound volumes, baskets of vellum scrolls, and faded manuscript pages, some as fragile as dried autumn leaves.

Philippe Beaumont pulled the heavy draperies closed and turned away from the window. He scanned the shelves that contained arcane secrets brought here to the kingdom of Fontine from the earth's four corners.

The flickering light limned his high cheekbones, his strong jaw and stubborn mouth. He refused to believe that the knowledge he sought so desperately was lost forever.

If there were only himself to consider, he might have given up the search long ago. There were times when his spirits flagged and he wondered if he would ever find what he sought, and others when hope blazed in him like a torch. He was suddenly fired with it now. He *would* find the means to end the curse before it destroyed him and everything he held most dear.

His dark eyes burned with fierce determination. "The answer is here. And I *will* find it!"

But *where*?

And, God in heaven—*when*?

Selecting a large tome written in a language long dead, he lost himself in his search, and lost track of time as well. Intriguing hints led him through the pages as the fire burned low in the hearth and shadows danced over the walls like giant moths.

The first strike of the clock caught him totally unprepared. Philippe looked up from the yellowed pages and muttered an oath. Midnight was upon him.

He pushed back from the worktable without bothering to mark his page. He'd almost made it to the door when the first stab of heat and pain transfixed him. Steadying himself, he dragged in a few ragged breaths, then raced down the winding steps to ground level and out the iron-barred door, his blood pounding in his veins.

Mountains black as onyx held up a spangled tent of sky. He loped across the stone bridge that spanned the moat with a runner's easy grace, lean muscles rippling. He was almost at the edge of the forest when another spasm caught him in midstride, leaving him drenched in sweat and gasping for breath.

He stripped off his clothes, and the moon rose above the tallest peaks, bright as a silver mirror. A bolt of energy shot through Philippe like lightning, leaving him blind and deaf. His body arched, muscles stretched taut in agony.

When the flare of power faded, he was in a world transformed. The beauty of the Midnight Country burst upon him in a textured mosaic of shapes and colors, of sounds and tastes and scents.

The cool air slid over him, wrapped around him like silk. Philippe lifted his face to the seductive moonlight, embracing his fate as if it were a lover.

1

"THE KEYS TO your automobile, mademoiselle."

"Thank you." Jenna D'Arcy took the keys, discreetly slipped the concierge a small white envelope, and walked out into the brilliant sunshine.

The coastline of Fontine was spread out before her, all tumbling cliffs, white beaches, and nodding palms. It was the most beautiful place on the Riviera, a storybook kingdom that ran from ice-crowned mountains in the north through castled green hills, down to the dazzling lapis sea.

Jenna had fallen in love with it at first sight.

At the moment, though, as she pulled away from her hotel in a sleek red rental car, she scarcely noticed the view. She was on a quest.

Slipping on a pair of sunglasses, she turned away from the bay, where white yachts bobbed at anchor and bikinied vacationers lined the strand, browning like cookies in the late August sun.

Within minutes she was zipping along the heights high above the city, with the sea only a silver shimmer in her rearview mirror. The wind from the open window ruffled her chestnut hair, and her blue eyes sparkled behind the dark lenses.

Her destination was Beaumont Foret, a small village high in the mountains. Her ancestors had left Fontine to start over in northern California—and from what she'd learned, they hadn't left willingly. Now that the International Conference of Art Conservators was over, she intended to do a little digging among the roots of the family tree.

She'd uncovered the journal when she was fourteen, cleaning out her grandmother's attic. It was inside a worn trunk under the eaves, tucked away with a christening gown and cap and a packet of lavender blossoms that disintegrated to dust when she touched them.

The opening lines of the first journal entry were engraved on her heart.

Not even the smiles of my little son can ease my heart. It is one year ago today that we were forced to leave our homes in Beaumont Foret, sent into exile forever.

Tears ran down our cheeks, but those left behind were pale and dry-eyed as they watched us go. Impossible to know what dark thoughts were in their minds!

When we reached the rocky ledge high above the valley, I turned for one last look, but not even the tallest towers of the chateau were visible. The forest had already closed in behind us.

And so we began our exile, our purses heavy with silver and gold, our hearts with sorrow . . .

The stark emotions in those first few paragraphs had haunted Jenna ever since. She didn't know the reason her ancestors had been exiled—but she intended to uncover it. And the conference had given her all the excuse she needed to fly halfway around the world on this search for the past.

The landscape began to change dramatically, and Jenna had to concentrate less on her quest and more on the steep and twisting road. Massive rock formations thrust straight up, their towering summits crowned with crumbling fortresses; villages of pale, glimmering stone cascaded down their steep sides like frozen waterfalls.

An hour passed, and the views grew increasingly breathtaking and more than a little terrifying. Mountains rose in jagged tiers, their distant peaks covered in bald gray rock or blinding white sheets of ice and snow. The villages were few and far between, almost inaccessible on their rocky heights or hidden deep in their isolated valleys.

She pulled off the road beside a tiny village and called her brother on her cell phone. As usual, Paul was gone and all Jenna got was the tinny voice of his antiquated answering machine. She left him a message.

"I'm getting into the mountains and likely going to be out of range soon, so I thought I'd check in. I'll try to call you this evening from Beaumont Foret."

Three hours later, as she neared her destination, Jenna's hands were locked to the steering wheel in a white-knuckled death grip. Signs warned of hairpin turns and falling rocks, and every now and then she passed a fresh spill that covered half the roadway.

Ahead, the tall peaks glittered like carved crystal far above the treetops. She wondered which one of them had given her family's home village its name, which translated as "beautiful mountain in the forest."

Rounding a tight curve, Jenna downshifted and slowed, looking for the turnoff marked on the old map she'd brought with her from home.

"Yes! There it is."

Her relief vanished. The road split just as the old map showed, but there was no third road leading off to Beaumont Foret.

And no indication that there ever had been one.

A worn sign nailed to a post said it was seventy kilometers to St. Anne. The old map isn't drawn to scale, Jenna reminded herself. The turn-off to Beaumont Foret must be a little farther on.

The road plunged into a twilight world, all black tree trunks with sunbeams slanting like spotlights through gaps in the highland forest. Half an hour passed, and she couldn't decide if she should turn off or keep going. She was glad she'd topped off the gas tank earlier, and wished now that she'd gotten something to eat instead of deciding to press on.

Her heart lifted when she broke out of the thick trees and spied a small village ahead. As she drew closer she saw a weathered wooden sign bearing the words HAUTE BEAUMONT.

She gave a cry of triumph. Either this was the place or it was close by.

As she turned into the village and drove along the cobbled street, however, Jenna was disappointed. She'd been certain that when she reached her destination she would recognize the place by sight, a sort of ancestral memory that would resonate in her bones. No such magic happened.

Haute Beaumont looked like any one of a dozen other picturesque little villages she had passed earlier. It wasn't very large, only a handful of buildings in the center, with a few stone houses and a church. Other homes and small farmsteads were scattered here and there in the higher meadows.

She filled her tank at a tiny gas station, glad she'd packed a warm jacket and sweater for this excursion, and parked across the street outside a half-timbered inn. The interior was warm and welcoming, smelling of wood fires and wine, and she realized that she was famished. The aroma of caramelized onions and coffee led her past the taproom to a small dining room. It was almost deserted, except for a laughing young couple in one corner and a white-haired man in a warm sweater by the window.

Jenna took an empty table by the window and ordered the *plat du jour*. While she waited, she took the two maps from her handbag and spread them out on the tablecloth. One was a modern map provided by the rental company, the other a photocopy of the hand-drawn map she'd found in her grandmother's attic. According to it, she'd driven too far west.

Frowning, she retraced her route. Everything on the modern map matched up with the one drawn generations earlier by her ancestor—except for the missing third road. But sometimes not all little country roads were marked on maps.

A shadow fell across her table. She glanced up, expecting to see her waiter with the cup of coffee she'd ordered. Instead it was the elderly man she'd noticed earlier. He had twinkling dark eyes and a warm smile that helped banish her shyness and put her at ease.

"Perhaps I may be of assistance, mam'zelle?" he inquired. "You are having difficulty in determining your route, perhaps?"

"Not exactly. My problem is that the place I'm looking for doesn't appear on this map at all. Are you from Haute Beaumont, monsieur?"

His smile deepened. "Indeed I am. I was born and raised here, and my family before me. I know this area of the mountains very well, and would be honored to assist you in any way."

Jenna thanked him and invited him to sit down. "I'm doing some genealogical research. My family originated in these mountains, in the village of Beaumont Foret, and I came to look up the old records."

He looked at her in astonishment. "I fear that you are on a wild-goose chase."

"Then this village was never called Beaumont Foret?"

"No, mam'zelle."

Jenna thought he seemed oddly hesitant. "But," she persisted, "you *have* heard of it?"

"Yes, mam'zelle. But I regret to inform you that Beaumont Foret does not exist—except in fairy tales told to amuse children."

Jenna stared at him. "That's not possible. My relatives, for many generations back, were born in Beaumont Foret."

"No, mam'zelle. It is what *you* say that is not at all possible."

"But look." She showed him the photocopy. "Here's an old map of the area handed down in the family. It was drawn by Henri D'Arcy, my great-great-grandfather."

The old gentleman glanced down a moment, then back at her. "But see here, mam'zelle!"

He stabbed a finger at the drawing spread out on the table. "There is St. Anne, and there the road leading here, to the village of Haute Beaumont. Other than that, there appears only a squiggly line with a circled 'X' at its end. Beaumont Foret is mentioned nowhere upon this drawing."

Jenna nodded. "Yes, I do realize that. I was always told that the 'X' marks Beaumont Foret."

The old man shrugged. "Tales handed down for generations tend to become distorted with time, mam'zelle," he said gently. "Perhaps the gentleman who drew the map, he made a little joke for his children, and they believed it to be an actual place. In time, that joke became a part of the family history."

She turned her blue eyes on him with interest. "You mentioned a fairy tale?"

"Yes. Perhaps it is not well known these days, but we of the older generation were weaned on the story." He waved the gray-haired waiter over. "Pierre, this young lady wishes to know about Beaumont Foret. Can you tell her what you know of it?"

"Beaumont Foret? But of course. It is an enchanted castle, deep in the heart of the mountains, guarded by wolves. Those who stumble upon it never return."

A shiver feathered up Jenna's spine. "That's a bit somber for my taste," she said lightly. "I prefer my bedtime stories with happily-ever-after endings, not something guaranteed to give nightmares."

The waiter shrugged. "But, you see, it is meant to warn the children so they do not wander off and become lost in the forest."

The diners at the other table signaled and Pierre went back to his duties. The old man gave Jenna a sympathetic smile. "Console yourself, mam'zelle. It may be that your family actually originated right here in Haute Beaumont. Then your journey will not have been in vain."

Jenna thanked him for his trouble, and he rose with a gallant bow. "I must be on my way. *Bonsoir*, mam'zelle."

When he was gone she turned back to the maps, not at all discouraged. The old gentleman was wrong.

There was too much evidence pointing the other way. The front of the old family Bible she'd found in the attic was filled with spidery writing in faded inks; births, marriages, and deaths were listed there in different hands, over several generations. Each entry was noted as having taken place in the kingdom of Fontine, in the village of Beaumont Foret.

If it was a joke, as the old man suggested, it was certainly an elaborate one. She didn't believe it for one minute.

Over the *plat du jour,* sausage and ratatouille, Jenna came to a conclusion. Somehow she must have missed the turnoff to Beaumont Foret. There was only one way to know for sure. She would have to drive back up the road to where it split and see for herself.

If the road to Beaumont Foret was there, she'd find it.

A few minutes later she was back in the rental car, heading up the road in the slanting sunlight of late afternoon.

The old man who'd spoken to her at the inn had just reached his home on the edge of the village when Jenna drove away. He stopped by the door of the old stone house and watched the red car vanish into the thick stand of pines that lined the road.

"So," he murmured, "the American mam'zelle does not stay in Haute Beaumont." He hoped that she had abandoned her search, but he somehow doubted it.

A large dog looked up from his cozy place on the hearth rug and thumped his tail in greeting as the man entered.

"Ah, yes, you are wanting your dinner, old friend." The dog scrabbled to his feet, and the old man leaned down to stroke the Alsatian's proud head.

"I was detained, you see. A foolish young woman came searching for the lost village. I fear that she has not given up her dangerous quest. She is very determined, that one."

He unwrapped the parcel of scraps he'd brought back from his dinner, along with the soup bone Pierre had thrown in. As he filled the dog's dish, his thoughts were still with Jenna.

"It has been a long time since anyone came looking for the lost village, my friend. Before your time and mine. Perhaps it is really out there, hidden in some deep valley bounded by the mountains, waiting to be discovered again."

The dog lifted his muzzle and gave a muted bark. He took two steps in place, almost dancing with excitement, and barked again.

His owner sighed and rested his hand upon the creature's strong back. "Easy, my old friend. Yes, yes. If you could speak I know what you would say: Better she than you or I."

When the old man straightened up, his eyes were shadowed. "And if she *should* somehow stumble upon Beaumont Foret! Ah, then may *Le Bon Dieu* and all the saints protect her!"

2

PHILIPPE BEAUMONT CAME back from the stableyard in a restless mood. His horse had been skittish, and their brisk gallop across the meadows had done nothing to soothe the wildness in either one of them.

Although snow glistened atop the jagged mountains ringing Beaumont Foret, the August sun bathed the deep valley in molten light. He crossed the courtyard and entered the château by a side door. It was refreshingly cool inside the thick stone walls, and he felt some of his tension drain away.

He tossed his riding crop and hat on a table and spotted his majordomo hovering in the hall like a mournful ghost. "So sour a face, Gaston? You look as though you've been sucking lemons."

The old man sent him a look of gentle reproach. "You have been gone long and are back late, monsieur. I was beginning to worry."

A wry smile turned up the corners of Philippe's mouth. "Did you think I had run off again? Where could I go, Gaston, that Fate would not find me?" He ran long fingers through his tousled hair. "I am no longer the foolish boy you once knew. I am a man. I know my duties."

The butler smiled. "I have no doubt of that, monsieur. Will you dine now?"

"Later, perhaps. I have no appetite today. Where is my son? Has he returned from the village?"

"Yes, monsieur. He is out on the lawn, throwing sticks for his dog to chase. He will sleep well tonight."

"Good. I'm glad that one of us will."

Philippe went up to his suite to change his clothes. He stopped on the landing, where the latticed window stood open to a view across the château grounds and the graceful bridge that spanned the moat. Beyond it the dusty road wound alongside the river, past meadows and cultivated fields. Wide violet swaths bloomed in neat rows, and the scent of sun-warmed lavender came on the soft breeze.

If this is hell, he thought, at least it is beautiful.

He started to turn from the window when he heard barks and shrieks. A moment later Claude ran laughing in the late-afternoon sun, with a great dog beside him. He tossed a stick into the moat, and the creature lunged after it, splashing silver drops of water high into the air.

Philippe's heart ached with love. Burned with anger. He should be down there with his son, laughing and playing, sailing toy boats upon the moat, not locked away for hours with his stacks of books and manuscripts.

And yet, he thought, what choice have I? I must do everything in my power to change the future for Claude, so that he can live a full and normal life. I cannot hold time back forever.

But Philippe felt time ticking away with every beat of his heart, and he knew it would run out soon.

Jenna shifted gears and stepped on the accelerator. The little red car responded immediately, tackling the steep grade without difficulty. She imagined it grinding its teeth with renewed determination as it climbed up the road that wound between sheer cliffs and thick pine forest.

When she reached the split in the road, she pulled off as far as she dared, then got out and slammed the door behind her. The trees and brush were dense and made the going tough, but Jenna persevered and finally broke through into an open spot.

That rock formation down to the right—it looks like the unidentifiable symbol on the old map, she thought. This has to be the right place!

Sunlight poured down the mountainside like gold dust, making it difficult to see. Shielding her eyes, she scanned the scene from side to side. There appeared to be nothing but scrubby undergrowth and bare rock rising up to form high cliffs on one side and a straight plunge over the mountain ledge on the other.

Beyond the cliffs, staggered ranges of sharp-toothed mountains ran east to west, great jagged walls of fiercely crumpled rock that could hide any number of valleys. And then, when she'd almost given up, the slanting rays slid further west, illuminating the curious rock formation.

With shadows cast over it in high relief, it looked like a crouching wolf.

Her heart gave a leap. "Guarded by wolves!"

Then she spied the "third road"—two thin, parallel scratches along the rock that veered off abruptly into the alpine vegetation, exactly like the road in her drawing. They disappeared between a steep cut in the rocky walls to her right.

Jenna laughed at herself. She'd been looking for a modern road, not an overgrown cart track. It probably hasn't changed much since Yvette and Henri D'Arcy traveled it together four generations back! she thought.

And if she hadn't had the old map, and hadn't been in this spot at exactly this time of day, she would never have found it. Climbing into the car, she backed up just enough to make the angle between the boulders. With a leap of faith and a spurt of raw adrenaline, she drove into the cleft.

The road dropped away before her, into the depths of the forest. The dark pines closed in, swallowing everything. She was forced to switch on her headlights. The path zigged and zagged through the trees to cut the steep incline into something more manageable, but the descent was still hair-raising. Finally the car broke out of the heavy forest, and Jenna found herself braking above a valley so deep and narrow it looked like an axe cleft between the sheer battlements of stone.

Jenna suffered a moment of vertigo, brought on by the dizzying sensation that there were only two directions, straight up and straight down. When she mastered it and took in her surroundings, she got a nasty surprise: all signs of the old track had completely vanished.

Turning her head to the right, she got a second unpleasant surprise: night fell suddenly in these high mountains. The sun that had still been high in the western sky when she'd left the inn was ominously low, a flaming orange ball, impaled on the ragged peaks.

"This wasn't a bright idea," she said. "I'll turn around at the first good spot."

Except there didn't seem to be one.

Blue-violet shadows stretched out to infinity, and the sun was sinking like a stone.

3

Philippe was restless, unable to concentrate on his reading. He looked up and noticed the colors reflected in the silver inkstand on his desk. He rose, opened the doors to the balcony, and stepped out. A cool breeze gusted, tugging at his thick, dark hair.

The night sky above the wide valley was suffused with a pale, eerie glow. In some places it shimmered like a transparent veil, in others it rippled like silk. Pulses of green and violet shot across the heavens, waxing and waning, dancing to music that no human ear could hear.

Philippe mistrusted their siren call. Despite their beauty there was a hint of menace in those subtly shifting hues. Something was disturbing the barrier surrounding Beaumont Foret.

A moment later Philippe saw something even more unsettling—lights where no lights should be, not at this time of night. When darkness fell across the mountains, only fools and drunkards left the safety of their homes.

The lights grew brighter, flickering like fireflies through the evergreen forest that spilled down in the distance. They vanished briefly but appeared again, lower down. Philippe cursed beneath his breath. It had been a long, long time since anyone from the outside world had ventured so close to the invisible boundaries of Beaumont Foret.

He drew in a deep breath and went completely still, willing his senses to find the interloper, hurling them across the wide river valley like lightning bolts.

The grass of the lawn and the rich soil beneath, the garden flowers with their complex emanations. Ripe fruits of the earth and the fields of lavender ready to harvest. Then the damp and mossy stones that edged the river, the icy clarity of the water, the hardwoods that gave way to pungent evergreen needles.

He ignored the squeak and skitter of nocturnal creatures, the whispering breeze and bolder gusts of cold air from the surrounding peaks, and focused on the purr of a finely tuned engine.

He detected notes of honey and ripening fruit—and beneath them, the warm scent of woman. Memories rose to haunt him.

A moonlight terrace . . . the air redolent of lavender and mown grass . . . the soft stirring of a breeze, promising rain by morning . . .

It was early summer, and he was young and foolish and very much in love. Perhaps as much with the idea of being in love as with the woman he courted so ardently.

He smiled when he heard light footfalls behind him, the glide of her satin slippers across the stone-flagged terrace. He took in a deep breath, inhaling the heady bouquet of her perfume, and turned, reaching out for her . . .

Cold seared his skin. The vision vanished instantly. It was not warm flesh beneath his hand but the chilled limestone coping of the balcony.

Philippe blinked and shook his head. It had been years since he'd felt such a rush of emotion. Such eager anticipation and burning hunger.

But that was long ago. Another lifetime.

His mouth curled in a bitter smile. *What a fool's paradise I lived in then, thinking I would be different, that I could change everything by wishing it so.*

He took a deep breath. He must not think of what was lost and gone. He must think of the future that was approaching with the speed of a freight train—and the present, which held its own dangers.

The lights on the mountain moved down along the old track from Haute Beaumont, then halted abruptly. Philippe cursed beneath his breath. He knew exactly where the woman was: the sharply descending part of the track, where the old path had been purposely obliterated.

"Turn back," he murmured. "Now, before it is too late."

But the vehicle moved down from the valley's rim with the inevitability of fate. He watched the lights jerking along toward the rocky ledge and certain disaster.

They stopped at last, and he let himself believe that his worries were for nothing. She had seen there was no road continuing down.

The lights jerked into motion, bounced lower and stopped again. The woman's scent came stronger now, underscored by the spiky tang of fear.

She is afraid, he thought. And with good reason. She is realizing that there is no turning back.

4

JENNA'S STOMACH LURCHED, and her hands were clamped to the steering wheel. One moment the pine trees and sheer stone escarpments were dusted with rosy, golden light; the next they were flat black shapes against a backdrop of blazing stars.

"Damn it!"

She was furious with herself. It was too dark to continue, or to back up safely. In her eagerness to find Beaumont Foret, she'd committed Mistake Number One in the Stupid Tourist Handbook: going out into an unfamiliar countryside without checking the local conditions—and without telling anyone where she was headed.

She had expected this adventure to have its hazards, but this was pushing the odds. She reached into her purse. Thank God for cell phones!

Jenna took out the slim yellow case, pressed "O" for operator, and put it to her ear. If she was lucky, she was high up enough that the mountains wouldn't block the signals.

There was nothing, not even a crackle of static.

She swore again. Evidently a communications satellite would have to be right overhead for it to work.

There was no way that she would compound her foolishness by trying to hike up to the road in such rugged terrain, but she wasn't happy to be spending a night locked in the car on a dark mountainside instead of sleeping in a cozy bed.

A car that proved to be damnably uncomfortable. The backseat was too small to even attempt lying down, and the console and gearshift made it impossible to stretch out in the front. She pushed the seat back and resigned herself.

At least she had a full tank of gas and could run the heater. She listened for strange noises over the hum of the engine and tried not to watch the clock.

If only the moon was up, she thought. It would be ironic if I sit here all night twiddling my thumbs when there's a wider space where I could turn around beyond the next stand of trees.

The only safe way to find out was on foot. Leaning across the other seat, she opened the map box and took out the flashlight the rental company had provided. The batteries were fresh and bright. She couldn't get disoriented if she stayed in sight of the car's headlights. If her scouting expedition was unsuccessful, she would simply have to grit her teeth and wait until morning.

Jenna got out and made her way over the uneven ground, following the beam from the headlights. The temperature had dropped considerably, and the air was sharp with the scent of snow. She walked carefully along the path of the beams to where they began to fade, and then she stopped short. Barely a yard away the ridge ended and a bottomless black void began.

She backed away and went off to her left, sweeping the flashlight from side to side. Suddenly she stopped. There was movement in the night downwind of her. Something large and stealthy, moving up toward the ridge where she stood.

As she stepped backward her foot twisted on a fallen pinecone that skittered out from beneath it. She fought to keep her balance, and succeeded, but the flashlight flew out of her hand, bounced once, and went out.

• • •

Deep in the valley, Philippe was watching it all with sinking heart. He winced when the single light broke away from the twin beams of the vehicle's headlights, knowing the woman had left the safety of her vehicle.

The light moved slowly, and he imagined her picking her way carefully over the rocks toward the drop-off, unaware of her growing danger. He saw the lone light make a wide arc against the black backdrop of the mountains and then wink out. It brought back a nightmare time, ten years ago, when another woman had been lost at almost the same spot.

His hands curled into fists as he struggled to hold back the memories. He might as well have tried to stop an avalanche. Images tumbled into his mind, shattered him with remembered pain.

Not again! He thought, and reached for the bellpull. It must not happen again.

Gaston answered his summons, looking surprised. "I thought you had gone out for the evening, monsieur."

"Not yet. I've been watching lights on the mountain. Some fool of a woman has driven down the old track and stranded herself there. She hasn't breached the barrier guarding Beaumont Foret yet. But she's very close to the edge of the precipice and may not see her way clear of it."

Shadows of the old tragedy flickered through Philippe's eyes. "Alert the men. Tell them to bring whatever they may need in case of accident. I'll set off ahead of them and try to avert trouble."

The butler looked grave. "But . . . monsieur!"

Philippe flushed. "Can't you see I have no choice? No one knows that terrain better than I."

"But the danger . . ."

"Don't be concerned. If I reach her in time, I'll do my best to persuade her to remain safely inside her car until morning."

"And if you do not arrive in time?"

A hardness settled over Philippe's features. "Then I will have no choice but to bring her here, to Beaumont Foret—dead or alive."

5

JENNA GOT DOWN on her hands and knees, feeling for the dropped flashlight among the litter of dried needles and pinecones. There was no sign of it anywhere.

If only the moon would rise over the peaks! Moving methodically, she swept her gloves in wide arcs in the area where she thought the flashlight had fallen. After a thorough search she realized it was useless.

"Thank God I had the sense to leave my headlights on, so I can follow them back to the car!" she said out loud.

But when she scanned the mountainside for their beams, she couldn't spot them at all. Jenna took several deep breaths of icicle-sharp air, trying to slow the frantic pounding in her chest.

"Where the hell is the car?"

Pushing down her panic, she convinced herself that the thick trees and huge rocks were blocking the lights from view. She would soon locate them if she moved across the ledge. She knew she had to hurry. Her jacket was warm enough, but the unlined leather gloves she wore weren't made for freezing temperatures and her fingers were already numb with cold.

She heard crackling in the encircling forest. Her imagination went into high gear. Frosted twigs snapping in the cold? Stealthy footsteps? Or a predator seeking its prey?

The sounds grew louder and headed in her direction. The nape of her neck prickled.

"Who's there?" she called out, first in the French dialect of Fontine and then in English.

There was no answering voice, only the soft *pad-pad* of something closing in.

She turned her head, scanning the dark mountainside in vain for the beams of her headlights. As she was deciding which way to go, an eerie sound lifted the hair at her nape—a low, growling moan that she felt in her bones as much as heard.

A wolf?

She thought of the waiter's words: "Beaumont Foret . . . an enchanted castle deep in the heart of the mountains . . . guarded by wolves."

A crack of thunder split the air, and Jenna felt the ground shift beneath her. She flailed for her balance, but fell, hard. The thick layers of fallen pine needles cushioned the worst of it, but the wind was knocked out of her.

While she lay stunned, she felt herself sliding forward and down—then realized it was the very rock beneath her that was moving. The ledge beneath her was breaking away from the mountainside in a skitter and hail of bouncing stones.

A single clear thought shimmered in her dulling brain: What a stupid, stupid way to die.

For a moment she was weightless, a leaf on the wind.

Then, although she could see nothing but air beneath her, her fall was gently cushioned. For a disbelieving instant she rested in space above the void. Jenna felt it give, heard a soft *pop*! Her invisible support gave way abruptly.

The night erupted in a silent explosion of scintillating lights of vivid rose and violet and green. She was falling again, caroming into entwined branches that cracked and snapped beneath her weight. Grasping desperately, she caught at one, but her gloves were ripped from her frozen hands. She was gaining momentum, tobogganing over the ice-glazed rock.

A stunning blow stopped her wild descent. Surprisingly, there was no pain, only a flash like a strobe light. Then everything was blotted out by darkness, far deeper, far blacker than midnight.

Philippe threw himself forward to block the women's wild descent and winced when he heard her body strike a glancing blow off the tree trunk. For a split second he lay there, panting with the effort and fearing the worst.

He rolled away and pushed himself up to examine her. She was limp and unmoving, her face so white it seemed that every bit of blood had drained from her body. He said a prayer to a god in whose mercy he no longer believed and touched the angle beneath her jaw. Her pulse beat frantically against his fingertips, and she took in a soft gasp of air.

Mon Dieu! She is still alive! he thought.

Not, he realized quickly, that there was any guarantee she would remain that way. She was injured and in shock, and it was a very long way down the mountain to Beaumont Foret. There was little he could do until his men worked their way up with the equipment, except to try and keep her warm with the heat of his body.

It had been years since he'd held a woman so close. Her breath ruffled against his cheek, and the scent of her hair and skin once again evoked memories he'd pushed to the back of his mind. A warm summer night . . . paper lanterns illuminating the garden . . . music and wine . . . the taste of apricots and first love . . .

Bitterness filled him. Those fleeting moments of golden promise had turned to lead, and all these long years later, he was still dealing with their consequences.

He'd made faulty decisions then, and now he wondered if he had erred again. Taking a stranger, a woman, to the château was a risk—yet how could he do otherwise?

He pushed the pale hair from her face and a scent rose around him. Now he knew why the memories had battered him so strongly tonight—it was her perfume, with the warm fragrance of apricots, taking him back to a summer eleven years ago.

She looked touchingly fragile, like a snowflake that would melt at his touch. And very, very beautiful. Her lips were blanched but beautifully shaped, and her thick lashes cast shadows on her lovely cheekbones. What cruel trick of fate had caused this exquisite creature to stumble out of her world and into his?

His knuckles grazed her cheek. Why are you here? What in the name of heaven—or hell—has brought you to this dark mountainside?

And, he thought with a sudden sense of foreboding, what am I to do with you when you awaken?

If you awaken.

She aroused all his chivalrous instincts. He thought, with a swift stab of pity, she must live.

And for that to happen he would need all the available resources at the château. He knew that once again he was rushing in where angels feared to tread.

Philippe shrugged. It is said that *Le Bon Dieu* watches out for fools and children. I will worry about the consequences later.

But try as he might, he couldn't dismiss the feeling that disaster was sure to follow.

Just as it had before.

6

JENNA SWAM IN the darkness of a twilight world. Was that snow melting on her face, or her own tears?

And then, miraculously, she realized that she was no longer alone. She felt the touch of a leather-gloved hand on her cheek. A thick blanket was wrapped around her. Heat radiated from it, cocooning her in warmth and safety. She sank into it, and into soothing oblivion.

Fleeting sounds and sensations roused her, danced through her hazy awareness. The scrape of a chair, a man's deep voice and a woman's soft reply. The closing of a door. Later there were gentle hands, a cup of cool water pressed to her lips.

She woke gradually, and struggled against an overwhelming lassitude. In the silence she heard the hiss and crackle of flame, smelled the deep, smoky fragrance of a wood fire. Her eyes fluttered open. She saw a lovely, candlelit room and glimpsed the reflection of a handsome, dark-haired man in the mirrored armoire.

I'm dreaming, she told herself. And a very nice dream it is.

Later, when she awoke briefly, the man was gone, the candles snuffed. She didn't know where she was or how she'd gotten there. The room was shrouded in deep shadows, the only light that of the banked fire in the hearth. She looked toward it and gasped.

An enormous beast was stretched out on the rug before the hearth. At her sound, it turned its head and regarded her steadily. Its eyes glowed like burnished coins.

Her heart constricted with a leap of atavistic fear. The creature stared at her a moment, then lowered its head.

Jenna stared. Then she realized what it was: a very large dog, its face framed by a ruff of pale, silvery fur.

For a split second, she'd thought it was a wolf.

The next time Jenna awakened it was to filtered daylight. She was disoriented for a moment, as she struggled to free herself from a nightmare in which was running, wild with fear, across an alien landscape.

As the fear receded, an awareness of pain took its place. Her left shoulder and ribs felt bruised, and her head ached abominably. There was a bandage on her temple and another on her arm.

She was in a bed, a high tester bed with elaborately carved posts and hangings of pale gold brocade. The draperies were partially open, and the unfamiliar view through the tall windows revealed a wide green valley tucked in the embrace of lofty mountains.

She turned her head and winced as pain lanced through it.

The man standing before the marble fireplace heard her sharp intake of breath and whirled around. He was dressed casually but expensively, in gray slacks and a crisp shirt, open at his tanned throat.

Something teased at the back of her mind. Recognition came to her slowly. He was the man whose reflection she'd seen in the mirror.

He strode across the chamber to the bedside, looking very much in control of the situation. She was suddenly and intensely aware of her disheveled state, with the white gown slipping off her shoulder and her tousled hair.

Although his eyes were dark, up close she saw that they held a golden light in their depths. He inclined his head. "*Bonjour*, mademoiselle. How do you feel?"

Jenna licked her dry lips. Her voice was hoarse when she answered. "Like I fell off a cliff. On my head."

"You came very close to doing so. It was only by the grace of God that I arrived on the scene in time to prevent it."

"I'm sorry that I don't remember it . . . but I'm very grateful to you."

He regarded her intently. "You recall nothing of the circumstances that brought you here?"

"I'm afraid not. The last thing I remember was leaving my hotel."

"That is not unusual, given what happened. You were wandering about on the mountainside and fell, striking your head. You've been in and out of consciousness for the past day and a half."

Jenna stared at him. That was a shock.

She raised her hand to her head and felt the bandage at her temple. "I don't remember—except that you were here when I woke earlier."

"Ah." His dark eyes were suddenly wary. She had the impression of shadows flickering through their depths. "So you remember that," he said. He lifted a red glass goblet from somewhere out of sight and held it to her lips. "Drink this. It will ease the pain."

"Not if it will put me to sleep again. I need to sort things out. Is this some sort of hospital or rest home? Are you a doctor?"

He laughed and suddenly looked younger. "The answer to both your questions is no, mademoiselle. This is my home." He made her a low bow. "Philippe Beaumont, at your service."

"I'm Jenna. Jenna D'Arcy. I wish I could remember . . ."

She frowned as images tumbled through her mind, like out-of-focus photographs in a stranger's album. Night . . . a narrow track . . . trees . . .

His eyes fixed on hers with peculiar intensity. "So you do remember something of it, mademoiselle?"

"Jumbled bits and pieces." She shook her head to clear it. Pain exploded behind her eyes, leaving her shaken and dizzy.

Philippe watched her with concern. Her skin had gone as pale as her gown, and her lovely face was drawn. With her blue eyes shadowed and her hair in a wild corona of curls, she looked touchingly young and vulnerable.

"Don't try to force your memory," he advised. "The important thing is that you continue to rest and recover."

He lifted the red goblet once more. "Drink this down, if you please. It is an old family recipe, and heals the body as well as soothing the mind. When you've slept a bit you'll feel much better."

She didn't refuse this time, but sipped the bittersweet brew. It smelled of oranges and honey and something distinctly medicinal. "I hope when I do wake again that I'll remember more."

He took the empty cup from her hand. "Sleep is a great restorative. But you must understand it is very possible that your memory of the accident and its aftermath may never come back in its entirety."

At least he sincerely hoped, not anytime soon.

7

WHEN BERTHE, THE white-haired housekeeper, came in to remove Jenna's breakfast tray, she carried a long dress-maker's box under her arm.

"I've brought you a change of clothes."

She put the box down on the settee, removed the lid, and pushed back the silver tissue paper.

"All the way from Paris, and never once worn," she grumbled, shaking out a gown of sumptuous peach silk, trimmed with points of lace. The housekeeper pursed her lips and draped the gown and a matching robe at the foot of the bed.

Jenna stared. It was straight out of the 1930s. She wondered what other treasures were hidden away in the château's attics. "It's gorgeous."

Berthe gave a disapproving sniff but didn't reply.

"I'm very grateful to you for everything. I know my being here has meant more work for you," Jenna said. Her words didn't have the desired effect.

The older woman nodded vigorously. "It is not a good thing, your being here. The sooner you leave, the better it will be for everyone." She turned on her heel and bustled out.

Jenna lay back against the pillows and closed her eyes. So much for international diplomacy. When she heard the door open a moment later, she thought it was Berthe returning. But the footsteps were far too quick and light.

She opened her eyes as a boy of about ten years slipped in and tiptoed to the bed. He was neatly dressed, with thick dark hair, and looked like a miniature version of Philippe Beaumont—except, she thought, there are no shadows in his eyes.

"Good morning," she said aloud.

The boy froze, his eyes wide with alarm. Recovering quickly, he made what Jenna thought was a comically formal bow for someone so young.

"*Bonjour,* mademoiselle. I hope I did not wake you?"

"No. In fact, I'm happy to have a visitor. My name is Jenna."

"Yes," he said shyly. "I know. I am Claude." He hesitated. "I only meant to look in on you. It is not often that we have guests."

She smiled. "That was kind of you. Can you tell me where I am, Claude?"

"But of course, mademoiselle. You are in the south wing, in the room that was my grandmother's. She was not able to manage the stairs, you see."

Jenna tried not to laugh. "I mean in the larger sense. I can see trees and mountains in the distance, but the view is totally unknown to me."

The boy blushed. "Ah, I understand you now. You are my father's guest, mademoiselle—and this is Château Beaumont Foret."

"Beaumont Foret," she said slowly. "An enchanted castle—complete with wolves?"

It was the boy's turn to look startled. "It is best not to speak of the wolves."

He would have said more, but the door opened and Philippe entered. "Claude! You are supposed to be at your lessons."

"Yes, Father. I am on my way." He stood very close to Jenna and lowered his voice. "I would not mention the wolves. My father would be very displeased."

She gave him a wink. "It will be our secret."

"*Au'voir,* mademoiselle." The boy gave another little bow, then turned and hurried out.

Philippe shut the door behind him, still frowning. "My apologies, mademoiselle. My son has been too indulged. I expected he would know better than to disturb you."

"He didn't disturb me, and his manners are charming." Her curiosity was aroused. "I look forward to meeting the rest of your family."

"There are only the two of us," he said curtly. "Claude's mother died soon after his birth."

Jenna saw a quick flash of emotion in his eyes, the flicker of an old grief.

"I'm very sorry."

"You couldn't be expected to know of the circumstances." His gaze flickered over her face. "You look more rested."

"I am. In fact, I'd like to get up."

"I see no reason not to. Perhaps you'd care to sit for a while on the terrace? The afternoon is warm, with a pleasant breeze."

"I'd like that very much."

She threw back the covers and sat up. Philippe kneeled and put the embroidered satin sippers on her slender feet, then rose and helped her into the peach silk dressing gown.

Jenna took a tentative step and caught her foot in the hem of the robe, but Philippe swooped her up in his arms before she knew what was happening. One second she was standing, the next her cheek was pressed against his shoulder, her senses besieged by the sudden intimacy. Her deep breath of surprise drew in the subtle fragrance of his aftershave, the crisp, clean scent of his linen shirt, and the warm, male muskiness of his skin.

"I'm not that weak. I can walk," she said.

"You are a bit unsteady yet." Ignoring her protests, he carried her effortlessly toward the glass doors and out to the terrace beyond.

She felt the initial awkwardness give way to pleasure. It was nice, for once, to let someone else be in charge, to feel weightless and protected in his arms with her head cradled against his shoulder.

He carried her to a cushioned chair in the shelter of a rose trellis.

"You'll be warm but shaded from the worst of the sun here," he said as he settled her into it.

She couldn't meet his eyes.

The château was situated on high ground, and the land fell away down to the floor of the main valley, where a river wound through fields and meadows and stands of forest. It was a dizzying view. Other valleys branched off, surrounded by high plateaus, and over all loomed the protective bulk of the mountains, their summits wreathed in clouds.

She glanced back at the château itself and was captivated. It was beautifully proportioned, the stone facade pierced with Gothic windows of leaded glass and the roofs and peaked towers tiled in a deep shade of blue. On the other side of the terrace, green lawns ran down to a moat where swans rippled the reflections of the reeds.

"It all looks too perfect to be real," she said. "An enchanted place, where the scullery girl changes into a princess with the wave of a magic wand. I expect Prince Charming to ride up the road at any moment."

Philippe looked down at her gravely. "Such optimism deserves to be rewarded. Alas, there are no fairy godmothers here."

Or happily-ever-afters.

She'd noticed the quenching of the light in his eyes. "Perhaps you haven't looked hard enough," she said. "With all this atmosphere, there must be one lurking about somewhere."

"Ah. You are a romantic at heart."

The air between them shimmered with summer heat, and something more. Jenna smiled. "I wouldn't be here if I weren't. I came looking for Beaumont Foret—and now I've found it."

Philippe paled beneath his tan, but his voice remained level. "You surprise me, mademoiselle. We don't usually attract tourists in our remote little valley. May I inquire why you've ventured so far from the beaten track?"

She noticed the way his color changed, but didn't comment on it. "My family originated in Beaumont Foret and lived here happily for many generations. I imagine that some still do."

He frowned and shook his head. "I regret very much to tell you that the line died out several generations ago. There are no longer any D'Arcys in Beaumont Foret."

That jolted Jenna to the core. "None?"

"I am sorry."

There was such finality in his tone that she knew he spoke the truth. Disappointment choked her, and it was several moments before she could find her voice again.

"I'd hoped to find cousins here . . . talk with them about the past and see if they knew anything of why my ancestors left. My great-grandfather, like his father before him, was a surgeon, and his brother was an apothecary who ran the chemist shop in the village. Then one summer they packed up with their wives and children and left for California."

"Ah." He smiled. "Many left in those times, for the adventure of starting anew in a young country rich with land and opportunity."

"Not in their case," she told him. "They were given no choice in the matter. My great-grandmother wrote in her journal that they were 'sent into exile forever.' "

"Exile." Philippe considered it. "That is a poetic word. Your ancestor was no doubt homesick. I believe you are reading more into it than was intended."

"No." Jenna was adamant. "I'm not. And I want to find out why they left."

He gave that Gallic shrug that could mean anything from total agreement to utter disbelief. "It might have been anything. A family quarrel, perhaps. Or a falling-out over an inheritance."

"It was something more serious," she said. "There were other families beside my own. A group of men, women, and children who emigrated to America together from Beaumont Foret."

He didn't volunteer anything, but Jenna had a feeling that he knew something. Something that he didn't intend to share with her.

"I managed to get in touch with a few of their descendants," she told him. "Among their surviving documents—diaries, letters, reminiscences—the same term is used: 'sent into exile.' Unfortunately, not a one of them mentions *why*."

"And so your quest for information has led you here, mademoiselle?" His dark eyes glinted. "That is quite a coincidence. It is not easy to find Beaumont Foret without a guide. If not for your unfortunate accident, you might never have done so."

She lifted her chin and smiled. "It might have taken longer, but I would have found my way here eventually. I come from stubborn stock. We don't give up easily."

Philippe returned her smile. "Neither do I, mademoiselle. Perhaps it is a trait common to the inhabitants of Beaumont Foret."

Once again she had the impression that he knew more than he intended her to find out. "I'd like to spend a few hours going through the village records." The blue eyes regarded him innocently. "I'm sure a word from you would smooth the way."

She felt a spurt of triumph. There. That put him on the spot.

"Ah." He lifted his hands, palms up. "You must forgive me, mademoiselle. It is out of my power to assist you."

"Really? I find that difficult to believe. You surely have influence in the village."

His dark brows snapped together. "True. But, you see, the church records and those of the village meetings were kept at the rectory of St. Marie Madeleine. I regret to tell you that the church and rectory burned to the ground in my father's day. All the contents, including the records, were destroyed."

Jenna felt her color ebb. To come so far . . .

"You are naturally disappointed," he said.

She bit her lip. " 'Disappointed' is too tame a word."

Philippe offered her a crumb of comfort. "The churchyard is still intact, with all its headstones. You may be able to gather some information on your family there, before you leave."

That caught Jenna off guard. "You've been very kind," she said, "and I've imposed on you too long already."

"Not at all. You must stay on at the château until you are fully recovered, mademoiselle. But September is almost upon us, and the change of weather sometimes brings snow to the higher elevations. Should the pass leading down from Haute Beaumont become blocked, there would be no way in or out of this valley until the spring thaw." He flashed his charming smile. "I do not think you wish to prolong your visit until then."

She returned his smile, upping the wattage. "Winters must be long in Beaumont Foret—although I imagine that it might have its compensations. I can't think of anything cozier than roasting chestnuts on the hearth during a snowstorm, or curling up by the fires with a good book and a glass of wine."

"I see that you have a decided turn for the romantic, mademoiselle." He didn't know why, but that pleased him. "However," he added, "I assure you that even such pleasant activities can pall after a while."

"I'm never bored as long as I have something good to read."

"Perhaps you would care for something to read now, mademoiselle, while you enjoy the sunshine?"

"Thank you, but I'd rather sit here and enjoy the view," Jenna said.

"Then I will take my leave of you. I have urgent business that demands my attention. The bell upon the table will summon Berthe should you require anything."

She watched him cross the terrace and vanish into the château. She was glad to be alone again. It was easier to think without his magnetic presence pulling her toward him like a lodestone.

Philippe Beaumont is an intensely attractive man, she mused. And an intensely troubled one.

He tried to hide his unease behind an urbane mask, but it was apparent to her in the set of his jaw, and in the shadows that flickered like heat lightning in the depths of his dark eyes.

One thing she knew for certain: Philippe Beaumont was very anxious to be rid of her.

8

PHILIPPE WENT INSIDE and through the bedchamber to the corridor beyond, thinking of his uninvited guest. She was beautiful, clever, and full of lively curiosity. All three qualities made her dangerous to him, but for very different reasons.

The first was his strong attraction to her. The feelings of pity and protectiveness he'd experienced on the mountainside were resolving themselves into a deeper interest. Jenna D'Arcy reminded him that he was a man, with a man's needs for companionship—and more.

When she'd spoken of winter at the château, he'd had a sudden image of her curled up in a chair by the fire in the salon with a book upon her lap. For that split second he'd imagined himself in the chair beside hers, a snifter of cognac in his hand, watching the light dance over her lovely face.

He'd rather liked that vision of her curled up near him by the fire. In his bed, nestled against his chest, within the circle of his arm. How could he not think of such things, when he still remembered the feeling of her slender body curved into his as the rescuers worked their way up the mountain?

He banished it as quickly as it came. His interest in her could, he knew, never amount to more than a passing thought, an idle daydream of what might have come to pass if circumstances were not as they were. Since he couldn't alter them, he must adapt himself instead.

But if Jenna D'Arcy stayed too long, there would be no way he could hide his other secrets. There were bound to be slipups—and that was the second danger.

The third, and most volatile, was the quest that had brought her to Beaumont Foret. He would have to find a way to satisfy her curiosity about the village's past history, while convincing her that there was no use in digging further into it.

Fortunate indeed that the old church burned to the ground.

The most urgent need was to hide the truth from Mademoiselle Jenna D'Arcy's lovely eyes until she was safely away from the valley. And that would be only a matter of a day or two. Then she would be gone from Beaumont Foret, and life would slip back into its daily rhythms.

The thought should have filled him with relief. Instead it left him feeling bleak. If he had been free to indulge his likes and dislikes, he would have wanted to get to know his pretty guest much better, to see if there was as much wit and cleverness behind that lovely face as he imagined. To discover if the tension that shivered in the air between them might develop into something more interesting.

Philippe shrugged. What he wanted made no difference at all. He had no choice, must be rid of her as soon as possible. Then he could go back to being not a man but a stone, with no emotions to stir him other than love for his son—and the desperation that fueled his long hours of isolation surrounded by crumbling manuscripts.

Gaston stepped out of the shadows. "Monsieur LeFevre has arrived. He is in the estate room."

"Thank you." Philippe crossed the wide hall and went down a side corridor to the estate room. It was a masculine room of paneled wood and leather, where records of business were kept.

Armand LeFevre, his cousin and right-hand man, was standing at the window with his back to the room. He was thin and dark, with a quality of barely restrained energy even when he was at rest.

"We found the mademoiselle's automobile."

Philippe raised his eyebrows. "And—?"

"The old road out of the valley is gone in a massive rock-slide. And her vehicle with it. It is a miracle we found it at all. The driver's side and rear of the vehicle were crushed beyond hope." He shook his head. "Had she been inside it, the mademoiselle would be dead."

"A lucky escape for her." Philippe said, picking up the crystal decanter on the desk. The thought that Jenna might have been killed upset him, but his hand and voice were steady. "What of her luggage?"

Armand gestured toward the table, where he'd placed a square leather box with a carrying handle, a laptop computer in its protective leather case, and a trendy handbag. Nearby a garment bag was laid over the seat of a tapestry chair. "This is all we could salvage from the wreck."

Philippe poured the amber liquid into two glasses and handed one to his cousin. "Is there anything of the vehicle that can be seen on the road from Haute Beaumont?"

"No. The overhang and the pile of rubble make it impossible to be seen from above."

"Good. At least we won't have to worry about anyone coming to retrieve it." Philippe sipped his brandy.

"Gaston tells me she has made a rapid recovery. You could take her across the valley and up the hidden road to St. Anne this afternoon."

"She is not recovered enough as yet. Perhaps by Friday."

Armand frowned. "But you said you meant to be rid of her as soon as possible."

"The matter is more complicated than I first imagined." Philippe swirled the liquid in his glass. "Mademoiselle D'Arcy did not come to Beaumont Foret by accident, but by design."

"*What?*" Armand's jaw dropped. "This is a joke, no? You cannot be serious!"

"I assure you that I am." Philippe leaned against the mantelpiece. "Her family was among those who left the valley before the barrier went up—perhaps that's why she was able to penetrate it. She told me she came here to research her family's roots."

Armand was visibly shaken. He took a healthy swallow of brandy. "What are we to do?"

"String her along just enough to satisfy her curiosity. I told her that the records were destroyed along with the church." Philippe watched as relief flooded the other man's face. "But she won't go happily until she sees the ruins and has a chance to wander among the headstones, looking for her ancestors."

"The longer she stays, the more dangerous she becomes!"

"I don't need you to remind me of that, Armand." Philippe tossed off the rest of his brandy. "Leave it to me. I will escort her about the village—that way she will see only what I wish her to see. I hope it will be enough."

"I hope so too—for all our sakes." His cousin eyed him shrewdly. "Berthe and Gaston say she is very beautiful."

Philippe refilled their glasses. "She is."

"In that case, I could set aside my pressing business affairs long enough to take her back," Armand offered. A twinkle lit his eyes.

"How good it is of you to offer," Philippe replied wryly. "However, you needn't make the sacrifice. As soon as she is well enough to travel, I'll drive Mademoiselle D'Arcy back down to the coast—and vanish the moment she is safely inside her hotel."

Something in his voice alerted his cousin. "Ah. So you are interested in her, are you? My dear cousin, is that wise?"

Philippe felt a quick flash of anger. Was it wrong of him to wish to enjoy an afternoon's drive with a beautiful woman? To create the illusion, for a few pleasurable hours, that life was the same for him as for other men?

"Spare your breath." Philippe set down his glass with more force than he intended. "I am too old for your lectures. And you know I have no choice. Am I not sworn to do everything in my power to rid Beaumont Foret of its affliction?"

Armand acknowledged that was true. "I do not envy you your position. It cannot be an easy one."

"There will be no trouble, I assure you. I'll see to that."

"I hope you may be right." He shrugged. "Meanwhile, there is another problem at hand. I rode down to the old mill this morning to help old Louis oil the turbines for the hydropower. I found fresh wolf tracks. I followed them all the way to the river, where they vanished."

Philippe turned to stare at him. "How many?"

"Just a single wolf. Not fully grown, from the size and depth of its marks. But it is a bold one."

"Indeed." Philippe rubbed his jaw. "One of ours?"

"I don't think so. We would surely have known if one appeared near the village."

"That is so." Philippe knew there were small pockets in the most remote mountains where wolves still thrived, but they rarely ventured in close to Beaumont Foret except in times of famine.

"It had to come over the mountains and down from the higher elevations," Philippe said. "There was a dynamite crew blasting rock last week for the planned resort on the other side of Haute Beaumont. Perhaps the noise disoriented the creature, and it became separated from its pack. Were there any signs that it was ill or injured?"

"None that I could see. What do you want me to do?"

"Nothing yet, except to send out a warning. My guess is that it's a young wolf and merely curious. If it returns, we'll have to frighten it back up into the mountains, where it belongs. I would prefer not to take stronger action unless it's absolutely necessary."

"I'll see to it."

"Good. Will you stay to dine with me?"

"Thank you, but I promised Marie that I would be home early." Armand fixed him with a sharp glance. "Do you feel the need for a chaperon?"

Philippe laughed. "Not at this stage of my life. Tell me, would it be convenient for you to take my son to stay with you for a few days? I am afraid that in his innocence he might say the wrong thing in front of our unexpected guest."

"I have been meaning to ask if I might have Claude come to stay again. I promised him I would do it soon. Shall I take him back with me today?"

"Tomorrow morning will be soon enough." He hesitated. "Marie does not mind?"

"She dotes on the boy."

The same thoughts crossed their minds. Marie would have been a wonderful mother, if circumstances were otherwise. Philippe put his hand on Armand's arm. "You are both young enough. If I can find the cure . . ."

"If, if, *if*!" The older man said with a crooked smile. "I do not hold my breath, hoping. But if you should succeed—ah, how different all our lives would be."

When his cousin left, Philippe gathered up Jenna's belongings. He saw that the leather case wasn't closed tightly, and lifted the lid so he could shut it properly.

"What the devil?"

Instead of the cosmetics he'd expected to find, the inside of the case was carefully fitted with brushes, tweezers, magnifying glasses, several pairs of white cotton gloves, and vials of powders and fixatives. He looked at the labels more closely. Each one bore the same legend in gold letters: "D'Arcy Industries."

Curious, Philippe extracted the glossy pamphlet tucked into one side of the case. It wasn't the manufacturer's brochure that he expected, but a program for a seminar that had been held in Fontine, by the International Society of Museum Conservators.

He turned it over, and his gaze was immediately arrested by the photograph of the keynote speaker. Her hair was longer in the photo and slicked back, the rioting chestnut curls subdued at her nape—but it was definitely Jenna D'Arcy.

There was no personal information about her beneath the photo, only a list of credentials and a short blurb.

Mademoiselle D'Arcy is Curator of the Archives of Ancient Texts at the Avery Library Museum in Sacramento. Her seminar will introduce the innovative D'Arcy Method, which has been successfully tested on manuscripts previously considered to be damaged beyond hope of restoration.

He stared at the words, unable to take them in until he read them over again. So, Jenna D'Arcy is an expert in restoration. The irony of the situation struck him. His unwanted guest was in a position to help him. The price of it was risking the safety of all those he held most dear.

Still . . .

After a moment Philippe closed the case and rang for his butler. "Gaston, please see that these items are taken to Mademoiselle D'Arcy's room."

"Very good, monsieur."

Philippe walked to the window. He stood there, staring out over the green lawns toward the moat, considering events from every angle. The temptation was almost overwhelming.

He shook his head. But no . . . I cannot do it. I am a Beaumont. A man of honor. And, setting that aside, there is still far too much at risk. Too many people depend upon me. I must tread carefully.

But then his son came into view, all gangling arms and legs and boyish energy. Claude flung himself down in the shade of a tree and took out a pocketknife. As the boy sat whittling a stick, Philippe's priorities fell into their proper order.

Philippe frowned and turned away from the window, brooding. He would have to consider all options and then make a choice. One based on clear logic, untinged by sentiment.

In bringing Jenna D'Arcy to Beaumont Foret, Fate had handed him a gift on a silver platter. He would be a fool if he didn't take it.

9

JENNA SAT IN the sun, letting the warmth soak into her bones. I'm at an ancient château in the village Beaumont Foret, she thought, smiling contentedly. A place I was told didn't even exist.

She could almost believe that it *was* all a mirage. The air held the soft-edged, golden glow of a summer daydream. Past the meadows, cultivated fields and neat orchards basked in the sun. In the distance she saw a thick stand of trees and what might be chimneys and the tiled roofs of the village, but they were too far away for her to be certain.

And inside the château, she thought, is the most intriguing and attractive man I've ever met.

For a moment she let herself remember the way he'd lifted her in his arms, the hardness of his body beneath the finely tailored clothes. The sudden surge of pure physical attraction that burned invisibly around them like a flame.

He would be a wonderful lover. Romantic and tender, yet passionate and demanding.

Her blood heated, thinking of it. She felt the rush of it through her veins and pushed the thought quickly away. The strength of him, combined with such gentleness, had had a powerful effect on her, but she didn't want to go weaving fantasies about Philippe Beaumont. Their worlds were very different. Their paths might be destined to cross briefly and then diverge.

A restlessness came over her. The gentle breeze on her face was real enough, as was the bandage at her temple. Jenna rose and strolled along the terrace. As she passed the trellis, she paused to pluck one of the climbing roses. She'd never seen a more perfect flower. It was thornless, with a light, faintly spicy scent and velvety petals shading from palest pink to deepest rose. It was so beautiful it didn't seem real.

Jenna loved flowers, but she wasn't an avid gardener, so it took her a minute to realize that something wasn't right. She eyed the myriad pink roses twining among the glossy leaves, wondering what it was that arrested her notice.

It dawned on her slowly. On any rose plant, there should be flowers in every stage, from furled buds to overblown blossoms past their prime.

That wasn't the case here. Each petal was perfectly formed and curled, each flower at the height of bloom. And every one of them identical to the others.

She stared at the one in her hand. The gardener who created this rose, she decided, was a genius—or a magician.

Sounds of barking distracted her. They came from somewhere out of sight, beyond a wing of the château. They grew louder, and then Claude came over the grass with a large dog racing at his side.

Seeing Jenna, the boy altered his course and came up on the terrace to join her. His face was open and happy. This is how his father must have looked once upon a time, she thought. Before his eyes became filled with shadows.

"This is Roland," he said, The dog came up to Jenna and sniffed.

"Yes," she said, rubbing the dog's muzzle, "we've met before. You were in my room one night."

The boy shook his head. "Not Roland, mademoiselle. He sleeps in my room and never stirs until morning." The dog lost interest and went off, sniffing after an interesting scent.

"Have you finished your lessons so quickly?" Jenna asked.

"They were canceled," he told her, "so I took Roland for a run instead. He is young and too rambunctious, Gaston says." He looked over his shoulder anxiously to check on the dog's whereabouts.

Jenna hoped he would stay and keep her company for a while, and she tried to draw him out. "Do you have your lessons here at the château, or do you attend school in the village with the other children?"

Claude stared at her. "There are no other children."

The dog began barking urgently, and the boy turned around. "Oh! He has treed one of the kittens! No, no, you silly creature!"

He ran off to the rescue, leaving Jenna to puzzle over his words.

10

JENNA GREW RESTLESS and regretted her refusal of something to read. She remembered seeing a stack of books on one of the tables in the bedroom and decided to look for something to hold her interest. She crossed the terrace and went inside—and found herself in the wrong room.

A long table sat at right angles to the window, and the wall opposite was covered with open shelves holding rows of books. They looked old, and Jenna's professional instincts drew her across the room to examine them. One row was red, another green, but there were no titles on their bindings, only consecutive years from 1960 to the present.

Ledgers of some sort, she thought with disappointment.

As she was turning to leave, her eye was caught by a slender volume lying on one of the shelves. The label was yellowed with age, the black ink faded to purple but still legible:

Beaumont Foret, 1880.
Census and Vital Records

Jenna's heart filled with excitement. Not every parish document had been destroyed, and here was the proof of it. Inside there might be something that touched her own past.

Carefully opening the cover, she glanced at the first page. The entries weren't alphabetical, and she went down them scanning for her family name.

Amboise, Louis (farmer); wife—Isabelle, 7 children
Amboise, Charles (farmer)—unmarried
Deschamps, Marthe (widow)—no issue
Langlois, Rupert (silversmith); wife—Clotilde Amboise, 2
    children
Brun, Henri (farmer); wife—Marie Amboise, 6 children
Hubert, François (weaver)—unmarried, 1 natural child
Hubert, Amelie (weaver)—unmarried

"I see that you have changed your mind about wanting something to read," a voice said coldly.

She looked up to see Philippe framed in the open terrace doorway, his face severe. Her cheeks flamed with embarrassment.

"I was looking for the bedroom, and entered this room by mistake," she said quickly, "but I realize I can't offer any acceptable excuse for examining what is, after all, a private document—only my deepest apology for abusing your hospitality."

The frown was still there as he came forward. "You would find it dull reading," he said. "This is the estate room, and the book is nothing but an inventory."

"It's a census record," she confessed, "and I was looking for my family's name in it."

"I'm afraid your hopes must be disappointed." He lifted it from the shelf and turned it over. The back cover was gone, the other pages a fragile, soot-blackened mass. "I found this earlier today, after we spoke. It is the only record to survive the church fire. I suppose I should dispose of it."

He touched his finger to the last page, and pieces of it flaked away like black snow.

"No!" Jenna's hand shot out to clasp his wrist. She could feel his pulse beating strong and steady beneath her fingers. "Please! You mustn't destroy it. It can be preserved with proper care."

"I beg your pardon?"

"My profession is restoring damaged manuscripts."

"Ah. I then can appreciate your concern, mademoiselle." Philippe looked down at his tanned wrist, still ringed by her slender fingers. "If you will unhand me, I'll do my best to set the ledger down without causing further damage."

She let go of his wrist at once, feeling awkward and rude. 'I'd be happy to try and stabilize the ledger for you. As a way of expressing my gratitude to you."

He put the book down, and when he turned back to her, his charming smile was back. "There is no need to do so."

"There is every need. I can't forget that you saved my life," she said.

"You must not put yourself out, mademoiselle."

Philippe watched the frustration flicker over her face. "However," he continued, "you might be in a position to render me a great service. There are some other old documents that were damaged in the fire and that could be of immense importance to me. If you would render your opinion on how they should be treated and if they are salvageable, I would be deeply in your debt."

This is a gift from the gods, Jenna thought. Who knew what treasures she might uncover? "I'd be very happy to look at them."

"Excellent. But now you must rest. Come, I'll guide you back to your bedchamber."

He escorted her out into the corridor. The walls of the hallway were paneled in carved pearwood and hung with vibrant tapestries and paintings. She thought she glimpsed a Fragonard in a dim alcove, a Chagall through an open door. Jenna wondered what other treasures the château held.

He led her to the second door down. "Here we are. I'm sure you'll be happy to be reunited with your garment bag and a few of your other belongings."

She looked up at him swiftly. "My car's been found?"

"Yes."

"Thank God!"

"Unfortunately," he went on, "it is buried beneath a rockslide and damaged beyond repair."

Jenna bit her lower lip. "Thank God for insurance."

"And that you were not in the vehicle when it plunged over the ledge." Philippe took her hand and kissed it. "Now that your mind is relieved, I suggest you rest until dinner. You must be very tired after being up so long for the first time."

"A little," she admitted.

"If you feel up to it when you've rested, will you dine with me tonight?"

Jenna smiled. "Yes, thank you—now that I have something a little dressier to put on than this gown and robe."

"You look charming. Like a film star from Hollywood's Golden Age."

She felt herself blushing, something she couldn't remember doing in years, over a simple compliment. She changed the subject.

"I need to make some phone calls to arrange matters, and I've lost my cell phone."

"We have no land lines in Beaumont Foret, and I've never bothered to get a cell phone," he said.

"Really?" Jenna raised her eyebrows. "That seems strange in this day and age."

"To you, perhaps, mademoiselle." He smiled. "We are content with the old ways here, for the most part. Life in Fontine, especially here in Beaumont Foret, moves at a leisurely pace, compared to the outside world. Business within the valley is conducted face-to-face and with a handshake; business beyond is done mostly by letter."

"Then I could call from the inn in Haute Beaumont," she said, "if you'd arrange for me to be driven there. There was a phone outside the dining room."

His smile faded at the edges. "I regret that I did not make the situation clear, mademoiselle. The rockslide that destroyed your vehicle, mademoiselle, also closed the old road from the château. I've set some men to the task of building a way around it, but it will take some time to do."

"Are you saying we're completely cut off?"

"No, there is another way out at the far end, which comes out ten miles from Haute Beaumont; unfortunately it is rugged and only negotiable on horseback."

Jenna listened to his calm explanation, her mind working furiously beneath her calm surface. He was relaxed and casual, yet everything he said confirmed her growing suspicions. Something was more than a little odd about this place.

"Rest now. We will discuss this later in detail."

"Very well."

He touched her cheek with the back of his fingers. "Until this evening, then."

She closed the door and leaned against it for a moment, feeling light-headed. She tried to fool herself into believing that the mental image of the rental car buried beneath a rockslide was the cause of it.

No, she admitted finally. It was the look in his eyes when he smiled and touched my cheek.

She took a deep, steadying breath. Philippe Beaumont was a very handsome, charming, and virile man. She couldn't deny that she was attracted to him. And judging from the way he had looked at her just then, the attraction was mutual.

That could work for or against her.

Her face set in determined lines. Either way, it wouldn't stop her from pursuing her real purpose in coming to Beaumont Foret. But, she admitted to herself, I might find out that I'm on a fool's errand.

Her purse was on the table beside the bed, and she looked inside it for her cell phone. She couldn't recall if she'd put it back inside its pocket, or left it on the car's console. Jenna sighed. Either way, it was gone.

As she slipped off her robe, she heard something fall softly to the floor at her feet. Jenna looked but didn't see anything at first because the long hem of her nightgown hid it from view. She moved and her foot came down on it squarely, grinding it beneath her slippered heel.

"Oh! The rose!"

She stooped down to retrieve the flower, expecting to find a mass of crushed leaves and bruised petals. But the rose wasn't ruined after all. Her fingers brushed the blossom. Despite the trauma, it looked and felt as fresh and perfect as if it had just been plucked.

Beaumont Foret, she thought, really is a *very* strange place.

11

On his way down to dinner Philippe looked in on his son. Claude had taken his meal early and was now working on a complicated creation of wood, metal gears, and thick rubber bands.

"I'm building a mechanical rabbit," he said. "I thought it might amuse the mademoiselle."

"I'm sure it will." He picked up the sanded wood and turned it over in his hand, revealing the carved body. "Who taught you to work with gears so skillfully?"

"Monsieur LeFevre. He said I have a true talent for it. He's promised to teach me everything he knows, since his son has no interest in it."

A pang of guilt stabbed Philippe. In a better, saner world he would be the one teaching his son such things, instead of burying himself among the books in the tower room. He ran a long finger over the smooth surface.

"It's very impressive."

Claude's face lit up at his praise. "Perhaps I shall be a sculptor when I grow up."

"Perhaps you shall, indeed." He set the rabbit back on the desk.

"I must go down to dinner," he told the boy. "I'll stop by again before your bedtime."

Claude went back to his task. Philippe watched him from the doorway for a moment, then went out. As he strode along the corridor, he felt the familiar anger. If he didn't succeed in finding what he sought, what future would there be for his son?

But he dressed for dinner in an optimistic frame of mind. For once it seemed that Fate was on his side. Mademoiselle Jenna D'Arcy might be the catalyst for change.

The shelves in the tower room were full of learned works of the philosophers, scientists, and alchemists of other ages. His father had been sure the answer was in one of them, but Philippe himself had always had a terrible feeling that the answers he needed were to be found in an old clay urn, fire-damaged and fragile.

If that was true . . . and if she could salvage them . . .

As he went down the staircase he struggled against the hope rising within him. So many times he'd thought he was near to discovering the cure. So many times he'd failed. But now, the woman whose life he'd saved might offer him hope of salvation in turn. If she would agree to his proposals.

Philippe acknowledged that her professional skills were only part of the reason he'd told her about the manuscripts. *I am a man, not a monk. It is no surprise that I am attracted by her fresh beauty, by the quick intelligence in those intriguing sapphire eyes.*

There would be difficulties, of course. And dangers.

And he would deal with them when they came.

Gaston stepped out of the shadows and coughed discreetly.

Philippe raised his dark brows. "Yes? What is it?"

"If I may be so bold, monsieur—is it permissible to ask when the mademoiselle will be leaving?"

A small smile played over Philippe's mouth. "There has been a change of plans, Gaston. Mademoiselle D'Arcy will not be leaving. She will be staying on . . . indefinitely."

12

PHILIPPE KNOCKED ON Jenna's door and heard footsteps crossing the floor inside. When she opened it, the pale waif was gone, replaced by a chic and slender woman in a silk dress the same devastating blue as her eyes.

Her transformation stunned him. He stopped short on the threshold, then proceeded into the room when he'd caught his breath again.

She didn't notice his reaction—she was having trouble enough controlling hers.

The whiteness of his linen shirt heightened the effect of his brilliant smile against his deeply bronzed skin and his exquisitely tailored suit. He looked very much the lord of the manor—handsome, elegant, and supremely confident. But beneath that civilized surface lurked an air of mystery and danger that raised her pulse and sent a thrill dancing up her spine.

"You look rested," he said, and saw a flicker of disappointment cross her face. "And very beautiful."

She thanked him with composure, but his compliment brought a fresh rush of color to her cheeks. He took her hand as if he hadn't noticed, tucked it over his arm, and led her out of the room.

They dined by candlelight in a small salon done in muted colors to match the Aubusson carpet. Jenna was relieved when the last course was removed. Afterward she couldn't even remember what they'd eaten. Gaston removed the dessert plates and set out a tray with a crystal decanter and brandy snifters.

"Shall I leave you to your brandy?" she asked.

"I would much prefer that you stay and have a glass with me. How did you become interested in restoring manuscripts? Is it perhaps a family tradition?"

"Not at all." She smiled across at him. "I'm the first D'Arcy in three generations who didn't follow an interest in medicine. My parents are doctors, involved in genetic therapy, and my brother is a chemist and heads a pharmaceutical research company."

He looked at her across the rim of his glass. "What made you decide to follow another path?"

"I enjoy a more personal angle to my work. It began with my great-grandmother's journal." Jenna sipped the brandy. "I looked up other old diaries in the local library's collection. One thing led to another—and to Beaumont Foret."

"I think you will be very pleased with the library here."

After they finished their brandy, he escorted her down a long hall to the base of the north tower. The tall double doors were thrown open to a large room with a cavernous fireplace on the far wall. Every wall was filled with books and exquisite paintings.

Philippe took her around the room, telling her the history of its treasures. The highlights were an early Bible, an exquisitely painted Chinese scroll, and his favorite—an illuminated Book of Hours, gloriously gilded and intricately painted by a master's hand.

Jenna admired them, lingering over the Book of Hours, but he noticed that her gaze still roamed the room, as if searching for something more. "You seem disappointed."

"How could I be? Any museum would be over the moon to have a single one of these. But they're all remarkably preserved," she added. "I don't see anything requiring my talents."

"Ah, so you are looking for a challenge? Excellent. I have one that I hope will interest you."

He took her through a door and up a steep flight of winding stairs. "The thick stone walls keep this room cool in summer and warm in winter," he told her, "but there are special controls to keep the manuscripts at an unvarying degree."

Jenna was breathless before they reached the room on the top floor—and then she was speechless.

She walked along the shelves, taking in the handwritten manuscripts, rare books, and scrolls. "But . . . some of these are ancient and incredibly valuable! They should be in a museum."

"Someday they will be. But not until I've found what I'm seeking."

He went to a wooden chest and opened the lid. The fragrance of aromatic wood wafted out, with a dark undertone of smoke. "I imagine that these will interest you."

Jenna peered inside. It held three pottery jars containing charred vellum scrolls. She could make out a few of the Latin words and phrases.

"*Afflictions and Diseases . . . Cures . . . The Relief of Evil Humors in the Blood . . . Methods of Surgery*," she translated. "Why, these are medical texts."

Jenna read part of a line that was half obliterated. "And from what I can make out, they're copies of Greek originals that were far older."

"Yes. From the ruins of Pompeii. They were found inside a deep stone niche, beneath thick layers of ash. The unglazed jars helped preserve them."

"It's a shame the ash didn't protect them. It usually acts as an insulator."

"They were intact at the time of their discovery," he said, his voice deep with regret. "The curé purchased them on a pilgrimage to Rome, as a gift for my father, and brought them back here to Beaumont Foret. The night of his return the fire I spoke of earlier broke out. These scrolls were charred by the flames that destroyed the village records."

But not before the old curé had read enough to convince him that the cure we have sought so long was in them, he thought.

Aloud, he said, "They've been kept undisturbed for decades, in hopes that one day the technology would be available to restore them."

"It *is* available," Jenna said. "I know two universities that might undertake the project, if you're interested in contacting them."

"No." Philippe's voice was firm. "The scrolls cannot be taken from the château. Not until they've been restored and deciphered."

Jenna tried not to show her eagerness. "I see. And this is the challenge you mentioned?"

"You said earlier that winter at the château might have many compensations. Perhaps you would consider this one of them?"

"Yes." She slanted a thoughtful look his way. "But I imagine it might also have its complications."

His dark gaze met her clear blue one, and a smile lifted the corners of his firm mouth. "Any decisions are entirely in your hands, mademoiselle."

His words were simple enough on the surface, but beneath them lay a wealth of meaning. He was open to the possibility of a relationship outside their professional one—but she would be the one who made the choice.

She pretended to consider his offer, but she'd already made her up her mind. A professional opportunity like this came once in a lifetime, and then only to the lucky few. Added to her private agenda, it was almost too good to be true.

"I have to agree that moving them could present problems. They're incredibly fragile. But it's a huge project . . . I'd have to take a leave of absence."

Philippe closed the lid. He wasn't fooled. She radiated sparks of excitement. It occurred to him that it would be a delightful thing to see her light up that same way when she looked at him.

"There is no need to rush," he said. "We'll discuss terms later, and you can think about whether or not you would like to accept my offer over the next few days."

Later, back in her room, that was all that Jenna *could* think about.

Do I really want to spend the winter couped up in a fantastic château in Beaumont Foret, with an abundance of rare manuscripts, carte blanche to restore them—and a handsome, intriguing man like Philippe Beaumont?

The answer, of course, was a resounding "Yes!"

Philippe went down to the village to inform his cousin of what he'd done. The news was not received well.

"You invited her to stay on?" Armand was incredulous. "Have you lost your wits?"

"You forget yourself," Philippe said coldly. "You know my sworn duty. I will do everything in my power to see that the responsibility handed down to me is fulfilled."

The old man sitting in the corner nodded at his son. "And it is your duty, Armand, to help Philippe in any way you can. His task is not an easy one."

His cousin didn't like it, but he had to accept it. "As you will. But, for the love of God—be careful!"

Philippe smiled. "Have no fear. I can control Jenna D'Arcy. And I'll keep her so busy she has no time for anything else."

He took his leave of them. When he was gone, the old man tapped his son on the knee. "Do not worry. He is brave, that one, and wise beyond his years."

Armand shook his head. "Yes. But he is also a damned fool, because he is falling in love with her. I know the signs. He will bring ruin to us all."

13

AFTER GOING OVER the same paragraph three times without taking in a word of it, Jenna set aside the book she'd been trying to read. For the first time in years she felt out of her element.

The room seemed overly warm, and relaxing proved impossible. There were so many circumstances beyond her control. She could be sure of only two things.

The first was that she could salvage a good deal of the charred scrolls. The second was the certain knowledge that if she stayed on at the château, she and Philippe Beaumont would become lovers.

He was the first man ever to have that effect. For years she'd been driven by research and work. But there was something in him that attracted her strongly. It was more than the primal pull of his handsome face and steel-hard body. More than her pleasure at the keen intelligence that burned in his eyes, or the quick humor that touched his mouth.

God! That mouth! From the first moment she'd tried very hard not to think of what it would feel like, gliding over her skin. A flush of heat filled her and images rose to tantalize.

She imagined his arms wrapped around her, his mouth on hers. She could almost feel the pressure of it as it changed from soft seduction to the bold insistence of passion. Feel it moving along her jawline and down her throat . . .

A flush of heat rose from deep inside her, spreading through her veins. She went to the terrace doors and opened them to the cool night air. The stars looked huge, brighter than she remembered ever seeing them. Their reflections floated like candles on the surface of the moat, and fireflies flickered above the opposite bank.

If ever a place was enchanted, she thought, it would be Beaumont Foret.

Jenna stood there, letting the beauty of it fill her. As she watched, the moon crested the dark silhouette of the mountains, rimming them with silver.

The breeze picked up, skimming over her skin like a lover's hands. She grew restless and unsettled. I won't sleep tonight, she thought.

Taking the stairs down to the lawn, she moved through swaths of inky shadows and spears of pure white light. Her body ached to be held and touched, and she wondered if Philippe felt the same hum of desire that coursed through her. She wondered what would happen if she went to his room.

Jenna knew she could find it if she tried . . .

She turned back toward the château, and that was when she saw something. It was on the far side of the moat, near the woods. Certainly the biggest dog she'd ever seen.

The great head lifted, and the fur rippled like molten silver in the moonlight. Suddenly she knew the creature for what it was: not a dog but a wolf.

Its glowing eyes regarded her for a moment. Then it was gone, vanishing into the night.

14

PHILIPPE STOPPED IN the shadows between the old mill and the river. The bulk of the stone building loomed against the stars as he neared the water's edge. The breeze dropped. There was no sound but that of the river dashing and splashing over the rocks below the narrow dam.

Moonlight illuminated the tracks he'd come to examine. A young female, running lightly over the moist ground, then stopping to drink her fill. But why alone? That was unusual and disturbing.

Something has driven her down from the mountains, he thought again, and wondered what it could be. If she came from the blasting site near St. Anne, she was in unfamiliar territory. That could be dangerous.

He followed her trail as it went up past the mill and into the orchards, zigzagging through the trees. He lost it on a stretch of rocky ground near a low stone wall, then across the field toward the village the tracks picked up again, circling the houses at a distance. She'd done it more than once, obscuring her trail.

Something must have frightened her then. Her tracks ran straight past the ruins of the old church and headed back toward the château as if drawn with a ruler.

There was no use searching any further tonight. She would likely find her way back up to her pack. Philippe loped back toward the bridge.

He was skirting the edge of the forest when he heard something crackling its way through. A good-sized creature by the sound of it. At any other time he would have investigated, but then he saw Jenna descending the steps from the terrace in her light-colored gown.

She moved as gracefully as the reeds trembling in the breeze.

His breath came more quickly as need flooded him, tangled with admiration and alarm. She was lovely and clever and different from any woman he'd known. And she wanted him with a woman's passion. He imagined the heat of her molded against him, the yielding of her soft mouth. The sharp nip of her teeth upon his bare skin.

The decision would be hers, he'd said, and he would abide by the rules he'd set. The heat of desire warred with a bittersweet anticipation. How long would they stretch out this charade? How long until she was in his arms and in his bed?

He realized she'd turned her head and was staring across the moat to where he stood. Philippe melted back into the black mass of the forest, wondering exactly how much she'd seen.

15

PHILIPPE POURED HIMSELF another cup of coffee and looked across the breakfast table at his son. "Between estate business and our guest, I shall be more occupied than usual for a while. Armand and Marie have invited you to spend a few days with them. Would you like to go?"

"Oh, yes!" Claude set down his glass and grinned with boyish excitement. "Marie said she would make lemon tarts the next time I came to stay with them. And Armand promised to take me tracking with him in one of the side valleys."

"Then it is settled. Ask Berthe to pack up what you need for three or four days."

Claude was affronted. "I can pack my own things without bothering Berthe. And," he announced, "I can ride down to their home myself. There is no need for Armand to come for me. I am almost grown now, after all."

Philippe smiled, but his eyes were sad. "Yes, you are."

While Claude went off to pack, Philippe stared into his cup, wishing he could read the future there.

After taking care of some estate business with Gaston, he went in search of Jenna. She wasn't in her room, but he found her down by the moat, throwing bits of her breakfast roll to the swans.

"I was hoping to find Claude," she said. "But I haven't seen him or his dog."

"My son has gone to spend a few days with my cousin and his wife on the other side of the valley. As for Claude and Roland, they are inseparable. Where one goes, the other is bound to follow."

Jenna was disappointed. She liked Claude and looked forward to spending some time with him. Plus, she acknowledged, he would have been a good source of information about the château, the village, and their inhabitants. And his father.

Philippe scrutinized her as she tossed another morsel to the swans. She was dressed in tailored black slacks and a simply cut white silk shirt, with her hair neatly pulled back with combs. Her crisp appearance didn't fool him, though. Her skin was pale, despite the touch of lipstick and blusher, and there were shadows beneath her eyes.

"You did not sleep well, mademoiselle?"

"No. I was troubled by dreams," she admitted. She looked off across the moat toward the far shore. "At first I was running through a dark forest, with dogs baying somewhere behind me. I ran and ran for miles. Later I found myself up on a ridge so high that I could see the entire valley spread out at my feet like a map."

She tossed the last crumb of roll to a pair of ducks that swam up, braving the wrath of the swans. "But no matter how I tried, I couldn't find my way down again!"

Jenna shivered, remembering the icy splendor of the lonely mountain peaks and the cold wind that had blown through her dreams. "It was so real that I thought I was actually there when I woke up. It was a relief to find myself safely in bed."

Philippe's concern showed in the line that formed between his brows. "I hope your nightmare has not given you a distaste for Beaumont Foret."

Jenna shook her head. "It was only a dream. But I have come to a decision. I accept your offer. I'm due for a sabbatical. I'll stay on at Beaumont Foret and work on your manuscripts."

He felt the tension flow out of him. If he'd known she would take him up on his offer, his own sleep would have been less fretful. "I am delighted."

"I have only two conditions," she said. "One is that I'm not disturbed while I'm working, and the second is that no one cleans my lab except me."

"Fair enough. I have two of my own. No one leaves the château after nightfall—it is not safe. There are still wolves in the mountains, and one has been seen lurking about in the valley. Second, I am never to be disturbed at night once I've retired. Gaston will notify me in an emergency."

"Like Bluebeard?"

He laughed. "If you like."

"I have no trouble with either of your conditions," Jenna said.

"Then I am in your debt, mademoiselle."

"Not yet," she teased. "But you will be. I'm shockingly expensive."

A smile lit his eyes. "Most good things in life are. You must let me know what you require in the way of equipment and supplies."

She took a sheet of paper from her pocket. "I've made a list of everything I'll need. If there's a room you can set aside for my laboratory and an old table you don't mind ruining, I can get started right away."

He scanned the list in surprise. "Distilled water, paraffin, white vinegar, rubbing alcohol, cornstarch, fuller's earth—this looks like one of Berthe's lists for cleaning supplies and pantry items!"

Jenna laughed. "Yes, that's the beauty of it. They're mostly ordinary things that can be found in any household or general store. It's the materials in my kit that make the difference—and a little goes a long way."

"How clever of you to have invented it."

"I can claim only partial credit. The initial idea was mine, but it was my brother who refined it."

"Ah, yes. He is a chemist, you said. I should like to meet him one day."

She glanced up at him through her thick lashes. "Perhaps you will. One day."

The swans chased the ducks away in a great splashing and beating of wings, and Jenna turned away from the water. "When would you like me to begin?"

Philippe finished reading the list. "It will take me a day or two to get everything assembled. Meantime you must rest and conserve your energy until you're fully recovered. I will do my best to keep you entertained."

He was a man of his word, and devoted himself to Jenna for many hours every day. They walked through the château gardens and took the blue rowboat out on the moat, moving like the swans did through the water lilies. In the evenings they listened to music, discussed favorite books, and talked of their lives.

Jenna thought his must have been rather lonely, with long hours spent studying his books and estate management. Hers was fairly hurly-burly by comparison, romping with her brother and a dozen cousins who all lived nearby.

One day he came in from riding and found her in the salon, reading Daphne du Maurier's *Rebecca*. "That was one of Amelie's favorites," he said, looking over Jenna's shoulder. "She loved to read. Romance, mystery, fantasy."

Now that the topic was opened, Jenna felt free to ask about his wife. "She must have been very young."

"She was not quite nineteen." He lifted a silver-framed photograph and handed it to her. "This is Amelie, the night we met. We were both on holiday in Switzerland and went to the same party. We fell head over heels and decided to make a runaway match of it, knowing our parents would not approve. And rightly so."

He gave that shrug she was coming to know so well. "We were not suited. I know that now. But we never had time to discover that and become embittered. Less than a year later Amelie was gone."

"I'm very sorry. Had she been ill long?"

Philippe's brows came together, and it was a moment before he answered her. "It was an accident that took her. She was hiking out on the mountainside and became lost in one of the side valleys. She lost her footing and fell to her death."

Trying to escape from a reality that was worse than anything her imagination could conjure, he thought silently.

"I'm sorry," Jenna repeated softly. There was little she could say to an old tragedy, and nothing she could do to change the past.

"You've never married?" he asked.

"No." She lifted her shoulders. "The timing was never right."

Jenna picked up another framed picture. Philippe and Amelie on horseback, looking happy. Philippe rested an arm on the mantel. "Do you ride?"

"Yes, although it's been quite a while since I've been on horseback."

"Good. Perhaps we might ride down to the village one day when you are stronger."

"I'd like that. You ride out every afternoon. I've seen you from my window."

"Perhaps you might accompany me today. Would you like to visit the stables? There's a chestnut mare I think you might like."

They went out into the gardens. Phillipe led Jenna through an arch and into the stableyard. An old man sat outside in the sunlight, mending a harness, while another sluiced down the cobblestones. They smiled and answered Philippe's greetings, and eyed Jenna when they thought she wasn't looking.

She pretended not to notice their obvious interest in the newcomer to the château.

But the moment they entered the stables, the animals grew restive. The mare snorted and whinnied, and dun-colored gelding lashed at the door of his stall with flashing hooves. The others moved uncertainly, their graceful nostrils flaring and their eyes showing too much white.

"Something has happened to upset them," Philippe said, trying to calm the mare as a stable hand attempted to soothe the dun gelding.

Jenna saw the fine black horse with a white blaze on its forehead down at the end. He tossed his mane and snorted in warning as she neared.

Philippe whirled around. "No! You little fool! He'll kill you."

Before he could stop her, Jenna entered the box. She lifted her hand to caress the horse's velvety muzzle and whispered to him. The trembling stopped, and the animal went still. Then he whickered softly and nudged her.

"He won't harm me," she laughed, when she saw Philippe's face, white with fear and fury. It was true, and the other horses calmed down almost immediately.

"You have a gift for soothing them," Philippe said with amazement.

She smiled. "I've always had a knack with animals." She ran the palm of her hand over the horse's neck. "This one is your particular favorite, isn't he? I've seen you riding him from my window."

Philippe was astounded to see the creature so tame beneath her hand. "Yes. His name is Lion-Heart, but the undergrooms call him Devil's Seed. Usually he is the most high-spirited of them all."

In fact, only Philippe and his head groom could control him.

As Jenna stroked Lion-Heart's muzzle, the animal gave a soft whinny. Philippe watched as the horse nuzzled Jenna's neck. "I've never seen him so eager to please. It is almost as if he knows you."

"I imagine he can be a rare handful. Would you trust me to ride him?"

"Ordinarily I would not let anyone else even attempt to mount him, but I would have no qualms about you after seeing the special rapport you have with him."

Jenna patted Lion-Heart. "We understand one another. We speak a common language."

The next few days flew by, and Philippe kept her entertained, although the excursion to the village was put off more than once. Formality vanished between them, but Jenna was sometimes aware of a slight air of reserve in him.

They walked in the gardens in the cool of the mornings, talking about a dozen things that neither of them could recall afterward. In the afternoon, when the heat was greatest, they retreated inside the thick stone walls of the château, setting up Jenna's workspace.

The evenings were best—dining by candlelight, laughing, talking, or lapsing into the deep silences of two people who, given enough time and the right set of circumstances, might find themselves falling in love.

16

Every afternoon they went for short rides near the château, but whenever Jenna suggested riding down to the village, Philippe found an excuse: he had a meeting with his steward, Jenna looked tired, the heat was too intense.

By the fourth day they still hadn't gone into Beaumont Foret, but things were almost completely set up for Jenna to start working. She looked around in satisfaction. She had glass measuring cups, bowls, and tools set out along the long worktable. Two large sheets of glass covered part of it, with her case of chemicals and fixatives beside them.

She heard the sound of hoofbeats and went to the window in time to see Philippe ride out on his black horse. Once away, he let the horse have his head and they went from a brisk trot to a canter, then to a gallop across the green meadows. When they vanished from sight, she turned her gaze in the direction of the village.

Tomorrow, she thought. Tomorrow I
have to go alone. Jenna had a good view
window. It looked like a watercolor, all
distance. Remembering the opera glasses she
moire, she went down to fetch them for a bet

What she saw through them on her return pe.
rather, what she didn't see.

The village square was empty. No young wives with babies
or older men and women sat in the shade of the ancient trees.
No laundry hung from the limp clotheslines, no children played
in the overgrown gardens.

She panned the houses from east to west. The shutters were
closed on most, perhaps to keep the heat of the day out. Or
because no one lives in them? she wondered.

Then she saw movement. A boy and a large dog running
through the empty streets. She swung the opera glasses to follow Claude, as he turned and skipped along with his shaggy
pet toward a cream-colored house with blue shutters. Was that
the home of Armand and his wife, Marie?

An old man sat on a bench outside, smoking his pipe, and
she glimpsed a woman of about fifty through an open window.
Jenna saw other signs of life nearby: a man repairing a wheel-
barrow, two older women, one picking beans from a wire support and the other hulling them.

All in all, it seemed that a dozen houses out of the thirty or
forty were occupied. The other people must be in their shops
in the village or out in the fields with their crops, she thought.
Otherwise there would be only about sixty or seventy people
in all, Jenna calculated. No, that can't be right. That can't be
the entire population of Beaumont Foret!

But in her heart she feared it was. Like so many out-of-the-
way villages, Beaumont Foret was dying.

A short time later Jenna went out to the stables in an old pair
of jodhpurs and some tan riding boots that Berthe had un-
earthed the day before. "I'm taking the mare out," she told the
groom.

The old man scratched his chin. It was true that monsieur
Philippe had said the lady was to ride the mare, but no one had

would be today. "Very well. I will saddle her up
mademoiselle."

na thanked him, and a short time later she was on
eback, heading across the bridge. I'll be sore tomorrow,
e thought. But I won't put it off any longer. I'll stop by and
see how Claude is doing.

She took the road toward the village, then cut off across the
meadow and entered it from the side that seemed uninhabited.
The first two cottages looked fine from a distance, but as she
approached she saw that the flowers beside them were really
wildflowers, tiles were missing on the roofs, and glass in the
windows was broken.

Then she came to a burned-out foundation and by the cross
and the inscription on the blackened cornerstone realized that
she'd found the ruins of the old church. The churchyard was
beyond it, backing up toward the rocky cliffs. Although the
roofs of the houses rose past the trees, there was no steeple
visible to indicate the site of a new church.

Dismounting, Jennifer tied the mare to a tree and wandered
among the headstones. They were lovingly tended, the grass
clipped short and every stone fronted by a kind of small, pale
blue flower that she'd never seen before.

She moved among them, noting the names and dates. The
D'Arcys were on a knoll topped with the wide-arching
branches of an ancient tree. Even here, she saw, the little flowers bloomed. Someone still tended them with care, although the
last D'Arcy had died sixty years before. It touched her deeply.

Jenna jumped as a shadow fell over her. She gasped and
looked up to find Philippe glaring at her.

"You should not have attempted to ride so far alone, the first
time!"

Now or never, she decided. "It was too tempting to resist,"
she said. "Tomorrow I start working on the texts, and today is
just so perfect . . . and I was beginning to wonder if you ever
meant to bring me here."

He grimaced and ran his tanned fingers through his hair. "I
suppose I have been avoiding it. My family have been the lords
of this valley for hundreds of years. Love for this place, for its
people, runs deep in my blood. In my heart it is as it was when
I was a boy—still full of life and hope."

Jenna listened, her heart breaking for him. When he s͓. of his boyhood his face was soft and filled with abiding aﬀec-tion. Then it changed, became hard and wintry, and his mouth flattened in a bitter line.

"But as you see, the vigor of Beaumont Foret is gone. It is withering away, like fruit left too long on the vine."

She sighed softly. "I noticed that there seemed to be no one under the age of thirty or so, except for Claude." She hesitated, gazing through the trees at the sun-drenched orchards, the stone houses clustered on either side of the winding road.

Philippe's eyes were dark with emotion. "You are very ob-servant. My son is the only one of his generation in this entire valley."

Hearing it put into so baldly makes it so much worse, Jenna thought. "Claude told me that there were no other children in the village. I didn't understand at the time."

He stood in silence for a moment, staring into a past that only he could see. Jenna was sorry she'd broached the subject. Philippe blinked and came back to the present. "Shall we con-tinue into the village, then?"

"No . . . I'd like to go back to the château. I'm . . . I'm tired."

"As you wish." He helped her mount the mare, then swung onto his own horse. As they rode away, his gaze raked the village with its empty houses, the fields that were unused and going back to nature.

God knew, he was tired too.

Then he glanced over at Jenna riding at his side, the sun gleaming on her chestnut hair. Her presence brought life to the château, and hope to him.

And, please God, life and hope for all of Beaumont Foret.

17

Jenna WENT DOWN to dinner in a Deco-inspired dress of red jersey, caught at the midriff with a circle of rhinestones. Three narrow straps held it in place on either side of her shoulders, and the curves of the bodice molded to her own. As the draped hem swirled against her legs, she felt elegant and sophisticated, like the heroine in a thirties movie.

The two dresses she'd brought with her to Fontine were lovely, but nowhere near the same class. And this one, like the peach ensemble, had never even been taken from its box.

Philippe met her at the foot of the stairs with a smile of approval. "Enchanting!" he said. "And the color suits you admirably."

"Thank you. It's another one more of the thirties confections that Berthe continues to produce from her stores, like a magician pulling scarves from his sleeve."

"There is an attic devoted solely to them," he told her. "One of my grandmother's great aunts was addicted to fashion, and had far too much time and money on her hands. She went to London or Paris several times a year. I recall as a boy seeing her return with enough trunks and bandboxes to outfit a caravan. She never wore half of them."

He swept another admiring look over Jenna. "And they would not have been nearly as charming as they are upon you."

Dinner was a quiet affair. The long windows were open to the warm summer air, and the candle flames flickered in the light breeze. There was a curious intimacy, and it seemed to Jenna that time had no meaning, that she and Philippe had dined like this hundreds of times in the past, or even in the future.

The realization hit her. I'm falling in love with him— No! I'm already in love with him.

Yesterday that would have panicked her—she hadn't always chosen wisely in the past. Tonight it seemed part of a romantic dream. She and Philippe were two of a kind, equally matched in spirit and mind.

It feels right and good, she thought. And magical. Something that was meant to be.

She smiled at him across the table, her eyes like stars in the candlelight. Philippe took a deep breath. He sensed that they were on the brink of something too lovely and too delicate to put into words. For now they must live in the moment, with no baggage from their pasts and no expectations.

From time to time they made conversation, then drifted back into their own reverie's, which although separate, twined around each other like the vines on the garden walls. The silence was contented, punctuated by the clink of silver on porcelain, the chime of crystal as her wineglass touched the rim of her plate.

"When will Claude return?" Jenna asked as Gaston brought in the dessert course.

"The day after tomorrow," Philippe replied. "I saw him today in the village and he asked to stay on a bit. He enjoys a change of scene, and Marie LeFevre indulges him with all her motherly instincts." He stopped short, realizing what he'd said. Poor Marie.

Jenna hesitated until Gaston left the room. "Have you ever thought of sending him away to school?"

All their ease fell away. Philippe's face went rigid. "Claude is happy here."

Jenna felt chilled despite the warm night. She realized she'd breached a boundary of good manners, but she couldn't change her course—or her feelings.

"I've offended you, and I'm sorry for that. But he needs the company of other children. Someday he'll have to go off into the world."

"You will allow that I know best when it comes to my son's welfare," Philippe said.

She couldn't hold back. "He can't stay here forever, like Peter Pan and the Lost Boys."

"You know nothing of the matter." His voice was colder than absolute zero.

Jenna paled but held her chin up as she finished her wine. This time, when she rose to leave him with his brandy, Philippe didn't urge her to remain and share a glass with him.

When she was gone he sat clenching the crystal brandy snifter in the palm of his hand. He was furious with her, because she was right.

But then again, so am I. She knows nothing about us!

He hoped to God he could keep it that way.

Philippe went to the salon in search of Jenna, prepared to find she'd retired for the night. He'd lingered a long time over his brandy, turning over in his mind the little scene that had played out between them.

I did not handle the situation well, he thought, and wondered if she would change her mind about staying on. And exactly what he would tell her if she insisted on leaving Beaumont Foret.

When he entered, the room was empty, and he felt a keen pang of disappointment, followed by anger at himself. Then he saw a flutter of red just beyond the terrace doors and went out.

Jenna stood looking up at the sky. She was glad the moon wouldn't rise above the peaks for at least another hour. It seemed as if there were more stars above Fontine than anyplace she had ever seen. In the clear mountain air they looked immense and very, very close to earth.

She sensed Philippe behind her. "I could reach out my hand and touch that largest star," she murmured.

"I would gather them all for you, Jenna, and lay them at your feet—if you will forgive me."

She whirled around to face him. "It was my fault. I spoke out of turn."

He shook his head. "You spoke the truth. It is not something that I can discuss with you—or with anyone—just yet. But the truth can be painful."

Her smile was genuine, and just a little sad. "Yes."

It wasn't planned or even a conscious move on either part. The next moment she was wrapped in his arms, her head against his shoulder. Philippe lifted her chin in his hand and bent his head, claiming her lips with his. A simple kiss of reconciliation that suddenly changed, deepened, and turned into something more.

She heard a soft sound and realized it was her own voice, a low moan of surrender and need. It caught her off guard, sweeping her up in a flood of desire. The same currents swirled through him, tides of passion washing away everything else. Nothing mattered but this.

The circle of his arms tightened, and he felt the softness of her breasts against his chest, the slender arch of her back, the soft flare of her hips. For one moment of sanity, he tried to stem the flood. Her arms wound around his neck, pulled his mouth back to hers.

Their breath mingled and their hearts pounded in rhythm. They were submerged in a river of rising need, and it was too late, too late to hold it back. His mouth caught the tender place below her ear, slid smoothly down to just where the pulse beat wildly at her throat.

Jenna sighed and gave herself up to his lips and hands. This was the moment they'd been heading for from the beginning. That it came too soon made it no less welcome. She curved her body against his, gasped as his hands cupped her breasts and his mouth took hers again, in a ravaging kiss.

He lifted his head and looked down into her eyes, read the willingness, the longing, the deep, upwelling need. Then he swept her up against him, crushing her to his chest. It was only a few quick strides across the terrace to the doors of her room. A thrust of his shoulder and they were inside.

He started for the bed, but they never made it that far. Her mouth was hot on his, urging him on. He tilted her body, let the supple curves slide through his hands until her feet touched the ground. With his kiss still lingering, Philippe stripped off his jacket and shirt, then tugged at the straps of her dress, exposing her smooth shoulder to his lips.

A quick zip and the bodice loosened, spilling her breasts free to his caresses. She ached with pleasure as his mouth found them, and she stretched and arched and almost purred beneath his touch.

The brush of his hand against her, the strong muscles of his arms and chest beneath her fingers, inflamed her more. Soon, they were entwined on the carpet in a lush tangle of limbs, seeking and tasting, giving and taking, teasing and pleasuring.

Her breasts were ripe for his tongue, aching for the tug of his mouth. She felt the pull of it deep in her loins as her body went liquid beneath him. He tantalized her, brought her to the edge of rational thought and drove her far beyond it.

He knew the exact moment that she was ready for him, but held back. The touch of his hand, the thrust of his fingers had her slick and wild. She grasped at him, wanting more. Faster. Then she was out of control, her nails raking down his back as she cried out, her mouth against his hot, hot skin.

He took her there again, flung her higher into the bright flare of heat that rose around them. Just when she thought she was done, that there was nothing left of her to give or take, she felt him slide inside. She fought to hold him without losing herself in him. Not yet, not yet.

As she molded herself to him, her fingers danced and teased across his chest, leaving trails of flame. At her signal he thrust deep and hard, taking his cues from her arousal. Holding himself back by sheer willpower.

Their bodies paced one another, moving instinctively to heighten sensation. Her hips lifted to welcome him, urged him to ride her long and hard. He met her, need for need, passion for passion, heat for heat. The world ignited. Turned molten as they melted into one another, forging something bright and new and strong.

When it was over, they lay slick and sated. But not for long. This time their joining was a slow dance, a celebration of pure physical sensation. The climax was more glorious than before, taking them higher and higher until they reached a shattering crescendo. She abandoned herself to it, enveloping him in heat, thrusting up with a joyous cry.

For a long time they lay together, kissing. Neither spoke. She fell asleep with her cheek against his shoulder.

Jenna dreamed.

She was a silver wolf, running through a world of rainbow scents and infinite colors. The sheer joy of it was overwhelming, the pure physicality an intoxication.

A shape moved out of the shadows, thick fur rippling over muscles of steel. Eye glowing golden. She knew him, of course. The alpha male. Sure of himself, regal in his power.

She would have laughed if she could have. A quick glance of invitation and she was off, running wild and free. Let him catch her if he dared.

He did.

They leapt and wrestled in the moonlight, reveling in the knowledge of how it would end. He rose over her at last, victorious. She bared her throat in surrender and he growled his pleasure.

Their mating was fierce, the release intense . . .

And Jenna awakened to find herself slick with sweat and stretched out, naked, across her bed. Her body felt liquid and languid and ready for more.

She reached out, but her questing hand touched nothing but cool linen. She rolled over and sat up.

Moonlight poured through the open window, and Philippe was gone.

18

JENNA SMILED AS Philippe came into her laboratory. Every time she looked at him she thought how very lucky she was. She'd never expected to find a lover so suited to her. Handsome, ardent. Her equal in every way.

If only he would trust me more, she thought, then everything would be perfect.

But night after night he left her side. He would never say why he didn't stay beside her. He would never talk over the worries that shadowed his eyes. They'd been growing day by day.

He looked somber now. "Gaston said you needed me."

She went to him, sliding her hands up over his shoulders, letting her fingertips trail along the back of his neck. "I always need you."

She'd hoped for a like rejoinder, and frowned as he pulled away. "What is it? Is something wrong?"

Taking her hands in his, Philippe took her over to the window, where the golden autumn light shone brightly. In the valley far below, the leaves were just falling, but there were bruised clouds rolling in from the north, hiding the highest peaks.

He looked down into her eyes. "Are you happy, Jenna?"

"Deliriously."

His eyes raked her face, searching for signs of distress. There were none. He dropped her hands and turned to look out over the valley. It was so hard to know what was right and wrong, and where his loyalties lay. His love for her was overwhelming. If he lost her— *No!* The pain of it was unthinkable.

He took a deep breath.

"If I asked you to leave . . ."

"Philippe!" It was a cry of protest, ripped from the heart of her.

She reached out to him for assurance, but he shook his head. "I have to know, Jenna. If I asked you to leave, would you go?"

"No." She didn't hesitate.

"Then . . . what if I *told* you to leave?"

Jenna saw the fear he was trying to hide, and laughed softly. "I would ignore you. And then I would make mad, passionate love to you until you were too exhausted to speak."

He laughed too, but the darkness was still there, eating at him. The longer she stayed, the closer she came to discovering everything he wanted to hide. With their growing intimacy it was inevitable.

His face became serious. "I think you should leave Beaumont Foret, Jenna. Today, before it's too late. There will be snow by morning. If you don't leave today, it will be many months before you have another chance to go."

"You're awfully anxious to be rid of me," she said.

"No. But I would rather have you go now, with good feelings, than to stay and . . . and change."

She stepped so close that his arms gathered her in from habit. "I love you, Philippe, and I intend to stay."

He closed his eyes and kissed her with a fierce protectiveness. "I love you too, Jenna. I have from the very beginning. Never forget that—whatever happens."

She cradled his cheek against her palm. "And never forget that the decision to stay was mine—whatever happens."

Jenna moved away, her eyes gleaming. "Did Gaston say why I wanted you to come up here?"

"No."

She lifted the protective cover off the table. Yesterday the pieces of glass had held sections of charred scroll, flattened by one of the chemicals in her kit, and still unreadable. Today, what were once vague coppery marks and unreadable squiggles on the dark brown parchment had been transformed to flowing black words against a pale ocher ground.

"Unbelievable!" he said. "You are a magician!"

She tipped up her head and smiled. "No. It's just the magic of science."

"My God!" He came over to examine them. "I can make out a word here and there."

"But not enough. Don't worry," she said. "The fixative is unstable at first, and some of the chemicals have to evaporate. By tomorrow the words will be crystal clear."

Philippe's first excitement calmed a bit. The text wasn't what he'd expected. "They look like extracts from works on herbs, or gardening—"

"Try this one." She indicated her laptop, humming on the desk. "It was still faint, so I scanned it in and ran the enhancing software. The writing is very ornate and difficult to read, and the language is one I've never seen before."

"Ah, but I have. It is a coded form of Old French and Latin, used by mages and alchemists." Tension stretched his muscles taut. Had the moment finally come?

For the first time he faced the fears that had hovered like a specter, haunting all his hopes. Perhaps the burned documents held no answers to his prayers. Perhaps his father had told him so only to give him courage to go on with his life.

He scanned the first page of the scrolls that had been uploaded into the computer, frowning in concentration. The ornate writing, with all its loops and flourishes, was difficult enough to read, much less translate.

Jenna was impatient. "What does it say?"

"It is a sort of introduction to the 'wonders and marvels' contained within the document." A slight smile curved his lips.

"Along with a good deal of bragging by the author that he is the greatest alchemist of his time."

Philippe scrolled down further, and his heart gave a leap of excitement. He read aloud:

> *In this work will be found stunning spells, enchantments, and philters for the use of those who have studied philosophy and medicine. First come the simple cures for ailments of the heart and uneasy breath, lung fever and other afflictions of man; then those that protect against the Red Death and the Black Death, scrofulous fevers and wasting disease, and those that hasten childbirth.*
>
> *In the third part will be found such as can calm a madman, turn a simpleton into a paragon of wisdom, and other miracles of nature derived from alchemy. And lastly are those that only the most experienced of mages should attempt: the summoning of angels; the alterations of weather; the changing of man into beast, and back again.*

He tried to move the cursor further down, but it wouldn't budge. "It's the end of the document," he exclaimed. "Where is the rest of it?"

Jenna made a face. "I don't know, but I certainly hope it's in one of the jars, with the other scrolls."

That evening, as he and Jenna and Claude played Concentration with two card decks in the salon, Philippe's gaze was attracted by movement at the window. He looked up and saw it was snowing heavily.

He rubbed his neck and let the tension ease out of him. For good or ill, Mother Nature had taken the decision out of his hands.

"I have another match! And another." Claude exclaimed, as he picked up another king of hearts and the nine of diamonds. His cheeks were rosy and his eyes almost overbright.

"You win. You've beaten us again," Jenna said.

Philippe congratulated his son, and they played another game before his bedtime. He joined in the spirit of it, his mood buoyed by the knowledge that Jenna could not leave him now. Not until spring.

Pray God that she will uncover the cure before she uncovers my secret.

That night, for the first time, he stayed in bed with Jenna.

She'd fallen asleep in his arms after their heated lovemaking, her body tangled with his. When she awakened in the night, she was surprised to find him still there.

She stretched and got up, tiptoeing to the window. The valley was ermined with snow, and stars burned bright in a moonless sky.

Somewhere a wolf howled, its eerie cry borne to her on the wind. Jenna shivered and wrapped her arms around her shoulders.

Philippe murmured in his sleep and turned over.

After a while Jenna walked back to the bed and stood staring down at him. There were so many words unspoken between them. So many questions left unasked. She was afraid that she would ruin everything by wanting too much, too soon.

She slipped into the bed beside him and fell asleep with her head against his chest. When she awakened next it was dawn, and he was gone.

19

"I'VE FOUND ANOTHER part of it," Jenna said excitedly as she burst into the estate room where Philippe had been working late. Outside the wind howled and February sleet drove at the windows.

He looked up in astonishment as she set her laptop down on the desk beside him. "The manuscript?"

"Yes. From the color of the vellum and the handwriting, I think it's a scroll belonging to the first set of those I restored."

He turned to the screen she propped open, trying to keep his hand steady as he scanned the lines.

" 'For the changing of man into wolf,' " he translated. " 'In a goblet of rock crystal, let it be half filled with the crests of white stallions and let there be placed twelve threads from the garments of a holy man, add the distilled essence of twenty unicorn horns and a breath of winter . . .' "

Philippe was sick with disappointment. He pushed the laptop

away and rose. "All nonsense," he told her. "The ravings of an unsound mind!"

But Jenna was frowning and paying no attention to him. Excitement unfurled inside her. "There's nothing I like better than solving a mystery. Unicorn horns: that's an old nickname for the allium plant. The crests could be its white flowers . . . and monks are holy men . . ."

"What are you talking about?"

"Monkshood," she said. "The plant called aconite. But I don't know what the 'breath of winter' might be. Do you have any botany books around?"

He looked down at her in wonder. "Where do you come by all this strange knowledge?"

"It's not strange in my family. Aunt Alys is a gardener and herbalist, and she was always teaching us to make face creams and body lotions and herbal teas from the things that grew in our backyard. Her influence is one of the reasons my brother became interested in chemistry. We were always out picking things for her—chamomile, witch hazel, cherry bark. You name it, and I can probably tell you what it's good for; John could tell you all its chemical components, too."

Philippe put his hands on her shoulder. "My darling Jenna, how much more of this scroll do you have to restore?"

"Five, maybe six strips. I can't tell until I unroll them."

He pulled her into his arms and kissed her. "What a fortunate day it was when you came into my life."

One thing led to another. The ledgers and the laptop were forgotten in their haste to go upstairs and celebrate.

Jenna was awakened after midnight by a rapping on her door. She looked over for Philippe, but he was gone, as was usual after their lovemaking.

She slipped on a robe and unlocked the door. Berthe stood there in her nightgown and terry robe. "It is Claude. He is doubled over with stomach pains, and asking for you."

Jenna hurried out into the passage and followed the housekeeper toward the stairs. "Is Monsieur Beaumont with him?"

"No." Berthe bit her lip.

"Has he been sent for?"

"He has gone out."

"At this time of night? It's almost three in the morning."

"Nevertheless, he has gone out!" Berthe flung open the door to Claude's room.

The boy was tangled in his sheet, his legs curled up to his chest and his face pale. "Oh, mademoiselle! I hurt so."

She was glad that she'd learned a lot just observing her mother. Jenna leaned down and touched his forehead. No fever. That was good. She felt his stomach and side the way her mother had when she'd been a young girl with appendicitis. No rebound tenderness.

"What did you eat for your dinner?" she asked.

"Onion soup," he managed between moans. "And two stuffed cabbage rolls."

"And a slice of raisin pie," Berthe added.

"No," Claude said, rolling from side to side. "*Three* slices of raisin pie. With fresh cream."

Jenna laughed despite herself. "I believe this is the mystery solved. A bad case of indigestion is my diagnosis. Nothing that can't be cured by a dose of antacid."

"Do you think so?" Berthe managed. "Oh, mademoiselle, I am so glad you were here tonight. I was quite distracted with worry."

She hurried off to fetch a bottle of liquid antacid. Once Claude was dosed he began to feel better quickly. He fell asleep before Jenna could finish the story she was weaving for him, about kindly dwarves who mined gemstones, a wicked queen, and the lovely princess who came to live in their cottage in the woods.

"It is almost dawn. I'll stay with him," Berthe said, with a warm smile for Jenna.

There is nothing like overcoming a crisis together to bond two women, Jenna thought. Unless it is love for the same small boy.

Once he was settled Jenna tiptoed back toward the head of the stairs. The light of dawn was seeping into the corridor as she passed the room that was Philippe's. She turned the corner and gave a squeak of surprise as a shape lunged out of the shadows toward the door of his room.

For a confused moment it looked like a great gray wolf standing on its haunches. She gasped in shock, before recognizing Philippe. He was swathed in a fur cloak that covered him from the crown of his head to his feet.

"I told you never to come here!" he said angrily.

Jenna tried to speak and couldn't. As the light came through his windows into the corridor she stared at him in shock. The illusion of a cloak vanished. His body was covered with thick fur, his long hair flaring out behind his neck and flowing down along his spine into a wolf's raised hackles.

20

PHILIPPE TOOK HER wrists in hands like steel and pulled her into the room. She didn't move as he shut the door and thrust the bolt home. The bedchamber was huge, with a massive bed canopied by a faded tapestry, and dark furnishings. The draperies of red brocade were swagged back to let in the light.

He stood where sunbeams fell across the floor, watching her reaction as the fur that covered him began to vanish like mist, revealing the tanned and solid muscle beneath.

Jenna observed it all, as if from a far distance. It wasn't the transformation of him from werewolf to man that had her frozen to one spot, it was the red that stained his skin. At first she thought it was only the glow of sunrise through the windows.

Then she saw it was blood. Fresh blood.

It smeared his mouth and jaw and ran in rivulets down his throat. The hot, metallic scent of it filled the room. She recoiled from him in horror.

No, no, no!

She didn't realize that she'd spoken aloud. Philippe saw her stricken face, the anguish in her eyes. "Hush! Jenna, you must listen to me . . ."

He reached out to clasp her shoulders but she stepped back, stretching out her palm to block him. She couldn't bear to have him touch her. Not now, not with that bright red blood drying on his lips. "Keep back!"

He stepped forward, into the light from the window. It was only then that Jenna saw that the source of the blood was a deep gash in his cheek. More blood ran down his chin and jaw.

"You're injured!"

Philippe heard the relief in her voice, and smiled in irony. "Yes. The blood is mine. To whom did you think it belonged— some hapless villager?"

"You'll have to forgive me for jumping to conclusions," she said in a tart but slightly shaky voice. "It's not every morning that I accidentally stumble upon a bloodied wolf turning back into a man before my eyes."

He laughed suddenly. "You're remarkably calm, given the circumstances. I only wish Roland had been as calm. He got loose somehow and came upon me as I was transforming back. He was confused to smell my scent upon a wolf, and thought I had fallen victim to a savage beast. I had to lock him in the garden shed."

"You can tell me all about it later. First I'd better clean that gash." Jenna took a thick wash cloth from the linen cupboard folded it neatly and pressed it against his cheek. "Keep that in place while I find some antiseptic and bandages."

"Don't bother. It will soon heal itself"

He took her wrist and pulled the makeshift bandage away. Jenna blinked. It was true. The wound was half its former size, and closing before her eyes. In another minute or two it would be gone.

"What are you?" she whispered. "Who are you?"

"I think you've guessed by now." His jaw tightened. "I am the *loup garaou*. What you would call a werewolf. The product of an experiment gone wrong. It was supposed to improve the strength and endurance of the human race—not turn a man into a monster."

"This is the reason, then, that you never stayed the night with me." The reason for the urgency in his face at times—and the despair at others. "I imagine this is the reason you told me there was no way out of Beaumont Foret during the winter months. So I wouldn't try to leave if I discovered your secret."

Philippe looked suddenly weary. "No. If you had wanted to leave, I would not have stopped you from doing so. I told you that to protect you. So you would not become lost on the mountainside trying to flee this place, and die. That is the truth of Amelie's death."

She frowned. "She was leaving you?"

"How could she not? When we married I believed that I was one of the lucky ones, that I could escape the curse that lies over this valley. That we could live anywhere in the world, untouched by it. You see, there is only one *loup garaou* in each immediate family. The alpha male, he would be called by scientists studying a wolf pack. When the father or oldest male in that group either dies or his powers wane, only then is the trait activated in his successor."

"I see. You thought you had time on your side, and you tried to grasp happiness while you could."

"Exactly. My father was a healthy man in his prime and the alpha male. There was no reason to think that Amelie and I could not live twenty, thirty, forty years before I would inherit the transformation."

Jenna sat down on the edge of the bed. "And so you ran off with Amelie and married her, without telling her the rest of it."

He shook his head. "I didn't want to take the chance of losing her. Also, there was some speculation that I, like my cousin Armand, might not have inherited the trait. What a fool I was!"

His face altered, and she could see in it all the tragic reflections of the past. "What happened?"

"My first change occurred on the first full moon after I became twenty-one. Claude was only two months old, and we had just come to live at the château. I was totally unprepared for it." His voice was heavy with grief.

"I awakened in the night beside her in agony, thinking I was suffering some kind of seizure. And then I saw my hand change, felt my teeth lengthen to fangs. I knew then that I had not escaped the curse—and that my father was dead."

His eyes grew dark with sorrow. "When she saw what I was, she was terrified. I tried to explain to her that I was still Philippe. Still her love. But her love for me was dead, killed by her fear of me. She threatened to take Claude and leave me."

"Can you blame her?" Jenna exclaimed. "Everything she thought she knew was a lie. The husband and child she loved were doomed to a fate she couldn't alter or even understand."

"Yes. I had to make her face the facts, and I pointed out that Claude would be certain to inherit the transformation gene. And that even though I was now alpha male of the entire pack living in Beaumont Foret, whether she was given permission to leave rested with their vote. We have been hunted and killed too many times. She left the next night while I was sleeping. You already know the rest."

Jenna propped her chin on her elbow. "What of me, Philippe? Will you let me leave the château? Or am I to remain here, a prisoner?"

His face flushed with anger. "Your knowledge of what I am is a danger to me, but I will accept your word that you won't give me away. I won't hold you here against your will. The moment that the road is clear, I'll take you to Haute Beaumont and arrange for you to be driven down to the coast."

She hid her emotions behind a mask of stone. "How can you be sure I won't reveal your secret?"

"Because I know your heart," he told her. "Because I know your soul."

"Do you trust me so much, then?"

"I do." He came toward her and touched her cheek. "I am trusting you with more than my secret, Jenna. I am trusting you with my life." His dark eyes looked down into hers. "And with my son's."

A shiver went through her. "You can't force me into exile, the way my ancestors were. I'm not going anywhere just yet," she said.

He misunderstood. "You wanted to know what sin your ancestors had committed, to be forced to leave Beaumont Foret?" His laugh was bitter. "None! It was those who were left behind whose blood was tainted.

"Those who were of the *loup gareaux* remained behind in Beaumont Foret, isolated from a world that would have destroyed them had their secret been known. They pooled their resources and sent the rest away, so they could live normal lives, marry, and have children who were free from the stain."

Jenna's pulse pounded in her throat. "What you're saying is fantastic."

"Nevertheless, it is true. Perhaps there are others like us, but the *loup gareau* has existed in Beaumont Foret for less than three hundred years, the product of ignorance—and arrogance."

"I don't understand," she whispered.

"The Beaumont line is an ancient one, my dear Jenna, with a history of dabbling in alchemy and magic. You've seen the texts they've written and collected. Especially those of Hugh Beaumont. It is he who is to blame for everything, with his conceit and messing about with concoctions whose properties he didn't understand."

Jenna had seen several of Hugh Beaumont's writings. "Eye of newt and mummy powder? I'm afraid I can't take that too seriously."

"Do you recall the pink roses that bloomed on the terrace well beyond the first frost? Their beauty is due to Hugh Beaumont's efforts. As you have seen," he said, indicating himself, "some of his experiments were less successful. But both the roses and the *loup gareau* arose from his meddling. Not the result of patient genetic breeding but of magic."

"Magic . . ." She remembered thinking that only a genius or a magician could have created those perfect, almost indestructible roses. "It would be hard to convince most people of that."

Philippe's mouth thinned. "You do not believe me?"

"Are you saying that your ancestor was responsible for your . . . condition?"

He nodded. "Yes. Remember that the superstitions of one age become the science of another. Who would have believed that voices and pictures could be transmitted around the world, or that men would walk upon the moon? Or that a young woman could get inside a metal tube in California and exit it in Fontine?"

That brought a smile to her lips. "You have a point," she agreed. "How did your ancestor cause this? And why?"

"You are familiar with the old saying that good intentions pave the way to hell?"

"Of course."

"Well, it was Hugh Beaumont's good intentions that created the werewolf. Like many of man's most horrible inventions, it was a product of war. Enemy armies occupied Fontine and threatened our peaceful valley. What could a village of farmers do against armed and well-trained warriors?"

"And with a wave of his wizard's wand," she said wryly, "he changed them into werewolves?"

"Nothing so easily reversible. Hugh found an ancient manuscript that promised to turn men into 'creatures like wolves, fierce and invincible.' My ancestor took that as a metaphor for strength and courage. He brewed a great batch of the formula and gave it to every man and boy of fighting age in the village at midnight, when the moon was full."

He smiled wryly. "You can imagine his great dismay at the results! When the moon rose over the mountains, everyone who'd taken the potion was affected.

"There was a time when men were closer to the animals than now. In becoming civilized, most humans gave up skills that are still common to most beasts—superior sight and hearing and the ability to distinguish the faintest of scents. To survive and thrive in the harshest of environments. To attack or defend with the fiercest of animal instincts.

"These are the traits that my ancestor tried to revive with his potion, but he was not a scientist like your brother, carefully combining ingredients in a controlled environment. He was an alchemist, mixing raw chemicals together with the glee of a child. Whether it was some impurity in the products he used or a chance combination of the proper proportions, his formula altered the subjects of his experiment on the most elemental level."

"How can you possibly explain it?" Jenna's throat was dry, her voice raspy. "It goes against all nature."

Philippe frowned. "Does it? No one questions a furry, multilegged caterpillar turning into a delicate-winged butterfly. Perhaps because that is a beautiful transformation. But if this change is possible, why should it be so different that a man becomes a wolf? Surely that is equally extraordinary!"

"Yes. But a butterfly stays a butterfly once the transformation is over. It doesn't change back again."

"I wish I could prevent changing back! Man or wolf, either one. But we have been ruled by the phases of the moon for all this time, helpless to change our destiny. The decision was made to let our line die out. I was to have been the last of our kind. But we were young and heedless—and so my son was born. He is the last of our line. This half-life . . ." Philippe shrugged. "It is no life. It is a doomed and lonely existence."

"It doesn't have to be," Jenna said. "If you want me to stay— if you want *me*, not just someone who can save your precious manuscripts, not just a lover and companion but *me*—then I'll stay here with you for the rest of my days."

Philippe's heart turned over. "I want you, Jenna. *You!* I love you more than words can say."

For a moment he glimpsed happiness, shining like the sun. Then reality snuffed it out. "I want you in my world, but you are not of it—and I love you far too deeply to let you make that sacrifice. Go back to the life you had before we met. Forget you ever came to Beaumont Foret."

He started to turn away. Jenna ran lightly across the floor and put her arms around his neck. "I can't. I won't!"

"Please, Jenna." His voice was anguished. "Don't make this any more difficult. There is no need for it."

"There is every need." Philippe tried to move out of her embrace.

She hung on, lifting her face to his, and her eyes shone bright. "You see, my love, you aren't alone. There are others who share your powers of transformation—and I'm one of them."

21

PHILIPPE STARED AT her blankly. Her words didn't sink in.

Jenna laughed. "Did you think that you and the handful of others in this valley were the only werewolves left? Do you know why I really came to Beaumont Foret? To find out if there were others like me still living here."

"How can that be?" he asked. "Those with the curse remained behind, in this valley. Only those free of it emigrated to America."

"Not entirely. You see, my great-grandmother and great-grandfather both carried the recessive gene for the *loup garaou* trait, without having the change of form themselves. When they had children, their genes combined and altered to produce a new generation. And this mutation affected women, too. The same thing occurred in fifteen other families who left Beaumont Foret for California.

"That's why they went so heavily into science and medicine in succeeding generations: in hopes of finding a way to prevent

384

the physical change from occurring, and to avoid its being passed on to future generations."

Philippe couldn't believe what he was hearing. She put her hand on his arm and looked up into his face.

"You're not alone anymore, Philippe, nor is Claude the last of your kind. There are more than three hundred of us now, descendants of the original settlers from Beaumont Foret, spread all along the West Coast from San Francisco to Vancouver."

Philippe shook his head, like a man waking from a dream. "I have no choice in when I change; it occurs with moonrise. But you *don't* change. I know, Jenna, because I was in my wolf form when I found you on the mountainside that first night. But you—you were a woman still, even in the full light of the moon."

She smiled. "I can change," she told him, "or I can prevent it from happening. And so can you—and Claude, and anyone else who carries the trait. Those small metal vials in my case aren't for my work: they're the serum developed by my parents and specially manufactured by my brother's company." Jenna laughed at his astonishment.

"Haven't you guessed yet?" Her eyes shone. "I didn't come to Fontine just for the conference. I came to look for Beaumont Foret, hoping to find proof that this is where the *loup gareau* began. Hoping that if there were others of our kind still living here, we could help them."

"You've known I was one all along!" he exclaimed.

"No, but I guessed. Oh Phillipe! There was a wildness in you that called to me. The pain I saw mingled with the love in your eyes when you looked at your son." She tilted her head. "And after we became lovers you never stayed with me after moonrise. Rather insulting . . . unless you know your lover has a damned good reason for it!"

His smile was tender. "I wanted to, my darling—and I did, that first night after you were brought here to the château. After that I went to any extreme to be far away from you before the change occurred."

"Now everything has changed, Phillipe. You don't have to hide here in your secret valley. Once you begin taking the serum, you can go anywhere, at any time, and be free. Or you can let the change occur by skipping the weekly dose, as I recently did. It was hard on me to give up my secret life of the Midnight Country, with all its richness, for so many months, and I finally gave in to it."

Jenna saw understanding dawn. "Yes. Two nights ago we ran together in the moonlight. We raced through the valley and along the ridges—all the way to that mountain meadow high above Beaumont Foret. We almost made love there, you and I in our wolf guises."

He shook his head. "No. I should have recognized you in any form. Especially by your scent."

Jenna laughed. "I thought of that, and I rolled in the lavender beds first, to throw off the scent and confuse you."

The certainty in her voice penetrated his disbelief. His heart swelled with joy. Jenna had brought more than hope to Beaumont Foret, she'd brought a cure. There would be no more need for concealment. No need to restrict travel to only those few nights when the dark of the moon occurred. No more fear that friends and loved ones would be hunted down for being something that was beyond their control.

She watched the burden lift from him, the light come back into his beloved face. And then he laughed aloud, a free and joyous sound like none she'd heard from him before. He enfolded her in his arms and kissed her until they were breathless.

Then he took her into his room, and they made love in the great canopied bed. For the first time there were no shadows, no secrets between them. They abandoned themselves to the joy of it, and the flame of their mutual passion burned white-hot.

When their blood finally cooled, they lay entwined and spoke their love in soft words. "Are you happy, love?"

"More than I ever believed possible." Jenna sighed in contentment. "When I first came to Fontine, it was only to bring the cure to any who suffered from it. I never thought I'd find anything like this."

He smiled down at her. "I certainly never thought I'd find anyone like you!"

Epilogue

Jᴇɴɴᴀ ᴄᴀᴍᴇ ᴏᴜᴛ on the terrace where Philippe and Claude were throwing a ball for Roland to chase. The land was golden in the rich autumn light. The dog barked and ran to her, almost knocking her down in his eagerness.

"You were right," she told Philippe. "With the new satellite links they've launched there's not much of a time gap. We can use cell phones and modems to communicate with the outside world twenty hours out of twenty-four."

"Have you tried it?" Philippe asked.

Jenna laughed. "For the past hour I've been downloading E-mails from my family and answering them. I wrote to my brother, and he thinks we're on to something with the monks-hood and aconite. He thinks they'd be a better substitute for what he's been using to manufacture the serum—and he wonders if we would be interested in planting and harvesting it here in Beaumont Foret."

He lifted her hand and kissed it. "New hope, new jobs . . . and new life for a dying village."

"Some of the families in America are considering returning here." She grinned. "I told them there was plenty of free housing in the village."

They stood side by side, imagining the village square filled with happy people. Young people, old people—and most of all, children.

"I have good news, also. Marie is pregnant," Philippe said. "She wants to tell you herself, so look surprised."

"I will," Jenna promised. "Don't worry, I'm good at keeping secrets."

"Don't I know it?" He tipped back his head and laughed, sounding as happy and carefree as Claude, who was racing Roland back down to the moat. "How your coming to Beaumont Foret has changed things, Jenna! It's like magic. The good kind of magic."

Philippe shook his head. "All the years I searched through the old manuscripts, working backward through time, while your family was working toward the future."

"There was no guarantee we would find the answer by our method before you found it through yours. And the one method verified the other."

She trailed her fingers along his arm. "There are other wonders buried deep in your collection. We'll find them eventually, and we'll find them together."

"When we are not making love." He took her hands in his, kissing them. "Ah, my clever Jenna. Because you came to Beaumont Foret, I can live again. And my son will have a good life. A normal life."

"And so will your new son—or daughter."

"What?" He caught her face between his hands. "Is it true? Or are you merely speaking of the future?"

She kissed him. "The future," she said, and watched the disappointment fill his eyes. "About seven months in the future! Claude will have a brother or sister early next summer." She glanced up from beneath her lashes. "I'd like our child to be born here, in Beaumont Foret."

"But first we must be married," he said. "We can hold the wedding in the château's chapel, if you like."

THE MIDNIGHT COUNTRY ⟩ 389

"Or you could come with me to California."

Philippe laughed. "Yes—I could! Now that it's safe for me to travel again."

Jenna wound her arms around his neck. "But from time to time, we'll skip the serum injections . . . won't we? It won't harm the baby, either way."

"Yes. We can't give up our runs through the Midnight Country—now that we know there's always a safe way back."

The whole world was opened up to him once more, but now that he had it in his grasp, Philippe realized that all he wanted was to remain here in Beaumont Foret. With Jenna.

Philippe put his strong hand out protectively, over the soft curve of her belly. There was a precious new life growing there, a symbol of a new life and hope for them, and for all the people of Beaumont Foret.

"It's time to make it official then." He held her close and his dark eyes were warm as he smiled into hers. "I don't care where we exchange vows, my love, as long as you marry me. And I insist that it be as soon as possible."

Jenna felt her heart swell with love for him. "I'd like it to be here in Beaumont Foret, with all my family present," she said, snuggling into his shoulder. "Here, where it all began so long ago."

"Wolves mate for life," he said softly.

Jenna laughed. "I'm counting on it.

The old case clock chimed, its deep tones echoing along the silent halls. The last of the wedding guests were gone, and Claude—and Roland—safely tucked away for the night. Philippe reached out to Jenna.

"It is time."

Stars glittered and danced in the clear night air as they stepped out through the terrace doors and went down into the dappled gardens. They were naked beneath their warm cloaks. He led her into the shadows, then unclasped his cloak and let it fall. Starlight haloed his dark hair and outlined his body as he smiled down at her. Her heartbeat quickened in anticipation. She undid the clasp and her velvet cloak fell in folds around her slender ankles. Jenna gasped at the cool caress of the autumn breeze.

Hand in hand they waited, until the moon rose over the high, crystalline peaks, silver and serene. As the first moonbeams touched their skin, the transformation swept over them. The pain was intense but brief, and quickly rewarded. The world had transformed as well, from black and silver silence, into an incredible tapestry woven of sound and scent and shimmering color.

Jenna's heart leapt with eagerness. She inhaled the deep green perfume of the pines and the rich loamy fragrance of the earth, the pungent aroma of late-blooming flowers and the clear, cool blue of water. Philippe's scent surrounded her, familiar and seductive, and now incredibly rich and complex.

He spoke to her wordlessly and his voice echoed in her mind. "Come, my love. Run with me!"

Together they went through the silent gardens warmly clothed in lush fur, their graceful lupine bodies slipping through the chateau's gardens with incredible grace and agility.

The breeze ruffled the grass and the river sang softly as it sped along on its journey from the mountains toward the distant sea. The sky above blazed with constellations invisible to the naked human eye, and iridescent veils and plumes of light flared high above the mountains.

Intoxicated with joy and freedom, they raced through the silver night, deep into the heart of the Midnight Country.

Turn the page for a preview of

Key of Light

the first book in
the new Key trilogy from

Nora Roberts
coming in November 2003
from Jove Books

THE STORM RIPPED over the mountains, gushing venomous rain that struck the ground with the sharp ring of metal on stone. Lightning strikes spat down, angry artillery fire that slammed against the cannon roar of thunder.

There was a gleeful kind of mean in the air, a sizzle of temper and spite that boiled with power.

It suited Malory Price's mood perfectly.

Hadn't she asked herself what else could go wrong? Now in answer to that weary and completely rhetorical question, nature—in all her maternal wrath—was showing her just how bad things could get.

There was an ominous rattling somewhere in the dash of her sweet little Mazda, and she still had nineteen payments to go on it. In order to make those payments, she had to keep her job.

She hated her job.

That wasn't part of The Malory Price Life Plan, which she

had begun to outline at the age of eight. Twenty years later, that outline had become a detailed and organized checklist, complete with headings, subheadings, and cross-references. She revised it meticulously on the first of each year.

She was supposed to *love* her job. It said so, quite clearly, under the heading of CAREER.

She'd worked at The Gallery for seven years, the last three of those as manager, which was right on schedule. And she had loved it—being surrounded by art, having an almost free hand in the displaying, the acquiring, the promotion and set-up for showings and events.

The fact was she'd begun to think of The Gallery as hers, and knew full well the rest of the staff, the clients, the artists and craftsman had felt very much the same.

James P. Horace might have owned the smart little gallery, but he'd never questioned Malory's decisions, and on his increasingly rare visits had complimented her, always, on the acquisitions, the ambiance, the sales.

It had been perfect, which was exactly what Malory intended her life to be. After all, if it wasn't perfect, what was the point?

Everything had changed when James had forsaken fifty-three years of comfortable bachelorhood and acquired himself a young, sexy wife. A wife, Malory thought with her steel-blue eyes narrowing in resentment, who'd decided to make The Gallery her personal pet.

It didn't matter that the new Mrs. Horace knew next to nothing about art, about business, about public relations or managing employees. James doted on his Pamela, and Malory's dream job had become a daily nightmare.

But she'd been dealing with it, Malory thought as she scowled through her dark, drenched windshield. She'd outlined her strategy and it had been to wait Pamela out. To remain calm and possessed during this nasty little bump until the road had smoothed out again.

Now that excellent strategy was out the window. She'd lost her temper when Pamela had countermanded her orders on a display of art glass, when she'd seen the perfectly and beautifully organized gallery turned upside-down with clutter and ugly fabrics.

There were some things she could tolerate, Malory told herself, but being slapped in the face with hideous taste in her own space wasn't one of them.

Then again, blowing up at the owner's wife was not the path to solid job security. Particularly when the words *myopic, plebeian bimbo* were employed.

Lightning crashed over the rise ahead, and Malory winced as much in memory of her temper as from the flash. A very bad move on her part, which only showed what happened when you gave in to temper and impulse.

To top it off, she'd spilled cappuccino on Pamela's Escada suit. But that *had* been an accident.

Almost.

However fond James was of her, Malory knew her livelihood was hanging by a very slim thread. And when the thread broke, she was sunk. Art galleries weren't a dime a dozen in a pretty, picturesque town like Pleasant Valley. She'd either have to find another area of work as a stop-gap, or relocate.

Neither option put a smile on her face.

She loved Pleasant Valley, loved being surrounded by the mountains of western Pennsylvania. She loved the small-town feel, the mix of quaint and sophisticated that drew the tourists, and the get-away crowds that spilled out of neighboring Pittsburgh for impulsive weekends.

Even as a child growing up in the suburbs of Pittsburgh, Pleasant Valley was exactly the sort of place she'd imagined living. She'd craved the hills, with their shadows, their textures, and the tidy streets of a valley town, the simplicity of the pace, the friendliness of neighbors.

The decision to someday fold herself into the fabric of Pleasant Valley had been made when she'd been fourteen and had spent a long holiday weekend there with her parents.

Just as she'd decided, when she'd wandered through The Gallery that long-ago autumn, that she'd one day be part of that space.

Of course, she'd believed her paintings would hang there, but that had been one item on her checklist she'd been forced to delete rather than tick off when accomplished.

She would never be an artist. But she had to be, *needed* to be, involved and surrounded by art.

Still, she didn't want to move back to the city. She wanted

to keep her gorgeous, roomy apartment two blocks from The Gallery, with its views of the Appalachians, its creaky old floors and its walls jammed with carefully selected artwork.

And the hope of that was looking as dim as the stormy sky.

So she hadn't been smart with her money, Malory admitted with a windy sigh. She didn't see the point of letting it lie in some bank when it could be turned into something lovely to look at or wear. Until it was used, money was just paper. Malory tended to use a great deal of paper.

She was overdrawn at the bank. Again. She'd maxed out her credit cards. Ditto. But, she reminded herself, she had a great wardrobe. And the start of a very impressive art collection. Which she'd have to sell, piece by piece, and most likely at a loss to keep a roof over her head if Pamela brought the axe down.

But maybe tonight would buy her some time and good will. She hadn't wanted to attend the cocktail reception at Warrior's Peak. A fanciful name for a spooky old place, she thought. Another time she'd have been thrilled at the opportunity to see the inside of the great old house so high on the ridge. And to rub elbows with people who might be patrons of the arts.

But the invitation had been odd. Written in an elegant hand on heavy stone-colored paper, with a logo of an ornate gold key in lieu of letterhead. Though it was tucked in her evening bag now along with her compact, her lipstick, her cell phone, her glasses, fresh pen, business cards, and ten dollars, Malory remembered the wording.

**THE PLEASURE OF YOUR COMPANY IS DESIRED
FOR COCKTAILS AND CONVERSATION
EIGHT P.M., SEPTEMBER 4
WARRIOR'S PEAK
YOU ARE THE KEY. THE LOCK AWAITS.**

Now how weird was that? Malory asked herself, and gritted her teeth as the car shimmied in a sudden gust of wind. The way her luck was going, it was probably a scam for some pyramid scheme.

Warrior's Peak had been empty for years. She knew it had been purchased recently, but the details were lean. Some outfit called Triad, she recalled, and assumed it was some sort of corporation looking to turn it into a hotel or mini-resort.

Which didn't explain why they'd invited the manager of The Gallery, and not the owner and his interfering wife. Pamela had been pretty peeved about the slight—so that was something.

Still, Malory would have passed on the evening. She didn't have a date, just another aspect of her life that currently sucked, and driving alone into the mountains to a house straight out of Hollywood horror on the strength of an invitation that made her uneasy wasn't on her list of fun things to do in the middle of the workweek.

There hadn't even been a number or contact for an rsvp. And that, she felt, was arrogant and rude. Her response in ignoring the invitation would have been equally arrogant and rude, but James had spotted it on her desk.

He'd been so excited, so pleased by the idea of her going, had pressed her to relay the details of the house's interior to him. And had reminded her that if she could discreetly drop The Gallery into conversation from time to time, it would be good for business.

If she could score a few clients, it might offset the Escada and the bimbo comment.

Her car chugged up the narrowing road that cut through the dense, dark forest. She'd always thought of those hills and woods as a kind of Sleepy Hollow effect that ringed her pretty valley. But just now, with the wind and rain and dark, the less serene aspects of that old tale were a little too much in evidence for her peace of mind.

If whatever was pinging in her dash was serious, she could end up broken down on the side of the road, huddled in the car listening to the moans and lashes of the storm, imagining headless horsemen, while she waited for a tow-truck she couldn't afford.

Obviously, the answer was to not break down.

She thought she caught glimpses of lights beaming through the rain and trees, but her windshield wipers were whipping at the highest speed and still barely able to shove aside the flood of rain.

As lightning snapped again, she gripped the wheel tighter. She liked a good, hellcat storm as much as anyone, but she wanted to enjoy this one while she was sitting inside, anywhere, and drinking a nice glass of wine.

She had to be close. How far could any single road climb up before it just had to start falling down the other side of the mountain? She knew Warrior's Peak stood atop the ridge, guarding the valley below. Or lording it over the valley, depending on your viewpoint. She hadn't passed another car for miles.

Which only proved anyone with half a brain wasn't driving in this mess, she thought.

The road forked, and the bend on the right streamed through enormous stone pillars. Malory slowed, gawked at the life-sized warriors standing on each pillar. Perhaps it was the storm, the night, her own jittery mood, but they looked more human than stone, with hair flying around their fierce faces, their hands gripped on the hilt of swords. In the shimmer of lightning, she could almost see muscles rippling in the arms, over the broad, bare chests.

She had to fight the temptation to get out of the car for a closer look. But the chill that tripped down her spine as she turned through the open iron gates had her glancing back up at the warriors with as much wariness as appreciation for the skill of the sculptor.

Then she hit the brakes and fishtailed on the crushed stone of the private roadbed. Her heart jammed into her throat as she stared at the stunning buck standing arrogantly a foot in front of the bumper, and the sprawling, eccentric lines of the house behind him.

For a moment she took the deer for a sculpture as well, though why any sane person would set a sculpture in the center of their drive was beyond her. Then again, *sane* didn't seem to be the operative word for anyone who would choose to live in the house on the ridge.

But the deer's eyes gleamed, a sharp emerald green in the beam of her headlights, and its head with its great, crowning rack, turned slightly. Regally, Malory mused, mesmerized. Rain streamed off its coat, and in the next flash of light, that coat seemed white as the moon.

He stared at her, but there was nothing of fear, nothing of surprise in those glinting eyes. There was, if such things were possible, a kind of amused disdain. Then he walked away, through the curtain of rain, the rivers of fog, and was gone.

"Wow." She let out a long breath, shivered in the warmth of her car. "And one more wow," she murmured as she stared at the house.

She'd seen pictures of it, and paintings. She'd seen its shape and silhouette hulking on the ridge above the valley. But it was an entirely different matter to see it up close, with a storm raging.

Something caught between a castle, a fortress, and a house of horrors, she decided.

Its stone was obsidian black, with its juts and towers, its peaks and battlements stacked and spread as if some very clever, very wicked child had placed them at his whim. Against that rain-slicked black, long, narrow windows, perhaps hundreds of them, all glowed with gilded light.

Someone was not worried about the electric bill.

Fog smoked around its base, like a moat of mist.

In the next shock of lightning, she caught a glimpse of a white banner with the gold key madly waving from one of the topmost spires.

She inched the car closer. Gargoyles hunched along the walls, crawled over the eaves. Rainwater vomited out of their grinning mouths, spilled out of clawed hands as they grinned down at her.

She stopped in front of the stone skirt of a wide portico, and considered, very seriously, turning back into the storm and driving away.

She called herself a coward, a childish idiot. She asked herself where she'd lost her sense of adventure and fun.

The insults worked well enough to have her tapping her fingers on the door handle. And the quick rap on her window had a scream shooting out of her throat.

The white, bony face surrounded by a black hood that peered in at her turned the scream to a kind of breathless keening.

Gargoyles do not come to life, she assured herself, repeating the words over and over in her head as she rolled the window down a cautious half-inch.

"Welcome to Warrior's Peak." His voice boomed over the rain, and his welcoming smile showed a great many teeth. "If you'll just leave your keys in the car, Miss, I'll see to it for you."

Before she could think to slap down the locks, he'd pulled open her door. He blocked the sweep of wind and rain with his body, and the biggest umbrella she'd ever seen.

"I'll see you safe and dry to the door."

What was that accent? English, Irish, Scots?

"Thank you." She started to climb out, felt herself pinned back. Panic dribbled into embarrassment as she realized she'd yet to unhook her seat belt.

Freed, she huddled under the umbrella, struggling to regulate her breathing as he walked her to the double entrance doors. They were wide enough to accommodate a semi and boasted dull silver knockers, big as turkey platters, fashioned into dragons' heads.

Some welcome, Malory thought an instant before one of the doors opened, and light and warmth poured out.

The woman had a straight and gorgeous stream of flame-colored hair—it spilled around a pale face of perfect angles and curves. Her eyes, green as the buck's had been, danced as if at some private joke under dark, slashing brows. She was tall and slim, garbed in a long gown of fluid black. A silver amulet holding a fat stone of misty green hung beneath her breasts.

Her lips, red as her hair, curved as she held out a hand sparkling with rings.

She looked, Malory thought, like something out of a very sexy fairy tale.

"Miss Price. Welcome. Such a thrilling storm, but distressing, I'm sure, to be out in it. Come in."

The hand was warm and strong, and stayed clasped over Malory's as the woman drew her into the entrance hall.

The light showered down from a chandelier of crystal so fine it resembled spun sugar sparkling over the twists and curves of silver.

The floor was mosaic, depicting the warriors from the gate and what seemed to be a number of mythological figures. She couldn't kneel down and study it as she might have liked and was already struggling to hold back an orgasmic moan at the paintings that crowded walls the color of melted butter.

"I'm so glad you could join us tonight," the woman continued. "I'm Rowena. Please, let me take you into the parlor. There's a lovely fire. Early in the year for one, but the storm seemed to call for it. Was the drive up difficult?"

"Challenging. Miss—"

"Rowena. Just Rowena."

"Rowena. I wonder if I could take just a moment to freshen up before joining the other guests?"

"Of course. Powder room." She gestured to a door tucked under the long sweep of the front stairs. "The parlor is the first door on your right. Take your time."

"Thanks." Malory slipped inside, and immediately thought *powder room* was a very poor label for the plush, roomy area.

The half-dozen candles on the marble counter streamed out light and scent. Burgundy hand towels edged in ecru lace were arranged beside the generous pool of sink. The faucet gleamed gold in the fanciful shape of a swan.

Here the floor mosaic held a mermaid, sitting on a rock, smiling out at a blue sea as she combed her flame-colored hair.

This time, after double-checking to make certain she'd locked the door, Malory did kneel down to study the craftsmanship.

Gorgeous, she thought, running her fingertips over the tiles. Old, certainly, and brilliantly executed.

Was there anything more powerful than the ability to create beauty?

She straightened, washed her hands with soap that smelled faintly of rosemary. She took a moment to admire the collection of Waterstone's nymphs and sirens framed on the walls before digging out her compact.

There was little she could do for her hair. Though she'd drawn it back, anchored it at her nape with a rhinestone clip, the weather had played riot with the dark blonde curls. It was a look, she thought, as she dusted her nose. Sort of arty and carefree. Not elegant like the redhead, but it suited her well enough. She reapplied her lipstick, satisfied the pale rose had been a good investment. Subtle worked best with her milkmaid coloring.

She'd paid too much for the cocktail suit. Of course. But a woman was entitled to a few weaknesses, she reminded herself as she straightened the slim satin lapels. Besides, the slate-blue was right for her eyes, the tailored lines pulled it all together into a style both professional and elegant. She closed her bag, lifted her chin.

"Okay, Mal, let's go drum up some business."

She stepped out, forced herself not to tip-toe back down the hall to drool over the paintings.

Her heels clicked briskly on the tile. She always enjoyed the sound of it. Powerful. Female.

And when she stepped through the first arch to the right, the thrilled gasp escaped before she could block it.

She'd never seen its like, in or out of a museum. Antiques so lovingly tended their surfaces gleamed like mirrors, the rich, deep colors that demonstrated an artist's flare, rugs, pillows, draperies were as much art forms as the paintings and statuary. On the far wall was a fireplace she could have stood in with her arms stretched out to her sides. Framed in malachite, it held enormous logs that snapped with tongues of red and gold fire.

If the woman had looked like a creature from a fairy tale, this was the perfect setting for one.

She wanted to spend hours there, to wallow in all that marvelous color and light. The uneasy woman who'd huddled in her car in the rain was long forgotten.

"It took five minutes for my eyes to stop bugging out of my head after I walked in."

Malory jolted around, stared at the woman who stood framed in the side window.

This one was a brunette, with dense brown hair skimming between her jawline and shoulders in a stylish swing. She was perhaps six full inches taller than Malory's compact five-four, and had the lush curves to match the height. Both were set off with trim black pants and a knee-length jacket worn over a snug white top.

She held a champagne flute in one hand and extended the other as she walked across the room. Malory saw her eyes were deep, dark-brown, and direct. Her nose was narrow and straight, her mouth wide and unpainted. The faintest hint of dimples fluttered in her cheeks when she smiled.

"I'm Dana. Dana Steele."

"Malory Price. Nice to meet you. Great jacket."

"Thanks. I was pretty relieved when I saw you drive up. It's a hell of a place, but I was getting a little spooked rattling around by myself. It's nearly quarter after." She tapped the face of her watch. "You'd think some of the other guests would be here by now."

"Where's the woman who met me at the door? Rowena?"

Dana pursed her lips as she glanced back toward the archway. "She glides in and out, looking gorgeous and mysterious. I'm told our host will be joining us shortly."

"Who is our host?"

"Your guess is as good as mine. Haven't I seen you?" Dana added. "In the Valley?"

"Possibly. I manage The Gallery." For the time being, she thought.

"That's it. I've come to a couple of showings there. And sometimes I just wander in and look around avariciously. I'm at the library. A research specialist."

They both turned as Rowena walked in. Though glided in, Malory thought, was a better description.

"I see you've introduced yourselves. Lovely. What can I get you to drink, Miss Price?"

"I'll have what she's having."

"Perfect." Even as she spoke a uniformed maid came in bearing two flutes on a silver tray. "Please help yourselves to the canapés, and make yourselves at home."

"I hope the weather isn't keeping your other guests away," Dana put in.

Rowena merely smiled. "I'm sure everyone who's expected will be here shortly. If you'll excuse me just another moment."

"Okay, this is just weird." Dana picked a canapé at random, discovered it was a lobster puff. "Delicious, but weird."

"Fascinating." Malory sipped her champagne, and trailed her fingers over a bronze sculpture of a reclining fairy.

"I'm still trying to figure out why I got an invitation." Since they were there, and so was she, Dana sampled another canapé. "No one else at the library got one. No one else I know got one, for that matter. I'm starting to wish I'd talked my brother into coming with me after all. He's got a good bullshit barometer."

Malory found herself grinning. "You don't sound like any librarian I've ever known. You don't look like one either."

"I burned all my Laura Ashley ten years ago." Dana gave a little shrug. Restless, moving toward irritated, she tapped her fingers on the crystal flute. "I'm going to give this about ten more minutes, then I'm booking."

"If you go, I go. I'd feel better heading back into that storm if I drove behind someone else heading back to the Valley."

"Same goes." Dana frowned toward the window, watched the rain beat on the other side of the glass. "Crappy night. And it was an extremely crappy day. Driving all the way here and back in this mess for a couple of glasses of wine and some canapés just about caps it."

"You, too?" Malory wandered toward a wonderful painting of a masked ball. It made her think of Paris, though she'd never been there except in her dreams. "I only came tonight hoping I could make some contacts for The Gallery. Job insurance," she added lifting her glass in a mock toast. "As my job is currently in a very precarious state."

"Mine, too. Between budget cuts and nepotism, my position was adjusted, my hours trimmed back to twenty-five a week. How the hell am I supposed to live on that? And my landlord just announced my rent's going up first of next month."

"There's a rattle in my car and I spent my auto maintenance on these shoes."

Dana looked down, pursed her lips. "Terrific shoes. My computer crashed this morning."

Enjoying herself, Malory turned away from the painting, cocked her brow at Dana. "I called my boss's new wife a bimbo, then spilled her cappuccino on her designer suit."

"Okay, you win." In the spirit of good-fellowship, Dana stepped over and clinked her glass to Malory's. "What do you say we hunt up the Welsh goddess and find out what's going on around here?"

"Is that what the accent is? Welsh?"

"Gorgeous, isn't it? But be that as it may, I think . . . ."

She trailed off as they heard that distinctive click of high heels on tile.

The first thing Malory noticed was the hair. It was black and short, with thick bangs cut so blunt they might have required a ruler. Beneath them, the tawny eyes were large and long, making her think of Waterhouse again, and his faeries. She had a triangular face, glowing now with what might have been excitement, nerves, or excellent cosmetics.

The way her fingers kneaded at her little black bag, Malory went with the nerves.

She wore red, stoplight red, in an abbreviated dress that clung to her curvy body and showed off terrific legs. The heels that had clicked along the tile were a good four inches high, and sharp as stilletos.

"Hi." Her voice was breathy, and her gaze was already flicking around the room. "Um. She said I should come right in."

"Join the party. Such as it is. Dana Steele, and my equally baffled companion this evening, Malory Price."

"I'm Zoe. McCourt." She took another cautious step into the room, as if she was waiting for someone to tell her there'd been a mistake and boot her out again. "Holy cow. This place, it's like a movie. It's, um, beautiful and all, but I keep expecting that scary guy in the smoking jacket to come in."

"Vincent Price? No relation," Malory said with a grin. "I take it you don't know any more about what's going on than we do."

"No. I think I got invited by mistake, but—" She broke off, goggling a bit when a servant entered with another flute on a tray. "Ah . . . thanks." She took the crystal gingerly, then just smiled down at the bubbling wine. "Champagne. It *has* to be a mistake. But I couldn't pass up the chance to come. Where is everybody else?"

"Good question." Dana angled her head, charmed and amused as Zoe took a small, testing sip of champagne.

"Are you from the Valley?"

"Yes. Well, for the last couple years."

"Three for three," Malory murmured. "Do you know anyone else who got an invitation for tonight?"

"No. In fact, I asked around, which is probably why I got fired today. Is that food just to take?"

"You got fired?" Malory exchanged a look with Dana. "Three for three."

"Carly—she owns the salon where I work. Worked," Zoe corrected and walked toward a tray of canapés. "She heard me talking about it with one of my customers, got bent out of shape. Boy, these are terrific."

Her voice had lost its breathiness now, and as Zoe appeared to relax, Malory detected the faintest hint of twang.

"Anyway, Carly's been gunning for me for months. I guess the invite, seeing as she didn't get one, put her nose out of joint. Next thing I know she's saying there's twenty missing from the till. I never stole anything in my life. Bitch."

She took another, more enthusiastic gulp of champagne. "Next thing I know, I'm out on my ear. Doesn't matter. It's not going to matter. I'll get another job. I hated working there anyway. God."

It mattered, Malory thought. The sparkle in Zoe's eyes that had as much fear to it as anger said it mattered a great deal. "You're a hairdresser."

"Yeah. Hair and skin consultant if you want to get snooty. I'm not the type who gets invited to fancy parties at fancy places, so I guess it's a mistake."

Considering, Malory shook her head. "I don't think someone like Rowena makes mistakes. Ever."

"Well, I don't know. I wasn't going to come, then I thought it would cheer me up. Then my car wouldn't start, again. I had to borrow the baby-sitter's."

"You have a baby?" Dana asked.

"He's not a baby anymore. Simon's nine. He's great. I wouldn't worry about the job, but I've got a kid to support. And I didn't steal any goddamn twenty dollars or twenty cents for that matter. I'm not a thief."

She caught herself, flushed scarlet. "Sorry. I'm sorry. Bubbles loosening my tongue, I guess."

"Don't worry about it." Dana rubbed a hand up and down Zoe's arm. "You want to hear something strange? My job, and my paycheck, just got cut down to the bone. I don't know what the hell I'm going to do. And Malory thinks she's about to get the axe."

"Really?" Zoe looked from one face to the other. "That's just weird."

"And nobody we know was invited here tonight." With a wary glance toward the doorway, Malory lowered her voice. "From the looks of it, we're it."

"I'm a librarian, you're a hairdresser, she runs an art gallery. What do we have in common?"

"We're all out of work." Malory frowned. "Or the next thing to it. That alone is strange when you consider the Valley's got a population of about five thousand. What are the odds of three women hitting a professional wall the same day in the same little town? Next, we're all from the Valley. We're all female, about the same age? Twenty-eight."

"Twenty-seven," Dana said.

"Twenty-six—twenty-seven in December." Zoe shivered. "This is just too strange." Her eyes widened as she looked at her half-empty glass, and she set it hastily aside. "You don't think there's anything in there that shouldn't be, do you?"

"I don't think we're going to be drugged and sold into white slavery." Dana's tone was dry, but she set her glass down as well. "People know we're here, right? My brother knows where I am, and people at work."

"My boss, his wife. Your ex-boss," Malory said to Zoe. "Your baby-sitter. Anyway, this is Pennsylvania, for God's sake, not, I don't know, Zimbabwe."

"I say we go find the mysterious Rowena, and get some answers. We stick together, right?" Dana nodded at Malory, then Zoe.

Zoe swallowed. "Honey, I'm your new best friend." To seal it, she took Dana's hand, then Malory's.

"How lovely to see you."

Their hands were still joined as they turned and looked at the man who stood in the archway.

He smiled, stepped inside. "Welcome to Warrior's Peak."